THE
BOROUGH

HORIKEI

Horikei
3-5-13 Kichijoji Kitamachi
Musashino-Shi
Tokyo

For 'Her' whoever the fuck she is...

"It is necessary to fall in love - the better to provide an alibi for all the despair we are going to feel anyway."
Albert Camus

I'm real, the people in this story are real. Some of them are no longer with us, and some of them never really were. Some of them have become ghosts of sorts, not necessarily dead but merely impressions of people that were once a massive part of my life, and who have since faded to vague memory. The things that occurred are mostly true if sometimes exaggerated. Some of the events have been summarised or embellished, but I have tried my hardest to capture the feelings and the mood of the time. My memory is fallible and the past cloudy and indistinct, and I'm sure that if you talked to the people mentioned here within you would find a hundred different viewpoints, a hundred different explanations and rationales. I am as everyone else, merely an observer.

We were young. Fucking hell we were young and like all young people we had no idea where our lives would take us or how we would get there. We had no plans, no big ambitions or grandiose ideals. We had a bit of money and far too much attitude. Our parents weren't rich or poor, they worked hard and tried to raise their children correctly. Theirs was a different generation. They had a good work ethic and a strong moral compass and they did their best to make sure we had a future. When they grew up, there was a job for everyone and anyone with a decent wage could get a mortgage. They were raised on the Beatles and Bob Dylan, children of the summer of love and the hippie movement, before the Iraq war and nuclear proliferation.

This story could be about anyone. This town could be any small town in Britain and its cast of characters seen in any pub or supermarket up and down the country. We were all flailing about in the wind, trying desperately to grab hold of

1

something. We craved meaning and purpose. We wanted to be loved and understood and our actions were just a means to this end. We were good people. We did bad things, but our motivations were always pure and we always looked after each other. We were close, and we loved each other like brothers (and sisters) and we told each other this regularly. We were from different backgrounds and classes but all shared the same goal every young person in the UK had. We wanted to escape, escape from sobriety, escape from our shitty little town and escape from our virginities. Some of the following events are not in chronological order, but that doesn't really matter as in retrospect events get muddled up in time and unweaving the threads of each individual narrative becomes near impossible.

I have tried to use my voice. Not the voice that the people at work or the lady in the Co-op hear, but the one I used to use. The one I had when I didn't care what people thought of me, when I wasn't trying to project an ideal image of myself, the voice that still sometimes emerges when I've had too much red wine or when I lose my patience. It was my voice once and these people were once my friends, my life. I thought we would never part ways but in the end life had other plans for us. The vicissitudes of existence got in the way and so here we are. Some of us keep in touch, others have left the fold, but I still think about these people every day and the events you will read shaped us into who we are today.

We are all products of our environments and our upbringing, and even though we all grew up in the same place, our lives all ended up very differently. I have probably painted myself in a favourable (unfavourable) light throughout, though this has never been intentional. We all see events differently and time has a habit of showing the past through a filter. Things are grainy and details are missing but the big objects are clearly visible and easy to distinguish. Sometimes I have merged two or more people into one in order to improve the narrative and to make things less confusing. Our lives are touched by a great number of people and most of these interactions are profound yet fleeting. It would be an insurmountable task to detail and describe every such interaction and to ascribe every word uttered to a specific individual.

The events in this story take place between my fifteenth and 23rd birthdays. From the rise of Nirvana to the birth of the Spice Girls. It was a time before mobile phones and the internet. Before Netflix or Twitter. We had dial phones and cars without electric windows. Girls had perms and boys had long hair. My school was predominantly white, but there were a lot of Sikhs and Muslims. There was a bit of racial tension but generally everyone just got along.

It was a time of mix tapes and Gordon the Gofer, it was a pre Blair Britain. Lager and fags were cheap and televisions were expensive. Boy bands were on the rise and Starbucks was still a tiny coffee shop chain in Seattle. We were young and beautiful, impetuous and stupid. We had it all and yet had nothing. We drank and took drugs, did well at school and were polite to our teachers. We wore our hearts on our sleeves and took life as it came. We struggled, we cried, we fought and we grew. Like I said this could be anyone's story from any small town in Britain, but it's not.

This is our story.

PROLOGUE

The plane shudders as we pass through another bit of turbulence. I look to my right, at my son shrouded in blankets and fast asleep. His head rests upon a stack of small pillows and the red headphones I bought him at the airport duty free shop dangle from the headrest next to his face. He breathes slowly in and out, fingers twitching ever so slightly, tickled by dreams and I smile. I wonder how I will ever explain all of this to him, all that has happened, how she has so betrayed me, betrayed both of us, left us, cut all ties and burned all bridges? How can I ever bring myself to tell him how she chose something other than him, how she probably doesn't even care?

Is it even possible to condense the last twenty years into something clear and concise, to separate each delicately interwoven tendril and describe every subtle emotional nuance? It is the impossibility of elucidating a dream or bringing to life the untold stories we all harbour within the deepest recesses of our beings. We are made of time, crafted from the movement of the world around us and moulded by its vicissitudes. Was there another path I could have taken, another me waiting patiently in the wings, eager to be ushered onto this mortal stage? Was Baudelaire right? Are those precious vessels really impenetrable, the sarcophagi within so inured to our touch. Did I ever love her? Have I ever really loved? In the end does it even matter?

I watch the passage of our aircraft on the screen in the seat back, we are passing over the vast expanse of Mongolia and Eastern Russia, the readout telling me that we have seven hours remaining until we land at Heathrow. It's the 3rd of August 2018.

The flight attendant passes by and I take off my headphones and get her attention with a raised hand

すみませんビールも一本お願いしま, I ask her.

はい分かりました, she replies.

I down the drink that's left in my little plastic cup and sink back into my seat, placing my right hand on my boy's sweaty forehead. I gaze out of the window at the setting sun and the clouds haloed with gold and I feel the distance slowly beginning to numb the horror of the last few months. I exhale deeply and the flight attendant arrives with my beer. I pop the ring pull and it opens with a fizz. I pour the beer into my small plastic cup and take a few sips. The seatbelt light turns off with a ping and I close my eyes and think of the empty depths below me.

I think it started with the girl with the black eye, or perhaps it ended with her. It is impossible to tell. I am in essence two different people, two halves of the same life, two branches of the same existence, and she inhabits that juncture, appearing as my old life ended and my new one was about to begin, the eulogy for everything I had been and the portent for what I would eventually become.

A life isn't a smooth stream of events. It doesn't flow like a story. There is no clear beginning or end, no structure or meaning to any of it. It is a haphazard sequence of experiences and connections. The different periods of our lives only become apparent in retrospect, once we can parse the things that matter, to rip the significant from the mundane and build it all into some sort of narrative, to conjure structure from the ether and distill it into something linear. To know where we truly are, it is important to recognize how we arrived there.

The girl with a black eye... Lucy...

Her name was Lucy.

I met her back in 97 or 98. She was tall with long skinny arms and black hair cut into a short bob, and big almond eyes that peered out from below a short messy fringe. She was shy and a bit awkward, but by far the most beautiful girl I had ever seen, and from the moment I first saw her, I couldn't think clearly about anything else.

She worked in a pub in town called Bogarts, a trendy little boozer with wooden floors and bare walls, lots of good beers on tap. I always managed to end up in that pub every Friday and Saturday with my brothers and a group of friends. I would try to get served by her, try to catch her eye, and we would chat occasionally in that slightly awkward way twenty somethings are prone to do, about telly and music and films. I would drink too much, wandering home through the empty streets to fall asleep thinking about her.

Little by little she began to engulf me, her being seeping into my every thought and action. It wasn't lust, no it was something else, something weighty and tangible. When I looked at her, it felt as though I was observing myself, as though we were two sides of the same coin, as though I had met her before, long ago in an existence no longer accessible to me. She became the denouement to my anecdotes, the prelude to a future that still slumbered somewhere beyond the reach of my yearning.

I lurked in that dark little pub at the weekend, drinking and smoking, and laughing with friends, struggling to call up the courage to ask her out, a courage that I knew I may never possess. I would lean against the bar, my beer in hand, the delicately constructed scenario playing over and over in my mind.

I would walk up to the bar. She would see me and smile, and I would say something funny and make her laugh. We would talk until closing time, the pub slowly emptying out, me waiting by the bar as she emptied ash trays and placed glasses in the dishwasher. We would laugh and joke and drink into the night, just the two of us, the door locked, oblivious to the night outside and its dark children. We would reach into each other, exploring and coaxing, and as the morning sun crept slowly on, I would ask her.

In my head it always seemed so simple, but when it came to it, when she was standing there in front of me in a tight white t-shirt, her big brown eyes staring up at me from under that messy black hair, all sense and reason would immediately leave me.

In the summer my friends and I used to strip down to our pants and jump off the suspension bridge into the River Nene. That sensation of being about to leap, of being on the very edge, on the verge of letting go, but never quite giving in, as though your body wouldn't obey the commands from your brain. Instinct would kick in as you teetered on the brink, toes sticking out over that deep water. Talking to Lucy engendered these same feelings. She possessed within her all the happiness that I could ever imagine, and perhaps the simple fact of knowing such was enough. I could wait on the edge of the bridge and watch the river flow by below me, or leap into its depths and be lost forever, and so it went. Weeks then months passed by and I always hesitated, always backed out, too afraid to ask her that one simple question, that one precious utterance that was forever on the tip of my tongue.

One weekend, my best friend Tim from University drove up from Bath and we spent the days drinking, playing Golden Eye on the Nintendo 64 and sitting around my dining room table, hungover and downing endless cups of sugary tea as we talked and laughed. On the Saturday night we ended up in Bogarts, and Lucy was there, working behind the bar as usual. I felt good, confident and alive, the world around me sharp and clear for once, Tim as always egging me on. I had explained the situation to him and he had managed to instil in me the confidence I so needed. He was right, I needed to say something to her, needed to get this thing out of me, needed to voice the horrible beauty that possessed me.

It was getting close to last orders and I was buoyed up on cheap lager and the encouragement from my mates, and so I downed the remainder of my pint, quickly checked my hair in the window and strolled up to the bar. I looked back briefly, Tim smiling and waving me forward.

I asked the barman, a meaty bloke with tattooed fingers to call Lucy over. He nodded and tapped her on the shoulder, whispering something into her ear.

I stood, one hand on the bar top, my heart beating in my chest as she finished pouring a pint for a customer, wiped her hands on a towel, then walked over to where I was standing. She stood in front of me, arms awkwardly by her sides, her dark eyes on mine, her fingers picking a few strands of hair from her face, and I nervously cleared my throat then very tentatively and politely asked her out.

I wish I could remember the words she spoke to me, recall the exact answer she gave. I wish I could relive that moment, to distill it and lock it away safely somewhere, to be able to play it over in my mind, and live those few precious seconds again, but sadly all I have left is a shadow, a crudely reconstructed image, like artefacts accidentally preserved on an old film, or the soft shapes of golden fish below the surface of a frozen lake. All I remember is the word yes, that simple perfect syllable spoken in the depths of that ancient place, that and the movement of her body as she stepped over to the till and quickly wrote down her number on a small yellow post it note, folding it in half and handing it to me. The barman asked if he could see it and I showed it to him. He looked at the note with a little surprise and told me that it was indeed her real number. I told her I would phone her some time the following week and went back to my friends, a massive stupid grin on my face. Tim gave me a hug and in my bliss I bought everyone a round, the rest of the night passing in a wonderful blur, the sudden release of a tremendous weight at last granting me flight.

As we pushed out of the pub and into the night I saw her in the corner clearing up glasses and I shook her hand. It was a stupid gesture in hindsight, but I didn't know what else to do. She had made me immeasurably happy. I went home that night clutching that small bit of paper, so afraid of losing it that I didn't even dare put it in my pocket.

Sometime during the following week I was sitting at my desk at work, everyone else having gone to the pub for an early lunch and in my solitude I decided to phone her. I picked up the receiver, holding it between my head and shoulder and dialled her number from that small scrap of yellow paper. The phone rang several times and her mum picked up. She told me that Lucy was out so I gave her my work number, asked her to tell Lucy that I had phoned, and to call me back when she was home. I waited at my desk all day, that expectant tingle in my innards each time the phone rang, but when I picked up the receiver it was never her voice on the other end.

She didn't phone, not that day, nor the next or even the next. I began to doubt myself, to wonder whether I had given her mother the wrong number, or that perhaps she had forgotten to pass on my message. My initial confidence began to ebb and wane, my thoughts returning to our initial meeting, my wavering voice, and that stupid handshake. On darker days I imagined her standing behind her mum, my voice barely audible over the receiver, Lucy gesturing with her hands that she didn't want to speak to me.

At home I sat about in the dining room in the evenings trying to paint, my mind on the phone in the hallway, a tight anxious feeling in my bones each time it rang, listening intently from the large round dining table when someone else answered, wishing that it was for me, that it was her.

After about two weeks she phoned. I think my mum answered and called upstairs that it was for me, I picked up the phone and heard Lucy's voice on the other end. I felt nervous, excited and awkward, suddenly aware of my breathing, conscious of my beating heart. She said she was sorry that she hadn't phoned but she had had a lot of stuff going on. She told me that she was in a bit of a stormy relationship with someone else and that she had decided to give things another go with him. My heart sank at this, but I wasn't surprised, I tried to remain calm, telling her it was no problem, and that maybe we would bump into each other some time. We chatted for a bit longer before she told me that she had to go. She said sorry again and hung up the phone. I stood in silence in the hallway, her voice still in my ears, the brief conversation playing over in my mind. I distinctly recall the rubbery coil of the telephone wire and the bitter smell of the polish on the dresser where the phone sat, but I also remember an apologetic look from one of my older co workers and the creek of my office chair as I leant back. Time has a way of muddying the waters, of reshaping reality to fit our desired narrative, of stealing from us the physical aspects of events, the times and the places, the specifics of what was said. We are left with a feeling, a ghost of what happened, like the sensation that lingers upon waking from a vivid dream.

The whole situation played on my mind for a long time. I felt hurt, frustrated and utterly helpless. I remember watching the World Cup final a few months later, Brazil were playing, but I couldn't concentrate on the match. I just wanted to see her, to hold her. It felt like an insatiable hunger or thirst, a deep longing that I couldn't satisfy.

Drinking helped to numb the pain a bit, to soften the blow, but it would always return late at night as I lay awake staring up at my bedroom ceiling, the distant sound of traffic on the main road, my window rattled by the wind in its old ill fitting frame. I thought that if I could talk to her again then maybe she would give me another chance, that I could hang on to that thread that so tentatively tied us together, that perhaps she would phone me out of the blue one day, telling me she had changed her mind. As I drifted off to sleep, I would invent complex fantasy scenarios in which the doorbell rang and I rushed downstairs to see her through the glass of the front door, standing in my porch, arms shoved in her pockets, her messy black hair obscuring her face, or that I would save her one night in the pub from a group of drunken thugs, her tears soaking into my t shirt as I held her.

Anyway time passed as it always does and things started to feel a little better. I still went to Bogarts occasionally but Lucy wasn't working there anymore. I asked the other staff where she was but nobody really knew. The big bloke with tattooed fingers said that she was at college, others that her boyfriend was a violent idiot who sometimes beat her. It was all rumours and hearsay, snatches of drunken conversations, utterances made in the dark, conjecture, words spoken in hushed tones over half empty pints.

One night in Bogarts my brother came rushing over, telling me that Lucy was at a party in a house close by. We made our way over, throwing pebbles at the upstairs window until a bloke popped his head out and we pleaded with him to let us in. He eventually came down and unlocked the door and we made our way up the stairs. A girl with two broken legs stalked the hall on crutches, legs hanging beneath her like some bionic simian and we sat awkwardly in the living room smoking a spliff and chatting idly about various subjects. I asked after Lucy, and the girl with broken legs told us some girls had been here with a friend of a friend but had left hours before. We made our excuses and left, pulling our leather jackets around us as we ventured back out onto the cold streets.

She started to become less and less real, less tangible, a ghost, the remnants of a sublime dream that forever hung on the periphery of my imagination. I could still picture her in my mind but the image had become distorted and amorphous, a reflection in a misty window pane.

I made a conscious decision to try and put her to the back of my mind and concentrate on other things. I started to apply for jobs in Japan and learn how to drive. I had a couple of casual flings, and slowly I found myself thinking about her a bit less.

I received a job offer from a school in Japan and quit my job at the insurance office. I had a month off before I had to fly out, and spent the time catching up with friends and getting drunk with my brothers Hardy and Luka until

13

the small hours of the morning, smoking and listening to tapes on the old stereo in the garage.

A couple of days before I was due to fly out to Japan, I went to Charters with Hardy for a few beers. Charters was a big wooden barge that had been converted into a pub. It sat on the River Nene, near the town centre and was only a ten minute walk from my house. We didn't drink that much, the mood subdued and introspective, and we left shortly before last orders. It was a cool night in April and I had just turned twenty four.

Hardy and I were a bit drunk, laughing about something or other as we walked out of the pub and down the wooden ramp to the path. We stopped to light a cigarette or perhaps it was a joint and I saw Lucy coming out of the other exit. She was wearing black army trousers and a hooded top, her hair in that same messy bob. I called out to her and she came wandering over, a broad smile on her face. We talked briefly, both gazing at the ground, hands in our pockets, our eyes occasionally meeting. I told her that I was going to Japan in a week or so, and that I was really excited. She said that was cool and I made a joke about something or other and we both laughed. I told her she looked good and she self consciously fiddled with a string bracelet looped around her left wrist. We stood in silence for a few moments, the trees that lined the river rustling in the breeze above our heads, the silent movement of the water behind us. My inner voice was screaming at me to talk to her, to ask her to have a drink with me, that this was my last chance, that I was about to fly to the other side of the world and would probably never see this beautiful girl again.

14

I told her that I knew she had a boyfriend, but asked if we could go somewhere and have a quick drink together, you know just as friends. She thought about it for a second then told me to wait where I was. She disappeared back into the pub and I turned to Hardy, telling him to go home without me. Lucy reappeared after a couple of minutes wearing a black body warmer and asked me what I wanted to do. I asked if her friends were alright and she said she'd told them not to wait for her, that she'd make her own way home.

We walked in the dark, down by the river past the disused hulks of rotting steam trains from the abandoned railway museum and across the thin iron bridge that spanned the Nene in the direction of the field at the bottom of my road. We talked about music and Japan, about her old job and the vast future before us. I told her how nervous I had been asking her out all those months ago in Bogarts and she giggled, slapping me lightly on the arm. I relaxed a bit, slowly becoming myself once more, the fear and insecurities that so often held me hostage quietened by her presence. I made some jokes and she laughed. At some point my hand had found its way into hers and we walked like that, hand in hand next to the still dark waters, the weight of her body against mine.

We turned away from the river and onto the path that led through the field and up towards the road on which I lived. I asked her if she wanted to come to mine and listen to some music and hang out, but she said she probably shouldn't. I mentioned that it was quite late, so at least she should come back and phone a taxi. She agreed.

As we left the field we stopped in a small open area next to some garages and kissed briefly. I held her close for a few seconds and I whispered something I don't remember. We carried on walking and I told her I would write to her when I was in Japan, that we should stay in touch. She said of course.

We got to my house and she phoned for a taxi as I stood in the silent hallway staring out into the street through the window in the front door at the sleeping houses opposite. We waited outside on the front wall for the taxi to arrive, my arm around her slim shoulders, the odd word passing between us. We kissed again briefly and I held her. It was starting to get cold.

There was so much I wanted to say to her, so much that lurked in the deep solitude that I longed to voice, all that I had been and could be, the coveted, the secret, the divine, all that was ever spoken in my secret oubliette, and yet I remained hushed and reticent, too engrossed in flattering the present to pay heed to the future.

The taxi arrived far too quickly and she climbed in. I leaned into the taxi and kissed her again as she was about to close the door, telling her she was the most beautiful girl I had ever met. She smiled at me, shut the door and the taxi pulled away. I caught a brief glimpse of her silhouette in the back seat as the taxi turned onto the main road and disappeared, taking her into the night and I sat for a few minutes in silence on the front wall, breathing in the cool air, waiting for something I knew would never come.

A few days later I left England behind me and started a new life in Japan.

ANOTHER SATURDAY 1991

Sitting in the garage, drunk and a bit stoned, and wondering where Rod and Max have got to. We had been in town walking back from the pub and there had been, let me say a small altercation. This massive bald bloke and his mates were in line to get into a club. Think it was Ronaldo's, but it could have been any number of establishments. The Borough was full of clubs and pubs. Most of them played shitty pop and catered to the coloured shirt, short back and sides crowd that wanted to spunk their monthly pay on eight pints and a kebab then shag some tottering high heeled slut in Tesco's car park, bragging about it to their mates over hair of the dog beers in the local on a Sunday night.

Fights were common. Growing up I just thought that it was the done thing on a Saturday night. A bit of a punch up after a skin full always seemed like a good bit of punctuation to a fun night out, a few bloody knuckles and some hungover stories for your mates.

Friday was a bit more chilled. Punters wanted to drink away the soul sucking work week and hang out with mates, maybe grab a curry and a few after hours beers. There was always a good vibe on a Friday, lots of hugs and 'love you mates', talk of girls we liked and stupid work

19

related anecdotes. The work week was over and people were ready to cut loose and have some fun.

Saturday though was a whole different beast. A lot of couples done up in their best and a shit tonne of raging drunk wankers, off their tits on too many Stellas, blown out by all the tarts they had tried to pull the previous night and just looking for some poor twat to smash the fuck out of.

Anyway, we were on the way back to mine from some corporate boozer after a skin full of beers and the queue outside this club was long. The pubs had cleared out after last orders and the lucky ones had already jumped in taxis to head home and fuck the night away. People were looking for more alcohol to fuel their night and hopefully push them into a sweaty encounter against a wall somewhere.

People were spilling out on to the road and we had to push through the crowd to get by. My mate Rod was leading the charge as he was the biggest of us and had a 'don't fuck with me' face on him. Rod is a good bloke, in fact he's a fucking martyr. He has the heart of a saint and he sticks up for people. He never lies or rips people off, and I would trust the drunken bastard with my life. He does however suffer from one fatal flaw. The bloke doesn't have any fear, not of authority, not of the law and certainly not of drunken loud mouth wankers wearing too much CK1, off their heads on cheap lager.

So we were pushing through this crowd and Rod was getting a little too enthusiastic. I was keeping my head down but I heard a few grumbles and "fucking twats" thrown our way from some of the lads as we nudged our way through. Anyway one of them, a really meaty bloke in a bright red shirt with too much to prove got shoved a bit too hard and was not happy at all. He grabbed Rod by the shirt collar and they started a bit of back and forth. Like I said Rod isn't one to back down and even though the other bloke was way larger, Rod was holding his own in the struggle. Red shirt tried to punch him and Rod ducked out of the way as the crowd started to part, getting ready for the inevitable ruck. Red shirt was with a lot of mates and we quickly realised that this was not a fight we could win. Rod pulled free after some shoving and name calling and we cleared the crowd, dashing across the road, hands skirting the bonnets of some slow moving taxis and onto the other side. Red shirt wasn't ready to let it go though. There was a lot of yelling and blinding, and him and his mates pushing through the crowd towards us. Rod was pissing himself laughing, but the rest of us were shitting it. They were big blokes and I wasn't at all interested in getting my nose broken again, so Rod shouted a few more insults at them and we legged it. They finally broke free of the crowd and started to give chase. They were big fuckers, but luckily for us they weren't fast. One too many kebabs and too much lager in their fat guts.

So we were pelting down the high street, everyone carried forward on that mix of excitement and fear, the cold wind in our faces, lungs burning, laughing and swearing, drunk and two or three joints in. We could still hear the bastards behind us shouting and cursing.

Two more minutes down the street I took a quick glance behind me and knew that we were at last safely away from their meaty fists and polished Chelsea boots.

They were starting to slow and one bloke, a lanky cunt with greased back hair and a beer belly, was clearly puking into a shop doorway, vomit splashing all over the meatheads shoes. A couple of them were still running and punching the air but it was a lost cause if ever there was one and they knew it. We rounded a corner to catch our respective breaths and Tom pulled a box of Benson and Hedges from his jacket pocket, sparking one up.

Where's Max, he asked, looking around and taking a drag, coughing the smoke back up.

Dunno mate, thought he was right behind us, I replied.

Rod go 'n' have a look mate, he might be in shit, suggested Tom, still panting and out of breath, fag in his gob, his body bent forward, hands on his knees.

Let's all go, replied Rod, if those cunts have got im then I can't do shit on my own.

We made our way slowly back around the corner, peaking out from behind some low bushes that were liberally decorated with crisp packets and empty cans of Special Brew. We were expecting a bloodbath, but what we saw was Max's stupid giggling face framed by his shoulder length brown hair, facing us with his trousers round his ankles, showing our pursuers his white fucking arse.

Come and get us ya cunts, he was shouting or something along those lines.

This seemed to give red shirt and his mates a second wind and suddenly a collective tonne of drunken Ben Sherman and too much hair gel was bearing down on us again.

Run, someone shouted and we all started to leg it, only there was a bit of a problem. Max still had his trousers round his ankles and couldn't run for shit. He was bounding along like a cowboy who had just shat himself, struggling to get his pants back up over his sweaty arse. Rod wasn't helping either, pointing and pissing himself laughing.

Max mate we've got to fucking move old boy, I shouted.

I saw him finally get his trousers up, and him and Rod vaulted the wall into the multi story car park while we took off the other way down the street and through the bus station. We could here lots of effing and blinding in the distance and the echo of patent leather on the pavement. We kept running until we reached the underpass, running down into it and leaning up against the sloping wall to once again catch our breaths. Tom collapsed onto the concrete, doubled up laughing, on his back with his knees arched. My head was spinning with the booze and adrenaline.

My brother Hardy took a packet of Embassy cigarettes out of his leather jacket pocket and crashed me and Tom a couple of fags. We sparked up, but were breathing too heavily and laughing too much to take a decent drag.

You reckon they'll be alright? Pondered Tom.

They'll be fine mate, assured Hardy, Rod can handle himself and he won't leave Max on his own, they'll probably get back to ours before we do. Fucking Max getting his arse out, fucking mental man.

I know, agreed Tom, that was well funny man.

We all laughed and I got a bit of smoke in my eye. I winced.

Got any ganja? I asked my brother.

Fucking half ounce in my room old boy, was the reply.

Could well fucking do with a spliff, remarked Tom.

I flicked my ciggie into the bushes half done. It tasted stale and my throat was dry.

Let's go lads, suggested my brother, and we all walked out of the other end of the underpass and up onto Crescent Bridge

You ever walk over the top? asked Tom, pointing up to the familiar steel arches as we crossed.

Crescent Bridge is an old iron road bridge spanning the railway on the way into town. It's constructed from two massive iron semi circular arches that run perpendicular to the road and held up by steel struts riveted into place. The arches are both about a metre in diameter and about three or four metres above the road at their highest point. It's possible to climb up onto the wall at the foot of the bridge and walk over the top of the arches some twenty or so metres above the railway and without anything to hold onto. We sometimes do it on the way back from a night out. It's fucking stupid but quite exciting.

It was midnight, but there were still a few taxis bombing it down Thorpe Road away from town with their cargoes of sleeping drunks and the lucky few who had managed to pull. The offices of The Borough would be full of stories of drunken violence and fingering birds in pub car parks come Monday.

We got back to my house and walked up the gravel path that ran up the side of the house to the garage. I switched on the lights and put a tape of Led Zeppelin 4 into the old tape player while Hardy sat down and started to skin up.

The garage is an old two story outhouse at the bottom of my garden. We call it the garage, but in truth it hasn't had a car in it for years. I think it used to be used to keep chickens in, back when the house was built at the beginning of the twentieth century, but those days have long passed. My parents rarely come up here so we use the place to get stoned and drunk in, and the second floor is where our band practice. I sing and play guitar, my younger brother, Hardy plays the drums and my mate Eli plays the bass. We play loud grunge music every Friday and usually get quite a good crowd.

So there we are, half way through our second monster joint and who stumbles in but Rod and Max. Both laughing, both drunk and dirty, covered in mud and fuck knows what else.

What happened to you? Asks Tom.

What, were you worried? Rod teases.

Fuck off, I was hoping you got your heads kicked in, Tom answers.

Yeah, no chance of that, retorts Rod.

He is dressed in just a t-shirt, his plaid shirt tied around his waist, curly hair long and dark with sweat.

Those cunts nearly caught us thanks to this twat, accuses Rod motioning to Max who is still giggling and out of breath, Fuckin nutter.

Thanks to him we had to hide in a fucking bush for an hour while those fuckers looked for us.

Nearly found us too, adds Max

Rod kept fucking shouting out stupid shit like 'hellooo' and 'arooooo'. I thought we were going to get fucking mashed

Fuck me, says Rod. Blinding one all round lads,

Yeah, well good night, I agree.

By the way, happy fourteenth birthday Rod old boy, someone calls out.

Yeah happy fourteenth mate, we all chime in.

Now skin up another spliff Hardy and let's get messed up.

A PLAGUE O' BOTH YOUR HOUSES

Mate come here, shouts Tom excitedly, bursting through my front door and into the living room. Tom's family live right across the road from us and Kael and his twin brother Tony just a couple of doors down from him, none of our families ever lock our doors and we all pop in and out of each other's houses as we please. I'm eating toast, drinking tea, and watching Saturday morning cartoons.

What is it? I ask him.

Fuckin Kael and everyone are down at the end of the street outside Wilmot's house, reckon there's gonna be some trouble man, he replies.

Must be about yesterday, I exclaim, already on my feet.

Come here, he repeats, grabbing my arm and leading me out into the hallway, toast still in my hand.

We rush out of the front door and into the street.

It's a warm day half way through Easter holidays, the sun is out for once and a cool breeze blows my chin length hair into my face. I brush it away with my hand as I follow Tom out of the house and onto the street. I was planning to head over to 'Her's' this afternoon, but things seem to be going in a different direction. There are a few cars parked on the other side of the road and the bloke at number fifteen is outside, hosing the last of the foam from the windscreen of a brand new Austin Maestro.

I live on quite a wide street lined on each side with rows of large semi detached houses with big bay windows at the front. There is a hill at the far end of the street that slopes down towards a large field and the river. Looking down in that direction I can see a small white van. It's one of those vans that plumbers and roofers drive. It's got a ladder and a few pipes or something on the roof rack and it's sitting in the centre of the road, surrounded by a crowd of people. We jog up the street, Tom tying his long, thick black hair into a ponytail as we do, fat steel toe cap DMs on the ends of his skinny legs.

Wait, I think we need to back up a bit...

We call round for Kael, banging the brass knocker onto the blue door, standing around in his front drive in the sun. We hear the latch turn and his dad answers dressed in a tank top, that faded blue tattoo on his shoulder, a cigarette in his mouth. He turns and calls for Kael before disappearing back into the house. Kael appears a minute or so later, stepping out into the driveway, pulling the door shut behind him. Hardy tells him what happened with Rob and the skateboard, and how that bastard nearly killed him. Kael listens intently, his nostrils flaring, staring down the street in the direction of the Wilmot's house. He mutters something under his breath and goes back into the house, flinging the heavy door open, leaving it hanging on its hinges as we congregate out on the pavement. He emerges a few minutes later with a long

28

heavy piece of wood, a pick axe handle or something similar. We flock around him as he stalks down the street towards the end of the road, towards the Wilmot's house, that thick bludgeon of wood swinging from his right hand. None of us try to stop him. There are no voices of discouragement or appeals to logic, we know our friend, know that he is controlled by instincts stronger than our own, know that something lurks within him, driving him forwards, pushing him towards eternity.

We get to Wilmot's house and Kael walks up to the front door, past the gold Ford Cortina parked in the front drive, swings the pick axe handle up over his head and brings it down with all his strength onto the heavy wooden door of number 26...

Still not there... rewind...

Tom's dad runs out into the road as the sports car turns into our street, waving his arms for the driver to stop. The red Toyota pulls up to the kerb and the twat driving jumps out, slamming the door shut behind him, Wilmot's mum peering out through the tinted windscreen. The driver strides over to where we all stand, skateboards by our feet, my right hand turning the cold knife over in my jeans pocket. The man is dressed in acid wash jeans and a red ski jacket, his black hair slicked back over his head, a thick gold chain hanging around his neck. Tom's dad immediately starts having a go.

What do you think you are doing? You could have killed my boy, you idiot, he shouts, pointing his finger, a scowl on his face.

29

The man just looks at him, a slight grin on his face.

My dad wanders over and sits down on the bonnet of his car, one leg over the other, the short stub of a cigar between his lips. The twat doesn't like this one bit, pushing him away from the car and yelling. My fingers close more tightly around the knife, pulling the blade out a little with my index finger.

Actually that doesn't make any sense either, we need to go back further...

We are skateboarding in the street outside my house, we live on a sort of cul-de-sac and there is very little traffic so if it's a nice day we mess about on our boards out on the road in front of my house, doing tricks off the pavement or popping ollies over cardboard boxes. Rob, Tom's little brother is standing on his deck, the tail on the pavement, the front sticking out into the road, waiting for a couple of cars to pass when a red sports car driven by Wilmot's mum's boyfriend comes bombing down the street and swerves towards Rob, running right over his board, snapping it in two and nearly hitting little Rob in the process. We all start shouting and chucking stones at the twat but he speeds off up the road, Rob in tears, his expensive skateboard in bits.

Still not far enough...

The Wilmots live at the end of our street, at the top of the incline that slopes down towards the field and the river beyond. Wilmot is a weird kid, a year older than me,

30

tall and wiry with a massive mess of curly blonde hair. In fact the whole family all look alike, long blonde mullets, and sharp faces with hooked noses. His mum is always hanging about with this young Asian bloke, we see them all the time in the car together or standing outside the house during the day chatting on the street, him sitting on the bonnet of his red Toyota smoking a cigarette. Wilmot rides around the nearby streets on his silver Raleigh Grifter, dressed in a tank top and cut off jeans, his skinny white arms and legs covered with freckles and wispy blonde hair. He watches us skateboarding and hanging out with girls, always from a distance, perched on his bike seat, arms hanging by his sides. We sometimes chase him off and threaten him, but he always pedals away giggling and calling us names.

We are sitting around on Tom's front wall, talking shit and messing about when Wilmot speeds past on his bike, spitting on Kael as he passes, then pedalling away laughing. We give chase, but the twat is too fast and disappears down the side of his house and through the gate before we can catch him. That night Kael, me and Tom break into his back garden and trash all of his plants. The tune Oxygen by Jean Michelle Jar is playing in his back room as we dance in time, pulling trees from their roots. Kael drags a massive conifer out of the back and into Kirkwood close, the street that runs up behind the houses on my side of the street, a thin piece of grassy land separating our gardens from the road.

That's not it either...

We are all still in primary school and the long summers seem eternal, our minds still able to sculpt the ordinary and the quotidian into the sublime, we dig holes in the damp earth and our dreams nestle in the embrace of hollow trees. We live in a fantastic world of invisible monsters and powerful weapons crafted from dead wood and old fence posts. We move as one, talk in code and lay in the sun gazing up at the clouds, the damp earth cold on our backs. The small world we inhabit is our playground and we sculpt and reimagine every patch of grass and muddy hill, moulding them into fantastic landscapes in our imaginations. We play cowboys and Indians, cops and robbers, construct dens in the woods by the river and bathe in the sun, building houses in the trees or vast underground tunnel systems within the confines of our daydreams. Our skins are ruddy and freckled by the sun, our knees a mess of scabs and scratches, black muck beneath our nails that our mothers painfully pick out as we sit in tepid baths, clean pyjamas hanging from heated towel rails.

Gabriel got a skateboard for his eleventh birthday, one of those little plastic ones with big wheels and wobbly trucks. We take turns riding it down the slope at the bottom of our road, seeing how long we can stay on before getting scared and jumping off. One day we notice a long line of large stones placed down the hill where we usually skate. We reckon old man Wilmot doesn't like us playing so close to his house. We kick them all away and throw a couple at the miserable bastard's windows. He comes out and we try to run away, but I slip on the wet grass and he grabs me tightly by the arm. There is something about this man, something that scares us, he spits his words with anger, his grey eyes are full of spite. I answer him back and he tightens his grip pulling me forward towards his face, the stink of greasy food and cigarettes on his breath. Kael tells him to let go and he does, but his grasp leaves a bruise. As we walk up back towards my house, below the horse chestnut trees that grow in the garden of the old abandoned house Kael pulls me close and whispers something into my ear, his hand on my arm, making me promise not to tell...

Kael is down at the gravel pit, the area around the garages at the bottom of the hill, a large patch of ground surrounded by a few bungalows and covered in a loose black gravel which is perfect for doing skids on our bikes. We see how long we can slide for, pedalling as fast as we can down the hill before pulling our breaks with all our strength and standing up on our pedals as our bikes slide across the loose ground, dark scars left in our wake.

Kael is alone, trying to pull wheelies on his tiny little BMX when Wilmot rides over, leaning his bike up against the wall and walking over to talk to Kael. They talk for a bit and Wilmot shares a stick of gum with him. He tells Kael to follow him into one of the garages, that he has found something really interesting that he wants to show him. Wilmot lifts one of the garage doors, it swings up slowly, the stink of petrol and bike oil within, the cold concrete floor stained with emulsion paint. Wilmot leads Kael into the cool interior and closes the door halfway...

As we get closer to the van and the crowd surrounding it, I see Nails, his hair short, dressed in a green Bomber jacket and Kael, who's wearing his favourite plaid padded shirt, fag in his mouth, his blonde hair curly and unkempt in the middle of the group along with some other faces I recognise, others I don't. I think Donnie is there. He's a bloke from the year below me.

I don't really know Donnie that well, but everyone says he's hard as fuck. I watched him fight some kid from Bretton Woods school in the underpass on the way to town once. There was a big group of us and the two of them were in the middle. They both had their tops off, Donnie the much bigger of the two, and were about to go at it. This fight had been on the cards for weeks, both of them were top billing at their respective schools, hard bastards whose only skill was kicking the shit out of people, but at 15 years old that was all they needed. Donnie was there with some pretty red haired girl from the second year. I don't remember her name but rumour has it that she shat herself in Mrs Hill's English class once because Donnie had shagged her in the arse one too many times.

After a few minutes of posing and cheering on from the assembled crowd they finally went at it. Donnie went in fast and hard and fucking pounded the other bloke before he even knew what had hit him. The bloke's mates were over in a flash pulling him away and wiping blood from his unconscious mouth as we on the other team congratulated our man. A rather nervous old couple passed by, giving us all a wide berth and some disapproving looks but we couldn't have given less of a fuck. We were invincible and young and ready for anything. We walked into town together after that all feeling like fucking heroes and did a bit of shoplifting to pass the time. Donnie was a fucking King for a day and we were his loyal followers.

What the fuck's goin on mate? I ask Nails, sliding up next to him, a hand on his shoulder to get his attention.

Alright mate, he replies, eyes still fixed on the van and its occupants, fuck we were on our way round to Wilmot's, reckoned he could do with a smack for that shit with Rob, so we were gonna ring his doorbell then drag him out and kick his fuckin head in. You heard about Kael and the pick axe yeah?

Yeah, I answer, I was there mate.

The driver's side window of the small white van is wound down and there is some shouting and cursing.

Yeah what happened to Rob was fuckin well out of order, I add.

Yeah mate, well bad, he says, we were all hanging around outside his house deciding who should knock for him when this bloke pulls up in his van, Kam started to give him shit, told him to get the fuck out of here.

There are a couple of Asian kids among the group. I recognise the little one as Credit (he half inched his old man's credit cards one day and spent a shit load of cash on them) and the other is Kam, another mad bastard from a different school. He's one of Kael's mates. I heard he got arrested for fighting in town once and had to appear at The Magistrate's Court for a hearing. He was really late and didn't have any money so the mental bastard stole

35

one of the mini buses from the depot and tried to drive to court. Suffice to say he didn't make it far.

The driver of the car steps out and I see that it's Darren's dad. Darren is a good kid really but we never really got along. He hangs out with Wilmot too much and nobody likes him for that reason alone. His dad and Wilmot's are thick as thieves, always standing about on the pavement outside Darren's house, dressed in overalls, tinkering with a car engine or sharing a cigarette.

So anyway Darren's dad and Kam are exchanging words and things are starting to escalate. At this point in the proceedings Darren's dad calls Kam a monkey and tells him to get back up his tree. Everyone fucking loses it at this. Kam grabs the racist wanker and throws him up against the side of the van. His mate gets out of the passenger door and comes round to our side. He is trying to play it cool in an attempt to diffuse the situation.

Come on lads it's not worth it, he didn't mean it, he's saying

Kam let's go of Darren's dad eventually, but you can see that he's really fucking unhappy to say the least.

All of this is happening right outside the Wilmot's house and the old man of the family chooses this moment to make an entrance. He pushes open the front door, a large dent still in the blue paint and walks out into the street in a vest. He's a short wiry fucker with a mass of blonde curly hair like his son, and an enormous fucking mullet. He looks like one of the singers from Abba after no sleep and a serious bout of something serious.

He sees what's going on and wanders over. He catches Nails' eye, walking up to him and whispering in his ear.

Let's go into my back garden and fucking settle this, just you and me, he says.

I'm right next to Nails and hear everything. This is a forty year old bloke threatening a fucking 16 year old. Anyway Nails seems really keen on taking up his offer. Things are starting to get a bit out of hand. There is pushing and shoving and swearing. Everyone is threatening to kill each other and things are about to get interesting when the old bill turn up.

It's just one car at first and no one notices it turning onto our street. We are all too caught up in whats going on. It pulls up to the side of the road and a WPC gets out. She's not that fit but everyone starts to wolf whistle, and Kael is up there in a flash right beside her trying to fucking chat her up. She is having none of it. Her partner gets out of the passenger seat and he definitely means business. He's got his hand on his baton and I can hear the static from the radio through the open door of the car. The male police officer pushes a few of us aside and moves forward to talk to Darren's dad. Everyone is shouting their own version of the events into the poor bastard's ear and he's got his little notepad out desperately trying to take notes. Kael is up in his face telling the bloke that Darren's dad is a racist cunt and that he's going to smash his fucking head in. Wilmot's dad is hanging back with a fucking grin on his face. He points to me and half mouths, half whispers the words,

I know about your dad too, fucking alcky.

Rage fills me and I clench my fists. I'm going to smash that twat's head in. I can feel tears starting to well up in my eyes and I swallow hard. Nails puts his hand on my shoulder.

He'll get his soon mate, he reassures me, he'll get his.

Damn fucking right he will, I think to myself.

The cop and Darren's dad are chatting away and he's feeding him all sorts of shit. Out of nowhere, Kael takes a swing at Darren's dad and the cops jump on him bundling him roughly away. Kael is yelling 'get the fuck off me' as they are trying to restrain him. He's fighting and struggling and the cops are having a really hard time keeping him still. He finally breaks free and makes a dash back up the street towards his house. The pigs shout after him but they've got too much on their little plates to go legging it up the street after one angry teenager.

No one try any stupid shit! orders the WPC resting her hand on her baton, her other palm raised towards us.

The other cop is on the radio calling in for backup and Darren's dad is climbing back into his van mumbling and cursing.

We move over to the curb and sit down with our legs facing into the road while the core of the group continues to shout and bicker. Tom gets out a packet of Embassy Number Ones and passes around a few.

The bloke pig sees us and asks us if we are over sixteen.

Of course we fucking are, we reply.

Don't get lippy lads, he warns us, but he's too busy with the ensuing riot to pay us much more attention.

I get my matches out of my pocket and strike one on the edge of the pavement. We all light our fags and take a few deep drags. Kam is being questioned by the male officer and the rest of the crowd is still shouting and calling out, everyone relaying their versions of the events.

We all hear a siren, and a large white police van turns the corner onto our road and races down the street towards us. It pulls up to the curb, lights still flashing, and out jump some serious looking fuckers with broad shoulders and beer guts. They order us all out of the road and over onto the pavement outside Wilmot's house. I see a few curtains moving, and some of the neighbours have come out of their houses and are now standing in their front gardens watching the spectacle. Don't think this lot have had so much fun since the acid house party at number 16.

Officers are trying to calm things down as everyone is arguing and fighting over the details of what transpired. Darren's dad is back in his van and one of the other officers is attempting to take names but failing.

So which one of you is David Hasselhoff? I hear him asking at one point.

Suddenly there is the roar of an engine and a big white Toyota comes barreling down the road. It pulls up with a screech and Kael's dad comes flying out. He's wearing slacks and a polo neck, his thick greying hair in a mess, a half finished cigarette hanging from his lower lip. As he jumps out of the car the police step back. They know who he is and they know he is pissed off.

Mick is Kael's dad and everyone in The Borough knows who he is. He's from Ireland, County Cork originally I think and he's got a really thick accent. Everyone respects Mick. Kael told me he came over to this country when he was in his twenties, jumping ship before it had chance to dock, and swimming into London. He spent his time working where he could, finding jobs at nightclubs and casinos, and occasionally rubbing shoulders with the London underworld. He owns the Luckyleaf club in town, which has a blinding indie rock night on a Friday. He has a poker night on Thursdays at one of the buildings he owns in the city centre. I go along there sometimes with Kael. It's good fun to climb up onto the roof there and throw stones at the trendy cunts hanging around outside the Wayward Frog, a poncy wine bar on Bridge Street street next to the Town Hall.

Mick once won a Patek Philippe wrist watch in one of his poker games. Kael found it knocking around the house and thinking it was just a normal watch, decided to wear it one day. We ended up down at the field at the bottom of the road, getting stoned and playing some football and Kael, having no jacket decided to use the watch as a goal post. On the way back home he realised that he'd left it in the field. His dad was fucking pissed off. Turned out the watch was worth about twenty thousand quid. He gave Kael a deserved smack around the head and sent us all back down to the field with a torch to find the fucking thing. Luckily we located it eventually and as they say all's well that ends well.

So Mick starts on the WPC first.

What the fuck do you think you're doing? Don't you dare touch my fuckin son, he growls at her.

The other officers are trying to diffuse the situation.

Get back in your car please Mr Corrigan, says one of them, this has nothing to do with you, but he won't be coddled, he won't be consoled.

The WPC looks terrified to be honest. I don't think this is what she signed up for, probably thought the job would involve parking offences and settling minor domestics, not stopping potential riots. Still, something to cut her teeth on I suppose. We are all loving it. This is real, this is exciting.

After a long chat and a great deal of scribbling in little note books, Mick mumbles something, gets back in the car and floors it back up to his house. It's literally a minutes walk up the hill from where we are, but the mad bastard decided to drive rather than hoof it. It certainly made an impression I can tell you that. Darren's dad drives off down the street to where he lives and the crowd starts to disperse. People have plans and can't stand around all day in middle class Borough when there are drugs to be sold and shoplifting to be done elsewhere. We all say our 'goodbyes' and 'laters mate' and we part company. I walk back to the house with my brother.

The police are still at the end of the road talking to neighbours and getting names but things have quietened down. My parents are standing around in the front garden as we approach, concerned looks on their faces. My dad is smoking a cigar and has his jumper sleeves rolled up exposing his skinny forearms, pacing about the small patch of grass nervously. I walk up to him and give him a hug.

Are you both alright? Asks my mum.

My father's hand goes to the back of my head and he pulls me close. I can smell alcohol on his breath, hear the slow rhythm of his heart, and Wilmot's dad's words play through my mind. At that moment I make a promise to myself that one day I'm going to kill that fucking man.

FIRST KISSES, LAST KISSES

When you are sixteen years old and living in a small town with lots of time on your hands there is one thing that literally consumes your thoughts for the majority of your waking life. From the moment hair starts to sprout in other areas, your brain becomes focused on the pursuit of one goal: How to get a member of the opposite sex to touch your dick. It may sound vacuous and pathetic to anyone not cursed with that ridiculous organ dangling between their legs, that thing with a life of its own that grows and shrinks at will, but a teenage boy's life is governed by those few inches of extra flesh.

We are a good looking group of blokes and there are always a lot of birds hanging around. There are the girls from our school, and those from the private girl's school down the road. We climb over the wall late at night (it's a boarding school) and meet up with them in the grounds, clumsy sticky fumblings in the dark and kisses with too much tongue. Then there are the nurses who live in the dorm next to the hospital. They are bored and drunk and a lot of fun. They work on flex time and if we are out all night we sneak into the hospital, find their cards and clock them in early for a little extra pay. Favour for a favour as it were.

43

First there was Jen, she was in my class at school and used to go out with my mate James. I liked her and she liked me so when they broke up I asked her if she wanted to come over to mine and listen to some music and chill out. I had to go to my grandparents house in Scunthorpe that day and couldn't wait to get home and be with her. It was all I could think about in the car on the way home.

We got back at about five in the evening and I was too excited to eat any dinner. My mum excused me from the table with a smile and I rushed up to my room, dabbed on some Armani aftershave from a bottle someone's older brother had half inched from their job at Asda, put on my favourite paisley shirt and did my hair, setting it with a couple of liberal sprays from a big pink can of hairspray.

The doorbell rang at about six. My mum called upstairs Kei, Jen is here.

I could hear them both exchanging some small talk at the bottom of the stairs, as I came out of my room, trying my hardest to appear relaxed and quell the flushing in my cheeks. I walked down the stairs, stopping near the bottom, one hand resting on the banisters, the other in the pocket of my favourite tartan jeans.

Alright Jen, I said.

Hello, she replied, smiling.

She was wearing a tight blue jumper and a pair of jeans. Girls in the eighties looked great in jeans. They were tight and came up over the hips. If the bird had a nice arse, then a good pair of jeans was sexy as fuck. She had lip gloss on and her hair was cut into a short bob. My heart was beating quickly as I tried to swallow down that ticklish swell.

You want to come up and listen to my new cure tape? I asked.

Yeah cool, she answered.

We headed upstairs together, and I lead her into my room, pushing the heavy door shut behind us before perching ourselves awkwardly on the edge of my bed. I had a big, old, iron, double bed with brass fittings. When we were children we used to spin the bell-like knobs on the frame because they made a ringing sound. We called it the fire engine bed.

I got up and pressed play on the tape player, the first few chords of 'Catch' coming through the tinny speakers. We shifted further back onto the bed, her hands tucked between her knees, me leaning back, hands splayed out behind me. We chatted about school and homework and The Cure.

What's your favourite tune? I asked.

'Just Like Heaven', she replied and I agreed.

I was trying to maintain the conversation, but all I could think about was leaning in to kiss her. I watched her lips as she spoke, the sticky layer of gloss on her mouth and the tiny soft blonde hairs on her upper lip. I felt the soft hush of her words. She tucked her short hair behind one ear, put her hands under her arse and leaned back slightly. I could see the curve of her tits under her top and a tiny bit of her stomach above her jeans where her jumper had ridden up. There was a lull in the conversation as everything seemed to slow down, her chest moving up and down as she breathed and the tape

45

player clicking as 'Kiss Me Kiss Me Kiss Me' reached the end of side one.

There was a moment of silence and her lips parted as she began to say something. Before she could talk I moved closer, put my hand behind her head and kissed her on the mouth. She reciprocated. The first kiss was brief and gentle. She breathed deeply out of her nose as I pulled away and let out a small sigh. I kissed her again. This time my tongue found its way into her mouth and hers into mine.

We lay back on the bed with me on top of her, her legs wrapped around mine. We kissed, talking in giggles and whispers and kissed some more. We rolled over and my hands found their way onto her shapely behind. I tried to undo the top button of her jeans but she quietly said no, the soft touch of her whisper on my ear.

That's as far as it went. We were content with just putting our tongues in each other's mouths. We were still too young to really comprehend what it all really meant, too naive to engage in the messy potential embarrassments of something more. It was pure. It was beautiful. I was happy.

We started going out. We were barely 14, and going out just meant that I was her boyfriend and she was my girlfriend. We didn't go on dates and we didn't even really spend much time together. We would talk on the phone in the evenings and occasionally go to each other's houses and kiss, but that was about it. I don't really recall how our relationship, if you can even call it that ended, but it did. These things just seemed to fizzle out when you were that age. Soon enough she was going out with someone else and I had my sights set on another girl from school. No difficult breakups and no jealousy or regret. We were still friends and we still saw each other regularly. The only difference was that we didn't kiss anymore.

I bumped into Jen again much later in life. I had finished University and had an office job, something in insurance. I was in a club in town on a Thursday night and I had just been chatting to this bloke Sean, an old mate from years ago. We used to go to primary school together. He was a massive hard bastard with a bald head and a face only a mother could love. Kael used to call him Frankenstein, although not to his face. He went off to get in another round and there was Jen on the dance floor. She looked the same as ever and was dancing drunkenly to some generic nineties pop music. She saw me and came over. We chatted for a bit and pretty soon we were dancing together. I put my arms over her shoulders and her forehead touched mine. Max came over, pushing his way onto the crowded dance floor and told me he was heading home. I gave him a hug and told him I was staying. He nodded with a grin and patted me on the shoulder.

Jen turned around and started to grind her arse up against my nether regions. I put my hands around her waist and we danced like that for a while. She turned back to face me and in the middle of that crowded dance floor we kissed. I asked her if she wanted to get out of there and she said yes. So I took her by the hand and we weaved our way off the dance floor, out through the double doors and into the club's bright atrium. We made our way drunkenly down the carpeted stairs, hand in hand.

We left the club and walked out into the cold autumn air. My ears were ringing, the muffled thump of the music still audible in the quiet. It was late but there were a lot of people on the streets, a few excited shouts and the echo of heels on the pavement carried on the breeze. The weekend always started on a Thursday. Everyone would turn up to the office on a Friday morning with a raging hangover and colourful stories from the night before. It was a nice way to set you up for the weekend.

We stopped to kiss a few times in the street and I took my jacket off and put it around her, holding her to me for a moment. It was cold and windy, a light misty rain in the air and she was dressed only in a short skirt over a pair of black tights. She told me that she was living in a flat quite near the town centre so we walked the five or ten minutes to her place.

She unlocked the front door and we crept into the warm, quiet interior. I told her she had a nice place and asked her how long she had been living there. We exchanged pleasantries and then went to her room and fucked until the morning.

She fell asleep on my shoulder, just as the sun was starting to peek through the blinds. I extricated myself from the bed, making sure I didn't wake her and sat naked next to the open window smoking a cigarette. I could see the first few people making their way to work in the blue light of that drab October morning. The bin men were out and there was the occasional shout from the last of the previous night's drinkers. They probably had work in a couple of hours and would turn up to the office stinking of booze and fags, heads pounding, the last kebab of the evening constantly threatening to make a come back. They would finish the work day, go home, take a shower and then go through the whole macabre dance again. Like I said there isn't much to do in my town and if you don't keep numbing your mind with booze and drugs then one day you might just wake up and realise how truly fucked your sorry life has become.

Jen woke up at about eight and told me she would drive me to work. We were both late. I had fallen asleep again and neither of us in our inebriated state had had the forethought to set the alarm. There was no time for anymore funny business. We didn't even kiss. I put on the previous night's clothes, brushed my teeth with her roommate's toothbrush and we were out of the door by a quarter past. She was driving a really nice 7 series BMW with leather seats. It was her Dad's and he had insured her on it and let her drive it while he was out of the country.

She dropped me off outside my office, and I leant over from the passenger seat and gave her a peck on the cheek as I tightened the knot on my tie and climbed out. She told me to call her as I closed the car door and she pulled away to join the rush hour traffic, looking back briefly and waving as she drove away. I never really saw her again after that. We kept in touch for a while but slowly we drifted out of each others lives once more.

EDUCATION, EDUCATION, EDUCATION

My dad totalled the car turning into our street on the way home from work last night. Another car hit him from the left as it came down Crescent Bridge and onto the main road. He's fine, hurt his shoulder and was in hospital overnight but was discharged this morning. The car is a fucking wreck though, so we have to walk to school today. We are a little bit later getting in than usual but the bell hasn't rung yet so we are alright. I say 'see you later' to my brother and run to my classroom, taking my usual seat at the back, next to the windows. Mrs Hartman takes the morning register and we all sit around talking for a while as she busies herself at her desk. The bell rings for the start of morning classes and we all bustle out into the hallway, Mrs Hartman shouting over us not to run in the corridors.

Our morning lessons go by as usual and I eat my whole packed lunch at 10.30 during break time. My mum makes me cheese sarnies and packs a bag of crisps and a chocolate bar. I usually eat half the sandwiches at break time because I am fucking starving and save the rest for lunch. Today we are planning to get lunch from the chippy, so I wolf down everything in about five minutes. A couple of my mates go to find somewhere for a crafty ciggie, but I have a personal rule of no smoking before lunch. It's a warm day, the ground still wet with the morning's rain, so I just sit around on a bench between the Science and English blocks with some other mates and talk.

As we are sitting there this bloke from the fourth year comes running up. His name is Gav. He is a bit of a twat. One of those try hard kids who always sucks up to everyone. He thinks he's popular, but no one really likes him. I don't really know him too well but he seems to be in a bit of a panic.

I ask him what's wrong.

'Everyone is getting done for selling drugs', he blurts out excitedly.

'What do you mean?' I ask.

They've got a list of names and they're pulling everyone into the headmasters office and questioning them about selling hash at school. It's fucking serious man, he continues.

What do you mean they've got a list? What fucking list? I ask, a cold panic starting to come over me, the prickly fingers of foreboding working their way into my stomach.

I don't know mate, he says, reducing his voice to a whisper as a group of first year girls wanders by giggling about something or other. Tom's name is on it, and your brother Hardy, and you, and some others.'

'Fuck' I think.

And... I think there's a pig in the office too, taking names and shit, he adds.

'Ok, I say, don't fucking talk to anyone else about this alright? Yeah, yeah of course mate, he answers.

Now how the fuck did we get to this?

I first smoked hash when I was about 13 years old. Four or five of us had been hanging out at the bottom of our road where the abandoned old house stood. It was huge, four stories high and built on a slope so the garden was below street level. We would slide down the bank from the pavement and into the garden, getting into the house through a side door. We would take girls in there and smoke and get drunk. The floors were falling apart and in places there were holes that let you see all the way down from the top floor to the basement. The attic had some old rickety stairs that led up to a few floor boards that hung precariously over a large drop. There were rusty nails everywhere and the whole place looked ready to give up the ghost.

We had been talking about wanting to get stoned for a while. We all thought we were going to have this life altering experience the first time we smoked, that it was going to expand our minds, but like all teenagers, we were full of shit. We were all on board for buying some, but didn't really know where to get any.

There was an older bloke, must have been in his early twenties who was always hanging around our street. I think he might have been going out with Suzanne Brown's sister who lived at number 22. He was a good looking bloke, tall with long blonde hair, looked a bit like Tony Hawk.

As we were hanging around on the street we saw him walking down the road in the opposite direction. Kael crossed the road and ran up to talk to him. Max, Tom, my brother and I hung back nervously watching them. We could see them chatting away but couldn't make out what they were saying over the sound of the traffic. After a few minutes Kael came running back, announcing excitedly that he could get us an eighth of resin. The bloke had told him to wait there for fifteen minutes, that he'd be back.

Hash in Britain is always sold in ounces and divisions there of. The smallest you can get is a sixteenth and this would do you for a couple of joints. I don't remember how much it was going to cost but something like 15 quid. We all agreed and dug into our pockets for the money. We managed to scrounge together a few quid and Kael ran back home to tell his mum he wanted to buy some food from The Spa. He came back with a crisp fiver and between us we had enough.

After about half an hour the bloke with the blonde hair returned. We saw him stop at the top of the road and he signalled for us to come up. We all took off up the street, Kael in front, our hands shoved in our pockets. Kael looked around then handed over the cash. I remember thinking the bloke was just going to take the cash and fuck off, but he produced a small clear plastic bag with some brown lumps in it that looked like dark chocolate and turned it over to us. He said cheers, pocketed the money and walked away up the main road in the direction of Crescent Bridge towards town. It was about 2:00 in the afternoon on a lazy Saturday. Parents washed their cars in the street or took naps in living rooms, Saturday afternoon telly, Land of the Giants or Lost in Space on hot tube tellies.

Now what? We had rolling papers and tobacco but none of us had ever rolled a spliff and we had no idea what we were doing. Kael was rolling the resin around in his hand and sniffing it. He handed it to me. It had a thick pungent aroma and was actually quite hard. It was dark brown and a little sticky to the touch. I used my nail to break a bit off and ate it. It was really bitter.

Don't fucking eat it, scolded Kael, snatching the small brown rock back, we have to smoke it.

We went into Tom's house, wiping our shoes on the mat in the porch and down the hallway to the kitchen at the back of the house. His parents were out and his little brother was in the living room, watching telly, tucking into a large plate of bread and butter. We broke open a cigarette and lined a rolling paper with the tobacco. We then tried to break off small pieces of the resin but it was too hard.

Tom, said Kael.

Yeah mate, Tom replied.

You got a cheese grater?

So there we were in Tom's kitchen using a fucking cheese grater to try and break the resin into bits small enough to get into a joint. It was heavy going as the piece was pretty small, and to hold it tightly enough to get a good amount of friction meant scraping your skin off on the grater along with the resin. It was a fucking mess. There was resin on the floor and on the counter and blood in the cheese grater. We must have wasted at least a quarter of what was already a small piece. Anyway we finally got enough into the rolling paper to make a decent joint. Tom licked the edge, folded it over and we finally had our first ever joint.

Fucking spark it up Tom, urged Kael.

Anyone got any matches? He asked.

There must be some in the drawer, I replied.

We couldn't find any matches in the house so we decided to light it from the electric hob. Fucking thing set alight and Tom got some hot rocks down his sleeve.

Fuck, he exclaimed beating his shirt sleeves with his other hand.

He passed it round and we got a few drags out of it before the fucking thing disintegrated.

We all looked at each other and burst out laughing. Worst joint ever. We all went home without even a buzz and fifteen quid worse off.

I called round for Tom the next day and his younger brother Rob answered the door.

Tom coming out? I enquired.

He's grounded mate replied his brother.

What? Why? I asked.

Dad found a cheese grater with marijuana all over it in the sink and burn marks all over Tom's arm. He thinks he's been doing drugs, said his brother.

Poor bastard, I thought.

So the next couple of lessons go by and still no call from the office or the headmaster. I hear at lunch that Tom and Nugget had their names called and were questioned. My stomach feels tight and I can't concentrate on anything Mrs B is saying in geography class.

Imran, the crazy bastard was smoking in the hall just outside the class in between periods, and when the teacher turned up he did that little trick with his tongue where you flip the cigarette, or in this case cigar back into your mouth and keep it hidden behind sealed lips, breathing the smoke out through your nose. So we are in class and the teacher is explaining the formation of oxbow lakes and Imran has a fucking lit cigar in his mouth. I look back at him and he laughs a bit. A small puff of smoke issuing from his mouth. The classroom must stink but all the teachers smoke, so I doubt anyone can smell it, the staff room at my school is always swathed in a dense cloud of carcinogens and the bitter odour of coffee so I don't think any of the teachers has any sense of smell left. It all takes my mind off the office and the police for an hour or so but once the bell rings and we empty out into the hall again, the feeling of foreboding returns with reignited vigour.

The last class of the day is maths with Mr Gordon. The man certainly isn't much of a teacher, more of the 'turn to page 12 and do exercise three in silence' sort of bloke. I keep looking out of the window onto the school field, half expecting a police van to come driving up the hill.

The final bell rings. We put our chairs up onto the desks and wait to be dismissed. Those last five minute go by at a fucking snail's pace, but once we stand in silence for a minute or two Mr Gordon tells us we can go. He wishes us all a good weekend and I grab my bag, hoisting it up onto my shoulder and leg it towards the exit. I see a couple of teachers on my way through the halls, one of them telling me to slow down. I make it outside and walk the short path out of the school and onto the main road. The pavements are crowded with teenagers in school uniforms. They wander slowly in big groups, headphones on their heads, walkman's shoved in donkey jacket pockets, chewing on cheap chocolate bars from the machine in the swimming pool. The fifth year and six formers pull cigarettes from top pockets and share them around. There are cars parked at the curb, picking up sons and daughters and I say 'alright' to a couple of people I know. I get to the small patch of grass outside the flats at the top of park road and wait there for my mates. People are passing by on both sides of the street. The pavement gradually becomes more and more crowded with pupils from my school, most of them already having discarded unwanted items of uniform and changed into trainers for the walk home. Some of them are drinking from cans, others hanging around the Netherton shops talking and messing about.

The Netherton shops area is a large paved square surrounded by local shops, a god awful chippy and some small council houses. There are a few benches and a big grassy area further back in front of some grotty looking blocks of flats. The place is infamous for fights after school.

Jimmy Doyle got his head kicked in over there a few months back. He's a short stocky kid from the year below me with long curly blonde hair and far too much attitude. He's pretty tasty when it comes to a ruck (or so he says) and most of the kids in his year keep well away from him. He does a bit of kick boxing and is always getting into scrapes in and out of school. He used to hang around with Kael quite a bit but they weren't really friends. To be honest, Kael used to bully him a bit.

Doyle got into an argument with these two girls from my year. They are called D and M but everyone just calls them the twins. They are pretty fit actually, nice legs and big tits, and everyone gets on with them really well. They are gregarious and straightforward. Nice girls but they don't fuck around. I think Jimmy had been giving them shit about something and D had had enough.

We were hanging around outside the offy trying to decide who looked old enough to go in and buy some ciggies when we heard a bit of a commotion. D had Jimmy by the arm and he was telling her to fucking let go or else. He looked her in the eye and said he was going to count to five. D didn't let go. Jimmy started to count.

5... They both maintained eye contact. Neither wanted to look away, but Jimmy had his hard-man image to uphold. He was going to fucking punch her if she didn't let go.

4... a few bystanders were telling D to let go but she wouldn't back down from some jumped up little twat from the year below.

3... D's sister looked on, her eyes were focused and she said nothing.

2... Jimmy didn't struggle, he didn't want to look like a pussy. A crowd had gathered in anticipation of a punch up and they wouldn't be denied.

1... Jimmy brought his right fist back, ready to deliver a massive right hook to the side of D's head. Girl or not, he was going to knock the fucking bitch out.

O... D's sister came in fast from the side, her little fists flying into Jimmy's face. He pulled away from D and tried to fight back but D had his long hair in her left fist and the two sisters were pounding the shit out of him. Pointed shoes connected with his shins and M pulled his jacket up over his head. Both girls jumped on him and gave him a proper thrashing. The crowd was yelling and cursing. 'Fucking twat him'. 'Punch that fucking bitch Doyle', and then it was over. A few older kids from the sixth form waded in and pulled Jimmy from the fray. The girls were still throwing punches and kicks but few connected. Jimmy had blood on his face and his jacket, a pretty expensive ski jacket by the looks of it, was ripped to shit. The adrenaline was still pumping and everyone had to be held back. The girls were F ing and blinding and Jimmy was trying to regain a semblance of dignity. D had clumps of his blonde hair in her fist and she was spitting at him and calling him a little twat. A few of Jimmy's mates came over and led him away from the crowd. Arms around his shoulders in consolation. A few parents had come out of the surrounding houses and were threatening to call the police. The crowd started to disperse, people wandering off towards the grange, talking excitedly about the fight, the younger kids scurrying away home, big heavy backpacks swinging from side to side.

Jimmy never regained his former image as a hard bastard after this and people gradually started to oust him from their groups. He got arrested a few years later for making dirty phone calls to this girl Janet's 11 year old sister and he went to jail. Janet's parents had started recording the calls and Jimmy had to stand in court in front of his folks while they played the tapes back to him. Must have fucked him up more than the time he got, but whatever, he deserved it. I never really liked him.

Finally I see Tom, Nugget and my brother coming down the road. We all meet on the corner under the tree, chat for a bit and then head home. Tom and Nugget got pulled into the office shortly after lunch and they were both questioned about drugs at school and were asked who else was involved. They didn't say a fucking word, denied it all. In the end there was no evidence apart from here-say, so what could they do but give them a warning and a slap on the wrist. Have to keep our heads down from now on though I think.

MADE IN ENGLAND

We are in the kitchen just hanging out and talking. The kettle is on and we are making some cups of tea to take up to the garage with us while we have a smoke. It's me, my brother and Tom. It's a Saturday afternoon and we are all just waiting around until the evening to head down to Joe's garage for happy hour and then on to whatever the night holds. We hear footsteps outside on the gravel and the back door swings open. It's Kael.

Alright mate, didn't expect to see you today, thought you were skint, I say.

Nah mate, got hold of a bit of cash last night, he tells me.

Nice one, comments Tom.

Yeah mate, he continues, this fucking bloke who's always hanging around in the College Arms, I told him I was going to get him an ounce and he gave me a hundred quid and I just fucking pocketed it, so it looks I can come out with you lot tonight after all.

The College Arms was a big new corporate brewery pub that had recently opened on Bridge Street in the town centre. These places were springing up all over the UK at the time and they all looked the fucking same, big TVs

61

playing the footie, Carling on tap and full to the rafters with coloured shirts and shaved heads, and lots of tarts and office workers in for a pint after a boring day in a shit hole office somewhere. There were usually a few familiar faces in there and the lager was cheap, so it was often the first stop on the way into town. They were a bit strict about underage drinking, but we usually managed to sneak past the bouncers.

That was another thing I hated, pubs with bouncers. The thinking was that a couple of meathead body builders on the door would keep out any trouble. In fact, the opposite was actually true. They usually turned away the goths and the punks and anyone with long hair and let in all the clean shaven button up psychos. If you spent long enough in the College Arms on a Saturday you were almost guaranteed to get in a punch up. Kael and me almost got battered by some blokes around the back of the pub once.

The toilets in the College Arms were all the way down the other end of the pub and up a flight of stairs. It was rammed on Fridays and Saturdays, so if you needed a slash you had to push through hordes of wankers with neck tattoos and Calvin Klein shirts. It would take you at least twenty minutes and who could be fucking bothered with that? What we used to do was push open the fire door at the back and sneak out into the alley that ran behind the pub and the gym next door. When I say gym I don't mean a nice clean place full of students and trendy people with brand name sports wear and little flasks of organic, naturally sourced fruit juice, normal blokes and birds just looking to run on a treadmill and lose a few pounds so they can post a couple of pics on Instagram. In the early nineties they were rough old places, dark and sweaty and full of bouncers and fighters and other hard cunts.

So we were outside the back of the gym taking a much needed piss up against the wall, when these two massive blokes came out of the back door. They saw a couple of skinny stoners pissing on their building and they fucking lost it.

What the fuck are you doing? One of them growled.

His arms were so massive he couldn't even keep them by his sides. He looked like he was about to take flight.

Kael doesn't like bouncers. A couple of weeks earlier he had got into a punch up with one of the doormen at Ronaldo's. The twat wouldn't let him in for wearing jeans so Kael started to have a go at him. Bouncers generally don't take kindly to being abused by the clientele. It's a power thing as much as anything. They've got this image to uphold, the ultimate alpha fucking male.

So Kael and this bloke started exchanging punches right there at the entrance to this club and all hell was breaking lose. Everyone was drunk and a few punters were trying to put the boot in, while others saw the chance of a free entrance and started to push past into the club. Kael was doing alright considering the size of the other bloke. Both of them had blood on their knuckles. The bouncer then grabbed Kael by his bomber jacket and tried to pull him inside. There was an office just inside the entrance, and the meaty bastard was trying to drag him in there to give him a proper whipping. We saw what was happening and all grabbed hold of Kael, desperately trying to pull him back out.

Don't let him get me in there, Kael was shouting.

A few of the other blokes in the queue saw what was going on and they started to pull too. We eventually got him out of the bouncer's clutches and we all collapsed on the pavement. Kael was bloody and battered but the mental bastard was laughing his arse off.

It later turned out that Kael's dad was really good mates with the owner of Ronaldo's. They went way back, and when he found out about what had happened to his son he was ready to kill the twat that had done it. He had words with the owner of the club and the bouncer was soon on the dole. Couldn't get another job anywhere in The Borough after that. Probably fucked off to some other identical shit hole and got another identical job at another identical club. Like I said my town is nothing special. Kael probably did the twat a favour. If you didn't leave this place it would kill you eventually. Not quickly and humanely, but slowly eat away at your soul and your dignity until you were just another faceless clown downing eight pints on a Friday and working in Dixon's for fucking pennies. Like I said, nothing special.

So these two meat heads were seriously pissed off and had probably taken too many steroids. They had been in the gym all day and the testosterone coursing through their bodies had them hunting for some violence. I was all apologetic and trying to diffuse the situation, but Kael was having none of it. He turned round to face them, cock still hanging out of his flies.

Fuck off back to sucking each other off, he shouted full force.

I don't think the two massive bastards were used to getting anything back and they were a bit taken aback, but only for a second. That was it, we were going to get beaten shitless I thought. I turned to get back in through the fire door, but it had slammed shut and there was no way to open it from the outside. I could see a group of blokes downing pints and chatting as the two mountains of flesh bore down on us. I slammed my fist against the door to try and get someone's attention. I turned to see Kael standing with his cock out ready for a punch up. He wasn't a small bloke but compared to these two beasts he looked like a toddler. They would throw him around like a fucking dog toy.

Open the door mate, I yelled, motioning to the horizontal bar that you had to push to get the fire door open. A girl sitting with the group of blokes saw me banging on the glass and gave me two fingers then started laughing. She was all perm and too much fucking make up.

Fucking bitch, I mumbled under my breath.

An older bloke with a beer gut hanging out over his jeans came towards the door. He must have had the same idea as us, couldn't be bothered walking ten miles just for a fucking piss. He pushed open the fire door and I saw my chance. I grabbed Kael by the shoulder and pulled him through, back into the noisy sweaty interior of that corporate boozer. A couple of glasses got knocked over and make up bitch got a lap full of Stella Artois.

Fucking wankers, she yelled.

I didn't care. Kael and I started to push through the crowd towards the doors, but we could see the two blokes from the gym coming around the front of the pub, through the windows. They got to the entrance and were stopped by the doorman. He had seen too many blokes like this with roids in their veins and blood in their eyes, and he was having none of it in his pub. I could see them arguing, and the gym blokes were pointing into the pub. We back tracked to the fire door past the make up girl and her mates who were drying her off with a towel, pushed it open and escaped into the night.

We ran the opposite way around the back of the pub, weaving around metal beer barrels, crates of empty bottles and soggy cardboard boxes until we got to a high wall. Kael gave me a boost and I vaulted up and onto the top. I held out my arm and pulled Kael up, then we both dropped down into the car park next door. We walked between the parked cars and down the side of an office building. There were still people in there working, eyes glued to their computer screens, spouting about productivity and synergy and drinking too much cheap coffee, clocking out at the end of the day then downing a quick pint and off home to wank off over that sexy new nineteen year old tart in finance. Give it ten years and they might end up team leader with a shitty three series BM and a mortgage on a semi detached house in Orton, married to that bird in finance, but she's pushing thirty now and has really let herself go, too many pies and chips in the cafeteria and some other bloke's bun in the oven. Divorce and lawyers, fighting over who gets the fucking sofa, selling off the house and moving into a flat in

Bretton, drinking too much and finally dying lost and forgotten along with all the other poor fucking souls that tried so hard to stick to the plan. Nothing turns out the way it should. Life is just a chaotic mix of random events. Control is an illusion. Nobody is steering this thing. All you can hope to do is buckle up your seat belt, wind down the window, enjoy the view and hope you don't hit a truck coming the other way before you run out of petrol.

We sneaked through the fence at the end and onto the main road. Cars and vans roared past, lights reflecting off the wet tarmac. The cathedral bells sounded in the distance and a few stars peaked out from an overcast sky. We stood under the orange haze of the streetlights and Kael handed me a fag, taking a small disposable lighter out of his jacket pocket. He lit his cigarette then passed it to me to light mine. I looked at my watch. It was nearly half ten and I was starving.

Fancy a kebab mate? I asked.

Sounds good old boy, replied Kael.

By the way mate, I added.

What? He enquired.

Your fuckin knob's still hanging out.

Ain't he going to wonder where his drugs are? Asks Tom.

Yeah probably, Kael answers, he's a well scary bastard too, got 'Made in England' tattooed across his stomach.

Fuck me, I say.

Kael fishes around in his jeans pocket for a moment, then pulls a massive bag of white powder out. Everyone is wearing super baggy jeans these days, so wide that they cover your shoes, really good for concealing plastic bags full of drugs.

What the fuck is that? I ask.

Just a bit of speed, Kael replies.

A bit? Must be an ounce at least, Tom interjects.

Kael shrugs it off, Yeah, you got a blender or something Kei mate?

What? Mate you can't fucking mix that in here, my mum's in the front room watching telly, I tell him.

Don't be a cunt, I'll clean everything up, I've got to cut it with something so I can make some cash and give 'Made in England' his money back, he explains, but I'm unconvinced.

Fuck mate, I dunno, I tell him.

My brother opens the cupboard and brings out the small blender. It hasn't been used in ages, my mum always uses a whisk when she is baking and my dad doesn't really cook anymore. Kael takes it and plugs it in, then empties the bag of speed into it, taking a couple of licks of his fingers as he does so.

Speed is a horrible drug. We sometimes bang down a couple of wraps then head to the pub and drink. You feel fucking great for the first few hours, you are the most charming, confident bloke in the pub. Your mind is clear and everything has the volume turned up. You can't stop talking and things happen with a wonderful quickness and clarity, but the come down, fuck me it's rough. All you want to do is sleep. You are hungover and tired and the inside of your mouth feels like it's been ripped to

68

shreds, you've got mouth ulcers and your eyes are dry and itchy. At the same time your liver is trying desperately to process the eight pints of lager you drank, but you haven't eaten in twenty hours. Your stomach has shrunk to the size of a fucking pea and you are hungover, dehydrated and sick. The sun is beginning to peep over the horizon and you have to get up in a few hours. You hear the first chorus of dawn and the milkman coming down the street, milk bottles clinking in the back of his float. You go for a piss, dry heave in the sink a bit and go back to bed, shivering and hoping that sleep will take you, but it never comes and you walk through the next day like a fucking zombie. You finally make it back home after a rough old day at school and a friend phones up and asks if you are going out, everyone is going to be there. You look at your watch. It's Friday and it's five thirty. You are so tired you can't think straight but you still have a couple of wraps left in the drawer. If you bang those down, it might pep you up a bit, you think.

We don't have any baking powder so my brother gives Kael a bag of flour. Some people mix the shit with detergent or caustic soda and other nasty substances, but that shit will kill you, and Kael isn't out to hurt anyone, just wants to make a few quid. He puts the flour in the blender then turns it on. Speed and flour go fucking everywhere. He hasn't put the top on the blender and the kitchen is suddenly obscured behind a thick cloud of drugs and baking goods.

Turn the fucking thing off, I'm yelling.

Kael is trying desperately to snatch his precious shit out of the air with his bare hands, must be a good couple of hundred quids worth. Tom reaches over the work surface and pulls the plug out of the wall and the whir of the blender comes to a sudden halt. Kael's face and hair are white with flour and amphetamines. He is covered in the shit.

You look like you've trekked across the arctic mate, Tom jokes.

Kael brushes his hands through his hair, shaking out a fog of white powder and starts to laugh. Soon we are all pissing ourselves. There is speed and flour everywhere. We all get down on our hands and knees and start to try to rescue some of the precious powder from the floor, scooping it up into piles and then collecting it with the dustpan and brush. We are actually recovering quite a lot of it, and we are half way done when my mum walks in.

CHEKHOV'S GUN

Fuck me I'm wasted, I tell Eli.

Eli is a great bloke and the bass player in my band. He's a handsome bastard, got that James Dean vibe going on and the ladies love him. He's tall with an olive complexion, lots of dark freckles around his eyes. He's confident and laid back, one of those people who seems genuinely comfortable in his own skin. He lives over in Westwood with his mum, dad and little brother. His old man cleans carpets, did ours once, and his mum likes Cliff Richard. They've got a little white dog called Jazz, looks like a poodle, but I think it's some other breed. Apparently it's a pedigree.

We all got pissed one night and got a taxi over to his house. He decided he was going to have a party but it was a fucking Wednesday night, midweek, so of course no one turned up. It was just me, him, my brother and his dog. Eli ended up drinking a whole bottle of his dad's home-brew strawberry wine and getting really messed up, kept telling us he could get any girls we wanted. Me and my brother were stone cold sober and a bit stoned and I had to call it a day. I got a taxi back home, but my brother, the good samaritan hung around and watched Eli puke into a bucket all night. Fucking blinding night, as Nugget would say.

We are at Chloe's party. Chloe is the older sister of Debbie, Kael's bird, and me and her have been shagging for the last few months. She Likes my skinny, pale, hairless body, thinks I look like David Bowie or Jesus.

The party is being held in this big brightly lit community centre somewhere on Lincoln road. It's a chilly night in autumn, the pavements thick with damp leaves and everyone dressed in donkey jackets and benny hats. We are all crammed into this little events room, a big red velvet curtain hanging over a low stage at one end, the music playing loudly through an old black stereo. The graphic equaliser is fucked so it's really tinny sounding, lots of treble and very little bass. Doesn't really matter though cause the music is all shit, chart songs and crappy pop. The oldest of us are still only sixteen but there is a shit load of booze knocking about. My younger brother is here and everyone I know from school. The vibe is pretty chilled, lots of conversations over plastic cups of vodka and orange, a couple of rough looking tarts dancing away on the polished boards.

Me and my brother decided to walk all the way here, which was a mammoth trek. We purchased a half of vodka from The Spa on the way and took swigs of it on the walk here, hands thrust into our jacket pockets from the cold. By the time we arrived it was all gone and we were already feeling a buzz. Hardy tossed the empty bottle into some waste land behind a local pub, we lit a couple of fags and strolled through the heavy double doors and into the community centre, a hand drawn sandwich board at the entrance welcoming us to the party.

72

Since we got here we've been hitting the punch pretty hard, scooping it up with see through plastic cups and I'm starting to feel the booze hit me. I tell Hardy and Eli I'm heading out for a piss and I step outside for some air and a quick fag.

The cold bites at my nose and fingers and I pull my coat around me, sparking up and taking a few drags. looking around I see Imran leaning back against a tree. Imran is a bloke in my year. He lives up in West Town, near the chippy. We aren't really that close, but we get along pretty well. He's tall, skinny and a cheeky bastard to all the teachers at school. He is really into 'Her'. We both gave her valentines cards this year and he took the piss out of me because mine was handmade. I drew a picture of John Lennon on the front of it and she said she really liked it.

He looks pretty messed up and upset, so I wander over to see whats up.

You ok mate? I inquire.

Nah mate, he replies, just a bit drunk.

You don't look good mate, whats the problem? I press.

He looks at me. His eyes are glazed, his thick black hair messy and uncombed. He's dressed in just a t-shirt, goose bumps on his hairy arms.

My dad's really ill mate, he tells me, reckon he hasn't got long left.

I don't really know how to respond to this. I fiddle around with my long hair, curling the ends about between my fingers, eyes on the damp leaves by my feet and tell him everything is going to be alright. I lie. I look into his eyes, wet with tears, glassy below the orange street lights

73

as the dull thud of shitty party music filters out through a small open window.

He's gonna be fine old boy, I tell him drunkenly, the words awkward and unwieldy.

To be honest I'm not really with it. The world is a bit shaky and incoherent and my speech doesn't seem to be in synch with my mouth or brain. I take another pull from my cigarette and my head spins. I put my arm around Imran's shoulder to console him. It has started to rain a bit and it's getting really cold, the wind stinging my face and fingers. I hear the front doors of the community centre swing open, followed by a familiar voice.

Alright Kei mate, you got a light?

I turn round to see Liam strolling over, his hands in his pockets, unlit fag hanging from his mouth. His hair is long, tied up behind his head, a few strands blown in front of his face, a bit of a bum fluff moustache poking out from under his flat boxer's nose. He walks with his shoulders hunched up, his heavy Dr Marten's swinging from his skinny legs.

He's the coolest kid in my year, a snappy dresser who listens to all the newest bands and has always got a really fit bird with him when I see him out. He's one of those blokes who just decided early on that he was going to be the coolest fucker at school, and that's just how it turned out. His brother is a few years older and the hardest bloke around, or so I'm told. Everyone is shit scared of him. He's one of those blokes whose name is whispered secretly in school hallways or scribbled in marker pen on sexy older girl's pencil cases. We all have stories about

74

that one time we met him outside school or when he gave us a nod as we passed him on the street.

It's fine, I tell him, Imran is just having a moment.

Cheer up mate, Liam says to him, nothing to fucking worry about, it's a fucking party mate.

Leave him alone Liam, I say, he's having a shitty night.

Alright mate, he replies, fuck I just wanted to see if the bloke was alright.

He's fine mate just leave it, I urge, stretching out my hand and motioning Liam away.

Alright mate, I'm just having a fucking chat, don't have to get fucking shirty, he says.

Just fuckin leave him alone mate, I warn, too drunk to catch my tongue.

I'm not your mate alright, he bites back, pushing my hand aside.

And that's how easy it is. That's how it always starts.

There is a bit of pushing and cursing, Imran desperately trying to appease and pacify, but it's too late for that and before you know it we are at each other, punching, kicking and swearing. I hit him a few times and he hits me. He is wearing steel toe caps and lands a good few kicks to my shins.

Don't you fucking start on me you cunt, he keeps shouting as I punch the fucker a few more times and he punches me. I can't really feel a thing through the adrenaline and booze. Pretty soon everyone is out of the community centre and jumping on us trying to break it up. Eli is there and Mark Mayhew, and a few others. They are holding us back and Liam is still trying to kick me in the shins. His legs are really skinny and he's got these massive fucking clown shoes on. They fucking hurt though. We get pulled apart. Someone drags Liam off somewhere and Eli pulls me back towards the entrance of the community centre.

My town can be a hostile place just like a lot of the small towns in this country, misanthropic and aggressive. There is always someone looking to intimidate, rob you or just beat the shit out of you for the fuck of it, so in my infinite wisdom I decided that it would be a good idea to carry a knife. I bought it for a fiver off one of Kael's mates. It was about the length of my palm and had a fold out blade. When I was walking around at night I would turn it about in my trouser pocket with my right hand. It felt solid and weighty and gave me a feeling of safety and security. If someone tried to start shit I thought I would just pull it out and frighten them. I wasn't looking to stab anyone, but I was small for my age and thought I needed a bit of protection, something to even things out. I used to carry it with me everywhere, only leaving it at home when I went to school. A lot of kids in my school carried knives, they all had their specific reasons, different ghosts that haunted their souls. Kael's cousin once got attacked on his way back from town, a stupid drunken brawl and got stabbed through the arm with a bread knife. It got lodged between the two bones in his forearm. He couldn't pull it out because the blade was serrated, and he had to walk all the way to the district hospital with a fucking bread knife stuck through his arm.

So the fight's been broken up, but I'm still fucking raging. At this point my brother comes walking out of the community centre. Liam sees him and runs over, the anger from our punch up not yet satiated and starts laying into him. My brother is only fourteen and nowhere near as big as Liam. He has no idea what's going on. He's backing away trying to block the punches with his arms and get away. I see a few land, Liam's skinny fists connecting with my little brother's head and I fucking lose it.

I remember my younger brother Hardy being born, or at least I think I do. Memories are extremely unreliable, like Chinese whispers passed down though the years. We recall something and then later we remember the recollection. It's like recording music from tape to tape, again and again. Somewhere along the line the clarity gets lost and what was once crisp and clear becomes muddy and imperfect.

I was two when he was born and I seem to recall someone saying my mum was in the hospital and being aware of something going on. There were a lot of people milling about the house, dressed smartly, chatting excitedly and drinking cups of tea, alluring boxes of chocolates hidden away safely high up on bookshelves, away from curious fingers.

I remember him being in bed and having no hair. He had little fingers like tiny plump sausages and I would sometimes lightly bite them while he was sleeping.

He learned to ride a bike without stabilisers before I did. It was a little blue thing with white rimmed tires and his little chubby legs would propel him along the pavement outside our house at quite a speed. It got to the point where the stabilisers no longer touched the ground anymore and so my dad brought out an adjustable spanner and took them off. I remember feeling a twinge of jealousy at the time. He was younger and yet somehow stronger, more full of the drives that propel us through life, unrestrained by the hesitancy that so often held me back. The praise and hugs he received from my parents quickly spurred me on to do the same a few weeks later, but by then the achievement had already lost its edge. It had become diluted and peripheral.

He was a faster runner than me at school too. I remember him winning a lot of red ribbons at the school sports day whereas mine were mostly yellow and blue. He soon grew as tall as me, and by about the age of ten we were basically the same height. We didn't look at all alike really. I was skinny and had small, what my dad liked to refer to as elfin features, whereas he had a wide nose and a big head with masses of untameable blonde hair. He was stocky with thick legs and arms, while I was pale and bony, my beating heart visible between the ribs in my narrow chest. We would brush our teeth together in the evenings and look at ourselves in the mirror. The only real similarity we found was our ear lobes. Despite this we were really close, closer perhaps than I was with my older brother. We did almost everything together, and as we grew up our bond grew stronger. When I was about eight or nine we slept in the same room. The big bedroom at the back of the house with a sash window that looked out over the garden towards the tall trees that separated the houses on our street from Kirkwood close.

We had these big wooden framed single beds set next to each other with about a metre gap in between. We would have endless fun at bed time after mum had read us a story and turned off the lights jumping from one bed to the other or throwing pillows at each other. My dad would hear us messing about from the room below where he would usually be listening to classical music, Vivaldi's Four Seasons more often than not, and he would call up the stairs for us to be quiet. We would settle down for a bit, but then one of us would laugh or say something stupid and we would be back at it. My dad would eventually get tired of our shit and come up the stairs to give us a bollocking. We would hear his feet on the creaky bottom step and hide under the covers pretending to be asleep. I would make a little peep hole for myself out of the side of the duvet. We would always leave the bedroom door slightly ajar and I would see his bearded face with those big black rimmed spectacles as he got to the landing outside our room. He would tell us off for a few minutes and we would try very hard not to giggle or make any noise and then he would go back down.

Once we had been particularly noisy and my dad had already been up twice. He had told us that if we made him come up again we would both get a good hiding. We heard the door to the back room click shut and we lay in silence for a few minutes. Hardy soon got bored and threw a pillow at me that hit me square in the face so I picked up mine, pushed the pillow stuffing all the way to one end of the pillow case so it was nice and solid, and proceeded to whack him with it.

We heard my dad say something in a raised voice and come out of the back room. We jumped back into bed and I pulled the covers over my head. Hardy did the same. I made a little hole as always and waited.

My house was built in about 1909. It was old and most of the floorboards creaked. I heard my dad's steps as he climbed the stairs, and as he reached the landing I could make out the top of his head through the crack in the door and I held my breath. I closed the little hole that I had made in the duvet so he wouldn't see me. His footsteps stopped as he reached the entrance to our room, but he was saying nothing. He must be really mad I thought to myself.

After a few seconds I pushed the duvet up a little bit, breath held, trying really hard not to move too much, so that I could take a look.

There was a man standing in the doorway to our bedroom, but he wasn't our father. My heart started to thump. I could feel it in my throat. I wanted to call out to Hardy who was in the bed closest to the door, covers pulled over him, but I was too afraid. The man stepped into our room, pushing open the door as he entered. I was too scared to take a proper look and could only make out a pair of muddy shoes and dark trousers as he walked in towards our beds. He came over to Hardy's bed, wrapped the duvet around him and lifted him off the bed. I could see my brother struggling in the covers, trying to free himself, his screams muffled. I tried to shout out, tried to call to my parents, my mouth moving but unable to make a sound. The man effortlessly threw my little brother, still wrapped in bedding, over his shoulder, turned towards the door and walked out, banging into the open door as he left, the doorknob knocking into the wall, leaving a shallow hole in the plaster...

I awoke with the duvet over my face, struggling to free myself. It was hot and stifling and I was panicked and scared. I got my face free and pulled in a few breaths of cool air. It was dark and there was a little bit of moonlight shining in through a slit in the heavy curtains. I looked over and saw my brother sleeping peacefully in his bed, one small white hand hanging out of the covers.

I call out Liam's name, pull the knife from my trousers and unfold the blade. I want to fucking stab the cunt. I want to stab him until he's dead. There is so much rage in me that I just want to destroy and murder and smash things till they stop moving.

Leave my brother alone, I scream out.

A group of people pull Liam away from my brother and he comes back over, pulling free of the people restraining him. He sees the knife and comes at me again, kicking at my shins with those heavy fucking shoes. There are a lot of people outside now and a big group has surrounded us, trying to break up the fight. Liam is fucking yelling and screaming, his long hair half pulled free from his pony tail, a bit of blood on his knuckles.

You fucking cunt, pull a fucking knife on me will you?

A group of my friends quickly restrain me as I lunge with the knife and Mark grabs my arm, pulling it from my grasp. I think he cuts himself in the process, but he is just interested in disarming me. More people get involved and finally the fight gets broken up. Alec pulls Liam away and leads him off towards the street. I'm in tears. I'm so full of rage and regret and alcohol that I can't think straight. Eli puts his arm around my shoulders and leads me away around the back of the community centre.

It's quiet back here away from the traffic of Lincoln Road and the shouts and noise of the aftermath. Eli hands me a cigarette and I light it with a shaky hand, pulling in a big lungful of smoke and exhaling into the cold still air.

It's alright mate, Eli tells me, just take a breath old boy.

I nod and wipe a few tears from my eyes.

Mate, what are you crying for? He consoles me, a warm smile on his face. It's alright, shit's done mate.

I dunno mate, I stutter, I just... he hit my fucking brother. I look around searching for him, pulling free of Eli and heading back towards the entrance. Eli catches up with me, spinning me back around.

Nah mate, he urges, don't fucking go back there, he's alright mate. He's with Tom and Debbie, don't go back, you need some fuckin air old boy.

He leads me out of the community centre grounds and onto Lincoln Road. It's getting on a bit and the traffic is sparse, the occasional taxi and bus speeding past us, dimly lit under the orange street lights.

After a cigarette, a long chat with Eli and a walk around some of the back streets, I finally start to calm down. My head is still spinning with booze, but the rage has subsided. I'm starting to feel cold, the chill of the night working it's way to my core. We light another cigarette and head back over to the community centre. When I get there I see Liam. Eli makes us both reconcile, forcing my hand into his. Liam says sorry, but I know he doesn't mean it. I apologise too and we shake hands and hug briefly. I ask where my brother is and Mayhew tells me that he's fine, someone put him in a taxi and sent him home. He asks me if I want my knife back.

No mate, I answer, throw it in the fucking river when you get the chance.

Things are a bit weird at school for a while after this. I dread that Monday, having to go in and face everyone who witnessed my idiocy that night, my lack of self control. I see Liam a couple of times and we nod a few greetings as we pass in the halls, but we are never really mates again. There is always a coldness between us, we meet at parties and chat occasionally but we still both harbour some resentment, the bitter residue of that night tainting our brief interactions. A couple of the muslim kids from my year come up and shake my hand on that first morning, thanking me for sticking up for Imran, ignorant to the real machinations that guide me, blind to the shadows that set this all in motion.

Imran's father passed away a few weeks later but no one really noticed or cared. I still get flashes of anger in those moments before sleep takes me, picturing Liam punching my brother, but I am glad I didn't stab him. My life would be very different if I had. I never carried a knife again and Mayhew threw the one he took from me that cold night into a wheelie bin somewhere on the way back from the party, or perhaps he sold it on to someone else for a couple of quid, another lost lonely kid with something to prove to the world, just looking for a reason to lash out, to carve his mark into this bleak heavy mediocrity. I don't really know and I don't really care.

As for Liam, and what happened to him. His older brother was in the local paper years later for crashing into a taxi on his bike and fracturing his kneecap while he was pissed out of his head. There was a picture of him looking rough as fuck, his face skinny and covered in bruises. My mate Alec tried to track down Liam on a quick trip back to The Borough and eventually found him living in a council house somewhere in The Borough drinking and banging up.

FOR MY GIRL

Another night and another party. I think this one is at Tammy Krueger 's house. Tammy is a really fat American girl who just started at our school. Her dad is a semi famous American football player who has come over here to squeeze a few extra years out of his career. She's got a massive spotty face and a mess of curly blonde hair. She is fat, North American fat, and people in England aren't really used to it. Suffice to say she gets a lot of shit. I think because of this she is really trying hard to make a good impression. Her parents are away a lot, so she has parties at her house all the time. They are always pretty mental, lots of booze and drugs. Liam, Alec and Butcher are here. Everyone says that Butcher is the hardest bloke in my year. He's big and stocky with floppy blonde hair that he keeps in a centre parting. I'm good with people, able to talk to anyone, but Butcher always puts me on edge, everything he says coloured with a subtle condescending aggression.

Liam has got a new pair of glasses without lenses because he wants to look like Morrisey. He's got a daffodil tucked behind the left arm. The Smiths are on the stereo and everyone is singing along and getting pissed on MD 20/20. It's a horrible sweet alcoholic fruit juice that comes in various flavours. It's cheap as fuck and does the job perfectly. Ethan is drunk with Blake in the kitchen. He's cut his hand on a beer can and is squeezing the blood out. It drips in little rivulets down his wrist and makes dark stains on his yellow t-shirt. Alec has brought some porn on a grotty VHS tape, Star Wars scribbled across the half torn sticker along its spine. It's really old school 70's shit with lots of big titted blonde birds and waka waka guitar riffs. Some of it is pretty good though. Alec is sitting on the sofa having a wank right there in the middle of the party but no one really gives a fuck.

Whats wrong? Are you all fucking puffs or something? He challenges when someone notices him going to town on the old boy.

Jen is there and she is looking fine, dressed in her usual tight jeans and t-shirt, too much perfume and a new short haircut. She is going out with Marko though so no chance there. There are quite a few other birds knocking about, so there might be the chance of a snog at some point. The house is pretty big, most people crowded into the spacious living room, lots of chintzy ceramic dogs and crystal ornaments adorning the shelves and mantle piece. There's also a small group in the kitchen, skinning up on the work surface and rummaging through the cupboards for some snacks.

Me and Eli steal a bottle of white wine from one of the cupboards, sneak out of the back of the house into the cool night, and walk down to the underpass. We lean up against the angled walls, a mess of graffiti and scribbled names, love hearts with arrows through them, teenagers mistaking their first clumsy thrusts for something deeper and more profound.

We don't have a bottle opener so Eli smashes off the neck and we pour the contents of the bottle into our mouths, trying to avoid cutting our lips on the glass as the occasional truck rumbles over our heads. The wine is cool and dry, the hint of something metallic in it. We finish the bottle and toss it onto some waste land, wandering back through the empty streets, talking about girls and guitars. Eli produces half a spliff from the top pocket of his military jacket and we spark it up from a box of Swan Vesta matches, leaning up against a red brick wall in a narrow passageway between two rows of houses.

We head back to the house and go in through the back gate which swings shut with a clang behind us. We walk up through the garden where a few people sit cross legged on the grass, the glowing cherries from lit cigarettes in their hands. We walk into the smoky kitchen and Eli starts chatting to a group of lads from the year above us while I go upstairs to find the toilet. I walk up the carpeted steps, onto the landing and look about for the bog. There's a large group of blokes I don't recognise in one of the bedrooms, three or four of them huddled around something on the bed, the others, as if standing guard eye me through the half open door as I walk by. As I pass, one of them comes out and grabs me.

Hey mate come in here a second, he whispers, his hand on my elbow, leading me towards the door.

I'm halfway in when Eli appears and grabs me, pulling me back out onto the landing by my jacket sleeve.

Mate don't go in there, they'll fucking kill you, he warns, as he steers me away from the room and down the landing to the toilet.

I'm in the toilet. I'm having a piss and the small bathroom window is open. I am swaying back and forth, my eyes scanning the pristine white walls. There's a framed photo of a small girl on the wall to my left, her mouth in a wide smile, a tiny white poodle clutched to her chest. I can hear 'Big Mouth Strikes Again' by 'The Smiths' through the open window then a loud crash, something glass, followed by laughter and shouting. The door closes behind me and I'm on the landing again. Did I flush? Don't know.

Hello, I say to Tess as she passes me by on the hall.

She looks at me and smiles, actually Kei you're really good-looking, she tells me, her hand going briefly to the side of my face.

Damn she's fit. I think her parents are from Sri Lanka or something. She's got a dark complexion, A mass of black curly hair, big lips and a curvy body. I smile back and tell her something as I search for my ciggies. Where did I put my fucking fags? I look in my shirt pocket and find the crumpled box. I pull one out and spark up. No smoking in the house, 'fuck that' I think to myself. Big mouth lala la laaa. Tess isn't there anymore, doesn't matter, I'll catch up with her. Time to head back down to the party. Where the fuck are the stairs? Oh there they are.

You alright mate? It's Eli.

Fine old boy, I say laughing.

I'm at the bottom of the stairs and my arse is fucking sore, still got my ciggie though so life is good. Did Tess just tell me I was good-looking? I'm going to have to find her later. I think I cut my lip on that broken bottle, it stung as we wandered back. The streets were dark and I was thinking about 'Her' in her school uniform, tight black skirt, her hair in plaits... They had something in that room upstairs, something secret and full of bright light, I could have seen it, could have held it. If only I were brave.

Hey, Eli mate, that fucking new song we wrote today is well wicked mate, I tell him. I look down at my feet.

I stumble in the garden, my left trainer sinking into the soft mud of a flower bed. I leave muddy footprints across the living room carpet.

Eli has a massive quiff going on and it looks fucking excellent. The man truly is a gift to the world of women I think. He's got his tongue in some girl's mouth now. I think her name is Rachel. She's new. She's tall.

Cheers mate, I say to him.

Ethan comes over and hands me another glass of something and I down it. The music plays and a few people dance. Someone opens a window, knocking some books off the shelf as they lean forward.

My mum kisses me on the cheek as Eli and I leave the house and wander down the front path towards the road.

Don't be too late, she calls after us.

We are outside in the garden and Liam's pockets are full of daffodils. He's spinning round, head back, staring up at the firmament.

Back inside and Eli asks me if I've seen Butcher. Not for ages I think. The music is on loud and everyone is having a good time. The porn is still on the telly but everyone has lost interest. A fat brunette is on all fours getting fucked by Santa Claus.

89

The living room door opens and Marko comes running in.

Fucking hell Butcher is shagging Tammy, he shouts in excitement.

What the fuck, we all exclaim, as he gestures for us to follow him, too drunk to stifle our giggles as we all sneak up the stairs. Marko shushes us with a finger to the lips as we get onto the upstairs landing. We head down the hall to Tammy's parent's room, treading carefully along the thickly carpeted hallway, past old photos of men in American Football uniforms and vistas of vast mountain ranges topped with caps of white snow. We reach the end of the hallway, and Marko uses his foot to quietly push open the door which already stands slightly ajar. It swings slowly open, the handle banging gently against the wall and we see the two of them going at it. Butcher is on top of Tammy, thrusting away at that massive white lump of flesh, his spotty arse moving up and down, her feet, one still covered in a small white sock, wrapped around his thick hairy thighs. They are completely unaware of us, and we just stand, mouths agape, taking in the spectacle.

Suddenly Marko shouts, fucking nice one mate! And we all start to piss ourselves laughing.

Now Tammy is a big girl and she's got her dad's upper body strength. She pushes Butcher unceremoniously off her as she realises whats going on, his half naked body rolling off the bed, landing with a bang face up on the floor. She gathers the quilt around her, desperately trying to cover herself up, swings out of bed and comes lumbering towards us.

There is a small ornament on top of the toilet cistern, a figurine of an American football player, his face in a grimace. The thud of the music from below halts for a moment and I shift my weight on the soft carpet.

Marko slams the door shut just before Tammy can reach us and we all leg it down the stairs laughing and shouting down into the living room. The house is full of people now, half of them I don't even recognise, and we get a few angry complaints as we push through the crowd, spilling drinks and barging through drunken conversations to emerge shouting and laughing into the back garden. My head is swimming with booze and the fresh evening air, the rumble of the party drifting out through the open windows along with so much smoke that the house looks like it's on fire. I lose my balance, the ground swinging up to meet me and I can all of a sudden feel the kiss of the cool grass on my face, see the stars spinning out of control above me. So many stars.

Long before the ugly hulk of adulthood and all the darkness that it brings, I lay in the grass, unaware of the life that stretched out untrodden before me and of the complexities and bitter depth of it all. I gazed up at a sky strewn with wisps of white cloud and let the sun warm my skin. I imagined being upside down, hanging from the world with the deep blue sky and those puffs of white far below me. Peering to the side I could see our bikes, our cars, our chariots, the sun reflecting harshly off metallic paint. I could smell the cool dark earth below me as the long stems of the green grass passed in and out of my focus, caressed by the wind. As I lie alone in that dark empty garden I am

91

wonderfully oblivious to the fact that one day that simple
and seemingly banal moment will rob me of my breath.

Did Tess say that she liked me? I wonder if she's still here. I find my cigarettes in my trouser pocket and spark one up, lying there on the cool, damp ground, smoking and gazing skyward. Oscar Wilde once said that we all live in the gutter, but some of us can see the stars.

Christine and Millie come out into the garden, escaping the smoke and noise of the house for a private chat, propped up against the outside wall, short tartan skirts over black stockings and far too much makeup. They look over, peering through the night and see me lying there on the grass.

Are you alright Kei? Inquires Millie.

I'm really fucking well thank you girls, I reply.

I'm back inside and the vibe has changed. The music is quieter and the house has emptied out, those that remain sitting in tight circles on the living room carpet sucking on the butts of cigarettes talking, or collapsed on the sofa. Ethan is on the sofa watching Batman and smoking a joint. The house is a fucking mess. Roll up papers and tobacco all over the floor, wine stains and half eaten packets of crisps everywhere, the air heavy with blue reefer smoke. Tammy is nowhere to be seen, but Butcher is in the living room, drinking rum from the bottle and having a chat to Marko. Everyone is really wasted.

I plonk myself down on the sofa and someone hands me half a lit cigarette. Things move about me, sounds are muffled and echoey, like voices from the depths of a broken vessel. Events occur in stops and starts, like cogs with broken teeth that stick and then lurch forward once the pressure builds. I wipe my face, bringing my fingers down over my eyes.

Has anyone seen Tess? I ask.

Do it do it!

We are all at the bottom of the stairs shouting. Most of the booze has gone and Ethan has finished watching Batman and is now rewinding the tape of Batman Returns, kneeling in front of the telly, eyes watching the digital display count down. Butcher is up at the top of the staircase with one of the last cans of beer in his hand, taking a few swigs and pumping the air with his left fist.

Do it do it! We are all yelling.

He throws the can aside and leaps head first down the fucking stairs. He clears the top couple of steps then thuds down the remaining few headfirst. His jeans get pulled all the way down his legs and he's lying unconscious, arse out at the bottom of the stairs. Marko goes over and slaps him around the face a few times but he's not moving. Someone pours some warm beer over his head, but he doesn't budge. The bastard is out cold. We leave him there and stumble back into the living room to try and find more booze or perhaps another spliff.

The stars are out but I can't focus on them.

She is out there somewhere, beyond those tiny lights that burst and dance across the blackness, my body sinking into the cool moist earth.

Blake presses play on the video, the snow of a dead channel resolving into a grainy picture, and I look out of the window. The sun is coming up, the first birds singing out to the morning.

Do you reckon Butcher will be alright? I ask Marko

He's had a fucking good night mate, he replies, a wide toothy grin on his face.

Yeah a fucking great one, I reply.

I wonder if Tess is still here.

When they got to the house and in through the front door, moving quickly through a messy kitchen, empty bottles of alcohol on the table and work surfaces, they found him, cold and unresponsive in an armchair in the main bedroom. They checked his pulse and pupil response but both paramedics already knew it was hopeless. The police and the coroner were called and the paramedics sat in the messy kitchen drinking from flasks as they waited. The coroner arrived and declared the time of death.

3:45 am on the 9th of November 2006.

The police did a quick search of the house. They located the victim's wallet on a small table in the hallway. In it there were a few credit and bank cards, a gym membership, a few crumpled five pound notes, a diabetics ID card and a small photograph of a young girl. She must have been about four or five years old with wavy blonde hair, a stuffed elephant clutched to her body, a big smile across her face. The officer turned the photo over. On the back scribbled in biro were the words.

'Shirley Butcher June 2005'

OXFORD 1963

We are all standing in Mr Pateman's class at the end of the day. It's Friday, our chairs are on the desks and we are all waiting patiently to be dismissed. It's a beautiful afternoon, the sun shining on our backs through the large windows at the back of the classroom. We fidget and shuffle, our eyes on the round white clock above the door. There is a party tonight. It's Kirsten's seventeenth and a lot of people from school are going to be there. I think Kael and a few of my brother's mates are heading over too. It's in Bretton at the community centre.

Natalie Colby is standing at the desk next to me. I look over at her and she smiles. I love her. She is so fit. She is the best looking girl in my year by far, petite, long brown hair, an absolutely beautiful face, delicate features and large brown eyes, doleful and melancholy, as though always close to tears.

Hey Natalie? I whisper.

Yes, she replies.

Are you going to the party tonight? I ask.

Yes, I'm going along with Suzanne, she says.

Suzanne is her best friend and lives just a couple of doors down from me. The four of us Marko, Suzanne, Natalie and me have had sort of a thing going for a while.

We meet up in town in the evening and head over to the cathedral grounds, away from the people and streetlights, and sit on the grass behind one of the grave stones sharing a beer or a bottle of sweet white wine. Marko and Suzanne usually end up walking off into the dark to find somewhere safe and secret, while me and Natalie sit around chatting and sharing a cigarette. She's cool.

Ok I'll see you there, I tell her with a smile.

Is there a problem Kei? Calls out Mr Pateman from the front of the class.

No problem sir... um sorry sir, I say, blushing a bit.

Natalie turns and giggles at me from beneath her long brown hair and I grin back. The bell rings and we grab our bags and head out of the door.

I'll see you tonight, I call to Natalie as we all file out, bags on shoulders, loosening our ties, Mr Pateman wishing us all a good evening as we leave.

I turn back once as I catch up with James and Mayhew, and Natalie gives me a small wave.

We are walking there, all the fucking way to Bretton and it's far. It's me, Kael, 'Her' little brother Billy and a few others. This bloke Nathan from my year is swigging from a full bottle of vodka and has nearly finished half of the fucking thing.

Hows your sister? I ask Billy as we walk.

Billy is a good kid. He's four years younger than me but strong as a mother fucker. He beat Kael in an arm wrestle once and apparently he's also pretty handy, does a bit of kickboxing at the community centre on Thursday nights. He's short and stocky with thick wrists and broad

96

shoulders. He's got blonde, chin length hair and a gold hoop in his left ear, a big tanned face with chubby cheeks, just like his sister.

She's alright mate, he tells me.

She's not coming tonight, she's got some ice skating thing on.

I don't really like it when she ice skates to be honest. She's got some bloke who is her partner and they are pretty close. He's always picking her up by the waste and spinning her around and shit. Whenever she talks about him I get a twinge of jealousy, thinking of them together, of the secret things that pass between them, things that I'll never be party to.

We are on a long footpath somewhere in the heart of Bretton. The Borough is a so called New Town. It was designed and purpose built to attract new business and industry and the main districts were planned to be as comfortable and communal as possible. Bretton has a lot of seventies red brick housing, a lot of wide open spaces with footpaths and concrete cycle paths lined with trees, a community centre, a shopping area and a few god awful pubs. It's also home to some of the rougher bastards from my school. We are all walking down a wide cycle path, occasionally passing through flickery orange lit underpasses, graffiti scrawled across the walls, broken glass in the gutters, towards the community centre. It's a chilly day in the middle of March, the ground still wet with rain, the sky cloudy and free of stars. Nathan is starting to look a bit worse for wear. I think the half bottle of vodka is starting to take its toll.

You remember that twat from Bretton Woods? Comments Kael to Billy, bumping his shoulder with a gentle fist.

Yeah mate, the one who fucking half inched your shirt from the multi story, he replies.

Yeah that wanker, continues Kael, the twat lives around here somewhere, hope we bump into him on his bike or something.

Yeah mate, replies Billy, the bloke needs a smack.

Fucking too right mate, agrees Kael, stopping by the side of the path to blow some snot from his nose.

My Grandma on my dad's side lives around here. She's probably already in bed, or sitting in her kitchen, the blinds down, eating a dinner of gammon and chips at her little table with the plastic table cloth, watching Eastenders on that tiny little black and white tv of hers, the painting of a hamburger I did back in the first year, hanging on her wall, her noisy little dog Rory curled up in his basket by the tumble dryer.

Nathan looks a bit wankered, I remark.

Nah he's fine, reassures Kael reaching for the half empty bottle of booze hanging limply in Nathan's hand, give me some of that mate, he orders, plying it from his grip.

Kael hands the bottle around and we each take a massive swig. It's good stuff. Spa's own brand fucking vodka. Kael skinned up a couple of spliffs before we left. He pulls the last one from behind his ear, taps it a few times on the back of his hand then lights it up so we can all have a toke before we get to the community centre.

Billy takes a few drags as well and we all tease him. The little bastard is barely thirteen years old.

We turn up to the place a bit stoned and a bit drunk. The party is already in full swing. It's a horrible place. Lots of bright lighting and plastic school chairs. The booze and snacks are all laid out on a big foldable table topped with a nasty plastic white floral table cloth. There is some pop music playing through the loud speakers, a DJ who looks far too old to be doing this shit and he's probably thinking the same thing himself. A couple of drunken kids are having a spin on the dance floor, bottles of Newcastle Brown or plastic cups of punch in hand. I see a few people I recognise. Mark Jacobs is there chatting to a bird from our year. Her name is Janine.

I say hello to Mark and give a cordial nod to Janine.

I need a drink and fast so I go up to the bar to get a round in. The barman looks about twelve and his face is covered in acne. He pushes his wire frame glasses up his nose with a skinny finger.

What can I get you sir? He asks.

I'm no fucking sir, I can tell you that much. I order a pint of lager and a double vodka and coke. I'm standing with my elbows on the bar top waiting for the barman to hand me my drinks when Natalie walks up and stands next to me.

I give her a nod and a quick look up and down. She is looking great, lots of makeup, red lip gloss and too much eye shadow, smudged around the edges. She has on a really short skirt and black tights to keep out the cold. The girl is skinny but certainly has some legs on her.

Hows it going? I ask her, leaning in to be heard above the noise.

Pretty good thanks, she replies.

We have to shout cause the shitty DJ has everything playing way too loudly, all the volume sliders pushed up to max, the sound from the speakers distorted with far too much bass.

You want a drink? I ask her.

What? She replies, sliding closer to hear, her shoulder now touching mine. I can smell her perfume, a delicate sweet aroma over the stink of fags and stale beer.

Do you want a drink? I repeat, pointing to my pint.

Yes, Southern Comfort and lemonade please, I just make out over the din.

Ok, I reply.

I catch the barman's gaze again and he comes over. I order Natalie her drink and spark up a cigarette.

You want one? I ask.

Yeah cheers, she answers, smiling at me.

There is nothing comparable to that feeling, that slightly sickly excitement of liking a girl and her liking you back. There is a gradual warm cognisance that creeps on, an unspoken essence of something. You have both caught a whisper from another realm, a secret that only the two of you are party too. You pass each other in the halls or sit and eat lunch in a half empty room, tables covered with crumbs and wet circles from water bottles. There is a warmth and immediacy to everything, a focus, a chance to be something more. We chat all the time in Mr Pateman's English class. I make jokes and when she

100

laughs I feel like a proper person again, strong, alive and full of all the dreams that concern boys of my age.

I hand her a cigarette and pay for her drink with a rolled up fiver from my pocket.

I pass her her drink and we walk back to the table together.

We hear a bit of commotion as we sit down and both turn our heads to see what's going on. Nathan is wasted. He's throwing up into a blue plastic dustbin, his mate's arm round his shoulders comforting him. Poor bastard must have had three quarters of a bottle of vodka already. I look at my watch. It's only 8:15

I look at Natalie and we both giggle. Poor bastard.

There is a bit of a lull, the music stopping for a few seconds while the DJ slides a blue milk crate stuffed with old vinyl out from under the turntables and starts to thumb through them, occasionally pulling one from its sleeve and peering at it under the multi-coloured lights. Everything has a wonderful softness too it, like flopping down into a newly made bed or opening the door to a perfect spring day.

James comes over and sits down next to me, a vodka and coke in his hand, his long curly blonde hair pulled back into a pony tail.

This music is shit mate, he remarks, don't they have any Dinosaur Jr or Mudhoney?

Reckon you could ask mate, I reply laughing and looking over at the DJ.

He must be about fifty. He's wearing a pair of white fucking flares and sporting the least convincing comb over

I've ever seen. There's a big hand painted sign hanging in front of his turn tables. It simply reads 'Jim Axe's Disco'.

Yeah right mate, replies James, reckon the best we'll get out of him is some Def Leppard.

I'll fucking drink to that mate, I tell him and we down our drinks, holding the plastic cups between our teeth.

I shift my chair over closer to Natalie and lean in. She turns to me and brushes her long brown hair away from her ear.

You are absolutely the best looking girl at school, I say to her, but I'm cut off half way by Jim Axe the Dj introducing 'Living On A Prayer' by 'Bon Jovi' over the Mic. She leans towards me, ear pinned forward with her hand.

I said you look really... um great tonight, I shout to her again.

She shakes her head but smiles, turning away briefly to stub out her cigarette in a blue plastic ash tray with the Fosters logo on it, then turns back and looks at me, pinning her hair behind her ear.

You aren't so bad yourself, she replies, feigning a bit of an Essex twang.

She takes my hand and asks me if I want to dance. I'm no dancer but I reckon for Natalie Colby I can make an exception.

We move over to the dance floor, my shoes sticking to the linoleum slightly as we walk. The floor is crowded now, lots of drunk teenagers with fags in hand moving awkwardly to the awful music, the windows misted up, the cold of the night lying in wait for us. Mark is there with Janine and as they dance past he gives me a sly wink.

He knows the score. My hands find their way onto Natalie's hips and we dance some more. It's hot in the community centre and I'm starting to sweat, sweeping my long hair back away from my face. I feel good. I'm half drunk, a bit stoned and dancing with the girl of my dreams. Things are looking pretty rosy to be honest.

Her hand goes to my shoulder and she leans into me and tells me that she has to go to the toilet. I feel her breath against my face and her lips touch my ear ever so gently. I tell her I have to go too. It's a lie, I just don't want to let her out of my sight.

We both walk off the dance floor, pushing through the crowd, her leading me by the hand as I follow her out through the swing doors and into the brightly lit corridor. As the doors swing closed behind us the music immediately cuts to a muted thump and we wince under the fluorescent lights that line the low plaster board ceiling. There is a set of double fire doors at the end of the corridor that open out into the car park. They shudder lightly in the wind, the bar holding them shut rattling. There are a few posters for local events on the walls, a bingo night at the Creset, and a pantomime down at the theatre on the embankment. Someone has scribbled 'Douglas is a bender' on one of them in black marker pen.

My ears ring and my head spins, the lights and quiet of this empty space amplifying my drunkenness. Natalie wanders off to the girl's toilets, touching my arm briefly as she turns away as I stand in that empty corridor, rocking gently back and forth on unsteady legs, watching the branches rattle against the reinforced glass of the fire doors at the end.

I make my way over to the gents and stand in front of one of the large cracked mirrors hanging above the wash basins. I pull a hair band from my pocket and tie my hair up behind my head in a messy pony tail, then quickly take it back out again, slipping the band over my wrist. I lean forward and peer at myself in the mirror, into those eyes that have held my gaze for so long, into that face that even now seems strange to me, too real, too well defined, as though someone has moulded me from the wrong materials. I fiddle with the earring in my left ear, then wander over to the urinals and take a piss, head bent forward, eyes fixed on that little blue cube, the rhythmic sounds of the party audible from the next room. I leave, washing my hands briefly and taking one last glance in the mirror.

I get back out into the bright corridor and Natalie is already standing there, an unlit fag hanging from one limp hand. She smiles as she sees me and I wave stupidly to her. I walk up to her and stand in front of her, left hand resting softly on her hip. Under the lights I can see that she is wearing too much makeup, thick foundation and eye liner. Her hair is loose and hanging about her thin shoulders. She has a small mole on the left side of her neck.

Natalie doesn't need makeup. She has a great face, big eyes, a straight nose and perfect skin. She catches me staring at her and smiles.

Didn't your mother ever tell you it was rude to stare, she scolds, grinning.

I'm sorry but you are so fit, I tell her.

She comes over to me and all of a sudden we are kissing. My tongue is in her mouth and I can feel her heart beating through my chest as I pull her closer. We kiss for a while and then some more. I move my hand down to the top of her skirt and start to ease it down into the front of her knickers. She grabs my hand.

Not here, she tells me.

My mother went to her Oxford University entrance interview dressed in a smart blouse and a pair of trousers. She was interviewed by a panel of six men, one of whom commented on her attire. My mother simply asked him whether he had ever braved the English winters in merely a skirt. A couple of the other professors smirked and the questioning quickly moved on. The University made her an offer the following spring, and in the autumn of 1963 she began reading geography at one of the best universities in the world. She was the first of her family to attend such a prestigious institution and the local paper wrote a brief story about the local girl from a working class family and the changing gender roles, the arrival of the modern woman.

Her parents, my grandma and granddad had instilled a really good set of values in her from a young age. They were paid up members of the communist party, very frugal and hardworking, though never truly poor. My granddad was an accomplished pianist, his pianos being his only concession to anything approaching materialism. They were modest but headstrong and this attitude continued with my mother. My dad always used to tell me that mum was much cleverer than he, they used to work together, her in a senior position. I believe that that is how they first met. I think that if she ever read my story that she would be mortified by my apparent objectification of the opposite sex.

The thing is I was young. I was a teenager and the only women I had ever been exposed to were those on TV, in films, or in porn. I watched comedies like Carry On, in which women were just tits and arse. American action movies always featured the weak beautiful girl being rescued from her virginity by a strong, masculine bloke. When we were teenagers we boasted about the number of girls we got off with at a party or how many fingers we managed to get in. It's stupid and puerile and degrading and I freely admit that, but at sixteen it's your only option, it's the only reality that we had ever been exposed to. It was all about conquest. It was about notches on the bed post. It wasn't even really about sex at this point, that came later. It was about boasting to your mates on a Monday morning, it was the same as getting into punch ups, or half inching a packet of sweets from the local offy. It was the only way we had to express ourselves, to bare our masculinity, to stand up and shout to the world that we were sick of being treated like boys, that even though our bodies were thin and supple, that we had the appetites of men.

I am sorry mother.

Natalie takes me by the hand and pulls me into the girls toilets. Thankfully no one is in here and the music is now just a low thud thud thud. She pulls me closer and we start to kiss again.

I have wanted to snog you for fucking ages, I say to her.

She doesn't reply, just pulls me back and kisses me some more. I slip my hand down the front of her skirt and into her knickers. I can feel her pubic hair and the warmth of her vagina. I slip my hand a little lower and push my finger lightly into her. She exhales slightly and I kiss her some more.

I really fancy you, I say as I work my finger in and out of her.

I catch a glimpse of myself in the toilet mirror. My hair is long, messy and dark with beer and sweat. Both my ears are decorated with multiple gold hoops and my chin is starting to get a bit of hair on it. I'm dressed in my favourite paisley shirt, the collar still smelling of the clean laundry my mother folds up and places in my drawer every evening, and a pair of black army trousers, the pockets full of half cigarettes, crumpled five pound notes and a few heavy coins. I look skinny as fuck and white as a sheet. I smile to myself and kiss that beautiful girl again.

THE TYPEWRITER

Now some men like fishing and some men like fowlin and some men like to hear a canon ball rolling, but me I like music and especially when I'm drinking. My first love was The Cure. Everyone else at the time was into The Smiths and while I liked a few of their tunes, Morrisey never really did it for me. I think the first Cure song I heard was 'Killing an Arab'. It was catchy, bare, dark and had an attitude all of its own, also the Camus homage appealed to my wannabe intellectual side, and from that moment on I fell in love with their music. I bought 'Kiss me Kiss me Kiss me' on vinyl as soon as I had saved up enough money. I eventually had all of their albums on vinyl and started spending the weekends going to music shops and record fairs with James to seek out their more obscure records. I bought the red vinyl version of 'Head on the Door' and got my hands on some rare pre-release, not for resale demos too. I grew my hair long and back combed it to look like Robert Smith and would sometimes put on lipstick to imitate my hero.

I think it helped that Jen was into them too. I would go and hang out at the school tennis courts on Saturday afternoons and watch the girls play while me and Jen talked about our favourite tracks. It was shortly after the release of their latest album 'Disintegration' and the music press was full of pictures of the band and they even appeared on top of the pops. Robert Smith was on the cover of the latest Select magazine and Jen lent me her copy of it, I took it home that night and curled up in bed reading the article about my favourite band, the smell of Jen's perfume still clinging to my old black school jumper.

My older brother has a band. They got together a couple of years ago and started practicing in our garage. Every Saturday we sit in that old red brick building at the bottom of the garden, smoking and listening to them practice upstairs. They play 'Hardcore', a mix of punk and heavy metal, but without any of the makeup or affectation. It is pure and raw and loud and the moment I heard it I fell in love with the genre.

The lead singer John has an eclectic music taste and is always recommending bands to us. One day he brought over a new record. It had a black cover with a negative photograph of a band on the front. They all had long hair covering their faces, and exotic sounding names like 'Kobain' and 'Novaselic'. I thought they were a Scandinavian punk band.

John put on the first track 'Blew' and from my first listen they were my new favourite band. I had never heard something so dark and raw before. The production was sparse and the vocals were full of rage and heart. I realised at that moment that making music was what I wanted to do. I decided to teach myself how to play the guitar. I already played the bass so I knew the strings and the names of some of the notes. One morning I woke up, found my older brother's cheap acoustic and spent all morning practicing open chords. By lunch time I could play most of them reasonably well and decided it was time to make my own band.

My friend Gabriel, from the year above played the guitar so I asked him first. I had known him since we were little and we had always been really close. His parents had divorced a long time ago and he had lived with his mom and brother across the road from us for a while. He had long hair and a bit of a beard. He was different from everyone else. He liked his own things and didn't follow the crowd. He always introduced me to a lot of cool bands and comics. Some people thought he was weird, but he was always popular and had a big group of friends. He also had his own guitar and a small amp.

I asked Eli if he wanted to play the bass. He didn't play but was willing to learn and was excited about the prospect of being in a band and soon got the hang of the instrument. He practices hard and gets better every time I see him. My younger brother Hardy plays the drums. Miles, the drummer from my older brother's band always leaves his kit in my garage because it's too much of a pain in the arse to take it home. It's a really nice metallic red Pearl kit with Ziljan cymbals. We asked Miles if we could use it and he said ok, as long as we were careful with it. We came to an agreement that we would practice in the garage on Fridays and Luka's band would have the space on Saturdays. It's a good arrangement. We've got about ten or so really good songs so far and every Friday we write a new one. Hardy has taken to the drums like a natural and practices hard everyday.

We usually practice until nine. We are noisy as fuck and so have an agreement with the neighbours to end at an appropriate time, after which we send James down to The Spa to buy beers, usually bottles of Newcastle Brown Ale and get drunk and talk about music and girls. Gabriel always has a story and he is great at telling them. They always start with a mundane premise, unfolding into something much darker and more enticing.

Gabriel is involved with this bird called Sally in his year. She is one of those untouchable girls that everyone fantasises about asking out but no one dares. She is the kind of girl who goes out with blokes who have left school and have their own cars.

Gabriel and Sally had been close for a long time, they were in the same class for years and moved in the same group of friends, all popular, attractive and did well at school. Gabriel had always been a weird kid when he was younger, skinny and pale, fidgety and a bit of a daydreamer, always getting told off in class for gazing out of the windows or doodling on his text books. He was the son of a single mother and one of five kids so as a young child he had quickly learnt how to get his own way, how to adapt to a situation and manipulate those around him. He was good with people, an expert at shrugging off the clutter of emotions that holds so many of us back and shaping the world to his liking. It was a skill. He wasn't malicious, just trying to make life go the way he wanted. None of us are ever really in control, but some of us are good at adapting to the surprises and vicissitudes that life throws at us.

One time when we were about nine years old this kid Sean was going to beat the crap out of Gabriel. Gabriel had shut a door in his face or something equally inconsequential. I don't really remember. Anyway, Sean was pretty hard and Gabriel had been shit scared. He had devised this plan that he would pretend to beat me up in the playground, and when Sean saw it he would back off, thinking that Gabriel was also someone not to fuck with. I told him at the time that the plan would never work but he was adamant and so we went ahead with it.

Sean came round the corner and Gabriel pretended to punch me in the stomach. I feigned injury and fell to the floor pretending to cry and Sean backed off. From that moment on Gabriel never had anymore trouble with him.

Gabriel had grown up since then. He was a handsome bloke with long thick hair and a strong chin. He still had a bit of a nerdy side, still collected comic books and action figures but he was confident and outgoing now, happy in his skin and ready to face the world. His friendship with Sally had started to become something more, he had started to realise that he was getting feelings for her. He didn't want to tell her though. He liked her and didn't want to jeopardise their friendship and so he hid that part away, kept it locked up, and tried to forget about it.

Gabriel had a typewriter in his room that he was constantly messing about with. He was always immersed in his comics and fancied himself as a bit of a writer. One night he had been out in town with a couple of mates, and one of them had put his foot through a windscreen while running over the tops of the cars parked along the street. Gabriel had some headed letter paper from a solicitor's office that he had done a two week work experience placement at. He used one of the pieces of paper to type out an official looking legal letter, put it in an envelope and sent it to his mate as a prank. The letter said that the owner was aware of the damage done to the car and threatened legal action. His mate's parents freaked out and pretty soon the police and the solicitors were involved. The pigs went round to Gabriel's place to talk to him but he hid the typewriter and denied everything. The situation scared him and he vowed never to touch the thing again.

He was starting to get frustrated with his relationship with Sally. He wanted more, but had no idea how to pursue it. He wanted to get though to her somehow, to shake things up. One night, as he was sitting on his bed reading some comics he had an idea. He got the type writer out, fed some plain paper into it and wrote a letter to Sally saying that he was watching her and some other stalkerish shit. He didn't sign it of course, it was just his way of relieving some of the tension, a way to push back against what he saw as an unfair situation. Deep down perhaps he even wanted to hurt her in some way, to eek out a small amount of revenge, not necessarily against her, but against the harsh unbending world that held us all so tightly in its shackles.

He put the letter in an envelope and left it on the shelf above his bed, tucked between the first two cellophane wrapped issues of 'The Watchmen' where it sat untouched, whispering into the darkness.

At some point in our lives we all fall prey to our darker instincts, acting on those urges that exist somehow beyond us, callous acts guided by invisible hands. Occasionally the homunculus takes control and sets us on a different path. One day, and for no particular reason Gabriel grabbed the envelope from the shelf and casually dropped it into the big red post box at the end of his road as he walked to school.

A few days later Gabrielle was at home when the phone rang. It was Sally and she was terrified. She told him tearfully that she had received a letter and didn't know what to do. She and Gabriel were close and so she felt comfortable confiding in him, told him how frightened she was and of course he consoled her. He liked the fact that she had come to him to talk about her fears and so like some sort of twisted Pavlovian experiment he continued to send the letters. She would come to him for protection and solace and he would comfort her, tell her that everything was alright, that he would look after her. She gradually let him further into the deeper recesses of her being, into those lost places where our fears lurk, showing him her sorrow and her darkness, inadvertently providing fuel for Gabriel's correspondences. He started to feel their relationship getting closer and that at last they might be something other than merely friends.

One night he was shaving, using one of those disposable Bic razors and slipped and cut his chin. He got a bit of tissue and cleaned up his face, and as he looked at the dark specks of blood on the tissue he had another idea. He decided to dab a bit of the blood onto the next letter and send it out like that.

A few nights later Sally called him. She was really upset, almost in tears and in a panic. She told him that she had received a letter with blood on it and was terrified. Gabriel calmed her down, persuading her to come round to his so that they could talk properly about the situation.

She arrived at the door about an hour later, eyes glassy with tears, her concerned mother peering out from behind the windscreen of their small car.

Gabriel greeted her on the doorstep, waving to her mother as she drove away. He closed the door behind them and led Sally up the stairs to his room. He put on some music and shut the door. They sat down on the bed and she explained the situation. She told him that her parents were very concerned and were going to contact the police. Gabriel concocted some story to convince her that involving the police might not be a good idea, that they should wait, see what happens next. She thanked him and he held her as she cried. They kissed that night for the first time and he confessed to her that he really liked her. She told him that she felt the same. She slept in his room that night, wrapped in a patchwork blanket Gabriel's grandmother had made, the old typewriter sitting in plain view on his desk.

GLASS HOUSES

T here is a party at Chloe's and Debbie's house tonight. Kael and Debbie have been together for a while now and it's safe to say that their relationship is somewhat turbulent. They are either gazing into each other's eyes lovingly or threatening to kill each other or themselves. Actually, when I say staring into each other's eyes, I actually mean shagging like there is no tomorrow, whenever and wherever the mood takes them.

There is a club in town at the local football ground and they put on an indie night on Saturdays. A group of us usually walk down together, drink a few beers on the way and get in on fake IDs to dance the night away to the Soup Dragons and Stone Roses. A few weeks back, as we were queueing up to get in I saw Kael and Debbie 'at it' next to the turn styles into the football ground. It was early evening and still light. They were in plain sight and a small group had convened to watch.

Another time we were sitting in the garage having a smoke and they started kissing. Soon enough Kael had his trousers down and Debbie lifted her skirt and sat down on top of him. We didn't know whether to watch or look away.

Actually by now it has become such a common occurrence that none of us even notices anymore. We just continue as usual, smoking and chatting, barely registering the moans and grunts emanating from the couple entwined in coitus next to us.

Chloe and Debbie live outside a small village somewhere in the Cambridgeshire countryside. I should probably know the name of the place but at seventeen, the geography of the East Anglian region isn't very high up on my list of priorities. The house is big and white and surrounded by corn fields. There is a small road leading up to it and a large garage occupies the left side of the property. Chloe's parents have told her that the party has to be held in the garage. They don't want a bunch of stupid drunken teenagers running about in their house till all hours of the morning, and I don't really blame them. Loads of people have turned up. A lot from my year; me, Blake, Ethan, Chris , Marko, Millie and Butcher so far and also a large crowd from my younger brother's year, Debbie's friends. I see Allison and Janet and a few other girls. Me and Allison used to have a bit of a thing a while back. She would come over and we would snog and fool around a bit. She's a beautiful girl with shortish blonde hair and a slightly upturned nose.

Butcher is boasting about some fight or other that he had to go to court for. Can't really hear the details but Marko tells me it's probably bullshit. Blake is there too. I like Blake, we used to go skating in town together a lot and he's a really nice bloke. A handsome chap with a lot of blonde hair in a semi long centre parting. He's coming to the Reading Festival with us, and we have a brief chat about that before heading into the garage.

There is a table set up with booze and crisps and other snacks on it, and we immediately crack open a few beers and a few bottles. I don't know what the fuck people are thinking. Feeding booze to a bunch of teenagers is just asking for fucking trouble, but who am I to judge. Someone puts a tape in the stereo and The Cure's 'In Between Days' comes on.

Good fucking song this, I say to Blake, but he's not really listening.

He's already got his tongue down Janet's throat, a lit fag dangling from his left hand. Occasionally he comes up for air and takes a drag and then back to it. I knock back a plastic cup of something sweet and very alcoholic and walk over to talk to James and Eli. The sun is still pretty high in the sky even though it's nine o'clock in the evening, and I can still hear a few birds singing. I've got that lovely buzz that comes from drinking too much too quickly outside in the fresh air and everything has a crisp clarity to it. The music sounds good, the girls look good and I fucking love each and every one of these wretched bastards.

I can't stop looking at Millie. She's wearing a tight top and some really short shorts. She's got a fucking great body and I keep telling everyone around me how fit I think she is. At some point Butcher comes over and tells me to stop going on about it. Millie is going out with Ethan and he is starting to get really fucking annoyed with me. I go over to Ethan and apologise.

Sorry mate, I'm just really drunk old boy, I say, shaking his hand.

He tells me it's fine and I apologise again.

Ian turns up at about eight, pulling into the driveway in his Ford Fiesta. It's white with a massive spoiler and this horrible tinny engine. Sounds like a wasp trapped in a fucking tin can. He fucking loves it though. A few of my mates have got cars but most of them are into bikes. Mum has told me that there is no way in hell I'm getting one. She is too afraid of me falling off or getting crushed by a lorry. Shame though. As Tom often says, wounds heal and chicks dig scars.

Ian gets out of his car, slamming the door shut behind him, spinning the keys around on his index finger, and giving his pride and joy one last glance as he comes wandering over. He plonks himself down on the grass, his long legs arched in front of him and we lean up against a hay bale. I offer him a cigarette.

No thanks mate, he declines with a wave of the hand.

Fuck I keep forgetting you don't smoke, you should try it once mate, I tell him, lighting my own.

Nah mate, I'm fine, he grins, but I'll have swig of your beer though.

I give him the can and he downs a good few mouthfuls.

Keep it, I tell him.

He takes a look around peering into the garage where a large group of people stand around chatting, smoking and swaying to the music issuing from the shitty old stereo with a broken graphics equaliser.

Who else is here? he asks.

There's Ethan, Jacobs, Butcher and Blake, um...Marko's here too, oh yeah and Blake is already getting off with Janet, I report, so I don't reckon you'll get too much sense out of him.

119

Don't know where the fuck Chloe has got too but it's her party so she's probably sorting out food or something. Eli and Ethan are dancing in the garage, faces down, long hair thrashing about to Sonic Youth, and James and Mark are probably in the field somewhere getting stoned.

Any birds? he asks.

A few, I reply taking another big drag on my cigarette, a strong head rush hitting me. The sun has just started to go down, a few pink clouds hover over the horizon, the corn field taking on a bright luminescence as late afternoon slips towards twilight. The evening has started to creep on and it's getting a bit chilly, but it's nice. I feel alive and focused, drunk, but sharp and full of energy. I want to talk and dance and kiss a girl.

I'm heading into the garage to get some booze mate, you coming? He asks.

Yes mate, I reply, getting a bit chilly out here actually.

Things are fuzzy. I have that feeling of being so drunk that I'm no longer cognisant of events as they happen. Like images played from an old video tape, things stagger forward and repeat, the usual smooth flow of time interrupted and twisted somehow, my mind replaying events on a loop, the same intrusive thought coming and going. I'm having a piss in a cornfield, the heads of the golden plants swaying in the evening breeze, the headlights of cars in the distance dancing through the silhouettes of the trees that line the horizon... I'm inside the garage, talking to James about music. I have bitten one of my nails too short and I pick at the skin around it until it bleeds. I have another cigarette to clear my head but it

120

makes me cough. Actually I've been feeling really wheezy recently, should probably go to the doctors at some point, but it's too much of a fucking hassle.

There is an old mirror propped up against the back wall, full length, a thick dark wooden frame pulling apart at one top corner, another forgotten project, a chore set aside for a day off that never came. I stand in front of it and look at myself. I'm white as porcelain and my face is skinny, cheeks sunken and pale. My hair is long, nearly down to my middle back and light brown with that reddish hue that I got from my mum. I'm wearing a long black wooly jumper, frayed at the cuffs and far too big for me, my thumb poking through a large hole near the cuff, and green army trousers from the army surplus shop in town, cheap as fuck and pockets on the legs just big enough for a packet of twenty fags. I've got on my favourite six hole Doctor Martens boots and a cigarette hangs loosely from my thin lips. There is a bit of stubble on my chin and my sideburns are starting to grow.

You good-looking bastard I whisper to myself and laugh. I cough a bit and take another drag on my cigarette. A bit of smoke gets in my eye. The skinny bloke in the mirror shuts that eye and grins at me.

Fuck them all mate, he says to me, fuck them all, it's you and me from now on partner, just you and me.

I know deep down that he's right. This is all temporary, some sort of grand illusion, that eventually someone will stand up and tear the screen back, revealing the fleshy machine that keeps this whole thing moving. One day I will sit in my living room drinking beer as I watch whole villages swept away. I will touch the inside of a woman's skull, still warm from the crematorium, a women I spoke to a week before. We will pass her bones between us with chopsticks. I will have intricate designs carved into my skin and I will bleed but never truly heal. I will watch the birth of my child and hold his tiny warm head in my cold hands as the snow falls outside. I will fall in love and and wish that I never had. Every small decision I make will lead me down a path that I cannot possibly foresee. The intricacies and complexity of it all will astound me in retrospect, and had I known at this point what my future held in its secret realms then perhaps I could have altered its course, done things differently, held on more tightly to these precious moments. I look at my hands, hands that will one day nurse and comfort, carve and bring ruin. They look old and used, like hands that belong to someone worn and beleaguered. The fingers are bony and slightly bent and the nails have been bitten down to the tips.

I'm lying on the ground in the garage with Allison. we are kissing and I've got my hand up her top. She's got really nice tits, round and full but not too big. Blake is lying next to us still getting off with Janet. He is trying his hardest to shag her and I can hear him saying.

Of course I really like you. It's not like that, I think you are the one.

I giggle a bit and Allison asks me what's wrong. I've got my hand down the back of her jeans and I can feel the warmth from her pussy at the tips of my fingers.

I look back over at Blake and ask, how's it going over there mate?

Yeah not bad old boy, reckon I'm in ere, he replies.

Janet gives him a playful slap around the face.

What are you saying about me?

Blake gives her another kiss on the lips and tells her she is sexy and they start kissing again. Allison puts both hands on the side of my head, through my hair and pulls me in close to her. Her tongue quickly finds its way into my mouth again. Fuck me I'm wasted, I think to myself.

Janet is really into me, she always has been. She is a bit of a bigger lass, but I like that. She wears her curly hair with the fringe pinned up, held together with too much hairspray. We've snogged a few times and I played with her tits down at the field once. She was sitting on top of me and I had my hands up her t-shirt, and my brother came round and undid her bra. We stayed like that for ages, me fondling her massive boobs and her pushing up against my hard on. I was really getting into it when Tom came down and told us my dad had tea ready and we had to go back to eat. I told him to fuck off, but he said my dad was pretty insistent so I had to walk all the way back home with a massive stiffy.

Another time we ended up in bed together at a party. Things were going pretty well when this girl Kat came in and lay down next to us. Kat was a girl in my brother's year and she loved me. She used to follow me around at school and made a boat out of paper that she named after me. It still sits on a shelf in Hardy's form room. Anyway, she wasn't happy at all that me and Janet were in bed together. Janet told her to leave, but she wasn't having any of it. I waited and waited and finally Kat fell asleep. I turned round to get things going again with Janet but she was also dead to the world.

Janet looks over. I catch her eye and she smiles.

Hey Allison, she whispers to her friend, her left hand on Blake's chest, keeping him gently at bay.

Yeah, Allison responds, pulling briefly away from our embrace.

Um, you fancy swapping, she giggles shyly.

What? You mean you wanna get off with Kei? Allison enquires.

Yeah, you know I've always liked him, and Blake is a really good kisser.

I look over at Blake and he grins, his left eyebrow raised.

Well, that is true I suppose, he laughs.

So what do you reckon? Pushes Janet.

Yeah alright then, concedes Allison, as long as the boys are alright with it.

I'm cool, I reply, my eyes going to Janet's ample chest, what about you Blake mate?

Yeah cool man, he answers, I reckon Allison is well fit anyway.

I roll off Allison and onto my back and she gets to her feet, going over to lie with Blake, while I take Janet by the hand and head out of the garage and into the field.

I could make excuses. I could say that I have the utmost respect for these girls, that I regret the way I treated certain people and used them to get what I could. I could apologise on behalf of all of us, of all of the weak minded horny teenage boys that lie and coerce and try to fulfil their own filthy appetites with little regard for anyone else. I hate that I am shackled at times by my id. I hate the control that our base instincts have over us. I hate this puppet of flesh and bone, careening about this world with no one to control it. We all try our best to assert logic and to assign depth and purpose to our actions, but in the end we are all the same. The chemicals in our brain that produce the feelings of love and empathy are the same that engender lust and hatred. We are all blameless for our actions and yet entirely culpable for them. We can change and grow and regret, but we can never erase the past or predict the future. Nothing is written and existence is constant and chaotic. We all dip into solipsism from time to time and the automata that surround us occasionally bloom and flourish into something tangible and apparent.

It's dark now and pretty cold, but I don't really feel it. Janet asks if I like her and of course, I tell her I do. She tells me that she had a dream about taking a shower with me the other night and we start to snog again. We are lying in a newly harvested corn field, next to a hay bale and the sharp stalks are sticking into me. I don't care. We kiss and my hand goes up inside her t-shirt. She rubs her hand up and down the bulge in my trousers, whispering in my ear that she likes my dick. There is a light breeze blowing and my hair is getting in her face when I kiss her. She sweeps it away with her hand. I push my hand down the front of her jeans, her pussy is wet and warm and we kiss some more.

Things are foggy and hard to discern. I'm looking through my eyes, but I'm not really in control anymore. I don't know, perhaps it's the alcohol, or the drugs or maybe it's the voices from another time and place that seem to be pressing in on me, polluting my mind and poking little transient holes in this reality that I try so hard to inhabit.

We are lying in the field doing our thing and James is there at some point. I am talking to him, but I can't be. Janet looks up at me with longing in her brown eyes. A shadow of me dances in a wheat field watching Ian and Debbie making crop circles with some others. They can't make crop circles. They are just trampling the wheat. I can see the lights from the garage in the distance, hear the thump of drums and snatches of voices carried on the wind. They must be quite far away. Someone is lying in the wheat. Am I there? I don't know. I'm with Janet still. I'm telling her that I have always fancied her. She tastes like vanilla and strawberries.

Debbie is really drunk and she's lying in the field. She looks unconscious. Her reddish brown hair, flame like against the crushed pale yellow stalks of wheat, her short white dress riding up above her thigh. Ian is there. This isn't right. I should stop this. I can't. I'm a ghost. This is just a memory, words I once heard, thoughts that have been filtered through dreams, remnants and shadows of events, semblances of what once was or could have been. I scream into the ether but my voice is silent. This has happened before but it feels wrong. Something has come unstuck...

I wander alone and cold, my foot slipping into a muddy dyke, my shoes squelch as I walk, the tiny oasis of light and sound in the distance wavering and hesitant. I have to get inside. I think I voice the words, I feel them vibrate through my skull, but there is no one to hear. It's really cold and I feel dizzy. Am I there? Is this even me? It's not me. Janet pulls me close and I bury my face in her neck. Her curly hair tickles my nose. I'm inside now. I woke up and she was sucking my... I told her to stop. We were in the garage, prostrate on the concrete floor... I don't want to be here anymore. I want to be at home, in bed or at least inside. How can I get inside?

Chloe's parents are up and they are pissed off. Of course they are. This is a fucking nightmare. They let me in. I'm inside. Jacobs threw up in the punch at about seven and people have been drinking it all night. Is that funny? It is now, but in a few years when I've got more wrinkles and fewer friends, who knows. We want to get outside again. It's too fucking hot in here, locked in this bedroom, white wooden frame bed and Laura Ashley curtains. We get the window open and James jumps out, but times it wrong and lands on the fence. He looks hurt. Why am I inside? I was really thirsty. That's it, I was really thirsty and really cold and wanted to come in. I pleaded with Chloe to let me in. She did. Where is Janet? I'm sorry about this. I want to go back outside now. It's morning and I don't think I slept, or maybe I did, just for a bit. I need a cigarette but no one seems to have any. Can I go back out? What do you mean? What did he do to her?

I feel a bit sick and I cough up some nasty thick phlegm. Really have to get that seen to, I think. I cough some more and wipe my mouth with my sleeve. I see a smear of dark red blood on my hand. I grin and wipe it on my trousers.

Has anyone got any fucking fags? I ask.

●

I wake up. The sun is out and I can feel the grass underneath me. It's cool and refreshing and when I clench my right fist, I get a handful of it. There is a tree above me. I recognise it, but I don't know why. I sit up. I'm on a small patch of grassy land below some horse chestnut trees. The wind is blowing quite strongly and I get a bit of grit in my eye. I blink it out and get up onto my feet.

There is an old dark red Austin Princess across the road but it looks clean and the chrome bumpers sparkle in the early morning sunlight. It looks brand new. Where the fuck am I? I know this place but it seems different, brighter and more vivid. The air is warm as it passes through my nostrils and inflates my lungs. It's clean and crisp and invigorating, like being in a lucid dream when you are breathing air from somewhere else. An old lady passes by and gives me the once over. She smiles and says good morning. I say good morning back. I've got a bit of a headache behind my left eye. My hand instinctively goes down to my left jean pocket and I feel the weight of my phone there. I pull it out and look at the home screen, but there's no signal. I put it back in my pocket and make my way up the hill to my right. There is a big old house there with a huge garden that sits below street level. The house is dilapidated and the garden overgrown with blackberry bushes and weeds. As I make my way up the street

128

I see more old cars. A silver, four door Volvo, an MG with chrome bumpers and an old Morris Minor with wooden panelling. Something feels off. It's as if everything has shifted slightly to one side.

Ahead of me a man crosses the road. He's wearing a tight brown t shirt and has a thick black beard specked with grey. He has a lit cigar in his mouth and heavy, black rimmed glasses perched on his nose. He goes into the house opposite without knocking. I know him.

He's my father.

I know where I am.

I suddenly feel a bit sick and dizzy and sit down on a front wall to get my bearings. I take out my phone and look at the display. It says

16/07/1983 It's a Saturday... I know where I am

This is my street. This is where I grew up. There are a few cars parked on either side of the road, but other than that the street is empty. I can hear a bit of traffic from up the road and an aeroplane passing overhead. I take a deep breath and catch a hint of bonfire smoke on the breeze. It's quite warm and my phone tells me it's about 9:30 in the morning. I stand up and walk a bit further down the street. I am wearing jeans and a t shirt underneath a black linen shirt. I can feel the sun on my skin and it feels good, familiar somehow. I walk past the Wooly's house on my right. There is an Austin Maestro in the driveway and I can hear morning cartoons on the TV

129

through the open window, sounds like He Man. There are a few children further down the road, riding around on their bikes. There is very little traffic about.

There is some white dog poo on the pavement in front of me and I steer myself around it. I can hear children laughing and playing in one of the back gardens. A lot of the houses still have bottles of milk on the front porch and I imagine the occupants, peacefully asleep in their beds, unaware of the intruder casually walking down their street.

Is this a dream? It certainly has a dream like quality and yet things around me seem so substantial. The air feels thick as it moves in little currents around my body. Everything has a weight and structure to it. I take my phone out of my pocket, being careful that no one is around and open up Google maps. Nothing happens. I press the home button and return to the lock screen. Of course there is no signal. I have my wallet in my right pocket. It contains some money in Japanese yen and my ID but it's all written in Japanese. Luckily I'm wearing a long sleeved shirt as I'm sure my heavily tattooed arms would draw a lot of attention in 1983. I am dressed simply in dark blue jeans and a t shirt with a black shirt over the top. My hair is quite short and a little messy but I don't think that my appearance will be too out of place, as long as no one sees my phone that is. I look at the lock screen again and notice that I have about 73% charge left. The thing is pretty much useless here anyway, just an elaborate time piece really.

I walk all the way down the street to the end, where it meets the main road heading over Crescent Bridge and into town. I stop on the corner next to the solicitors office and try to work out what to do next. I can see people coming and *going from the hospital that dominates the land on the other side of the road. In front of it is the old courthouse, repurposed and now a pub and restaurant. It looks like a castle with tall towers at each corner and crenelations running around the top of them. I could really do with a pint, but the pub won't be open for a good hour and a half and besides I don't have any English money from 1983, the Japanese money I do have is less than useless. I am, to be honest, a bit fucked. I could really do with a glass of water and my stomach is starting to rumble. I wonder if I should hide all of my stuff somewhere, perhaps stumble into the hospital claiming to have lost my memory. Might not be a good idea if the police get involved though or if someone finds my ID and phone. I could probably steal some food from the hospital shop or from The Spa up the road, but again the risks if I were caught are far too great so I decide against it. I cross the road and start to walk back down towards my old house. I'm going to try and talk to my parents, try to convince them of what is happening, but I need to go through it in my head first.*

My father is a local councilor at this time and spends a lot of his time helping out in the local community. I remember people phoning our house at all times of night and early morning and my dad always being willing to help out. My mum is really kind and caring and would never ignore someone in need of help. I think if I can assure them that I mean no harm and that I need help then I might just have a chance. I stop at the top of the path that leads to the front door of the house that I grew up in, a house in which I spent the first twenty or so years of my life, a house that holds so many memories and ghosts from the past.

I walk slowly up the path towards the painted white front door, going over my story in my head and trying to look as normal and confident as possible. My heart is racing and I can feel my face flushing in anticipation. I can smell the yellow flowers on the laburnum tree to my right and hear an electric lawn mower somewhere in the distance. I stop in front of the door, pull my jeans a bit higher up my waist and press the large white doorbell.

BITTER SWEET THIEVERY

We are all heading down into town tonight. It's a
Saturday night and we have tickets to see a
band at the Luckyleaf. I asked my mum if I
could go and she said it's ok as long as I'm back
by midnight. She worries.

A few years ago I went to the new multi screen cinema
with some girls from my year. There were three of them
and me. I think I was thirteen at the time and the prospect
of being alone with three good looking girls was too much
to pass up. It was Suzanne Green, (who lives up the street
at number 22), her friend Corrine, and Natalie Colby. I
don't remember what film we watched, but the cinema
was pretty far out of the town centre and only really
accessible by car. My mum dropped me off, and I told her
I would phone her when we were finished. I met the girls
in the lobby, under the bright lights, the sweet smell of
popcorn in the air. We bought some overpriced drinks
and snacks and sat in the dark auditorium and watched
the film, me in between Suzanne and Natalie, the
tantalising feminine smell of hair spray and a few dabs of
their mum's perfume filling my nose.

The film ended at about 8:30 and we all wandered out
through the fire exit at the back and into the cool night.

We were hungry and wanted to get some food. I told the girls that I had to phone my mum and ask her to come and pick me up, but when I got to the pay phone, rustling about in my pockets I realised that I didn't have the right change. Suzanne suggested we walk back into town and get a pizza on the way. It was going to be a long walk but it was still early and I couldn't let these three girls go alone, besides I was really enjoying their company. We started the walk back into town but it was much further than we had expected. We talked about all sorts of stuff on the way. Suzanne asked me who I thought was the best looking. I blushed and said Natalie. They all giggled and teased me for a bit. I didn't care.

We probably got into town at about nine and made our way to the pizza place. By this time I had totally forgotten about phoning my parents, too absorbed in the girls, the rhythmic sound of their heels on the pavement, their painted greasy lips and the thick mascara that stuck their eyelashes together. For a short time I had been allowed into their world. They talked about boys and kissing with tongues, about tampons and tights and all the other beautiful mysteries of femininity.

We ordered two pizzas and ate them standing up outside the restaurant, watching the people pass by, the old men in suits, the young kids with Mohawks and leather jackets, cigarettes behind ears, arms around lovers, sitting on the steps by the guild hall, drinking from cans of Special Brew, a stereo by their feet playing punk music, and the trendy blokes dressed in tartan flecked trousers wearing trilbies and pink wool cardigans with thick collars.

135

The pizza was the best thing I had ever eaten, thick crusts topped with tomato sauce, cheese, ham and pineapple. We stood out on that street below the night sky talking and laughing. Natalie would occasionally look over and smile at me and the other girls would giggle and tease.

Suzanne and Corrine lived pretty close to me, Suzanne on the same street and Corrine a bit further away near the local chippy, close to where I went to primary school. Natalie lived in Longthorpe but she was staying over at Suzanne's house, so once we had finished the pizza we all set off home together. It was getting late and there wasn't much traffic as we crossed Crescent Bridge and made our way down towards my street. The girls all looked really good under the orange lights. They were growing up and so was I, the attributes of our adolescence slowly giving way to encroaching adulthood.

We said goodbye to Corrine, the other two girls giving her a hug as the remaining three of us turned into my street and walked down towards mine. I said goodbye to Natalie and Suzanne on the pavement outside my house, awkwardly receiving a peck on the cheek from both of them and turned blushing down the front path, past the laburnum tree with its seeds that looked liked little pea pods.

I opened the front door and walked in, a big grin on my face. The living room door immediately flew open and out stalked my father, his glasses pushed up onto his forehead, the stub of a lit cigar in his hand. He looked angry and upset.

It's past ten o'clock, where in the hell have you been? I remember him shouting, the words harsh and biting, but tinged with relief.

My younger brother looked on from the living room, shaking his head, a glass of orange squash and a plate of bread and butter on the arm of the settee.

Where's mum? I asked timidly

She went out in the car looking for you, came the reply from my dad, stroking his beard with his left hand, why didn't you telephone from the cinema?

I tried to explain, making excuses, redirecting the blame, but I knew I had fucked up. An hour ago I had felt indestructible and now I was embarrassed and defeated.

My mother came back a few minutes later. I heard the car engine vibrating the old glass panes of the front door and went into the living room, opening the curtains to peer out. I couldn't make out anything through the glare of the headlights. The engine went quiet, and I heard the slam of a car door. She came rushing in, seeing me standing in the hall and smothered me with hugs and kisses, angry and in tears. She held me and I told her I was sorry. She told me she had scraped the car getting into the narrow driveway because she had been too worried to think clearly. She held me by the shoulders at arms length and looked me in the eye, as if making certain that the boy in front of her was real. I could hear the relief in her voice as she told me how afraid she had been, afraid that she had lost me. She pulled me close and hugged me. I could feel her warm breath on my face. I started to cry.

We stop at The Spa and buy a couple of quarter bottles of vodka. We send James in as he looks the oldest. We stash the bottles in the large pockets on the legs of our army trousers and set off over the bridge and into town. The Queensgate shopping centre dominates the skyline, its sandy coloured walls and big dark windows reflecting the harsh yellow lights that line the bus station. The road is busy, late evening commuters on their way home and estate cars full of families taking advantage of the late night shopping. On the way we spark up a few cigarettes and pass the vodka between us, taking a few large swigs, the alcohol warm in our empty stomachs.

It's me, both Marks and James. We are going to meet a few others at the club.

Who's this band playing tonight again? I ask Mark Jacobs.

He bought the tickets for all of us and handed them out before we left mine. We stood around in the hallway next to the front door, chatting excitedly while mum went into her purse and extracted a crisp ten pound note, handing it to Jacobs. He gave me back seven quid and the ticket, which I folded and put into the pocket on my right leg. Mum told us all to have a good night and to bring back some change from that tenner. I gave her an awkward hug and she kissed me on the cheek as the others bustled out into the cool night.

The band are called The Verve, from up north somewhere, Jacobs tells me, meant to be pretty good actually. Might be a bit too Indy for you mate though, he adds.

I'm alright with anything mate, I reply. As long as it's good.

Mark Jacobs is big into the indie music scene. He likes jangly guitars and lots of effects. He loves Sonic Youth and The Jesus and Mary Chain. I like my music a bit more aggressive, but each to their own I suppose.

Jacobs is the bloke everyone wants to be mates with at school. He's got a cheeky face and a really laid back attitude towards life. He's always up for anything. He does alright at school, is good at football and all the teachers really like him. He keeps his head down, does drugs when they are about, listens to music, and generally enjoys life. He is open and honest and says shit just like it is.

The other Mark is Mark Mayhew. He's one of my best mates at the moment. He's got long, thick black hair that he keeps tied back in a pony tail. He's into bikes, often popping over to mine on his Yamaha AR50 in the evening for a smoke and a chat. He's really frank and straightforward, never lies or talks shit. Whenever I ask him about a girl I like or a new song I've written, he gives me a straight up answer. If the song's shit he will say it's shit. If there is no way I can get the girl then he will let me know. He's a good fucking bloke. I would trust him with anything.

James and I have been best mates since the start of secondary school. He's a broad shouldered bloke with long wiry blonde hair that he usually wears tied up. He's got fat cheeks, the teachers at school always accusing him of eating, or chewing gum in class. We like the same bands and used to paint lead miniatures together, you know those little knights and monsters that people use for fantasy table top gaming, that was before we discovered girls, music and booze. I used to stay over at his house most weekends and we would stay up all night talking about Warhammer 40,000 and Judge Dredd. We have the exact same taste in music and on Saturday mornings we often wander over the bridge into town and hang around in Virgin flicking through the records in the indie section, or head over to the town hall when there's a record fair on to pick up some rare Cure records.

The three of us are a bit drunk as we walk through the Queens Gate bus station, people waiting in the large glass atrium for buses back to Stamford or the surrounding villages. The wind is stronger here, funnelled through the passageway that leads through the bus station and into the city centre. We pause in an alcove to light some cigarettes, James a joint, and the conversation invariably turns to the usual topic.

Mate what's going on with you and 'Her'? Asks Mayhew, Blake said he saw both of you walking around Netherton on Sunday. You shagged her yet?

I blush and try to deflect the question.

It's not like that, it's just... I don't know. I don't reckon she's into me, I confess.

What are you on about mate? Laughs James, poking the roach into the end of his joint, you are over there almost every week. You must have got off with her.

We talk mostly, we've been close a few times, I reply, I don't know mate...

Jacobs interrupts, mate you've liked her for fucking ages, you've got to make your move or she's gonna blow you out.

140

I take another swig of the vodka. It's a cool night and the alcohol is warm and crisp. I can feel it go down my throat and into my empty stomach. I take a few drags of my cigarette and this starts a coughing fit. Deep wet and crunchy coughs that come from my chest. I spit out some phlegm and a bit of blood onto the bushes to the side of the path

Fuck me mate, exclaims James. Have you been to the doctor with that?

Yeah sounds like you're fucking dying mate, agrees Mayhew, chuckling.

I'm alright, just a bit of a cold, I reply.

I pull my black wool hat a bit further down my head. It's the end of summer and the nights are arriving earlier, bringing with them that familiar chill, the first delicate kisses of winter.

I had my hair cut recently. Under-cuts are in. That's when you grow your hair long and then shave it halfway up, so that the top is left long but the underneath is really short. I like it because when I wear my hat I look like a fucking skin head, but when I take it off I can let my long hair down and head bang. Not sure there will be much of that tonight but then again who knows.

We get to the steps that lead up to the second floor of The Luckyleaf and can hear some sound checks going on. The doors don't open till 8:30 and it's still only about 7:45 so we hang around on the wall outside the club, smoking and polishing off the last of the vodka.

Mayhew pipes up. Jacobs had a chance of shagging Sophia over the summer but he fucking messed it up, he says.

Sophia Alessi? I ask.

That girl enjoyed nearly mythical status at school. She was half Italian I think, with a head of shiny dark brown hair cut into a shoulder length bob, and a perfect, pale complexion. Her body seemed to have been moulded by some sort of evil daemon that specialised in torturing teenage boys. She had long legs, a round arse that perfectly filled the tight black trousers she always wore at school, big tits and the face of a Greek goddess. She had these big dark eyes with long lashes, dark pools filled with the promise of promiscuity, a teardrop face punctuated with full pink lips and a smile that had probably featured in a good few teenage wanks. She walked and talked with confidence and most of the boys at school were far too terrified to even consider approaching her. She was a princess. A teenage vision of sexual perfection. She was our Helen, our Cleopatra and the closest thing any of us got to seeing what sexuality wrought flesh was like.

What the fuck Mark? Chimes in James.

Jacobs just grins and shakes his head.

Fucking tell us, I'm dying here, I say.

Mayhew tells us the story.

We were down at Ferry Meadows (it's a big wildlife reserve with a lot of open parkland, grassy fields and a few moderately sized lakes. They are all man made and not too deep, so in the summer they are always full of happy swimmers) and we were all in one of the lakes having a swim. We didn't have any trunks with us so we just stripped down to our Y- fronts and dived in. We were mucking about in the water, splashing each other and fucking about when Sophia and a couple of her mates from the year above us came along.

We all exchange a few glances.

Sophia was looking really fit in a tight white t shirt and jeans. She saw us in the water and came over to say hello. We were all embarrassed as fuck, white as fucking China with skinny legs and dressed only in our pants.

Fucking hell that must have been a site to behold, I comment, laughing.

So Jacobs might not have the face of a movie star, he continues, but he's got it where it counts, if you know what I mean and his wet tighty whities are leaving nothing to the imagination.

Jacobs grins and takes a quick swig of vodka.

Anyway we can all see that Sophia has noticed too and she seems well up for it. Jacobs however is completely fucking oblivious to this. She even fucking asked him if he wants to go for a walk, but he says 'nah I'm fine just messing about in the water'.

Fucking hell Mark, I say laughing, you aren't gonna get a chance like that again.

I know chimes in Mayhew, she was well up for it n'all.

Fuck, I was having a good laugh, birds always get in the way, says Jacobs, although he has a deep look of regret on that cheeky face of his.

Yeah a bit like your knob mate, teases James and we all laugh, mine quickly turning into a rasping cough.

We finish off the vodka just in time for opening time at the club. There is a narrow staircase that leads up to a small doorway on the second floor. There is always someone on the door to collect tickets and mark your hand with a rubber stamp, that way if you leave you can reenter the club at anytime. We usually take a collection of marker pens to the club with us and one person buys a ticket, gets the stamp, and then comes back down the stairs to show us. We pick the appropriate colour and stand under a street light faithfully recreating the stamp on each of our hands. We then lick our fingers and give the thing a bit of a smudge for realism and it works every time, five people through the door for the price of one. Looks like my art A level might pay off after all.

Tonight we all have tickets and so we hand them over to the bloke at the door. He gives each of us the once over as we pass by, and although we are pretty full of ourselves and think we are proper fucking adults, he must realise that we are all underage. He just shakes his head slightly as this gaggle of skinny drunk teenagers passes through and into The Luckyleaf club for yet another pissed up night.

There is a DJ on first. He's playing mostly indie stuff, a lot of Sonic Youth and Pavement and some Pop Will Eat Itself. He also plays a couple of older Smiths records and some Cure. It's all good stuff and the place is starting to fill up. We are all downing bottles of Newcastle Brown Ale. It's pretty weak shit but cheap as fuck. There is a rumour that it's got arsenic in it, and that drinking too much will kill you, but then again drinking too much of anything will kill you, so there you go.

The band come on at about 9:00. The DJ plays another couple of tracks while they set up their equipment and tune up their guitars. You can hear them shouting to each other over the music in deep, Manchester accents. The club is pretty small and the stage is low, basically just a step up from the dance floor that dominates most of the club. We are pretty close to the front and practically eye to eye with the band.

Liam and Butcher have joined us. They turned up at about 9:00 stinking of cheap aftershave and looking a bit wasted already. Liam said they had stopped off in the Wortly for a few beers before coming here. Butcher has another story about some drunken brawl in some boozer somewhere, which he is shouting into our ears. No one is really listening and all eyes are focused on the band.

We all went to watch The Silverfish play in Cambridge a couple of weeks ago. It was a last minute thing. I think Eli got the tickets. We were all there with our long hair and black t shirts, stage diving and moshing and Butcher turned up in a shirt and tie. I think he had been doing some part time work at a local office, but he was moshing and stage diving like the rest of us, short back and sides and smart business wear in a small dark fucking club full of misfits. He was up on stage, arms raised to heaven above a sea of humanity as the bass rumbled in my chest and the distorted guitar rang in my ears. He leapt and the crowd cheered with open arms and received him. His attire didn't matter. His short hair and fuck you attitude didn't matter. For those few minutes he was one of them,

145

he was one of us, just another lost soul leaping into the void.

There is nothing like being in a band. It's not just the music, it's not just the attention you get from girls. Fuck the self expression and the artistic process, it's about creating something with people who share your vision. It's about shaping something together that is more than the sum of its parts, then putting it out there to be loved or derided or whatever, who the fuck cares? That feeling of applause after you finish playing a song can never be matched. You spend hours practicing, honing it to perfection, but the audience never see this. They don't experience the inception, the infighting, the hours of practice, the fuck ups, the blisters, and the broken strings. They see the finished product, sealed and delivered and when they love it there is nothing else that can match it. Fuck sex, cocaine or love. There is nothing like it.

I'm sure that when I'm forty years old and half drunk in a city on the other side of the world, a small perfect boy resting peacefully in the next room, I will laugh at the insincerity of that previous statement, but for now I am a drunk teenage boy in a small dirty club in East Anglia and that boy couldn't give a fuck about what the future holds. Fuck tomorrow. It is now, we are young and strong and we can do anything. We are invincible. Our super power is the ability to shape the future in any way we want. This is our town and our time. I think about 'Her' and wonder what she's doing. I wish she was here. She always said she only fancied me when I played the guitar.

The band plays. We dance and we drink. At some point someone is on stage dancing with the band. Maybe it's me, perhaps it isn't, I don't know if I'm even here. It might be a different night, another half forgotten time. Clouds of dry ice curl around us as we twist and bend to the music. It's good. It's food. The bass and drums hit me in the chest like rhythmic palpitations and the booze has me wrapped in a warm blanket of my own self. I see the lads dancing and singing along and I know that whatever happens I have them. There is no tomorrow, only now. My mind goes back to 'Her', the delicate white scar across her hand, of pushing through thick fields of golden wheat, of the silvery bark of the birch tree that stands at the bottom of the garden, the birds that peck at the hard earth on those soft winter mornings, of the smell of oil on the fretboard of my guitar and stepping into the cool shade of the garage on a hot summer's day and …

ピピピピピピピピピピピピピピピ

You alright mate? Shouts Mark in my ear.

Yeah I'm fine mate… just a bit wasted, I shout back.

I cough a bit and suddenly have a lot of phlegm in my mouth. I spit it out onto the floor. No one notices. Some bird in heels and a really short skirt dances right through it.

The band are on their last song and I realise that I am well and truly wasted. Things spin out of my control and the world is softened and muted. They end their set and everyone claps and cheers. Pretty good band to be honest, again not really my thing but good all the same. I'm hanging out on the dance floor talking to a girl from the year above about the band, and I see Mark and Liam chatting to the lead singer at the bar. He's tall and skinny, dressed in really wide jeans and a white t shirt, his long sweaty hair, half covering his face, a full pint of bitter in his hand. I can see them laughing and joking. I walk over and stand next to Mark. There is quite a crowd so it's difficult to get close. I see some nods of approval and shaking of hands. The drummer is up on the stage already starting to dismantle his kit and Jacobs and Liam walk over.

What are you doing? I ask.

We're gonna give the band a hand taking all their stuff back to the van, Replies Jacobs.

He is also clearly pretty wasted and rocks back and forth a bit on his feet. There is another entrance at the back of the club that leads down a narrow staircase to the car park at the back. The DJ is back on playing some more tracks and the band are heaving heavy amps and speakers off the stage and down the tight staircase. Jacobs has picked up the snare drum and Liam has one of the toms. I see them both disappear into the stairwell at the back and think about lending a hand. I'm far too drunk though and knock that idea on the head pretty quickly. James and Mark Mayhew are at the bar so I walk over to chat.

We talk shit for a while and I realise I've run out of ciggies. The shops will have closed ages ago so my only option is the vending machine in The Luckyleaf. Now this isn't some high-tech thing with flashing lights, a touch screen and a selection of different brands, this thing is far more utilitarian. It's basically a big wooden box with some metal trays with handles attached to them. You put your money in the slot. It's two quid for twenty Embassy number one (actually it's seventeen in a box made for twenty, the place has to make a profit after all). You put your money in the correct slot and then pull on the handle with all your might, and if your are lucky the thing doesn't jam, and a pristine box of fags comes out.

I buy my fags, and I'm on my way back from the machine when I hear a commotion. The singer of the band is shouting at someone and there is a lot of arm waving and accusatory fingers being pointed. Mark Mayhew is standing there bearing the brunt and he's got his shoulders shrugged and his arms raised in an 'I don't know what the fuck you are talking about' pose. I stroll drunkenly over and catch snippets of the conversation

Your fucking mate... runner with the fucking drums...is the fucking cunt...three hundred fucking quid. I barge through the group surrounding the singer to find out what's going on

Turns out that Liam has done a runner with the snare drum and the roadie has got hold of Jacobs in the car park. People are shouting and arguing and everyone is acting hard. There's pushing and shoving and a few drinks get knocked over. The head barman is over there trying to calm things down. I push my way out of the crowd and over to the bar and get the barmaid's attention. She's a young girl with blonde permed hair, one of the regulars from downstair's daughters.

What's goin on, she asks, as I order another bottle of Newcastle Brown and sit down on a stool at the far end of the bar and watch the chaos unfold.

Dunno, think someone half inched the band's drums, I tell her, everyone is well pissed off.

She shakes her head and goes back to collecting glasses and emptying ashtrays.

I take a big swig of beer and tear the plastic off my new pack of fags. The DJ is back on and people are still on the dance floor. 'Fools Gold' by The Stone Roses starts playing.

The following Monday at school everyone wants to know what went down with Liam and the drum. I bump into the two Marks at lunch time and a big group of us take a walk down to the chippy in Bretton, going over the events of the weekend.

We thought it was rock and roll, he explains as we all tuck into our chips and battered sausages.

We are standing on the footbridge that crosses into Bretton, elbows on the railing, watching the cars and lorries pass below us, occasionally tossing the odd chip down onto the fast moving traffic below.

We saw the Mary Chain only used a snare on Pyschocandy so that's all we needed, he continues, I didn't get too far. Liam hid the drum in the multi-storey car park and I was out the back of The Luckyleaf being held hostage by a roadie. I could hear Liam going pssst from the bushes.

He laughs at this and brushes his long curly hair away from his face, tucking it behind his ears.

The band were called back and we all went back to mine in their van looking for Liam.

You were in their van? Asks James, where did they take you?

I took them down The Grange for no reason whatsoever, replies Jacobs, didn't know what else to do. I was pissed and wanted to mess with them a bit. The lead singer, the skinny twat was acting all hard, he adds and we all laugh.

Jacobs continues, the singer from the support band found Liam and the snare drum curled up behind a car in the multi storey, and I just went home and waited for him to make his way over.

Fucking hell mate, I exclaim, did they call the police?

Nah mate. Replies Jacobs. Said they were going to, but once they got the drum back everything was cushdy. The same band are supporting Ride in Cambridge next weekend and I'm going, he states, I'll have to spend the night hiding from that twat of a roadie though.

Mark Mayhew throws the remainder of his chips at Jacobs and Jacobs ducks out of the way, batting the greasy paper away with his school bag.

They might have some good equipment worth stealing mentions James.

We all laugh.

Shit it's nearly one, states Mayhew looking at his watch and we've got Moseley's Enviro class after lunch.

We all leg it back to school despite the bellies full of greasy chips and battered sausages.

Richard Ashcroft and his band 'The Verve', later went on to become hugely popular in the mid nineties with hits such as 'Bitter Sweet Symphony' and 'The Drugs Don't Work'. Oasis sang their praises and their third album 'Urban Hymns' went on to sell over ten million copies, remaining one of the twenty best selling albums in UK chart history. I still occasionally play one of their songs to my five year old son in our small apartment in Tokyo, as the sun goes down and my wife spends the night in the arms of a man I hate, but all of that is a long way off, a story from another time.

INSOMNIA

There's the cunt, says Nugget, tapping me on the shoulder. He's pointing down the road towards the group of five or six lads twenty yards ahead of us. We've all had a skin full and tonight is fight night. There is something in the fucking air. I can feel it and so can everyone else. Town seemed sharp and aggressive, everyone stalking about with attitude and scowls on their faces. Sometimes you know that a night out is going to end with some spilt blood. Things just seem a bit skewed, there is a sense of something dark and unresolved in the streets and everyone glances over their shoulders nervously. Shouts of anger carry on the still night air and the police in their yellow high visibility jackets do nothing to quell the feeling of unrest.

But why these blokes? I hear you ask.

Well, my mate Max works in a pub called The Fox and Hounds. It's in a village that was absorbed into the city proper a long time ago and yet still retains some of its quaint village charm. There is a small white post office with a polite elderly lady behind the counter, some old and rather well to do houses, a few open park areas and the pub. It's a great boozer, quiet and dignified and has some comfy chairs and a fireplace.

Max works there on Saturdays and Sundays in order to earn some extra cash, and we sometimes pop in for a pint and to say hello. His dad knows the owner and managed to pull some strings and get Max a job there. He says it's alright, the pay isn't bad and there are always people from school popping in. There's this kid in the year below me at school. He's called Gav. He's a popular kid, good looking and good at sports, but most of my mates think he's a bit of a smarmy twat. He knows not to fuck with our group and always greets us with a bow when we roll into school. It's all a bit weird to be honest.

Anyway him and his mates got pissed in The Fox the night before last and made a fucking mess in the bogs that Max had to clean up. Max reckons it was deliberate because they were all laughing and mocking as they left, but then again Max can be a bit paranoid. Anyway that's not the fucking point. The point is that we want to kick someone's head in. There isn't any logic to it, no rhyme or reason. Everyone is pissed up and on their moral fucking high horses. Nugget has just had his head shaved and looks like a right fucking nutter and I think that is feeding back into his temperament.

We were at a party down by the rowing lake a few days ago and he kept goading me to push him into people so that he could start some shit. We were acting like twats and I'll freely admit it, but tonight we have a mission, a reason to deal out some righteous retribution.

We all turn onto the road that heads towards the Queensgate bus station and I look sideways at Nugget. His mouth is set in a hard line across his face and his pale grey eyes stare ahead unblinking. Things have already

154

been set in motion and it would take a much greater force than I could possibly apply to alter the course of tonight's events. My only choice is to give in to the current and let it sweep me along. A few of the girls from my year lag behind a few paces. They have tried to dissuade us but we are numb to their logic.

Fucking cunts, I hear Nugget grumble as we gain some ground on our targets.

Nugget lives just up the road from us in a terraced house on the way to The Spa. His mum is Irish and his dad is from Scotland, or maybe it's the other way round. He's one of six brothers and they are all massive. He's the second youngest, the oldest already in his twenties. His poor parents must have a nightmare of a time trying to feed them all at Christmas. His name is Aidan but everyone calls him Nugget. When he was in the first year at school he was short and fat, but he's six foot tall now and the nickname hardly seems appropriate anymore. He's planning on doing an apprenticeship down at Perkins Engines, a local factory that machines engine parts and such like, once he finishes his GCSEs. No sixth form for him. He's got that working class work ethic that my parents never really managed to instil in me and I really admire that about him. Like a lot of my friends, I've known him for a good portion of my life, and so we are more like brothers than mates. He's two years younger than me, but he doesn't look it.

We catch up with them as they turn into the bus station and Nugget immediately goes piling in on one of Gav's friends. The bloke crouches down and puts his hands over his head, desperately trying to defend himself. Eli has Gav up against a wall and is punching him repeatedly in the face. I can see blood and hear the rush of the sea in my ears. In my head I can see those boys from the children's home breaking my nose with a cast on a broken arm.

My fists clench and I feel a surge of anger and hatred, not with the group of boys in front of me but with all of it. I want to strike back at this backward little town and its atmosphere of violence and bigotry. I want to rise up above the streets and crush all those stupid little drinking holes and burn the place to the ground. I want this thing to slow down. I want to get off, but there is no stopping it, all I can do is hold on and hope for the best. I'm doing this from a place of love, I tell myself.

I grab one of the boys by the neck without even throwing a punch and bring my knee up into his stomach. He is much bigger than me, but a little over weight and he doesn't fight back. He doubles over clutching his stomach in pain and moans a few swear words.

Don't fucking swear at me you cunt, I yell, I'll fucking kill you.

Everything is a mess. Someone is on the ground and Eli and another bloke are shouting at each other. Strangely Nugget and a boy from the group are standing back against a wall having a smoke and a chat. I see Nugget laugh a few times and make a joke as he nurses his right hand.

The bloke I kneed in the stomach is still doubled over and his friend is leading him away by the shoulders. I am still buzzed with adrenaline and the events of the last few seconds keep spiralling around in my head. Nugget comes over and gives me a pat on the back then hands me a cigarette. I spark up. His knuckles are bleeding, but I don't think he really notices. There are a few concerned onlookers walking past on the other side of the road but they keep going. They don't want any part of this.

The girls walk past us and on down into the bus station. We call after them but they aren't interested. Fucking childish bunch of twats we are, we deserve it. I start walking after them and Nugget and Eli follow.

We are staying over at Kirsten's house tonight as her parents are away and she always has us over when the house is empty. It's a really big house at the end of a cul-de-sac and must have at least seven bedrooms. It's got a really big garden with a treehouse in it, which is a great little hideout for getting stoned in. We have been going over every night for a week or so. It's still summer so we have fuck all else to do.

I love staying over at Kirsten's, that feeling of being well and truly free, no school, no parents and lots of booze and drugs. There are always a lot of girls over too. I got off with Jen again a couple of nights ago. I was lying on top of her in one of the bedrooms and we were kissing. She told me she wanted to fuck me, and I thought things were going to get interesting, but we were interrupted when someone else came in to sleep on the floor next to us. We tried to find somewhere more private, but the house was full. Jen fell asleep in Kirsten's sister's room and I got up for a smoke.

Tom and me had been skinning up and smoking these herbal sleeping pills all night since we had run out of hash and I was having a bout of really bad insomnia. I stayed up all night while everyone else slept. The house was quiet and I went out into the garden at about four in the morning. The sun was already coming up and there was a cold layer of dew on the long grass. I took off my socks and walked out into the crisp morning air. There were a few birds singing and some wispy clouds hung in the sky. A jet plane blazed white in the early morning sun as it slowly traversed the 'bley' sky. I wished that I had my guitar and thought about waking up Eli and running back to mine to write a few songs, but the impulse soon left me and my feet started to get cold. I thought about Jen asleep in bed and wanted to curl up next to her warm body, put my arms around her and drift off into a deep sleep, to hold her close and dream of being on that plane high above the surface of the earth, hanging in the emptiness with the void below. However, I knew deep down inside that sleep would never come.

Kirsten, Rachel and Kyra walk about ten metres ahead of us, and me, Nugget and Eli go over what occurred. Events are blurred and surreal like the tail end of a bad dream and we need to get them straight in our minds so we can process what happened.

Yeah he went down hard mate, I tell Nugget, you fuckin decked him old boy.

I know mate, thought they'd put up a bit more of a fight to be honest, he replies, rubbing his knuckles.

Who was the bloke you messed up? Asks Eli, my mind flashing back to him doubled over in pain, clutching at his stomach.

I don't know mate. I've seen him about at school. I think Stuee knows him. I don't really give a fuck mate to be honest, I tell him.

Hairy muff, says Nugget, I reckon the birds are well pissed off with us though.

Yeah I reply, might not get sucked off tonight I reckon.

Nugget and Eli laugh, but I don't mean it. That comes from somewhere else, from someone else; the other bloke in my head that has hijacked my id and is taking it for a fucking joy ride. I cough and wipe my mouth with my left hand.

You sound worse than me mate, comments Nugget.

Nugget often kips on my floor when we've had one too many. He wakes up in the morning with a horrible rasping cough and spits massive globs of phlegm into the sink in the corner. I can hear a wheezing in his chest when he breathes, but who the fuck cares? To be honest I like the feeling of being tired and broken, like an old heavily used piece of equipment or some sleep deprived junkie. It makes me feel sharp and alive. It gives me focus and a sense of being that a healthy lifestyle never could.

I call out after Kyra, look I'm sorry, it was just a fight, those twats were asking for it.

I love Kyra. We talk about anything and everything. If we were attracted to each other, then I think we would probably get married, have kids and grow old together, but we don't think of each other like that. She is petite, gregarious and headstrong, and staying up late, smoking

159

cigarettes and talking to her is perhaps my favourite thing in the world.

She ignores me, they all do. I take the hair band off my wrist and hold it in between my teeth as I pull my shoulder length hair back into a pony tail. I hold the pony tail with my left hand and use my right to tie my hair back with the band, looping it around twice so it's nice and tight. I pull at it a bit to get it straight. Nugget's hand is swelling up around the knuckles and he has a few grazes on his fingers. Cars are flying by on Thorpe Road as we round the corner onto Kirsten's street.

Is it still alright if we come back to yours mate? Nugget calls out to Kirsten.

Do what you want, she bites back.

They really aren't happy with us.

So they we are sitting in Kirsten's kitchen. It's big like the rest of the house and has a large table in the middle. There is a glass panelled door that opens out into the garden and a utility room at the back where the family dog sleeps.

Nugget has a packet of frozen peas on his knuckles and he's sitting at the kitchen table having a beer and smoking a joint. I am relaxing in a comfy chair with my legs arched over the arm. The girls are making cheese on toast. They are still pissed off with us for ruining a perfectly decent night out, but their anger is waning. The digital clock on the oven reads 00:46.

It's started to rain, the drops working their way down the glass panes in the kitchen door, a strong breeze rattling the windows in their frames. The mood is subdued. No loud music or downing shots tonight I reckon. Just a few quiet joints and then to bed. The dog has woken up and has come out of the utility room. He is excited and hungry. He circles my chair and I give him a tickle behind the ears. His neck feels warm and solid, his ears are a little cold at the tips.

Somewhere far across on the other side of town a young lad is lying in bed and clutching at his still aching stomach. He is dreading going into school on Monday and having to see the people that attacked him and his friends outside the bus station. At the district hospital another boy sits quietly, his shirt splattered with blood, head in hands, as his teary eyed mother talks in hushed tones to the doctor in a busy emergency room. The doctor explains that they will have to operate on her son's nose and that his breathing may be permanently obstructed.
In another bed in another house a kid called Gav lies in silence, the orange light from his bedside lamp illuminating his bruised face. He sits propped up against the headboard, his eyes closed, his fat old cat curled up in its usual place by his feet, the waste paper basket by the bedside table half full of bloody tissues. He yearns for sleep, for the soft security of that black nothingness, but he cannot let go, his mind replaying events on an endless deafening loop. He sees flashes of the boys who attacked them, hears echoes of their angry voices and the rush of blood in his ears, feels the touch of the cold concrete beneath his feet as he relives those few seconds of abrupt, violent chaos. Why them? Why tonight? He wonders if he had insulted one of them at school somehow, or made

eyes at the wrong girl. He thinks of his friends. His parents wanted to call the police, but he pleaded with them to leave it. He winces in pain as he reaches for the cup of hot chocolate his mum left by the side of his bed. It's still warm. He is tired and afraid and sleep doesn't find him.

I'm sitting in the back room of my parents house and it is just as I remember it. There is a certain smell that a house possesses. It is the combination of all the lives lived within it. The meals eaten, the soap used, the carpet cleaner and the people themselves all have a specific aroma, and the cumulation of all these things gives each dwelling a specific and very individual smell. You don't usually notice it yourself. You are used to it. It's like breathing or the beating of your own heart. It is a smell that is only noticeable after a long absence.

We used to drive to France every year in a silver Volvo with leather upholstery and stay in a Chateau or Gite in the French countryside. On the drive back we would try to spot cars with that year's new registration plate or play eye spy. I would sometimes draw a picture, and we would irritate my dad by fighting or teasing each other in the back. He would turn round and tell us to be quiet or he would make us walk home. We would settle down for a while but a giggle or silly comment from one of us would soon rekindle our mischief.

We would turn into our familiar street with its neat little front gardens and children at play in the road on their bikes. My dad would reverse the car into the drive way and we would eagerly hop out, running across the small grass

162

covered front garden and into the porch. My dad would unlock the door and we would rush inside pushing and shoving and happy to be home. Upon entering we would always be met by that smell, that familiar and comforting aroma that marked the end of another holiday. Someone would always remark about the house having 'that smell', but it was impossible to describe. It was only our shared love and experience that gave it meaning.

I catch a hint of it now as my mum, who is probably the same age as I am, if not a little younger brings in a pot of tea and some cups and saucers carried on a round wooden tray. The cups are delicate yet understated and the pot and tray have a lovely familiar well used look to them. I remember every tiny thing about them. I feel a few tears welling up in my eyes and a large lump in my throat, but I suppress both and manage to express a quiet thank you.

You are welcome, she says.

She is still eyeing me with a fair amount of suspicion or it could be recognition. Something about me looks wrong. There is nothing that strange about how I am dressed or how I style my hair. It's something else that feels off. Something intangible. It's as though I don't belong, like plunging the negative end of a magnet into iron filings. The world somehow doesn't seem to want to fit around me.

And so you don't remember at all how you got here? she enquires.

No, all I remember is going to sleep last night and waking up this morning on a patch of grass at the bottom of the road.

She nods slowly, considering everything I say logically and carefully. My accent seems a little off she thinks to

163

herself. I am definitely English but there is a hint of something else in there. My dialect is definitely from southern England but there are some American or could it be Australian sounding vowels. Sometimes I soften my T's into D's like Americans do. I sometimes appear to be searching for words that should come easily. It's the accent of someone who has moved around a lot. It's the accent of someone who speaks another language.

Had you been drinking? she asks calmly taking a sip of her tea and setting the cup down gently on a small round table to her right.

I want to reach out and hug her. I want to tell her all of the things that I never had a chance to. I want to tell her that I am happy, that she raised me right, that I miss her more than anything. I want to tell her all the things that will hopefully one day come from the mouth of my own son, things that only a parent can understand, beautiful and pure things that only find form in the selfless love we have for our sons and daughters.

I catch a glimpse of something out of the corner of my eye. The door to the room is closed, but the top section is divided into two glass panels that provide a view down the hallway all the way to the front door. Standing just outside the door is a small boy. He looks about seven or eight but might just be small for his age. His hair is cut into a short bob and he wears a brown tracksuit over his skinny form. He has bright hazel eyes and an olive complexion from playing in the sun all summer. I briefly catch his eye and for an instant I am standing where he is...

...I am looking into the back room wondering what mum is talking to that strange man about. She only ever shuts the

164

door when something important is happening. I feel a little nervous, but mum seems happy and the man seems nice. I wonder if I have met him before. He looks familiar. It's ok because dad will be back from Tom's house soon. He went over to help his dad fix the lawnmower.

The door bell rang this morning when me and Hardy were watching transformers. It was a really good episode and we recorded it. There was a really cool bit with the Dinobots. I heard my mum answer the door and the muffled sound of voices. They were talking for quite a long time but we couldn't tell what about. We heard them walk down the hall to the back room. Megatron was fighting Grimlock and Optimus Prime was badly damaged. I really want to draw a picture of Grimlock. Gabriel has the toy and it's the best transformer I've ever seen. It's got all these transparent bits that you can see all his inner workings through.

I can see them drinking tea and talking. He must be the same age as my mum. Probably one of her friends from work. Doesn't look like he works at the Nene Housing Society though. He looks over at me and smiles and gives me a small wave. I blush and lower my head. Mum sees me and waves me away. I turn round and run back to the front room. Hardy is getting the Lego out. We keep it folded up in a sheet inside a big basket...

I take a sip of my tea, it tastes good, milky with a bit of sugar for sweetness. It reminds me of cold winter mornings before school, sitting on the carpet in the dining room with my back resting up against the radiator to keep the cold out of my body, teeth chattering and knees pulled into me, wishing I could go back to bed for another ten minutes and my dad outside in the dark cold morning, scraping ice from the window of the silver Volvo in the driveway, the heater on full blast to warm up the interior for the drive to school.

I wasn't drinking, I reply, or at least I don't think so.

I nervously run a hand through my hair and I notice a few strands clinging to my hand. I blow them away.

The front door opens and I see my dad walk in. His beard is long and bushy and black. He's wearing a brown t shirt a bit too small for him and some black corduroy trousers with slightly flared bottoms. His glasses are large and thick, his hair thinning around the front and swept back away from his face.

He sees me sitting in the back room and scowls a little in recognition. He walks briskly down the hall and into the back room where we are sitting. Leaving the door open behind him.

Hello dear, he greets mum before turning to me.

And who is our guest?

Can you sit down please Nigel? My mum politely requests.

He is starting to look a little concerned, but he complies, perching himself down on the edge of the large comfy chair that sits up against the wall.

Everything alright? He asks.

My mum doesn't answer. She turns to me and says,

Show him.

UNSTOPPABLE FORCE, IMMOVABLE OBJECT

Show him, urges Rod giggling like an idiot.

Ok mate, replies Kael, but keep it down, my dad is going to go apeshit if you wake him up.

We are in Kael's house and it's about 2:00 am.

Come and have a look at this Kei, he encourages, motioning with his head for me to follow.

I was in my living room watching late night telly, some film about a possessed bulldozer that was killing everyone. I've got a bit of a temperature and my cough has got really bad so while everyone else was out in town getting pissed, I was stuck at home on a Friday night watching a piece of anthropomorphic construction equipment committing deicide.

At about one in the morning I heard Kael's old red metro pull up to his house and a few excited voices, and laughing from across the road. I peaked through the curtains and saw Max, Rod and Kael disappear into Kael's house. I got up, went out of the living room and quietly unlocked the front door. I crept out onto the porch, pushing the door closed while turning the knob to shut it as quietly as possible. My parents' bedroom is right above the door, a large bay window overlooking the street. Mum is a rather light sleeper.

The road was quiet and most of the houses were in darkness. A taxi drove by the end of the street heading down Thorpe Road towards town and Crescent Bridge, but other than that the street was still. I jogged across the road and up to Kael's house. As I neared the front door I could hear muffled voices and laughing above the softened melody of 'The Pixies' 'Doolittle'. Kael's old red Metro was in the drive. I could still feel a bit of heat from the engine.

I knocked on the solid dark blue door. The voices suddenly went quiet and I heard footsteps. I could hear whispering.

It's not the fucking pigs you twat.

Shhh.

Just open the door...

If it is I'm legging it...

Shhh.

I heard the latch turn and the door opened slightly. It's a big heavy wooden door and like most of the houses down the street it's also about eighty years old so it takes a good old tug to get the thing open. I saw Kael's face grinning through the gap.

It's alright lads, just Kei, told you it wasn't the pigs, he said turning back to them, bunch of pussies were shitting it.

He opened the door, letting me in with a slap on the shoulder as I passed, took an inquisitive look out into the street then shut the door firmly behind me.

Max gave me a hug.

Kei mate, you missed a fucking wicked one tonight old boy, he explained, grinning like a fucking lunatic.

Alright old boy, called out Rod in his usual loud voice, smacking me somewhat hard on the back with his open hand.

Good night then lads? I asked. My fever was giving everything a slightly surreal feeling, like watching events through a filter or on an old TV.

We are sad tripping old boy, giggled Max.

Kael had an enormous cone of a spliff in his gob which he sparked up with a cheap plastic lighter. He looked really normal actually, but then again he always does. It's always difficult to tell if Kael is wasted. His id is always close to the surface. It drives him. He is a lover and a fighter. He's got a brain on him, but his existence is governed by something more primal, something raw. He is a creature of instinct, not some neurotic paranoid over thinker like yours truly. He sometime gets a bit fucking loopy when he's had too much booze, but everything else just seems to roll off him. He was grinning and his eyes were red but other than that he seemed just like he had that morning.

Deep down I wish I could be like him. He is single minded in his pursuits. He doesn't let fear of the future cloud his judgement or get in the way of him or his appetites. It may well destroy him at some point in the future, or it may propel him to greatness, who knows? Only time can shape us into the beings we will become. The future is random and cursed and full of beauty and death, and one day I will be taking a train into central Tokyo and thinking about a girl, the sun reflecting off the concrete houses that stretch away to the horizon. I will be sipping hot coffee from a can and staring at a picture of a model on one of the many adverts plastered over the inside of the bright carriage. She is beautiful, olive skinned with dark eyes and a wide toothy smile. She is the daughter of the man who will one day tear my life apart. Someday these things will occur or they may not. The future is fickle and events happen beyond our control. The monster under my bed is getting bigger and stronger and one day he will seize one of us and send us hurtling into the blackness. He is hungry. He's always hungry.

Really good acid actually Kei mate, commented Kael, got it off a bloke in The College Arms. Want some?

For a second I wondered if it might make me feel a bit better, might take the edge off this creepy feeling I had under my skin, but the prospect of tripping with a fever quickly lost its appeal. Things already seemed weird enough.

I'm alright actually mate, still a bit under the weather, I thought or did I say it out loud?

Come on old boy, sad good stuff, added Rod. He had his back to me and was putting a cassette in the stereo.

Lash it on mate, called out Max. Sad getting trails lads. Kael just grinned and took another drag of the spliff.

You hungry? He asked.

Fuck me, that's got to be a whole fucking warehouse full you fucking nutters, I exclaim.

What the fuck is your dad going to say when he wakes up?

It's alright, grins Kael, he likes doughnuts.

We are in the kitchen at the back of the house and I'm looking at about twenty blue crates of freshly baked doughnuts. The smell is amazing and my stomach immediately starts rumbling in anticipation. Rod is already tucking in, one doughnut stuffed into his gob and another in his left hand.

Sad good doughnuts old boy, he says, a cascade of half chewed baked goods tumbling from his mouth.

At school Rod has a lunch time ritual. We call it the three S's; a shit, a shifty, and a sarnie. He goes into the teacher's bogs on the first floor next to the stairs that lead up to centre point (the room for the sixth formers), locks himself in one of the stalls, unwraps his sandwich (usually cheese ham and mayonnaise) lights up a ciggie, and has a dump. We tell him it's fucking gross, but he won't listen. Like I said, some of us are governed by more base instincts.

In fact we all are. It's just that some of us choose to ignore them. We pretend that we are somehow better because we keep our fantasies and appetites hidden deep below, covered in a veil of politeness and niceness. It's the Great British way. People like Rod and Kael are different. They live to an alternate set of values. Their morality is not governed by a need to follow some set of arbitrary rules or to kowtow to an accepted conservative ideal of manners or behaviour. They live life, they consume and they grow. They are forces of nature that plow through this short existence without regard for its rules or societal pressures. It's how we should all live life, point our bows into the sun and set forth, eat when we are hungry, sleep when we are tired and laugh and play and fuck. It will soon be too late. Our bodies will begin to wither and our bright eyes will begin to fade along with the dreams and hopes they conceal within. The weight of losses we endure will line our faces, and hearts that once pumped the blood of youth, will clog and die.

Kael passes me the joint and I allow myself a long pull. The smoke is hot and burns my throat and lungs. I cough and hack up a thick glob of blood and mucus. I swallow it back down and nearly wretch. I take another drag. It hurts. It feels good.

So what the fuck? I ask, pointing at the doughnuts.

Max explains.

So me Rod and Kael were out for a few beers down at Bogarts and Kael gave us some acid, it's called Spider-Man or something.

Superman, Kael interjects.

Yeah right, continues Max, anyway we left the boozer pretty early cause we were all off our heads. We got back here and realised that we didn't have any fags, so me and Rod decided to take a walk up to the all night garage to get some. On the way we got a bit sidetracked.

Max and Rod start laughing at this point and Kael shakes his head.

They were gone for about two fucking hours, he says.

Yeah we were just hanging around outside The Spa. There was this lamp post and every time Rod went under it he looked really small, giggles Max, It was funny as fuck. Must have looked mental to anyone walking by.

Rod is looking at the TV, grinning and moving his hand around in front of his face.

So anyway, Max continues, we phoned Kael from a phone box just to check in. He was well pissed off cause he was alone at home tripping on his own.

Fucking nightmare mate, tripping my arse off and watching MTV, grumbles Kael, taking another pull on the spliff.

He told me he was coming to pick us up in the Metro and to stay where we were, continues Max.

So anyway Rod notices a lorry with its back open over at the bakery and a shit load of fresh doughnuts just sitting in there. He says to me 'let's sad rob them' and so we run over to the bakery and Rod grabs about six crates of the things. I can't even see his face because they are stacked so high. I do the same and at this point we see the red Metro pull up and Kael get out. No one says anything, but there's a sort of unspoken agreement between us that we chuck them in the back of the motor.

Hardly fit, interrupts Kael, couldn't even close the bloody boot.

So Rod is getting some more crates and Kael is getting pissed off, Max continues.

Fucking right I was mate, these two twats wanted to take the whole fucking lorry.

Rod laughs.

At some point Kael just decides to take off. So I jump in the car and we are off. The only problem is Rod is still in the back of the lorry getting more crates. He sees us leaving and leaps in through the boot. We take off down the road with Rod's legs fucking dangling out of the back. Max laughs

Fucking pussies sad did a runner, teases Rod, bits of doughnut still clinging to his fluffy chin.

You would have been there all night mate, accuses Kael.

Besides I reckon we've got enough.

Yeah, agrees Max.

I take a doughnut and bite into it. It's good, still warm.

Rod and Kael have always had a weird relationship. They are too similar in many ways, so they often clash, and when they do it's a nightmare. Neither will ever back down, so it invariably comes to one or several of us having to stand in and break them up.

Humans share a lot with other mammals. We hide our instincts well but when under the influence of certain substances (especially alcohol) these animalistic traits awaken. If we were a pack of wolves Rod and Kael would be the two vying for the position of alpha of the pack.

A while back when I was with Chloe, and Kael and Debbie were just starting out we were all over at the girl's house. It was me, Kael, Rod, Hardy and the two girls I think. I had been upstairs with Chloe fooling about in her room. We had a sort of understanding that neither of us would get serious. I fancied her and she felt the same about me, so we would shag when the mood took us, but try not to get embroiled in all that complicated relationship nonsense.

So me and Chloe had finished up doing what we were doing and had headed down to the living room. It was a weekday and I think we had skived off school or it was after exams, I don't really recall. The others were down there watching afternoon telly and smoking cigarettes. I plonked myself down on the sofa and Chloe sat down on my knee. I put my arms around her and she lit up a cigarette. Kael and Rod were having a heated discussion about something or other, I don't really remember what, but it was something pretty insignificant. Like always neither of them was willing to back down and so things started to escalate.

Who the fuck are you? The fucking terminator? Kael started yelling at Rod.

Fucking hell mate, calm down replied Rod trying to diffuse the situation.

There was no going back. Once Kael got like this there was no talking him down. No amount of moderation would stop the inevitable. The fuse had been lit.

Don't fucking tell me what to do, you want a fucking smack? Growled Kael.

Now Rod was standing up too, and who's going to give it to me? You?

Fucking right I will, shouted Kael.

What happens when an unstoppable force hits an immovable object?

So they were both yelling and swearing when Kael picked up the coffee table that was on the floor in the centre of the room. The sofa was arranged in an L shape around it, one of those big soft creamy settees with wide arm rests and floppy cushions.

He didn't think about it. He didn't hesitate. He hurled it full force at Rod.

This wasn't one of those flimsy wooden coffee tables from 'B and Q', this was a solid metal thing with a glass top. It was heavy and it was hard. Rod lifted his arms to defend himself but he didn't need to. In his anger Kael had tossed the thing blindly and it came right towards me and Chloe. I put my arms around her and tried to pull her back, but it was pointless. There was nowhere to go.

I heard Debbie yelling, Kael!

Luckily the thing didn't connect fully with Chloe. She had her arms outstretched and it sort of bounced away from her, banging into her shoulder and right cheek. It fell to the ground and the glass top shattered, pieces of glass flying across the living room. The leg landed hard on my left foot and I brought my knee up quickly in pain.

What the fuck man? Rod was yelling and Debbie was slapping Kael roughly across the shoulder.

You hit my sister, you hit my sister. She was in tears and Chloe was curled up on my knee hiding her face in her hands.

Kael looked around the room.

Debbie, I'm sorry I didn't... he started to say but Debbie wasn't listening.

She was shaking her head in disbelief, surveying the wreckage of the living room. I was checking if Chloe was alright and trying to sweep some of the glass up into a pile with my foot.

What am I supposed to tell my mum? Yelled Debbie hitting Kael across the shoulders again. This wasn't a playful girly hit, it was a full on punch. There was anger behind it. Kael shrugged it off.

I can't be doing with this shit, he said eventually, I'm going for a smoke, and with that he stepped over the glass and walked out of the living room.

READING

I think we passed it, I say.

My dad looks a bit pissed off, it's dark and a bit drizzly, early evening and the roads around Reading are jammed, people going home from work or making their way to the festival. There are about ten of us heading down in about four separate cars, various parents ferrying us down on a rainy summer night. Me, my brother and Kael are in my dad's car. Jacobs, Marko, James and Eli in another. Blake was supposed to be coming along too but he had to sell his tickets.

His parents went away for a couple of weeks so his house had become somewhere to hang out, get drunk and bring girls. It had been parties every night and this had inevitably taken its toll on the house. When his parents got back from their relaxing two weeks in Menorca they returned to a broken window, plants that had been scorched when we tried to light the barbecue with a can of petrol, cigarette burns in the carpets and sofas, and kitchenware and cutlery strewn across the back lawn. Suffice to say they weren't particularly happy with the state of their beautiful abode and they made Blake sell his tickets. He was well gutted because it's a fucking wicked set list. Nirvana, Babes in Toyland, Iggy Pop, Sonic Youth, De La Soul and a shit tonne of smaller bands.

We are going to meet my older brother's mate John (the singer in Luka's band) when we get there. He told us he would be in a silver dome tent with a white flag outside, so shouldn't be too hard to find.

Yeah I think we need to get off at the next junction, comments my dad.

We have been following signs to the festival but they seem to have run out, so we need to pull over and have a gander at the map. We pull off the road into a pub car park and the others follow us. There's still a bit of drizzle so my dad pulls up in the shelter of a large tree and everyone gathers around the bonnet of his Renault 25. We call the car Marvin because it can talk. It says all sorts of things, tells you if you aren't wearing seatbelts, if the doors are open, and if you are low on petrol.

Everyone seems to come to a sort of consensus regarding the route, maps are folded back up and we are off again. We are really keen to get there and dump the parents. Kael's got twenty tabs burning a hole in his back pocket and we've got bottles of vodka and Southern Comfort stashed in our bags.

After another hour or so stuck in Friday night traffic we finally reach the entrance to the festival and it's fucking rammed. Looks like everyone has decided to arrive at the same time. The first bands are on tomorrow afternoon and everyone wants to pitch their tents and get fucked up in anticipation. I roll down the windows and we all peer out over the crowds as my dad inches the car slowly forward. A group of girls walk past, hair wet with the rain, long wool jumpers down to their hips, short skirts and black stockings, six hole DMs with coloured laces on their feet. Eli taps me on the shoulder and grins. I really like the girl at the front of the group, brown hair and too much eye make up. I imagine us in the crowd, the sun setting behind the main stage, hand in hand, Kurt screaming into the evening. I hope there is a massive group of ladies with a tent right next to us. We pull slowly into the open field and my dad finds somewhere to park the car. We all bail out and take a look around. There are tents and cars as far as the eye can see. I feel a shiver of excitement run up my spine.

This is going to be wicked, grins Eli, standing behind me and looking out over the sea of fabric and humanity before us.

There are already a few bonfires going and I can hear Faith No More being played loudly on a shitty stereo somewhere. The rain has stopped and the air is close, warm and humid. We get our bags and tents out of the car, dumping them on the grass and forming a loose circle around them. My dad asks if we need any help with the tent. I tell him we will be fine. He gives me a hug and a kiss on the cheek

Don't do anything I wouldn't do, he winks at me, and find yourself a proud breasted young lady.

I grin, I'll try my best dad, I tell him.

He gives me a wink.

See you in three days Batman, he smiles.

My mates bid farewell to their respective mums and dads and the small convoy pulls away into the late evening. A couple of hands wave from open windows and there are a few shouted goodbyes and then we are on our own. A massive sense of freedom washes over me as we lose sight of our parents' cars and I smile.

Kael takes a small plastic bag out of his pocket and waves it between two fingers. Who wants some acid then lads?

The tents look like a sea of bright paisley laid out across the grey field, the patterns and colours shifting as I refocus my eyes. We have a fire going and its little neon tendrils flicker and snatch at the evening air. There is an occasional pop as a piece of wood explodes and sends little glowing embers up into the sky leaving trails of light behind them. Another rush runs through my body and I let it take me, nearly heaving up my guts as it passes. I cough and wipe my mouth. I can hear someone in the distance singing and strumming a few rough chords on a guitar, can smell the muddy earth below my feet. Marko isn't having a good time. The acid is strong and we can see him slipping into a bad one. He is doing well to hold it together but we are losing him to the darkness.

He flits between good and bad. He pulls himself together and starts to mellow out then something will trigger another plunge and we will have to talk him back. He's in the middle of a rough patch at the moment.

Eli mate, talk to me about my girlfriend, he half pleads, his arm on his friend's leg.

It's alright mate, reassures Eli putting his arm around him, just a bit of a rough patch, she's really fit mate, she's got a great arse and she is well into you, she...

Stop, urges Marko suddenly recoiling, give me some mellows, I need those mellows, he puts his arms out

180

towards the mass of humanity and wriggles his fingers as though tickling the air.

I feel for him I really do. I've had a couple of bad ones myself and it's well rough. Imagine being trapped in a room with your greatest fears slowly encroaching on you and there being no way out. Now imagine that that room is your own body, your own mind. You are trapped in a mushy organ inside a piece of stinking meat and there is no way out, and the more you try to shut out that sickly feeling of impending doom and claustrophobia, the more strongly it tugs at your soul. When people think about acid they think it's going to be like a Dali painting, like passing into another dimension. The reality is a bit more subtle. The drug is like an amplifier for the world without and within. Visual stimuli get bent out of shape or moulded into something slightly skewed. Colours blossom and swarm, like the rainbows on the surface of an oily puddle. Moving lights leave trails behind them, bright smudges across your vision. You notice the world in more detail, and things that never would have concerned you before become suddenly vivid and pregnant with significance. Sounds and music are imbued with a greater depth and the senses begin to merge, the visual becoming the aural and vice versa.

However, if you aren't careful then the darkness starts to encroach. It starts off slowly, triggered by something seemingly insignificant, an offhand remark or an intrusive thought, but once it takes hold, it's difficult to claw your way back. Everything becomes tainted with a vague feeling of dread that spreads out and starts to consume. The mundane and the usual become twisted and dark as your mind starts to wander to all the sullen places hidden in the recesses of your subconscious. An internal monologue begins, a struggle between two forces, two sides of the same mind.

I'm having a good time, we are at the Reading festival, I'm here with my fr...there is something wrong with you...it's a beautiful evening, I can hear people singi...you are going to die...the fire looks beautiful and I can see st...she will leave you, like they all do, she is fucking him and there is nothing you can d...the grass feels so soft and coo...he will take her away from you...

2011年10月から仕事を始めて子供と主人もいる、彼も奥さんがいてバツイチ、子供は三人。一緒には住んでいない。一人暮らし。一か月しないうちに関係が始まって、ほぼ毎日。翌年から逃げるようにアメリカへ帰国は短期間で70％以上は海外...

I'm going to die. It's all coming to an end. Who was that weird man talking to my mum in the back room? I know his face. He is my ...

Jacobs's hand on my shoulder jolts me somewhat back into reality and I'm staring into the fire. Marko has started to chill out a bit, lying back with his head against his rucksack, staring up at the overcast sky, a beer in one hand and a lit ciggie in the other, chatting to Eli. The sun is going down, a warm burst of orange above a horizon littered with tents and the twisting silhouettes of inebriated festival goers. Everyone has a camp fire going and the air is thick with smoke and glowing embers. The stereo is on loud and Nirvana's bleach is playing. *I'm a negative creep and I'm stoned.* James is head banging along and people pass by our tent chatting in loud voices, swearing as they occasionally trip over the guy ropes.

We borrowed the tent from some younger kids who live down the road from us; Tom's little brother's friends. Their parents were keen to point out that the tent was expensive and that we should take care of it. Now only four hours in it's already covered in mud and beer and who knows what else. The thing is going to be totally fucked in another three days. It's getting cold, so I find my black jumper in the bottom of my bag and throw it on. It's too big for me and riddled with holes, one of which I can push my thumb through, but I love it. It smells of the fresh washing my mum always carefully folds and puts in the airing cupboard. It smells of the love she has for her children.

She once made us all Star Trek pyjamas from scratch on the old sewing machine, cutting out the little logo they wear on their uniforms from felt and stitching it to the front. She had to watch old Star Trek episodes on the video, pressing pause at exactly the right time in order to get a good look at the blurry logo. She did a great job. Luka got red ones and me and Hardy got yellow ones. I loved putting on those pyjamas and climbing under fresh sheets on a Saturday night after watching tv downstairs in the living room and eating bread and butter washed down with orange squash.

Jacobs has got his old guitar with him and is banging away on it, some indie tune I think, might be Sonic Youth. His hair is long, curly and matted and hangs over his face in a greasy mess. Don't know where Eli and Marko have got to, they seem to have wandered off. *This is out of my reach.* The trails are getting more vivid and my mind keeps skipping to other tracks like a dusty record. My stomach is in knots. I haven't eaten anything all day, too much excitement and fags. I can feel the heat from our fire on my back.

Mate, come and play a tune, encourages Jacobs.

I turn to him, his big face grinning. I look at my hands but they seem too big to do anything. I've got stairway to heaven running around in my head and I can see the chords on the neck of Jacobs' guitar.

I'll give it a shot mate, I tell him, in a bit of a state though.

Jacobs laughs, the sound echoing and ringing in my head like loud music in a small room.

I feel good. The universe might have its plans for me somewhere down the line, but for now I am free of the shackles of fate. *So far so good, so far so good.* I am still in control, my life still somewhat in my swollen hands, but there is that little nagging sense at the back of my mind that things will at some point come crashing down.

My big brother always says that life is a string of losses and heartbreaks, occasionally punctuated by periods of calm and happiness, but then again he always has been a fucking cynic. I feel good tonight though and that's all that matters. All the tomorrows and the hurt and disaster that they will one day unleash are still safely locked away, buried within a cloud of a billion possibilities. The slow beep of a heart monitor, the violent shifting of the earth below me and the unstoppable wall of black water it brings, the young man hanging by his neck in an empty garage, the stiff white body with sallow cheeks and red curly hair, and the girl with a black eye who will one day steal my heart. They wait in silence, unmoving and lethargic, waiting to be stirred into life by the footfalls of an unwilling protagonist. The winds and waters of a yet unmasked future will at some point shape them into demons that will stalk and tear at me, but so far so good. I am paddling down a stream that ends with a waterfall, vast and deep and plunging into foaming waters, but I sail on blissfully unaware. The sun is out and fat koi with iridescent bodies flap and writhe in the clear crisp waters below my boat, the sunlight glittering and sparkling across the still water. So far so good. I lie back and let it carry me onward.

I play a few songs on the guitar, some Nirvana and some Zeppelin, but my voice sounds like it's coming from somewhere else. I put the guitar down and walk out into the night. Tents are everywhere and the throng and bustle of people carries me forward. They pat my back as I pass and one hands me an open can of beer. I drink it, the warm liquid sinking into my empty stomach. I am sitting at a fire. It's not ours. There are four other people, their faces covered with rubber masks of ex presidents. I'm talking to Reagan about the new Faith No More album, about sex and the end of the world. There is a girl spinning and twisting behind me. I occasionally glance back to look at her. I swear that her legs are on backwards. I'm in a car. It's a white Metro with the windows wound down. We are sniffing amyl nitrate and my head is throbbing and buzzing. I ask a question. Let's consult Mr Nitrate comes the answer. I stumble out of the car and take off across the field. I can see Eli and Marko ahead of me. They are staring off into the distance, scanning the horizon.

I can't fucking see our tent anywhere mate, Says Marko.

Perhaps that's it, replies Eli pointing through the smoke and bodies.

They walk off. I think about catching them up but quickly lose sight of them, swallowed up by the night. Jacobs is standing next to me. A rush of something strong passes through my body and I throw up.

You alright mate? He asks.

Fucking great mate, I reply in someone else's voice.

I wake up hot and thirsty below a pile of bodies. There are eight or nine of us crammed into a four man dome tent. It's late August and the timid sun is out for a brief period. I am ridiculously hot and thirsty. I glance around the tent for a flask of water. I can see one under Kael's leg. I shift a few groaning bodies out of the way and pull myself out from under the heap. I grab the flask, twist off the top and take a long swig. I can hear a few voices coming from outside. I wonder what time it is. The light has the quality of late morning, but it could be anytime. I literally have no idea how long I slept. I unzip the front of the tent and pull myself out through the opening, spilling out onto the moist grass. Marko, Jacobs and Eli are sitting around the fire with a few cans of beans and some tea on the go.

Morning mate, they say all at once.

Morning lads, I reply.

The beans smell good and my stomach is rumbling.

Have a cup of tea, offers Eli, pouring some of the hot brown liquid into a metal cup and handing it to me.

Cheers old boy, I reply.

Bit of a mental one last night wasn't it? I comment taking a sip of my tea.

It's hot and bitter, the warmth immediately spreading out from my stomach as I swallow.

Yeah, me and Marko got completely fucking lost, were wandering around until the sun came up, trying to find our tent, replies Eli, taking an exploratory sip from his own mug, ended up sitting around someone else's camp fire and chatting to these blokes who were all wearing masks of old British Prime Ministers.

Fuck, think I was there too mate, I say, didn't see you two though.

Kael and your brother were completely wasted, adds Jacobs, drank most of the vodka and were still out here next to the fire when we finally called it a night.

Reckon they'll be well rough today, comments Eli, grinning.

The sun feels good on my skin and I've got a hint of a hangover, hanging at the back of my head, a reminder of the previous night's excesses. The caffeine from the tea has pepped me up and I gaze around the camp site. People stand around the openings to their tents sipping on hot beverages and smoking. A few lads with long dreadlocks, dance half naked around a still smouldering fire, listening to distorted punk music from a tiny stereo. The bassy growl and thumps from the stadium carry on the air, bands getting ready, tuning up guitars and doing sound checks for the upcoming day. Groups of unwashed people, lank hair hanging over their faces step carefully among guy ropes, rolls of toilet paper in hand, cigarettes tucked behind ears.

What time is the first band on? Asks Marko.

About 11:00 I think, replies Jacobs, looking over the crumpled set list, some band called The Honey Thieves are on first, he continues, and then Babes in Toy Land and then fucking Nirvana mate.

Can't wait mate, I grin.

The sky is mostly clear, but there are a few grey clouds in the distance.

It's about three in the afternoon on an overcast Friday in late August of 1991 and me and the hundreds gathered around me are all here to see one thing. We are almost all dressed in army trousers and black t shirts with various grunge or death metal band names emblazoned across the front, the more esoteric the better. I made my t shirt myself, painted it with acrylics at the big round dining room table as my dad sat smoking a cigar and sipping a cup of black coffee. It's a simple white logo on a black long sleeved t shirt. I've always preferred long sleeves. I hate my skinny wrists and forearms. I wish I was taller and stronger. Fuck, I wish I looked like Kurt and could grow a decent bit of stubble on my chin. The logo across my chest simply says one word 'Nirvana'.

I love everything about them, the heavy guitars, the anger and the soul wrenching angst of Kurt's voice. I love the name. I love the logo. 'Blew', the opening track on their debut album 'Bleach' was the first song of theirs that I ever learned on the bass.

My dad bought me a bass from a local music shop when I was about fourteen. It was an ugly looking thing, all metallic grey with a sharp headstock and black hardware, but I thought it looked really rock and roll. I sat in my room for hours on end just listening and rewinding cassette tapes, trying to work out the bass lines. Blew was a good one. Not only was it a wicked riff, but it also began the song without any drums or guitar to obscure it. At first I found it really difficult, especially playing while tapping my foot as my older brother had told me was so important, but I soon got the hang of it, and by the end of that year I'm sure my entire family was fucking sick of hearing those same tunes, but not me. I listened to that record so much that I knew all of the song names, all of the lyrics, all the minor imperfections in the musicianship and recording. I drew the band's logo a million times, occasionally getting scolded by Mr Pateman who would point out politely that I should be concentrating harder on King Lear and paying less attention to Nirvana.

Mr Pateman is cool. Hands down the best teacher I've ever had. He is probably in his forties but still understands at a very basic level what it means to be a person my age. He isn't pretentious or a try hard. He just clicks with us. He is passionate about art and literature and music, that passion is infectious and we latch on to it. He is pen pals with Jello Biafra of Dead Kennedys fame and was at the famous Doors concert where Morrison got his cock out and was arrested. He loves poetry from the thirties and the Beat Generation of writers. He introduced

189

me to Hunter S Thompson and Jack Kerouac. He is big and friendly and full of life. He's got a handlebar moustache and long, red, shoulder length hair that's balding in the middle. He often pulls and twists at it as he explains to us the Intricacies of Mercutio or waxes about dialectical materialism.

So Kurt comes on the stage dressed in a leather jacket over a white t shirt and ripped jeans. He is unshaven and his hair is bleached blonde. He looks as rough as always but cool as fuck. I imagine running into him backstage and chatting about music, him asking me to play guitar in their band. We would tour the world and I could escape The Borough and all its small minded bullshit.

It's windy and they are tuning up their instruments, occasionally turning on a distortion pedal, filling the air with that familiar ear splitting crunch that runs up my spine like an acid rush, prickling the hair on the back of my neck. They've got another bloke with them up on stage. He has long dreadlocks tied back in a pony tail above his head, the sides of which are shaved short. He is shirtless and wearing striped trousers with braces that go over his shoulders. He has 'God is Gay' scrawled in felt tip pen across his naked chest in large blue letters. Dave Grohl introduces him as Kurt stands at the front of the stage, his amp omitting a loud growl of feedback.

'We have a special guest with us up on stage, his name is Tony and he's an interpretive dancer'

and then all hell breaks loose.

Kurt leaps into the opening riff of 'School' and the whole crowd rushes forward. I am carried up and along with it, there is no fighting it. I let it take me. I stupidly decided to wear my Doc Martens shoes this morning rather than boots and the ground is soft and muddy. One of my shoes gets stuck in the mud and is wrenched from my foot. There is nothing I can do. As Kurt starts to sing, I start to bang my head, my long hair lashing out in front of me. I can feel people shouldering into me and I get a couple of elbows to the head and face. I taste a bit of blood, but I don't care. This is the fucking moment I've been waiting for my whole life. This is what I want to do. I want to be up there on that stage with Kurt and Krist and Dave. I want this mass of humanity crammed together worshipping me. This is what life is about, not rotting away in some office or at a till in Sainsburys. I want to forge ahead like these twenty year olds from a small town outside Seattle. I want to make something of myself, to see my name in NME, to play live on The Word on a Friday night. I want to live fast, take too many drugs and die skinny and broken, surrounded by rotting angels on a plain white mattress. The media will take pictures of my broken form and teenage dolls will slit their wrists and bleed to death in bathrooms while their parents, numb to their children's angst drink red wine and listen to Phil Collins on their brand new CD players.

I catch glimpses of the band through the melee of hair and flailing arms. Krist is tall and thin, sporting a blue Dinosaur Jr T-shirt (another fucking great band I might add) and Kurt is screaming away into the mic, eyes half closed, tendons in his skinny neck straining. They play a lot of tunes off Bleach and some new songs I've never heard before. It's an amazing set and the crowd has more than doubled since the opening song. We are all head banging away and smashing into each other. I catch a glimpse of James for a few seconds. He reaches out his hand towards me, but is soon swept away in another direction, disappearing into the mass of hair, sweat and bodies. A few people emerge bloody and battered from the crowd in front of me and push weakly through the throng to the back of the crowd, desperate to escape the chaos close to the stage.

If you fight it then it soon gets scary. It's like a trip. If you relinquish control and let it take you then you will be fine. It's impossible to fight against the tide of the crowd, so you just have to give in and realise that the only way to survive is to accept that you are not in control. If you try to fight back then you will lose. The forces against you are too strong and you will end up trampled battered and panicking, pushed up against the front barrier, begging for one of the security guards to pluck you from the horror. I let it take me.

At one point I am only about three people back from the stage. I am so close I can see the individual hairs on Kurt's unshaven chin and the dents and scratches on the wood finish of Krist's bass. They End Negative Creep with a lot of feedback and guitars pressed up against amps. It's loud here and my ears are ringing, the bass in my chest, like a second heart beating deep within me. I have a moment to take a breath and get my bearings as the crowd rests briefly in anticipation of the next song. Kurt says something to the crowd, everyone cheers and then I am thrown back into the tumult. I thrust my hand skyward and yell Kurt's name at the top of my lungs. In my mind he hears me through the mass of other voices and turns to face me. He gives me a brief nod of recognition. A nod that tells me that we are all in this together, that we are all a part of this, that our being here is enough.

One day it will be me up there on that stage in front of these people. It will be me looking out upon a late August afternoon under a grey sky, alcohol in my blood and a black guitar slung over my shoulder. My hair will be long and unwashed and I will wear a long black jumper with holes in the sleeves. 'She' will be back stage watching me and telling the roadies how much she loves me. My friends will all have free tickets to attend the concert and after the gig I will do a few interviews, then go and get hammered with my mates until the early hours of the morning when I will slip between cool sheets against 'Her' warm body and sleep until the sun kisses us from our slumber. I will live forever like this, just me and my friends. I will buy my parents a nice car and pay for their holidays in France and I'll appear in trendy magazines speaking out against Bush and Dan Quayle and their war in the gulf. I will never grow old, a bullet through my head or an overdose will put an end to me and my blood will be washed off the bedroom walls by a porcelain skinned beauty.

I realise at this moment that there is nothing anyone can do to me, that I am already dead. As Camus said 'the act of suicide is prepared in the heart long before it happens, like a great work of art'. There is no reason or purpose to it, no catalyst or trigger. It does not matter how happy I am, or how my life may unfold, because some day this will all come to an end. It might be tomorrow, or it might be in ten years but I know it will happen. I have swallowed a secret burning thread, a fuse, that once lit can be smothered or even ignored, but never extinguished. I always get everything I ever want and no life can sustain that. One day perhaps I will look into the eyes of another and will know love, will experience the thirst that so firmly fetters those around me to this ethereal dream, but I fear that even that majesty may not be enough to pull me from the depths, to reclaim the scattered remnants of all I am.

I hear the opening bass line from Blew and so does everyone else. The crowd explodes and I am carried away on a current of bodies into the centre of the mosh pit. My vision is a mass of hair and sweat and bodies, the throng of humanity around me in constant motion and the mud beneath my feet cool and soft. The sound encompasses me, none of my other senses able to function. I know this song so well that I feel like it has always been a part of me. Kurt has looked into my mind and plucked this song from within. He is playing this song for me and for me alone. All of these other people are just onlookers, tourists. This is my fucking song. *You could do anything, you could do anything, you could do anything, you could do anythaaaaang...*

I hurl my arms into the air with the last refrain and collapse back into the crowd behind me. I am spent, exhausted and thirsty. I haven't eaten for at least twenty four hours and my legs are week and shaky.

194

As I stand in that crowd only tens of meters from my hero, so close that I can see his blue eyes, I have no idea that in a little more than two years he will be found in a small attic room above a garage, a massive bullet wound in his head and enough heroin in his system to kill a horse. I have no idea the impact this small trio from Aberdeen will have on the world, how they are about to change it for good, and how twenty five years later people will still be writing about that dive into the drums and that small bottle of cough syrup that Kurt is carrying around with him. Teenagers will hold vigils and light candles when he is gone and as his light begins to fade, Brit pop and boy bands will begin to take over. Seattle, the home of Hendrix and Kurt will become more famous for its coffee shop with the mermaid logo than for the music. The world will change and the children born from those that grew up in the age of Nirvana and grunge will wear t shirts just like the one I am wearing now, with no fucking clue as to the meaning of those seven yellow letters scrawled across their chests. This band will become a brand, a commodity, and just like everything else that begins with passion or a purity of purpose they will be rebranded and resold, a fashion accessory or a cool t shirt you can buy in Next. Those crack smoking, fudge packing, Satan worshipping mother fuckers will become kitty petting, corporate rock whores, but not through their own volition. It's the way of the world, to turn art into a commodity, to strip everything that is beautiful from it and plaster it all over a fucking product.

But this is before any of that.

195

It would be easy to say that standing there in that crowd in front of that stage, in front of Kurt and his band that we can feel that this is the start of something, that we sense the beginning of something, a fundamental shift in the universe, but that's bollocks. There is no fate or destiny to be discovered and our lives are all as of yet unwritten. Those of us there in that crowd are only alive in that moment, we only care about the music and yet there is a sense that we are all in this together, that we are one. When someone goes down, the sea parts and he or she is helped back up, given some reassuring pats on the back and then hurled back into the affray. There is no violence or malice in this crowd. It's a shared outpouring of aggression and anger, not against each other but against the beautiful world that so selfishly birthed us into it and all the pain it harbours. This is how we fight back. This is how we set our selves apart from all that is wrong and drab and without beauty. We want to inject a bit of chaos and disruption into the world. We want to rock the boat that carries us rushing towards the fall. Maybe we want to escape from this grimy existence for a short moment and focus our senses on something that gives us meaning or purpose or a sense of togetherness. Or perhaps we just want to get drunk, fuck and listen to some great tunes.

My foot is a massive heavy lump and my shoe a distant memory, luckily I have my Vision Street Wear trainers back in the tent. The band are playing a really heavy rhythmic tune with lots of screamed vocals and discordant guitar. It occasionally lapses into a slow soft chorus with phased guitars and Kurt's indecipherable lyrics sung in a low moan over the top. It is beautiful and dark, weird and haunting. Then back into chugging screaming distortion and howling.

Krist takes the bass off his shoulder and hurls it into the drums. It's a big heavy chunk of wood and it levels half of the kit. He is laughing and stumbling about as Dave grabs the instrument and flings it back. Everyone cheers.

Meanwhile Kurt is standing in front of his amp with that riff still chugging away. The air is full of feedback and yells from the crowd, blown about and distorted by the wind. Kurt walks slowly back towards the front of the stage and waits there for a few moments, his back to us, long unkempt hair tossed about by the wind. Out of nowhere, he runs and jumps headlong into the drums, guitar still around his skinny shoulders. Everyone in the crowd goes fucking mental, yelling and screaming, fists punching the air. Krist is swinging his bass about and we can see Kurt's legs sticking up into the air as the stage staff rush over and try to get him back onto his feet. The bloke beside me grabs me around the neck and we both roar at the top of our lungs. It's a roar of pure pleasure. It's a roar into the ether, into the unknown. It's a roar for Kurt and Krist and Dave.

I don't know where Jacobs or James or the others have got to, but it doesn't matter. I'm sure they are enjoying this from another vantage point. I am surrounded by friends. There is an overwhelming sense of oneness at that moment in time, our shared experience uniting us in one mucky dreadlocked mass. In front of me is a sea of raised hands and sweat soaked locks. The wind blows hard as Krist and friends exit the stage and Kurt extricates himself from the drum kit, picks up a small bottle of something from behind one of the monitor speakers and gives a small wave. The roadies rush on and switch off the amps.

The loud hum and buzz of live amps and mics suddenly cuts off and we are standing there in silence, an obvious noisy silence that jogs us all back into the world. It's like walking out into the daylight after an afternoon at the cinema or that moment at two in the morning when the lights in the club suddenly come on. The world looks a little more well defined and clear. Our ears ring and sweat stings our eyes and the cuts on our faces. People start to drift apart, making for the chemical toilets at the end of the field or to the beer tent. There are a few handshakes and high fives, acknowledgements of the short bonds formed in the muddy pit. I look around for my shoe as the crowd starts to thin out but there is no way I'm ever going to find it in this quagmire. I hang around for a bit and wander aimlessly about half searching for Jacobs and James. I walk up to the back stage entrance and light up a cigarette. I have a quick look in, searching for a glimpse of one of my heroes. The drummer from Sonic Youth peeps his head out and has a quick look about and then goes back in, beer in hand. No sign of Nirvana or Dinosaur Jr. I soon give up and decide to walk back to the tent. My foot is a wet mass of mud and grass and I've got bumps and bruises on my face. I search around in my trouser pocket and find a crumpled packet of Embassy number ones. I pull one out. It's broken about two centimetres down from the tip. I break off the end and ask a passerby for a light.

I like your t shirt mate, he tells me, as he lights my fag. Where did you buy it?

Actually I painted it myself, I reply.

Wow, he says looking surprised, Looks fucking wicked.

Cheers man, I say.

Nirvana played again the following year and we attended. It was their last ever concert on British soil. There were more drugs and more booze and our hair was longer. A crowd that in 1991 consisted of a few hundred swelled to thousands as Kurt and companions became easily the biggest band on the planet. Nevermind, which was unreleased when I lost my shoe to the mud went on to sell millions of copies, grunge fashion was on cat walks and high streets and Kurt was an LA celebrity with a new born baby, he and Courtney becoming household names, regularly featured in gossip mags and other trash media. The band were still writing great music and I still loved them as before, but nothing could compare to that summer of 1991 when they were still an unheard of group of young musicians, untouched by the cynicism and materialism of fame, just a fucking great band brimming with so much energy, potential and an enthusiasm reserved for the young. It was the last chance to see them as a band and not as the rock stars that they would soon become. It was the last time Kurt would be able to move freely through the world and mix with other people. He could walk the streets of Reading city centre and have a drink in a local pub. He could smoke in his hotel with the window open and nobody would point a camera at him or ask him a personal question. He was still a nobody to most of the world's population, just a scruffy American in a small rock band, wide eyed and excited to be playing in Europe for the first time. After this came Courtney and addiction and rehab, the band slowly falling apart as Kurt slipped ever closer to his inevitable demise.

I decide to have a wander about and see if I can meet up with Jacobs or James or one of the others while I wait for Dinosaur Jr to come on. The sun is out, and I grab a hot dog with lots of onions from a stand and sit on the ground at the edge of one of the smaller stage tents to eat and have a smoke. The warm sun feels good on my face and the hot dog fills that gnawing hole in my guts. You can't beat festival food, slightly over cooked meat on soft bread with lots of fried onions, or a deep fried doughnut. My mum would probably tell me that it was going to kill me, but like I said, I'm already dead. I have another little walk around, stopping at a stall that sells these weird posters. They look just like a random repeating pattern but when you stare really hard at them a 3D image emerges. At first I thought I was still tripping. It's pretty fucking cool. I think about buying one, but I've only got one crunched up fiver in my pocket and need that for drugs or booze.

The Reading Festival is held on some farmland outside the main city. In the middle there is a big fenced off area with the main stage in the centre and a whole host of smaller stages dotted around it. This central area also contains various stalls and food vans, a couple of beer tents, a cinema tent that plays films through the night, ideal for those who are suffering from a wicked come down, and a blanket shop called Joe Bananas that becomes a crazy rave at midnight, with lights and dance music and a huge amount of amyl nitrate being passed around.

I notice Dinosaur Jr coming onto stage and slowly make my way back over. I think about pushing my way to the front of the crowd, but after Nirvana I am so knackered I can hardly stand. I decide to watch from the periphery instead. I bet James is deep in there though. He loves this band. The wind is still blowing, a passerby losing her hat and scuttling after it across the muddy field. People are drunk and stoned, laughing and excited. It's nice. I feel warm and alive, a sense of freedom washing over me. I am on my own in the middle of a huge field, the blue sky hanging low above me and there is no one to tell me what to do. No parents, no teachers, and no one over the age of forty. There are a lot of girls about and I think about 'Her' briefly. I wonder what she's doing at the moment? Wonder if she is thinking of me, wonder if she can also see the sky.

I see some people wearing Captain America t shirts. They are a small indie band from Scotland and Kurt Cobain is always going on about them. Nirvana do a couple of covers of their tunes. I make a mental note to get my hands on one of those shirts. I watch Dinosaur Jr from afar and really enjoy the set. That bit in Freak Scene where the rest of the band drop out and it's just J Mascis singing,

'Sometimes I don't thrill you, sometimes I think I'll kill you, just don't let me fuck up will you, cause when I need a friend it's still you', really gets the crowd going and I feel the familiar sensation of the hairs standing on the back of my neck.

I imagine James in the middle of that sweaty mass of people, hands lifted high above him, singing along to that refrain and dancing like a harlequin. I bet he's having a fucking wicked time.

The Dinosaur Jr set comes to an end and I decide to make my way back to the tent, have a few beers and then come back for Sonic Youth and Iggy Pop. I realise that walking around with only one shoe on looks really stupid, so I take it off and dump it in a bin. There are a few people wandering around barefooted anyway so I reckon it's better this way. The ground is cool and still a bit muddy, but feels soft and comfortable underfoot. When I was little I used to spend a lot of time in the garden in bare feet, digging holes or chasing insects in the summer. I get that same feeling now.

As I near the tent, I see my brother and Kael sitting at the fire eating beans and sausages and smoking a joint. They don't even have tickets. They aren't interested in watching any of the bands, just want to get wasted and chill out. It's cool.

Marko and Eli are talking to the French girls who are staying in the tent next to us. They don't speak a lick of English, but the blonde one is pretty fit. I plonk myself down on the grass next to Kael and he casually hands me the spliff he's holding. His eyes are red and his face has a subtle grin across it.

What the fuck happened to your shoes mate? He asks, not even turning his head.

His blonde hair is curly and unkempt and he has at least a week's fluff on his chin. He's wearing a padded shirt, riddled with boulder burns and an old pair of faded jeans, frayed at the bottoms.

Lost them mate, I reply.

Shit, got any more? I've got some spares if you want, he offers.

Cheers mate, I reply, but I've got some other ones in my tent, Nirvana were fucking wicked mate, I tell him.

Kael nods, Yeah? Can't really get into that hardcore stuff myself. Give me some Bob Marley or a bit of trance man.

He's staring off over the field at a point in the far distance. The sun is starting to dip below the trees that line the field and the sky is aglow.

Marko and Eli are still chatting up the two French birds and I hear a few giggles.

Le oiseau dans l'arbre est le poisson dans la mer, says Eli in his worst French accent.

The girls laugh and Eli looks over at me and winks. Smooth bastard. I think to myself.

The sun has sunk below the horizon and a fresh breeze blows over the open field, rustling the canvas of the tents. I can hear music and laughter, excited conversation from the camp sites all around me. There is a party atmosphere tonight. Everyone has now arrived and the festival is in full swing. There must be twenty thousand people here. Someone breaks out a brand new bottle of vodka, noisily twisting off the cap, takes a swig and passes it around. Jacobs and James have returned after having watched Dinosaur Jr and James is on a massive high. He's got his shirt off and is sweating so much that he looks like someone just dragged him out of the river. His long sleeve t shirt is tied around his waist and he takes a massive swig of the vodka as I pass it to him.

Steady on mate, I say, we've got all night.

Jacobs has decided that he's going to boil a can of beans but we've run out of water. The tap is a good ten minutes walk through a sea of tents and mud, so he just goes round the back of the tent and fills up the pan with some of his own piss. He then plonks it down on the burner, puts the can of beans in, lights the burner with an old bic lighter and sits down. He looks up to see us all staring at him. Eli is shaking his head slowly and laughing to himself.

Oh sorry, says Jacobs, you want to go twos on the can mate? We all politely decline the offer.

Nah I'm good mate, replies Eli, cheers mate.

Everyone is buzzing from the vodka and joints being passed around. The French girls have gone off to the main stage to watch some music and the night has arrived bringing with it a bit of a chill. We duck into our tents and grab our jackets, putting them on and huddling around the fire. We talk, we laugh, we make jokes, nattering about birds and music and school. A group of girls walks past our tent and one of them stumbles on one of the guy ropes.

Careful love, comments Marko, giving her a smile.

How's it going with your bird then Marko mate? I ask.

Marko is half Italian, I think on his dad's side. He's quite a striking looking bloke with pale skin and dark features. He's tall, confident and has really thick, curly black hair that he usually keeps tied up in a pony tail. He is an expert talker and is going to make an excellent salesman someday, used to rent out porno mags to the younger kids at school for a quid a pop.

A while back he wanted to sell his AR50 motorbike. He was after an Aprilia or something with a bigger engine so he wanted to get rid of his old bike. A bloke from our year at school really wanted the bike and made him an offer. Marko agreed and told him to come round the following day to make the deal. As the bloke was about to hand over the money, Marko's dad came rushing into the room telling Marko that someone else had phoned up and given a better offer for the bike. The bloke was desperate for it, so he told Marko he would give him the extra fifty quid. Marko agreed and the bloke left with the bike and Marko had his money. Everyone was happy.

The thing is there wasn't another offer. The whole thing was a set up. Marko had asked his dad to come into the room saying they had had another offer just to push the price up. He's probably going to do really well in this world. He is really into cars and bikes and anything that goes fast. He bought a used Riley Elf a year or so back and when I was over at his we took it out for a spin around the roads near his house. He fucking floored it and was doing handbrake turns and doughnuts all over Longthorpe. For a 16 year old without a license, the mad bastard could certainly drive. I loved every minute of it, but I was certain we were going to die and breathed a massive sigh of relief when we finally pulled up into his driveway and he turned that little silver key, cutting the engine. The next day at school he told me that there were still dents in the side of the passengers seat where I had been holding on so tight.

Anyway, he went on a blind date a while back with this bird who must be five years his senior. Don't know who introduced them, but I think it was someone in the family. She isn't that fit, but she puts out and that's all that matters at the moment. I met them at a party a while back. Half way through Marko and her disappeared outside for a bit. When they came back he had cum stains on his trousers and a massive fucking smile on his chops.

She's good mate, he replies, don't know how long it's going to last though.

Why's that? I ask.

She's older than me and I don't reckon we are really into the same stuff. She's got horrible taste in music to be honest, likes Boyz 2 Men and that sort of bollocks. Gives a cracking wank though, he laughs.

Speaking of wanks mate, I giggle, remember when Billy had a wank in environmental science?

Marko slaps his leg and bursts out laughing.

What's this? enquires Kael.

He is skinning up another joint in the opening to the tent, my brother, holding a torch over him so he can see. He licks the edges of the rolling paper carefully and wraps it shut. Kael never does shit at school but he certainly puts his all into skinning up. This is artistry, pure and simple.

You should enter one of your joints for your GCSEs, I comment and everyone laughs.

Kael smiles.

Billy Hart, I add. You remember him don't you mate?

Yeah, Kael replies, think I know his brother Bradley, wiry little cunt, always riding about on his bike.

Yeah that's him, I say.

I heard their dad is a right twat, adds Jacobs, used to bash them or fiddle with them apparently.

Fuck, well that explains a lot, comments Marko.

By the way Jacobs how were your piss beans? Enquires Eli

Fucking great mate, grins Jacobs, you lot missed out. He rubs his belly and licks the spoon clean before tossing it back into the tent. We all look at him.

And you can calm down, they were in a fucking can alright, he continues, the piss never even touched the beans.

Well thats alright then mate, teases Eli.

Yeah you're still fucking gross mate, adds James laughing.

Tell them about Billy Hart, urges Marko.

Right, I begin, so we had an exam in Mrs Moseley's class. Some course work I think. The room was silent and everyone was writing. Marko was sitting in front of me a couple of rows forward, and he turns round to me and starts pointing at something. I don't want to get a bollocking so I try to ignore him and finish the test. But he's making these faces and motioning towards Billy. At first I think he's trying to give me the answers or cheat or something. Then he starts waving his right hand and he mouths the words 'Billy is having a wank'.

He fucking was as well, interjects Marko, already laughing hard at this point.

Yeah, I say, the dirty little bastard was fucking going to town under the desk.

Taking little Billy out for a test drive, comments Eli and we all laugh harder.

Kael looks up from his joint for a second, must have been an exciting fucking test, he comments dryly and we all lose it.

James half chokes on a mouthful of vodka, which makes us laugh even more. There is vodka coming out of his nose and his eyes are streaming, but we are struggling to contain ourselves. My stomach hurts. It's like those laughs you get during lessons at school when you know you have to be quiet. It's one of those uncontrollable laughs that you only feel when you are young, untouched by the pain and drudgery of adulthood, when your life is simple and free of worry, before taxes and mortgages or budgeting, before loss and death take their inevitable toll, when there is hope and innocence and the world is still malleable and expectant and you are surrounded by the kind of friends that share your life wholly and without judgment, the kind of friends that you expect to know forever.

We pull ourselves together after a few minutes, wiping tears from our cheeks and catching our breaths. Everyone passes around the spliff and we all take a few more drags. It's strong and the smoke burns as it goes down my throat causing me to cough. The laughter has died down and we are all watching the fire crackle and spit.

Eli takes another big swig from the now half empty bottle of vodka and passes it on.

He looks up at Marko and asks, so did he pass? And we all burst out into fits of laughter again.

I look over at Kael. He's sitting with his knees pulled up into his chest, a padded shirt pulled around his shoulders. He is smiling, staring off towards a point far off on the horizon, a point where the red sun will soon once again rise and fill the world with light and warmth.

James and Jacobs head back to the main stage to watch Iggy Pop, but the rest of us are staying. We are too engrossed in conversation and full of vodka, and the prospect of leaving the warmth of this fire to watch some ageing rock star doesn't really have much appeal.

Have a good one, we call after them as they disappear into the smoke and crowds. We can hear the distant rumble of a band tuning up in the distance, like the thunder that descends on a summer day. The vodka is almost done and I am in the warm familiar embrace of inebriation.

Kael and my brother have wandered off for a look around and me Eli and Marko are passing around the amyl nitrate and talking about Kerry Hadfield. She's a girl in Marko's class and let's just say she's got a very generous... she's got massive tits. Everyone I know has tried to get off with her at some point, but few have had any success. Eli met her at an indie night at the sports club on Lincoln Road a few weeks ago though and ended up in bed with her.

So I undid her bra and the things just came spilling out, he says, gesturing with his hands out in front of him.

We all listen on enviously and prod and poke for more details.

Did you finger her? Asks Marko inquisitively, grinning and holding two fingers up to Eli's nose. Eli pushes him away and laughs.

I'm not telling you mate, let's just say it was a good fucking night.

You shagged her didn't you, accuses Marko laughing, you dirty bastard.

Marko pushes his friend affectionately and Eli just smiles.

Eli used to have a quiff back in the day when everyone was into The Smiths, but he has let his hair grow long recently. He's a charming bastard and I love him to death. He's a hard worker and one of those blokes who is up for anything. He comes over every Friday to mine to have band practice in the garage. We always get pissed and talk about lyrics and music and birds. He's tall and dark with grey eyes and olive skin whereas I'm short skinny and pasty as fuck. We make a good team.

Kael and Hardy reappear at about ten thirty. Kael is high as fuck and unstoppable. He is rushing about screaming into the night.

I fucking love it, I fucking love it!

He comes over and grabs me, giving me a crushing hug and a wet kiss on the ear.

I fucking love you mate, he tells me.

Love you too old boy, I reply grabbing him by the back of the head and holding him for a second.

We part and he gestures to the small group around the fire.

Love all you fucking cunts, he shouts, Eli you handsome fucker.

Eli smiles and reaches out his hand.

Fucking love it! He yells into the night as everyone gathers together for a group hug. I love all of you you know, whispers Kael from the centre of the group.

The fire is raging, fuelled by something intangible and transient. I can see the red flicker of it in each of their eyes and feel the warmth of it on my face. I can hear Iggy Pop's set coming to an end far off in the distance and the sound of thousands of hands coming together. Marko puts a tape into the cassette player and 'Groove is in the Heart' starts playing.

Turn it up, yells Kael, fag hanging loosely from his mouth as he starts clumsily dancing.

We all start to dance. It's spontaneous and natural. I can feel the music pulsing through me and I feel fucking great. I love these people. I love their faults and their insecurities. I love their companionship and their warmth. I love that I belong here amongst this group of men. This gaggle of misfits and heroes. We are all so different in appearance and background. We like different music and have different politics and yet the thing that drives us, the bright core that ignites us and burns so brightly within each of us is the same. We are as one this night and nothing can touch us. This bubble that we inhabit is impenetrable even to the Gods that will one day smite us. We are strong. We are bound to one another through something corporeal yet unspoken, a glimmer of something beautiful that will one day be snatched away and hidden beneath that dark blanket of time.

The dance intensifies and the fire rages on, spewing its smoky embers nightward to compete with the stars, and our shadows flicker and parade across the canvas of the surrounding tents. Eli stumbles over a guy rope but Marko grabs his arm and pulls him back to his feet, and the dance continues. We dance and drink and scream and laugh.

The cassette in the tape player comes to the end of side one with a click, and all at once the music ends. We are left with the crackle of the fire and the background hum and rumble of twenty thousand souls.

Kael ducks into his tent and grabs something, then pulls on his baseball cap and stalks off back into the night. I watch him walk away into the throng of tents and people, and he is soon lost to the fire and the darkness.

It's hot and muggy in the tent and the sunlight casts geometric shapes through the tents and guy ropes onto the grass by the entrance. I kick my legs out of the sleeping bag and reach over for some water. I grab my flask and shake it, but it's empty. My mouth and throat are dry and I've got a fucking terrible headache. I unzip the front of the tent and crawl out into the morning, or is it afternoon? I am met by a refreshing breeze and the cool moist grass on my hands. I can smell the fire from the night before and the campsite is littered with beer cans and bottles. Kael and my brother are sitting on the grass, constructing the first spliff of the day. They are both wearing clothes from the previous day and I wonder if either of them has even slept.

Morning lads, I call out.

My throat hurts and I cough up a bit of phlegm, spitting it onto the remnants of the camp fire. They look up seemingly surprised at my entrance.

My brother sees me and smiles and Kael goes back to the joint.

Have you two been to bed? I enquire.

Dunno mate, replies Kael. He's pushing the small cardboard roach into the tip of the joint and patting his pockets in a search for matches or a lighter.

I slept for an hour or so I think, says my brother. I think I called it a day when the sun started coming up. Kael was still running around the place like a fucking lunatic when I turned in.

Kael smiles and runs a dirty hand through his blonde hair. He's got a sun tan and his face is covered with grime and freckles.

This place is pretty fucking mad, he mentions, I met up with some blokes in the other field and got wasted. They had this massive bag of speed with them and when they all fell asleep I taxed it. It's in the tent if you want some mate.

I'm alright actually mate, I reply, bit early in the morning for all that.

I could really do with a drink though, you got any water?

My brother reaches for his flask and hands it to me.

There's a drop or two in there, he offers.

213

I twist off the lid and drink the stale water. There's barely a mouthful.

Kael tucks the joint behind his ear and stands up.

There's some beer in my tent mate I think, he suggests, or we could just go and fill up the water bottle. I could do with a wander.

Alright mate, let's go, I agree, I'm fucking dying.

He goes into his tent briefly and brings out the huge plastic water container. It must hold at least four gallons and is heavy as fuck when it's full.

There are taps dotted all around the camp site but there is usually a queue, especially in the morning as everyone is nursing hangovers and eager to make tea and coffee. We walk off in the direction of the closest one. It's in the corner of the field on the other side of the dyke that intersects the two fields. There's a small bridge that connects both fields, but that's a ten minute walk in the other direction. Our plan is to just jump the dyke and then walk back round once we have filled the container.

Reckon I'm getting a cold, Kael says sniffing as we wander off towards the trees at the far end of the field.

Yeah me too, I reply

We have to walk carefully because there are guy ropes and tents everywhere. We walk slowly with our eyes to the ground, lifting our knees high and pointing out obstacles to each other.

I reckon I'm going to blow out Debbie, announces Kael matter of factly.

What? I reply, thought you two were inseparable.

Nah mate, she's a fucking nutcase, he rubs his eyes and looks off into space.

214

I mean I love her but it's too much, if you get what I mean. I need to be on my own. He pauses, I need some fucking freedom mate.

I hear you old boy, I say, but I don't reckon she'll take it well.

Yeah, fuck it though, he replies, you know what I mean.

He stops briefly as though collecting his thoughts.

I love her you know, he half whispers.

I know mate. I do, I say, half to him, half to myself.

Who fucking needs birds anyway, he states brushing the thought away and we continue on, picking our way through the ropes and brushing up against canvas and occasionally tripping.

At one point his foot gets stuck under a guy rope and he yanks it free, pulling the peg holding it in place out of the wet earth. The side of the tent collapses and we freeze, waiting for an angry tirade of voices and condemnation that never comes.

We laugh and continue on.

We finally get to the dyke and it appears that our plan might be a little more difficult to pull off than we had previously thought.

It has rained a lot over that last few days and the dyke is full to the brim of not only rain water but also piss and shit and who knows what else. Kael points out a lone tampon floating across the filthy water like a tiny white battle ship.

We have to go round, I tell him.

We are right at the corner of the field and the tap is on the opposite side of the dyke. To get to it we will have to walk all the way down the edge of the field to the bridge and all the way back. It's a good twenty minutes walk but there really isn't another way.

Hold this, instructs Kael handing me the water container.

He is eyeing the tap on the other side and looking down at the brown lake of water in front.

You aren't going to jump that are you mate, I ask, surprised.

It's a good couple of metres and the bank we are now standing on is muddy and slippery.

You will never make it mate, I implore, let's go round.

I reckon I can do it mate, he assures.

He is rocking back and forth on his feet, testing the ground and getting ready to jump. I take the joint out from behind his ear.

Don't want to get this wet, I say.

Cheers mate, he replies.

You going to jump that?

There is a bloke in a tie dyed t-shirt on the other side of the dyke filling up his water bottle.

Fucking right I am, replies Kael

No way you can make that, says the bloke.

Wanna bet? Challenges Kael.

Tell you what mate, I'll give you a fiver if you do. The bloke takes out a crumpled note from his shorts pocket and waves it in the air.

Another group of people rock up to the tap and wait in line to fill up their collection of bottles and flasks.

What's going on, asks one of them, a short stocky dude in a Slayer t shirt and a shaved head.

That blokes going to jump the dyke, Tie Dye tells him.

No fucking way is he going to make that, comes the incredulous reply.

That's what I said, told him there was a fiver in it if he does.

Fuck, I'll chuck in a couple of quid too, says the bloke in the Slayer t shirt.

Hear that mate? You've got seven quid on it now, yells Tie Dye across the dyke.

A few people have gathered now and a couple of others agree to throw in a quid or two, crowding around the space on the opposite side of the dyke, dropping coins into tie dye blokes hand. What they really want is to see him fall into the dirty brown fecal water, to see him thrash and gag and crawl from the filth onto the muddy bank in front of them. They want a spectacle, some drama to tell their mates around the campfire after a couple too many. The thing is that they underestimate my friend. He doesn't lose a bet or back down from anything. If he says he is jumping the dyke then that is exactly what he's going to do. I put my hand on his arm. I can feel his tight muscles beneath his baggy sweat shirt.

Mate, what if they push you in or steal our container or something? I whisper quietly.

He looks at me and smiles.

Don't worry mate, he reassures, they can't fucking touch us.

He turns back to the assembled crowd on the other bank.

What's the pot looking like mate? He calls out to them.

The bloke in the tie dye has a hand full of cash. He gives it a quick count.

Looks like about twelve quid he replies.

Kael takes a few tentative steps back. He's got that look on his face, the same one he had when he faced down those body builders outside the college arms that time. It's a look of absolute resolution, of an unbending will and determination that I will perhaps never possess.

Say goodbye to your money hippies, he yells and then he leaps.

He slips on the muddy bank a little on the run up and for a second it looks like he isn't going to make it. It looks like the crowd on the other bank will get their wish, but like he said. They can't touch us.

He lands with both feet on the other bank and slides in the mud. One foot slips out in front of him and he starts to fall backwards. The bloke in the crowd with the cropped hair and slayer T-shirt darts forward and grabs him by the front of his faded sweat shirt, pulling him forward into the crowd. They all cheer, arms flung around his neck in congratulations. I shake my head in disbelief. Kael's got his arms in the air and everyone is slapping his back and giving high fives. He is a fucking king, standing there in the mud by that river of dirt and filth. Tie dye bloke slaps the money into his hand and gives him a congratulatory punch to the shoulder.

Nice one mate, he smiles, can't believe you did that. You fucking nutter.

Kael is grinning from ear to ear as he stuffs the money in his pocket.

Here catch, I shout.

218

I throw the water container over to him and he catches it. Someone turns on the tap for him and he starts filling it up.

The crowd starts to disperse and a long queue is beginning to form. Thirsty dirty people who need water for a drink and a quick wash before another day of drunkenness and substance abuse.

Kael fills the container to the brim, screws on the top then heaves it out of the way so the next people in line can get to the tap.

The tie dye bloke looks at the massive heavy container full of water and at the brown water in the dyke.

Now what? He asks.

I am tripping my balls off, we all are. We bumped into these couple of Welsh farmers who were wandering about the campsite. They were selling these wraps of mushrooms, all really fresh looking and cheap as houses, a fiver a piece. Suffice to say we all threw in some cash and bought about eight or nine wraps. I ate all of mine in one go and Jacobs was feeling a bit rough, and not really up for tripping, so I ate all of his too. The farmers told us to go easy on them because they were strong as fuck.

One wrap will do you just fine boys, I remember them saying, but fuck it I'm on holiday.

They took a while to kick in but once they did, they came on hard and strong. I started getting massive rushes that started in my toes and travelled up my body, taking my stomach with them as they passed. The world started to morph and change, becoming more solid, like an out of focus picture slowly coming into sharp resolution.

219

The fire is going again and spits trails of fire into the clear night sky. The firmament is awash with stars like a splash of paint across a pollock painting, and the darkness beyond our little camp feels thick and black and velvety. I feel nauseous and my teeth are chattering. The men in masks are back and grin at me from beyond the glow and safety of our tiny bubble. Everyone sits in a rough circle around the fire, staring and talking.

Do you feel it? Asks Eli, rubbing himself to keep warm against the chill of the August night.

Carter the Unstoppable Sex Machine are starting up and I can indeed feel the thud of a drum machine and the chug chug chug of a distorted guitar softened and diluted to a dull rhythm by the distance.

We made a brief trip to the main stage this afternoon and half heartedly watched De la Soul while we smoked a joint and drank a couple of beers. We popped into the tent selling those weird 'magic eye' posters and everyone had a go. My brother was pissed off that he couldn't see anything and kept accusing us of talking bollocks. We soon got bored and headed back to the tent, bumping into the Welsh farmers on the way back.

Someone throws on some music, slipping the cassette into the stereo and pressing play. I can hear the needle on the record used to make the recording and it prickles my body like a thousand tiny hairs. 'Just Like Heaven', the 'Dinosaur Jr' version comes on and I get another strong rush, my neck hair standing as though brushed with static. Marko and Eli are deep in discussion about something or other but even though I can hear the words, I have lost all sense of comprehension, they roll off me

220

like water on an oily surface. I know there is meaning there but I can't quite grasp it yet.

There is movement by our tent and four or five forms emerge from the darkness. Black faces and hands, and all clad in leather.

Need any drugs boys? Asks one of them.

Kael moves forward to talk to them. His body leaving a long trail behind it. A smudge across the darkness.

Could do with some hash actually. You got any? He asks.

I feel uneasy and self conscious.

Yo give the man some hash, the bloke in the leather jacket calls to his mate.

Only got an eighth mate, that alright

Yeah that's cool man, replies Kael

Ok, twenty quid. He says signalling his mate over.

Kael pulls out a couple of tens and holds them out.

The bloke in the leather goes to snatch them, but Kael reacts quickly, withdrawing his hand.

I want to see it first, he says.

The bloke in the leather jacket scowls but reciprocates.

Show him the stuff, he commands, sniffing and nodding his mate forward.

He passes a small bag to Kael and he takes it, turning it over in his hands, examining it for a few seconds using the flame of his disposable lighter. He shakes his head and laughs. I can feel a darkness creeping on, a sense of dread beginning to descend. Give him the money Kael, give him the money I repeat under my breath.

That's not a fucking eighth mate, that's barely a sixteenth, dismisses Kael, swinging the small bag back and forth between his thumb and forefinger.

It's a fuckin eighth alright and you touched it so you is buyin it, growls the bloke.

He scowls reaching out for the money that Kael still has clutched in his fist. His friends move closer, out of the darkness. Their white eyes glow yellow in the fire light as they dart around, sizing us up.

Fuck off, says Kael tossing the packet of weed back to the bloke's friend and pocketing the cash.

The lead bloke in the leather jacket comes forward unzipping his jacket and his friends move up behind him.

Now give us the fuckin money, he commands.

Kael turns to him and looks him dead in the eye. Everyone is silent and still. Even the fire seems to have died down. Give him the money Kael, give him the fucking money I repeat the mantra over and over, but things are spiralling out of control. I can feel the world shrinking around me. I look over at Jacobs and he stares back.

Go fuck yourself, spits Kael

Things move quickly. Someone reaches into a jacket and we all see something black and metallic reflected in the fire light. Marko jumps forward and snatches the money out of Kael's hand, tossing it to the bloke in the leather jacket. He snatches it out of the air and pockets it. His friend picks up the packet of drugs from the grass and puts it in his jeans, his eyes fixed on us as he slowly bends down, then they all silently creep back into the night. The leader is the last to go and he gives us all one last look, before he too fades off into the darkness.

Everyone is in silence. We are all still tripping, but the edge has been taken off. I can feel some of us slipping into a bad place, that sense of wonder and carefree happiness replaced by something sinister and dark. A blanket of smothering doubt and paranoia is descending. We eye each other with suspicion, everyone tense and on guard.

What the fuck are you doin man? Shouts Kael, pointing an accusing finger at Marko, that was my last fuckin twenty quid.

Mate, they were gonna fuckin kill us, retorts Marko, wiping his long curly black hair away from his face.

They weren't gonna do nothing, spits Kael, you fuckin owe me twenty quid mate.

Whatever mate, replies Marko, throwing his hands in the air, I was doing you a favour.

Kael stares him in the eyes for a minute, neither of them moving, the fire spitting and popping. Kael has his right fist clenched against his hip, eyes set in a scowl, lips tight, nostrils expanding and contracting as he breathes steadily in and out.

Gradually his face starts to soften, his hand loosening, the tension in his body starting to dissipate. A look of resignation on his face as he slowly shakes his head.

Bunch of fuckin pussies, he grumbles as he turns away.

Kael walks over to the stereo presses play and takes a few swigs from a bottle of m/d 20 20 that rests on the ground next to one of the tents.

What are you all standing around for? He says. Let's get this party going.

I reach into my pocket and let my fingers settle around it. It's warm from being in there pressed up against my leg, and its weight and smooth surface offer me a modicum of comfort. I pull the old leather wallet from my pocket and set it down in front of me on the arm of the settee. My parents eye it with suspicion in the way my cat used to watch the movement of a leaf or plant in the wind. I unfold it and run my finger across the edges of the cards considering my next move. I reach in and pluck out my foreign resident's card. It's all written in Japanese but has my photograph, date of birth and name written in English clearly across its face. It's the card I showed my mum about an hour ago. She looked at it and at me. She didn't speak, just held it out in front of her, eyes moving back and forth over the unfamiliar text, occasionally looking back at me. She didn't move, she didn't smile.

I hand it to my dad and he takes it with a polite thank you. He looks at it in much the way my mother did. This is going to be a hard sell I think to myself. My parents are both Oxford graduates, atheists, logical and skeptical. He nods to himself in understanding then turns to me.

What the bloody hell do you want? Is it money?

I am a bit taken aback. I'm not used to hearing my father swear.

No... I mean of course not da... I mean Nigel. I honestly don't know what's going on. I don't know why I'm here. I thought this was a dream at first, but now I'm starting to doubt that. I woke up in a patch of grass at the bottom of the road and made my way up here. That's all I know. I promise.

224

My father shakes his head, handing the card back to me between his middle and index fingers. I take it back and set it down on my lap beneath my hand.

You can see why this is so hard to believe, says my mum, looking deep into my eyes where I hope she can see me, the real me, the boy she raised, the boy whose puke and shit she cleaned up, the boy that she held close when his stomach was on fire, waiting for an ambulance, the boy who will one day hold her swollen hand as she slips away, the boy with long hair that stayed out too late with some girls after the cinema and worried her half to death.

I know, I half whisper, I don't reckon I would believe it either.

My dad takes a cigar out of the box in his shirt pocket and lights it, taking in a deep drag and wiping his lips with the back of his hand.

His hair is quite long and swept back over his head. He is thinning at the front and there are some flecks of grey in there. He has a big bushy black beard that he fiddles with as he smokes.

Are you after money? Is that it? Asks my dad again, peering at me through his thick rimmed glasses which he occasionally pushes back up his nose with his index finger.

No, like I said I'm not interested in taking anything from you. I just didn't know where else to turn. You have to believe me, I say, turning to my mum and looking into her eyes. Mu... Veronica it's me, you must be able to see that, I plead.

I think about showing them my phone. That would definitely convince them. It's got pictures of Uncle Roger, and Aunt Catherine and Richard on it from last summer, standing in my brother's kitchen. There are pictures from

225

when I was young that my dad's friend recently scanned and sent to me. If nothing else then they would have to believe that a device like that could never have been produced in the 1980s. But something stays my hand. Part of me is hesitant, part of me wants them to believe it's me without any more proof. Part of me is also worried about the police being called and me being dragged away to some facility somewhere. What the fuck would the government make of my iPhone and my Japanese ID?

I don't even know why he's still here, mumbles my dad to my mum. This is all obviously a load of bollocks, a time traveller, Jesus Christ Veronica, you can't honestly believe this.

My mum seems to consider this for a moment.

Look Nigel whatever this young man's story is, she replies, it's obvious that he needs our help.

My dad sighs and takes another deep drag from the cigar before crushing it out in the big brown glass ash tray on the mantle piece.

He shakes his head.

Look why don't we go through into the dining room and have a bite to eat and try to get to the bottom of this... and you, he says looking me directly in the eye, if anything happens then I'm calling the police, do you understand?

I understand, I tell him.

Veronica, can you go and makes sure the children are alright?

I'm with Jacobs at the edge of the mosh pit and Neds Atomic Dustbin have just come on. They are a really interesting five piece from The Midlands with two bass players, melodic new wave punk music with a humorous edge. I used to love this band and they are one of the reasons why I chose to start learning the bass rather than the guitar, but since Nirvana came along my enthusiasm for them has waned somewhat.

It's already evening and the events of last night have faded. We have had time to talk and assess, to go over the 'what ifs' and 'if onlys'. Kael was pissed off about losing money, but a few joints and a half bottle of vodka soon cured that. We all came to the main stage a couple of hours earlier and caught the opening few tunes from the Senseless Things, but we ended up drifting back to the camp site and smoking a few joints. Neds are the last band on this weekend that I'm really interested in seeing so Jacobs, James and me headed over here about twenty minutes before they came on, James pushing forward to the front for a better view while me and Jacobs hung back. It's a bit of a chilly night and everyone is dressed in leather jackets or those German style green army coats. We are standing just behind the main crowd having a beer and watching the show. There is a bloke In front of us, dancing like a lunatic, throwing his arms around and thrashing his head like a maniac. He keeps knocking into the line of people in front of him, but they just push him back and shrug it off. He's really drunk and holding a foil bag of wine ripped from one of those boxes adults usually have on the kitchen work surface at parties. At least he's enjoying himself I think.

The mushrooms from last night are still there. That is, the feeling remains. The real world has a thin film over it that distorts and intensifies things. I occasionally get trails from the cherry of my cigarette and the music has a tangible quality to it, chewy and obvious like hard caramel at the back of my mouth. The stars are out and the wind is blowing, warping and phasing the heavy pound of the drums and bass. Jacobs looks really stoned. His eye lids are heavy and puffy above his red eyes, and he has that semi permanent half smile of someone who has had too much of the green stuff.

You alright mate? I enquire.

Yeah cool man, he replies, just a bit wasted.

You're not going to have a whitey are you? I tease him.

Fuck off, is his short reply.

The drunk dancing bloke has stopped and is looking around. Looks like he needs a piss and good luck to him. The closest toilets are way back at the entrance through a massive crowd of people and mud.

He starts to undo his flies and I nudge Jacobs on the shoulder

Fucking bloke is going to take a piss right here, I tell him.

He better not piss on me, replies Jacobs grinning.

So the bloke gets his knob out and is standing there with it in hand, swaying from side to side when he starts to piss right up the back of some poor bastard's leg, a big bloke in jeans and a leather jacket who is standing right in front of him. At first the bloke doesn't respond, must be too engrossed in the band, but the feeling of warm urine flowing down the back of his jeans soon reaches his brain and he reacts suddenly. He turns round and sees the drunk bloke, cock in hand, piss still flowing in a steady stream onto his jeans and shoes, gives him a brief stare, then head butts him with such force that Jacobs and me recoil, voicing a string of expletives. The drunk bloke goes down hard into the dirt, piss still dribbling from his dick and into the mud. He isn't getting up anytime soon that's for sure. The bloke that attacked him doesn't say a word. I catch his eye briefly as he turns back to the stage, not even bending down to wipe the piss from his jeans.

Fuck me, says Jacobs you reckon he's alright?

Fucked if I know mate, I answer. Do you fancy fucking off back to the tent?

Sounds like a good idea replies Jacobs, unconsciously rubbing his own forehead.

We turn and walk back through the crowd leaving the drunk bloke unconscious and covered in his own piss and blood, lying in a field of mud as a band from Stourbridge with two bass players launch into another song.

We wake up at noon the next day, eat a breakfast of cold beans and drink a couple of beers before packing away our stuff and taking down the tent. The thing looks a state, covered in mud and the exhaust fumes from the car parked right next to us. Might be some explaining and apologising to do later for that. My dad said he would meet us at the entrance at about two in the afternoon so we have a couple of hours to get our shit together and walk over there. The camp is a sea of activity as people pack away their shit, putting out fires and dumping cans and bottles into black bin liners, keen to beat the rush to get out. Others have a more relaxed approach. There are a lot of people still sitting around their tents, drinking and listening to music. Might have been fun to stay another night I think, but I don't reckon my brain or stomach could take it. I need to get back to my bed and sleep for a fucking year.

Jacobs is standing in front of the half disassembled tent with a mug of tea in hand, watching a girl at the next camp site as she brushes her long luxurious blonde hair. She has her head bent forward so that her hair falls down over her face and is combing it with long strokes, pulling out the knots at the ends.

Kael wanders over and stands next to us, the tail end of the last reefer in his gob.

What are you two up to? He enquires.

That bird over there is really turning me on, brushing her hair like that, replies Jacobs, eyes still fixed on her.

Kael takes a look over and starts to laugh.

The girl finishes brushing her hair and lifts her head.

She's got a pretty nice beard too mate, teases Kael nudging Jacobs with his shoulder.

Fuck me Jacobs it's a bloke, I call out laughing.

Jacobs is grinning and shaking his head. He's embarrassed but hides it well.

Fuck me, he exclaims, I'd still shag him though.

The bloke with the beautiful blonde hair and beard hears this and looks over, a big grin on his face. Me and Kael burst into laughter again while Jacobs just grins, shaking his head.

My dad turns up at about 2:30 in that familiar cream Renault 25 and pulls up in some space on the grass avoiding the mud and holes that riddle the ground. We all put out our cigarettes when we see the car and Eli hands around some gum for us to chew and get rid of the tobacco breath. My dad wanders over, a big smile on his face, rolling up the sleeves of his thin sweater. He's happy to see his sons.

Glad you are both still alive, he says, giving us both a big hug and kiss on the cheek.

It's a bit embarrassing and my mates grin and look away awkwardly.

Have a good time then? He asks

Yeah it was wicked, I reply, hauling my bag onto my shoulder and following him over to the car. I shake Marko, Jacobs and Eli by the hand and give all three of them a hug. They are getting a lift back with Eli's dad, who should be turning up soon. See you tomorrow mate, calls out Eli as we walk away.

Yeah mate, I reply, and Marko old boy, show me them mellows, I call out.

He gives me two fingers.

Jacobs gives me a salute as we walk off across the grass and I wonder if that bloke who got head-butted is still lying in that muddy field.

Dad opens the boot and we all throw our bags in.

I climb into the front seat and Kael, James and my brother get in the back.

You got everything? My dad asks turning on the ignition and starting the car.

I think so, I answer.

Actually I have no fucking idea, but I'm too knackered to really care.

Dad winds down the window and repositions the rear view mirror, then pulls away, joining the line of vehicles all making their way out of the festival parking area and onto the road.

He winds down his window and lights a cigar.

Hope you didn't drink too much, he says smiling.

Just a couple of beers dad, I reply.

There is a cool breeze blowing in through the open window. The lads in the back are chatting and giggling about something and I take a brief look in the rear view mirror. They all have a couple of days stubble on their chins and look unwashed and tired. I smile and stare out of the window.

My dad puts a Dire Straits cassette in the car stereo and turns up the volume. Brothers in Arms comes on and I close my eyes and think of lying naked in bed with 'Her', her long blonde hair draped across my shoulders, the smell of her still on my fingers.

WHITE HORSES

I get home at about 4:00, dump my bag on the floor and run upstairs to change out of my school uniform. My mum and dad are still at work. Mum usually gets back at about 5:30 and dad much later. He has to drive back all the way from Milton Keynes. I get changed into my green army trousers and favourite plaid shirt and stroll downstairs into the kitchen to look for something to eat.

Hardy gets back about 20 minutes later tossing his bag down in the landing and we go up to the garage for a quick smoke, a chat and a cup of tea. Hardy doesn't have any fags left so I crash him one. He promises to pay me back. He never does. Mum gets back at 5:30, reversing the blue Vauxhall Astra into the driveway. She gives us both a hug and a kiss as we meet her at the front door, and asks us what we want for dinner. I say it's alright I'm going to make my own food in a bit, after I've done my homework. I climb back upstairs and sit down at my desk. I just have to write up the results from an experiment for Environmental Science. Once I finish this I go back down into the kitchen and make myself some fish fingers, chips and beans. I like the beans a bit over cooked. I eat my food sitting at the big round dining table, reading a couple of pages of a music magazine as I shovel the greasy food into my mouth, washing it down with a glass of orange squash. I finish, put my plate in the dishwasher and decide to phone 'Her'.

The phone is in the hallway next to the dining room on a big dresser under the stairs. It's a really cool Bang and Olufson push button thing in grey with colourful buttons. My dad loves B and O stuff, a socialist at heart but with a penchant for the occasional middle class luxury. The stereo in the back room is also Bang and Olufson, think it was really fucking expensive, it's got these touch sensitive buttons on the control panel and is all brushed aluminium and tinted glass.

I make sure no one is around. Hardy is watching telly in the living room and my mum is reading the paper at the table in the dining room, drinking a cup of tea and browsing though a knitting magazine, her curly red hair tucked behind her ear.

I dial 'Her' number and wait anxiously for her to pick up, that familiar feeling deep in the pit of my stomach as I wait for her to answer, the ring tone playing over and over in my left ear, a sickly excitement deep within me. After about eight or nine rings I hear her voice at the other end of the phone.

Oh, hello Kei, she says.

You alright? I ask.

Yeah I'm fine, she replies, but I'm not really in the mood for talking tonight.

What's up? I enquire. I get the sense that something is wrong, that she is upset about something.

It's nothing really, she responds, trying to brush it off, I'll talk to you at school tomorrow.

Tell me, I insist. She sounds really weird, distant and close to tears about something.

It's just... my dad, she gives in, he's just an idiot, it's fine really, you don't have to worry about it...

What happened? I push. He didn't hit you did he? I ask

It's just...no nothing like that...look I can't...

I can hear an angry voice from the background.

Look I have to go... talk to you tomorrow, she utters before hanging up.

I immediately try to phone her back but there's no answer. I hang up the phone and walk into the dining room

Everything alright love? Enquires my mum

I don't know, I reply.

My mate Dan calls round at about 7:30. He lives quite close, and like for a lot of my friends, my house has become a sort of hub at which to meet. Everyone congregates and hangs out at mine, necking a few beers or a having a quick smoke here before heading out into town on a Friday or Saturday night. It's a Wednesday and Dan is just round for a cup of tea and a few ciggies.

His home life is a bit different from mine. His mum is divorced and the children live with her, but I think things are a bit tough with a full time job and three big teenage boys to look after. Dan is a really good bloke and a loyal friend. He's one of those people that you can really talk to. He won't judge or tease you. He will listen and help. He doesn't seem to be cursed with that need to fit in, that constant yearning to be one of the cool kids, to project some alternative version of himself. Most of us are just effigies, plastic dolls that melt and warp in the heat, the social pressures that surround us shaping us into new forms, fashioning new bodies for us to pilot and pollute, not Dan. He seems to have the bigger stuff already figured out, he knows who he is and is completely unapologetic about it.

He's got a brand new packet of Embassy 100s with him, those really long ones, so as usual we head up to the garage for a smoke. I sit down in the old comfy chair and Dan sits on the old guinea pig hutch, pulling his long coat around him and rubbing his hands together, blowing into them. He crashes me a cigarette and we both spark up. I take a long drag and exhale. The smoke hangs in the still air for a long time slowly drifting towards the open door and out into the crisp October air. I'm wearing my favourite donkey jacket, my knees pulled in to my body and Dan has on his old wool coat. He's a really tall lad and gets bullied a bit at school. Some of the blokes at school tease him a little, and give him stupid nicknames. I can sense the anger welling up in Dan, it's there under the surface, he's got a grip on it for now, but one day it will become too much for him, one day it will tear free and he's going to lash out.

Had a bit of a weird conversation with 'Her' just now, I tell him.

What do you mean? He replies.

Not sure, I continue from below my wrinkled brow, she was crying and kept saying stuff about her dad.

What about? Dan asks, taking another drag and blowing a couple of perfect smoke rings in the air.

Don't know mate, I continue... you don't reckon he's hitting her do you?

Fuck knows, replies Dan, what's he like, her dad?

I've never really met him actually, but he sounds like a bit of a twat as far as I can tell, I tell him, she always complains about him, says he drinks too much.

Shit, I bet you know what that's like, he comments, with a nod of recognition which I ignore.

He notices I'm getting down to the filter on my fag and opens the box to offer me another one.

One more mate? he asks.

Cheers old boy, I thank him, teasing another cigarette from the full pack and lighting it from a box of matches.

We sit in silence for a few seconds, smoking and watching the leaves blow around in the driveway outside. I watch the smoke from my cigarette curling up from between my bony fingers. 'She' always tells me that I have man's hands, blunt nails and calloused tips. They look like the hands of someone from a time beyond this one, a time defined by the caresses of things lost and forgotten.

You wanna go down? Asks Dan.

What do you mean? I reply.

Go down to her house and see if she's alright? He enquires, shrugging slightly, I mean she only lives up in Netherton in' it.

I think it over for a second, letting the idea take root, the situation playing out in my mind.

I reckon that's a good idea mate. Who knows what's going on, I say, that cunt could be beating her or something.

Yeah, he replies, reckon the twat could do with a good smack.

Fuck it let's do it, I announce, already standing up. I feel a wave of excitement, that sensation of something set in motion, that feeling of taking charge, of forging forwards. Dan's right. I could just sit around in the garage all night smoking or I could get off my fucking arse and do something. I grab a piece of wood from the pile in the corner and conceal it in my jacket. I picture myself rushing into her house, kicking down the door and rescuing her from her evil father. We will kiss and I will hold her to me and everything will be alright.

Let's go Dan, I say with urgency, let's fucking go.

Alright mate hold on, he replies, I'm coming.

We walk out of the garage and quickly down the driveway, crunching over the gravel below my bedroom window and out onto the street. It's cold and we can see our breath. The orange street lamps bathe us in their soft light. The night feels crisp and clear and full of purpose.

We turn left onto Thorpe Road and cross the street near The Sessions House. The pub is open and people are coming and going, a few cars are in the car park and the imposing harsh edges of the district hospital rise into the dark sky from behind the old court house buildings's crenelated walls. I can feel the hard comfort of the bit of wood tucked into my coat sleeve and another cigarette glows between my lips.

I'm going to smash his fucking head in if he's hurt her, I mumble to Dan.

Yeah mate, he replies, I've got your back old boy.

238

A big lorry rumbles past and up onto Crescent Bridge, throwing a mass of dry leaves into the cold air and blowing my long hair over my face, before everything once again returns to silence.

Hows it been going with you and 'Her' by the way? Enquires Dan.

To be honest mate, I'm not really sure, I tell him, I dunno if she likes me or not.

But you are over at her house every week at least mate, he says, you must have got off with her.

I sigh and take another drag of the cigarette, letting the smoke drift up out between my thin lips and back up into my nostrils, before flicking the butt, unfinished into some hedges that line the hospital car park.

This is where I nearly got my nose broken that time, I comment to Dan, pointing into the side entrance to the hospital.

The District Hospital is a really ugly building, all late nineteen sixties sandy coloured brick, dirtied and stained by the years, sharpe angles and a large staircase visible through an expansive glass frontage that stretches up to the top floor. It's easily the tallest building this side of crescent bridge, the white edged concrete roof visible from most of central Borough.

Those twats from the children's home? Enquires Dan.

Yeah, little fuckers, I growl under my breath as I grip the piece of wood hard through the rough wool of my coat.

I was with Tom and Chris, I tell him, you know Rob's friend who lives down the road?

Jodzie's brother yeah, says Dan.

239

Yeah mate, I reply.

An ambulance pulls into the slip road leading into the emergency department entrance, lights flashing, windows blackened against prying eyes, another victim of time or circumstance, a heart attack or fall, a tragic, meaningless end to another lost soul.

So we were walking down here on the way back from school, I continue, and as we went past the children's home a couple of them saw us and shouted some shit.

Dan pulls at his pony tail, tightening it behind his head.

Must have been bored or something, I add, anyway we just kept walking, thinking nothing of it...So as we get close to the hospital we realise that a few of them are following us.

How many? Asks Dan.

Dunno three or four, I reply, I realise that they are going to fuckin fight us and I'm with little Chris whose only about fucking eleven at the time and Tom who is two years younger than me and skinny as fuck, so what can I do?

What did you do? Asks Dan.

We are approaching the children's home and will soon pass by it. It's an ordinary detached house, set amongst the others that line this side of the street. The house is big with a large bay window at the front. It's painted black and has a neat little front garden, and a short stone path leading up to the front porch.

Nothing I could do, so I turned round and fucking walked up to them, I tell him.

I can feel a stirring of something as my anger begins to reignite, a dark rage that I keep locked up deep down

240

there. It is an anger that lies dormant, unfocused and nebulous. It isn't about the boys that attacked me, it's something else, something spawned long ago, a part of me that has been held back by this place, pushed into submission, stunted and damaged by this town, by this time. I know I have something in me, something bright and beautiful, that if allowed to blossom could at last free me from myself, free me from the anguish that keeps me forever bound to this slavish existence and propel me into serenity, but I struggle to grasp on to it. It is always just beyond my reach, beaten back and locked away, obscured by fear and angst, sullied and bruised. I must keep it secret, safely confined beneath an extrinsic layer of something harder and invulnerable.

I clutch the bit of wood tightly, imagining smashing those fucking twats with it. Pounding their stupid heads in till they stop moving.

So I tell Tom and Chris to go and hide in the hospital, I say, and I fucking walk back towards them. The leader comes up to me, a stocky lad with short hair, and I ask him what they want. He's got his left arm in plaster, must have broken it, I continue. He pushes me and I tell him to go fuck himself. The next thing I know he fucking punches me in the face with his plaster cast and my nose fucking explodes. There's blood all over the shop and he shouts at me. 'No one fucking swears at me' he says. Then they turn round and walk off back home, and I wander back to mine, nose dripping with blood.

Fuck mate, did you break it then? Asks Dan.

Nah mate, I answer with a smirk, don't think so anyway, I bend the end of my nose from side to side, something got fucked up though, cause I never used to be able to do this.

This is the place, I say as we walk past the old children's home.

It's been repainted and the lights are on in the living room. There are voices emanating from the front room window that is a little bit ajar and a twinge of anxiety runs though me. My walk slows as we pass the house and I grip the piece of wood even more tightly.

Fuck them, I think to myself. I've got more important shit to worry about.

We make our way up Aldermans Drive, towards my old primary school and into an area called West Town. A lot of Muslim and Sikh families live around here, a lot of Datsuns and Nissans parked on the road. The left side of the street consists of terraced houses, all with different coloured doors and front gardens full of kid's bikes and plastic toys. There is a really good chippy up here on the right just before you turn onto Mayors Walk, but the place is always fucking closed. I swear it's a bloody miracle if you can ever manage to catch it open. For some inexplicable reason they are always shut on a Monday, something about not being able to buy any fish. It doesn't make any fucking sense because every other chippy on the planet seems to manage. We walk past the chippy. There's a small sign on the door that says it's closed.

I giggle to myself.

We walk up Mayors Walk and past the Co-op on the left. There is a pub on the corner called the Westwood. My dad went through a phase of taking us there on a Sunday afternoon. He would have a pint and we would all eat sausages and chips. They had a really good juke box and my dad used to give us 20p each and we would play 'Take On Me' by Aha and drink our lemonades through stripy, bendy straws.

What time is it? I ask Dan as we pass the pub.

He wiggles his wrist out of his jacket sleeve and peers down at his watch.

Just gone nine mate, he replies.

Time for another fag I reckon, I say.

Reckon you're right old boy, he replies.

We hunker down outside the Co-op and Dan passes out the ciggies. We light them and take a few big drags. I cough a little and spit on the pavement.

Lets turn right and walk down through The Grange, he suggests.

Good idea, I agree.

I don't really like The Grange. It's a big area of grass between Netherton and West Town with a wide path that runs all the way through it. It's a popular route for a lot of the pupils from my school to take on the way home. There are a few swings, a slide and a roundabout on one side. I've been down there a few times just to get pissed on cheap booze and try and get off with birds, but I never really liked the atmosphere, always a lot of fights and stupid shit going on.

A while back this kid Spookie from Westwood decided that he wanted to kick the shit out of Rod. Spookie got a load of his mates together and they all jumped Rod as he and my brother, and a few other mates were walking home. There were about ten of them and Rod was vastly outnumbered. They had him on the ground and were

243

kicking and punching him, but Rod wasn't having any of it. He flung the fuckers off, shouting 'can't Spookie fucking fight for himself?' They all shat themselves and backed off after that. Like I said, Rod isn't afraid of anything and it's going to take more than a group of little twats who think they're hard to worry him.

You reckon she's alright? I ask Dan

Who 'Her'? dunno mate, why? you losing interest?

It's not that mate...It's just that... fuck it's getting on a bit and I don't reckon he's going to do anything fucking stupid. He's a bit of a twat but he's still her dad.

It's properly cold now, my breath mingling with the cigarette smoke as it leaves my lips. I get a sudden ticklish sensation that runs up my back.

When we were still in primary school we spent everyday out on our bikes. We would pedal around the local streets until the sun started to set when dad would wander out into the road to call us in for dinner. We had to take our bikes all the way up the drive to leave them in the garage, dumping them up against the wood pile before rushing out, desperate not to be last and tasked with turning off the light. When it was my turn I would always pause for a second after flicking off the switch, and stare back into the darkness. I would call out in my head for whatever demons lurked within the inky blackness to come and face me, like trying to scream in a dream when you have no voice. I would beseech whatever slept in the shadows to come and take me, to pull me apart, to rip the flesh and skin from this useless body and bleed my open heart.

My brothers would be halfway back to the house before I would turn and run as fast as I could towards the warm yellow light of the kitchen and the figure of my father cooking over the electric hobs, my legs carrying me across the rough ground, running so fast I was close to stumbling as the thing that lurked in the dark bore down on me, mouth agape, thin tendril like fingers inches from my back, the prickle of its presence running up my spine to the erect hairs on the back of my neck. I would rush into the kitchen, not once looking back and slam the door shut behind me, a shiver of excitement running through me.

I get the same feeling now as I turn to stare into the shadowy interior of the Co-op, the ghost of my face on the glass, my breath on the cold window obscuring the black shadowy outlines of rows of shelves stacked with packets of crisps and boxes of cereal.

Come on mate, thought you were well up for this, encourages Dan, pushing himself back to his feet and holding out his hand to help me up.

I take a deep breath and stub out my cigarette on the damp concrete, flicking the butt into the gutter, and scramble up onto my feet, brushing the back of my jacket clean with the back of my hand.

Fuck it, let's go, I say to Dan.

We walk up Mayors walk, passing the small church on the right, the date 1901 carved into a relief above the arched doorway, and plod on in relative silence.

We reach the entrance to The Grange and plunge into its dark embrace, leaving the comforting yellow glow of the street lights as we enter. Our eyes gradually adjust to the near blackness and I can make out a group of shadowy figures propped up against the wooden walls of the shed-like changing rooms. They chat and mutter amongst themselves as we pass, collars up, the red cherries from their cigarettes glowing like little fireflies. Dan nods in recognition to one of the shadows as we walk by, greeting the group with a muted 'alright lads'.

Who's that mate? I ask him once we are out of earshot.

You know, Blakey from the forth year, good mates with Donnie and that lot, he answers, looking back briefly.

Yeah I know him, I say, hangs around with Kael a bit, thinks he's well hard.

Yeah mate, replies Dan, smirking.

We exit the Grange, emerging onto Ledbury road, the barely audible hum of the street lights above us. I glance back into the inky darkness of The Grange, to the echo of muted voices within.

Dan taps me on the shoulder, holding the box of long cigarettes towards me, one poking out filter first from the rest of the pack. I pick it out and place it between my lips sucking the taste of unlit tobacco through the filter. Dan plonks himself down on the front wall of one of the bungalows that line the street, large white framed front windows, light seeping out of the edges of heavy curtains, and lights a cigarette. He hands me his lit fag and I hold the glowing cherry to my own and puff until I get a good lungful of smoke. I hand him back his cigarette and we continue on down the quiet street.

We pass by the Netherton shops across the road on our right, the smell of fried food emanating from the now shut chippy. We cross the top of Audley Gate, over the patch of grass where we all usually congregate after school and down past our school. The building is dark. A few security lights illuminate the main entrance and the bike sheds, but other than that the building is dark and still. I watch our reflections in the tall black windows across the wide patch of grass at the front of the building as we slowly traverse, Dan a head taller than me at least.

Remember when we used to come here to skate? I ask Dan, still staring absently into the dark.

Yeah mate, he replies, it's where I did my first kick flip, over by the tennis courts. He takes another drag on his cigarette, flicks it into the gutter and lights up another, offering me one too. I decline.

Remember? He continues, it was when you lent me your Jeff Grossman deck and I fucked up the graphics doing rail slides.

Yeah mate, I grin, I remember.

Soz about that old boy, he remarks.

We push on into the cold night. I pull up the collar of my donkey jacket and hunch my shoulders to try and keep the cold air from my neck. We walk down Audley Gate and turn onto Atherston Avenue. This is 'Her' street.

I take in a deep breath, the cold air in my nostrils, a rattle somewhere deep in my chest and cough a bit.

So mate... uh what's the plan? Dan asks retrying his ponytail again.

Dunno mate, I reply, um... ring her doorbell, make sure she's alright I suppose.

Alright, says Dan nodding.

We stop for a minute, leaning up against a waste high wall as Dan finishes his cigarette. There are a few cars

247

parked along the road. I look at myself reflected in the passenger window of an old red Ford Escort. My thin white face peers out at me. My long dark hair falls almost to my shoulders, my donkey jacket hangs from my bony frame and a bit of fluff grows on my upper lip. I push my arm out of my jacket to expose my skinny wrist and brush my hair from my face and sigh.

You alright mate? Enquirers Dan.

Yeah mate... I dunno, I mean it's just... I don't reckon she even fancies me mate, I speak, still peering at my own reflection.

Nah mate, you and her have got something, he tells me, remember I've got the eye old boy.

Perhaps... I remark.

The upstairs window across the road from us flickers with blue light, and the muted canned laughter of a post watershed comedy echoes in the stillness of the night.

I reckon we should head back, I say reluctantly.

It's late and it's getting properly cold.

You sure mate? Questions Dan.

Yeah I reckon, I tell him.

Alright then, why don't we head back to yours, he suggests, I mean she might be trying to phone you or something.

Yeah mate, I answer smiling, She's probably in bed by now anyway. I'll talk to her tomorrow.

Fuck it she'll be fine mate, assures Dan.

We push ourselves back to our feet and begin the long trek back the way we came. I take a brief look behind me, down the street towards her house and a strong sense of deja vu overtakes me. I hear a voice on the cold breeze, a hint of something yet to come, a call from a void far out beyond the place I now inhabit. The winter is creeping on and buried deep within it are the whispers of the forgotten, an image of 'Her', the same and yet somehow changed. The years line her face and her golden hair is flecked with white. We talk, but our voices are no longer our own. The edges have worn off and frayed, eroded and softened by things as of yet undiscovered. She shines as always, perhaps more strongly, a stark brilliance that defines and illuminates, that ties this moment to the next and the next, on and on into the vast distance. One day I will cry, perhaps I will never stop, forever teetering precariously on the edges of this tentative dream I have built, to replay these moments until, like an old record, the grooves lose their definition and I am left with the fuzzy hiss of whispers through the static. One day I will see. One day I will understand.

I turn to Look up to Dan pacing just ahead of me, his long ponytail tucked unintentionally into the collar of his jacket.

Cheers for this mate, I tell him.

For what mate? He asks, briefly looking back over his shoulder and I wonder for a fleeting moment if he feels it too.

You know, being a good mate and shit, I tell him.

Yeah mate, he says, fucking birds eh.

fucking birds...

We walk alone, the streets dark and empty except for the occasional car and the sky is black, the stars hidden behind a layer of cloud. I look down at my feet as we plod onward and in my mind I get a glimpse of myself, small

249

and skinny, my hair in lank strands about my face. I walk with my head down and my shoulders hunched, the cigarette in my mouth illuminating my hazel eyes. I loosen my grip on the piece of wood I'm still carrying and it clatters to the ground. I kick it into an alley way.

Dan tugs the hairband off his long ponytail and reties it, pulling his hair behind his head, hair band between his teeth and flicks his still burning cigarette into the drain.

I reckon my dad's an alcoholic, I say.

METAMORPHOSIS

There's a party at Max's house tonight to celebrate the end of school. His parents are away on holiday and we go round early to help get ready. We have all been to too many parties that ended with broken windows and cigarette burns in the carpets, so Max has decided he isn't taking any chances. We take all of the nice furniture into the garage, roll up all of the carpets, and nice crockery and ornaments are safely hidden away in cupboards or high up on shelves. Red wine is banned from the house and Max has stationed dozens of ashtrays in every room.

We start drinking early, popping open a couple of cans of Stella and leaning back on the comfortable sofa in the living room. The sun is still high in the afternoon sky and the smell of a barbecue wafts through the half empty house. We sit and talk, that tight sickly excitement in our stomachs.

We are already a few beers in by six o clock when the first few eager party goers start to arrive. 'Ice T and Body Count' are on the stereo and it's a beautiful summer evening. On days like this the sun doesn't go down until about nine or ten and there is a warm breeze blowing through the house from the open double doors at the back. The dogs, Max has got two golden retrievers (one is

251

about two years old and the other is a fat old thing with a lovely temperament) are safely locked away in the utility room at the back. It's ok they have lots of food and water and Max is going to go in and see them every so often. Everything is ready and it's time to get this thing going.

Blake, Marko and Ethan are the first to arrive. They all live really close by and can walk over in a couple of minutes.

How's your shoulder mate, I ask Ethan as they walk in, beers and a quarter bottle of vodka in hand.

Pretty good actually, how are you?

Not bad old boy, I say, think it's going to be a good one tonight.

Blake stops Body Count in the middle of 'KKK Bitch' and throws in a cassette of 'The Rolling Stones' greatest hits. 'Sympathy for the Devil' comes on and Max turns up the volume. We all crack open a can of Stella each.

Cheers lads, says Blake, and we knock cans as we all depart on another drunken night.

The place starts to fill up as the sun starts to set, and by 10:00 things are in full swing. Everyone has that lovely 'late summer three beers in' buzz going on and the holidays have just started. Everyone is well fucking chuffed that exams are over and it's hugs and singing along to our favourite tunes time. The back doors are open to try and ventilate the place so it won't be too smoky come Monday morning, a refreshing cool breeze blowing through the house. I hear the call of something beautiful carried on that mid summer wind, something soft and urgent, an almost pleading cry that fills that hollow space that so often swells in my chest. Perhaps it's

252

the naive happiness of youth or the absent knowledge of things far more profound, the elaborately carved and utterly beguiling intricacies of being anything at all.

I take another sip of my beer, the sensual fingers of inebriation working their way up my spine, smoothing out all the hard edges, imbibing everything with warmth and clarity. Max wanders over, a cheap bottle of white wine hanging limply from his left hand, fag in his mouth, his left eye half shut against the smoke. I reach out and pull him close.

Love you old boy, I tell him, as we hug, my hand on the back of his cool neck.

Love you too mate, he replies, almost in a whisper.

Fucking love all of you, I yell, pulling away from our embrace, Max's hand still on my shoulder. The music is loud now, blaring out of the meaty wood finished speakers, and people crowd the spacious living room, spilling out into the conservatory. The air is thick with smoke and the excited shouts and voices of my friends. I catch snippets of conversations, little windows into the lives that surround me, girl's and boy's names, plans for the summer, complaints about teachers or homework, conversations about music, about films, about the latest adverts on telly.

Marko grabs me by the arm, he and Eli lifting me up onto their shoulders and parading me around the living room like some pasty Incan king. Someone passes me half a joint and I take a big drag, the tobacco making the room spin, Marko and Eli struggling to keep their balance as my weight suddenly shifts. 'She's a Rainbow' starts to play on the stereo and I see Vicky, Kirsten and Kyra come in

253

through the front door, dolled up and already tipsy, a half empty cardboard carton of alcopops clutched in Kirsten's hand. I want to kiss them all. I want to kiss everyone in this beautiful fucking room. I never want this night to end. I never want these people to leave. I long to exist like this for the rest of eternity, my life just a constant unending party with the people I love. Fuck offices and deadlines and meetings with the lads from finance. Fuck mortgages and interest rates and home ownership. Fuck getting a car on higher purchase and arguing with the wife in Sainsbury's on Christmas eve over how many bottles of white to buy. Fuck 'Take That' and 'Boyz 2 Men' and watching top of the fucking pops on a Thursday night. Fuck the endless drudgery of the human condition and the impulse to jump headlong into the void. Fuck John Major and his team of grey little yes men. Fuck those wannabe hard men with shaved back and sides in their colourful shirts with the button down collars. Fuck sleep and sobriety and virginity. I want to live like this forever.

Hardy and Rod turn up at about ten thirty, pushing through the crowd towards us, shaking hands and receiving hugs as they pass. They have been at another party with their new birds, but they 'blew it out cause it was a bit sad boring' as Rod so eloquently puts it.

There was a girl. There is always a girl.

Her name was Beth, another stupid little teenage fantasy, a nice face and wide hips, another potential ornament for my bedraggled form, another player on the stage of my imaginings, the soft pull of those delicate adolescent daydreams and the ticklish excitement of

254

unexplored possibilities in my chest, the subtle sweet sickness of unknowing stirred within me.

It was a Monday morning, me and a couple of mates were in the middle of Centre Point (the lounge for sixth form students) playing table tennis, 'It's the End of the World as We Know It' by 'REM' playing on the stereo, when she walked in with a couple of girls from my year. They stood chatting by the stereo, she occasionally brushing her long light brown hair away from her face, tucking it behind her ears, and biting her bottom lip with slightly buck teeth. She was dressed in the school's black and grey uniform, a slim fitting pair of black trousers rather than the usual skirt and a wool sweater, cuffs pulled down slightly over her hands.

When Centre Point emptied out and it was just me, her and a few others I walked over and tried to talk to her, but my words came out stunted and censored, my true self as always smothered and speechless, my hands hidden away in my pockets, long mousy hair over half my face, mumbling a few insignificant words.

One night at The Luckyleaf, my nerve bolstered by four or five whiskeys and coke, I finally built up the confidence to ask her out. I don't recall the words I used or how she looked at me as I spoke them, but I do know that she said yes. I walked away from her and back into my warm circle of friends, a wide smile on my drunken chops.

Life, however is rarely simple, never so forgiving. It is full of nuance and ambiguity, we all grab at what we can, ignoring the hearts of others, clumsily pushing forward in a vain hope of clutching some of the bright blessed things that lie ahead, just beyond our grasp.

Kelly was an older girl, into alternative music and facial piercing. She was the older sister of one of my closest female friends and we had ended up in bed a couple of days before. It had been someone or other's birthday and she had come along with some bloke from her year. She was three years older than me and popular with the boys, so I never had any idea that she would be interested in my pale, skinny form. She had talked to me all night and as everyone parted ways, stumbling into various rooms to collapse unconscious into drunken dreams she took me by the hand and led me up the quiet staircase.

She was in The Luckyleaf Club the night I talked to Beth and soon found out about my newly found infatuation. I must have grossly underestimated her feelings for me, because she found Beth and threatened to kick the shit out of her and after that Beth didn't want anything more to do with me, and who could blame her really. I moped around the club drinking and wallowing in self pity before slipping off unnoticed into the night.

I've also been fooling around with Hardy's ex bird Jacqui for the last few weeks. She comes over to ours most weekends and we drink and chat. Once everyone is in bed, I put a mattress down on the floor of my room for her to sleep on and turn off the lights. We talk in the darkness and I listen to her breath as she creeps closer to where I lie, her hands soon reaching up under my quilt.

I had a feeling that Hardy perhaps suspected something, he and Rod had been really weird and secretive, avoiding me and going up to the garage to smoke and chat without me. I was worried that my brother might have found out, that he might be hurt, angry even. He and Jacqui had been really close for a long time, one of those couples at school who always turn up to parties together, or sit hand in hand on the school field.

A week or so ago in the garage we were a bit stoned and I decided I had to let him know. I had rehearsed the speech I was going to give in my head, softening the edges to make it more palatable, more weighted in my favour.

We sat down and I lit a couple of fags, passing the first one to him.

Hardy mate, I began.

Yes, he replied.

There's something I've got to tell you old boy, I continued, blowing smoke out through my nose.

What is it? He enquired, cause there's something I've got to tell you too, he added. I tilted my head to one side, grinning slightly in the corner of my mouth.

Ok mate you first, I offered.

You know that bird...um Beth you like? He spoke hesitantly, testing the waters, unsure as of how to proceed.

Yes, I answered, nodding, what about her?

He hesitated for a few seconds, taking a long drag on his cigarette, before stubbing it out on the wall and flicking it into the driveway.

Well it's... um, he began before blurting out, me and her are going out.

A big grin came across my face, and I shook my head knowingly from side to side.

I fucking knew it, I told him, you and Rod have been all fucking secretive and weird recently. I thought something was going on.

Sorry mate, he replied meekly, head hung, eyes on the old brick floor, is it alright?

Look mate it's fine, I admitted, really.

He looked up at me, brushing his chin length hair from his face and gesturing for another cigarette. I plucked the last bent cigarette from the box and handed it to him.

Mate, I've been shagging your ex bird, I announced as he was half way through lighting it.

He coughed a bit and then we both started laughing, the tension in the air immediately dissipating.

I thought you were going to be so fucking mad mate, he said, still chuckling, you don't mind do you?

Nah mate really it's fine, I replied through my last few snickers. She wasn't really into me anyway. Actually, I asked her out a few weeks ago in the Luckyleaf and that bird Kelly threatened to kick the fuck out of her, so I can safely say that that ship has sailed old boy.

How about you mate? I asked earnestly, the smile fading from my face, Me and Jacqui? Is it alright?

It's fine mate. We split up ages ago, he told me finishing his ciggie and stubbing it out on the floor.

She's probably only shagging you to get to me anyway, he added.

We both laughed at that.

Love you old boy, I told him.

Love you too mate, he replied, and I knew he meant it.

Rod and Hardy are alone and dressed in matching leather jackets. They look like a right couple of criminals. Rod is in high spirits as usual and he's brought along a six pack of '8.6', a really cheap lager that they sell at The Spa

258

on Williamson Avenue. It tastes like shit and is only good for one thing, getting you totally off your tits. It's called 8.6 because that's the alcohol percentage. It comes in a blue can with gold lettering, absolute class.

Last summer Rod and Hardy bought ten of them from The Spa and decided to drink them as they walked all the way to Oundle, the next village over. The walk is along a small footpath that cuts through fields and undergrowth, crosses small streams and leads through muddy fields full of large white cows. They took along a Walkman and a 'Joe Satriani' cassette, but no water or food. They polished off all the beer, got thoroughly wankered and almost died. Rod tried to chat up some bird on a horse, stroking its mane and patting its flanks like he was an accomplished e-fucking-questrian, declaring it a 'magnificent beast'. It was the middle of summer and they both nearly collapsed of heat stroke. They turned up back at mine at about five in the evening covered in mud and straw, faces burnt and peeling, triumphant and absolutely wasted. It's good stuff alright.

Have a beer old boy, offers Rod, peeling one of the offending cans from the plastic mesh.

Nah I'm alright man, I reply, I want to still be alive tomorrow.

Max comes over and Rod opens up a new pack Of Benson and Hedges and hands them round.

Fuckin B and H, someone complains.

Whats the matter mate? too skint to buy Embassy?

Fuck off, is the curt reply.

Rod pulls a zippo from his jean pocket and strikes it on his thigh and we all lean in to light our fags.

Where are the birds then lads? I enquire.

Left them at the party old boy, says Rod. I mean I love Tess, she's sad fit, but birds can be a bit sad boring sometimes. It's much better just the lads, he grins.

Rod is a fucking Legend. Everyone is friends with the old boy. He is a big lad for his age, tall with a solid build and thick wrists. Him and his Uncle Dave, who is only about ten years older than him work out all the time down at the gym in town. He was born in Hammersmith on the exact day that Elvis died (we sometimes joke about him being his reincarnation) and moved to The Borough about ten years ago with his family. He's got a bit of that cockney wit about him, never fails to make us all laugh. He likes a drink, thats for certain, but everyone always takes the piss out of him for being a lightweight. He's as tough as anyone I know though, and would never back down from a fight, no matter how fucking big you are. He doesn't appear to possess any fear.

A couple of months back we stopped in McDonald's for a quick burger on the way back from some boozer in town. It was late and all the pubs had already kicked out. Turns out that most of The Borough had also come up with the same idea, and the place was rammed. It was me, Kael, Rod and both of my brothers along with Nugget and Tom. Rod really needed a piss and so fucked off to the bog to relieve himself while we waited in line to order.

Kael, get us a Big Mac meal would you old boy? I'm just going to have a slash, he shouted back as he wandered off.

There was a group of townies sitting at one of the small tables next to the big window that looked out towards the town square, tucking into some big macs. They all had short hair, shaved at the sides, leather jackets and enough gold chains and bracelets to start a small jewellery shop. Apparently they took exception to a bunch of rough looking druggie bastards buying food from the same establishment as them. They were giving us the eye, wanting one of us to say something, give them the excuse to beat the shit out of someone. They picked the wrong people.

Kael caught the eye of one of them and stared right back.

What the fuck are you looking at? The bloke threatened, a big meaty fucker in an Adidas jacket, his hair cropped short.

Don't know, answered Kael, looks like that little gay cunt from E17.

Now I don't think the bloke quite expected that response and for a second he looked a bit taken aback. He probably thought Kael didn't look much, dressed casually in jeans and the red sweatshirt he always wore. It had holes all over it from burning rocks, the arms a little too long, the cuffs stretched from rolling up the sleeves. His hair was messy and he had a bit of blonde bum fluff on his chin, a few freckles across his nose teased out by the sun, but the thing you have to realise with Kael is that he doesn't give a fuck. You could be Frank fucking Bruno and he would have a go.

There was a bit more shouting back and forth and some posturing and threats, the bloke behind the counter and some of the customers starting to look decidedly nervous. At this point Rod came out of the toilet and walked back towards the counter. He had heard the commotion from inside the bog, saw the group of lads sitting at the table, and heard the back and forth between them and Kael.

I'm going to kick your fucking head in, one of the group growled.

You can fucking try, replied Kael.

He wasn't going to back down to these fucking posers.

Rod looked them over, then walked over to their table. One of them stood up as Rod approached, ready to defend himself. Like I said, Rod is quite a big bloke and can look quite intimidating if he wants to. Then casually as you like, Rod Martin who was born on the exact fucking day that Elvis Presley popped his clogs, sat down at their table, grabbed a half eaten burger from one of their trays and took a large bite. While he was chewing he looked around the table staring each one of them in the eye in turn. They had no idea how to react to this, and they didn't know what to do. They were bullies, used to intimidating people and they didn't know how to react when things started to go south.

Rod swung round in his seat, right arm hanging loosely over the back and calmly and casually called over to Kael, What do you reckon mate? Should we fuck em up or let em go?

Rod's got an older brother in the year below me at school called John. The two are very similar and yet nothing alike. Rod is big and strong, a physical being of meat and muscle, a slave to his appetites, headstrong and indestructible. John is smaller, clean cut and handsome. He is a talker not a fighter, a man gifted with the ability to use words and persuasion. The one thing they share is their confidence, it's not that false cocky, confidence that so many our age try to pass off as their own. It's a confidence that comes from truly knowing oneself, of knowing how life will turn out, of staying on track and following the road ahead. John is the nicest bloke I know and Rod absolutely loves him to bits. Some of my mates don't like him, mistaking his genuine wish to connect with people for something else. Suspicious of anyone that lays their heart on the line, of anyone that doesn't hide who they really are below a layer of affectations and trinkets. Their family are Jehovahs Witnesses and while John seems to follow the faith quite closely, Rod doesn't want anything to do with that nonsense. He just wants to meet girls, play music and get fucked up, and Rod my dear friend, don't we all. Him and my younger brother are best mates. They hang around all the time together, always off to Joe's Garage on a Friday evening for happy hour, dressed almost identically in dark jeans and leather jackets, short back and sides and far too much cheap after shave.

Mate come here, urges Max.

I've been drinking in the kitchen with Ethan and Blake and sniffing amyl nitrate in between beers. It's nasty fucking stuff. One whiff and you feel like your head is going to explode. It's a vasodilator and apparently gay blokes use it to relax certain involuntary muscles. All I

263

know is that it gets you off your head. A girl in my brother's year filled up a water pistol with it once at a party and we all started squirting each other. She spilt a shit tonne of it down her t shirt and ended up curled in a ball under the shower, puking all night.

I follow Max out of the kitchen, lit fag in hand and into the living room. There are a lot more people here than before. The stereo is on loud, playing 'Fugazi' and some people are dancing. Everyone is shouting and laughing, and I can make out a few couples snogging in the dimly lit conservatory at the back. The air is thick with smoke, the smell of cheap booze and cheaper perfume. We may have cleared the house out, but we are still going to have a hell of a fucking time cleaning this shit up tomorrow.

Max's hair is long, tied up behind his head in a pony tail. He's wearing black army trousers and a quilted shirt from the army surplus shop in the arcade in town. He's got a fag in his mouth and a grin across his face. Max is a quiet lad, a thinker, genuine, and trustworthy. We all love Max. He's everyone's little brother, that bloke you can rely on, the bloke you would call if you were in the shit, the bloke you talk to when your other mates won't listen, but like all of us he has his demons.

He had a sister. She was beautiful and popular, always hanging about with the cool kids at school and invited to all the best parties. She was a couple of years older than me and I used to see her around school, but I don't think we ever met.

It was around Christmas. It might have been 1989 or perhaps 90. The decorations were up in the house and

264

there were presents around the Christmas tree. It was the holidays and school had finished. It was cold and people were in the pub around the fire drinking, or snuggled up on the sofa in the living room with the Radio Times, watching Christmas telly and drinking Bailiey's Cream liqueur.

Max's sister had been poorly, a bit of a temperature and complaining of a headache. Her parents thought nothing of it. It was winter and lots of kids had been off school, complaining of similar symptoms. That night she had been feeling particularly bad. Her headache had been getting worse, but it was Christmas and none of the surgeries were open, and it was hardly worth going to the emergency room for a common cold. She had gone to bed early and her mum had tucked her in, probably telling her that she would feel better in the morning. At around midnight the rest of the family turned off the lights, went to the bathroom, brushed their teeth and went to bed.

At about one o clock in the morning, everyone was awoken by a terrible scream, Max's parents sprung out of bed and rushed to his sister's room where they found her unconscious and unresponsive. They called an ambulance and while they waited, trying desperately to revive their daughter, Max stood in the hallway, watching on in silence. The ambulance arrived and took her to the hospital. The doctors fought for her, but in the end they couldn't revive her and she was pronounced dead. She died of hydrocephalus brought on by bacterial meningitis. There was nothing anyone could have done. No one touched her room and her presents remained wrapped below the tree that Christmas morning.

265

I find it very difficult to begin to understand the amount of anguish and pain caused by losing a loved one so young and so unexpectedly at such a time and we all carry this knowledge with us. It is at the back of our minds when we are with Max. I hope that it doesn't make us treat him any differently, as I'm sure he would be horrified to think so, but we love him and know deep down that nothing we can offer or provide can ever fill that hole.

Off the living room is a small room that Max's dad uses as a study. Max's dad is a psychologist, looks a bit like Hunter S Thompson with his bald head and wide rimmed glasses. There is a a lot of shouting and yelling coming from inside. I push open the door and walk into the humid little space, packed with people.

Rod and Valentine are in the middle, both with their tops off, lit fags in their grinning gobs. Someone pulls a small table over from the wall and they kneel down, rolling their shoulders as they get ready to arm wrestle. This should be good. Rod is a strong fucker with a muscular physique, always in the gym and striking poses in the middle of class. He always preaches that you won't get anywhere in life without abs. Valentine is the biggest bloke in my year.

Valentine is everyone's friend. He's a giant, but the gentlest bloke you will ever meet, really funny too. Always getting a bollocking at school for doing stupid shit. One time in geography class when he thought the teacher was out, he started stalking around from desk to desk, squawking and pretending to be a chicken. The teacher had only popped out for a minute to talk to someone and was standing in the doorway watching for five minutes as Valentine walked around pecking people with his pretend beak, while we all nearly died laughing.

Tess's little brother is reffing and has the two opponents lock hands, making sure their elbows are placed firmly on the small table. They both take a couple of swigs of beer and Rod yells out into the small room, muscles in his arm tensing.

We all count down from three and Tess's little brother releases their hands.

The room explodes into shouts and howls as the two opponents strain against each other, veins in their muscular arms protruding, tendons in their necks taught, mouths set in hard grimaces. At first Valentine seems to have the upper hand, pushing Rod's arm to about forty five degrees off the table. Rod alters his grip slightly, his free hand clenching beneath the table and pushes back, bending Valentine's wrist back and forcing the larger boy's arm back to within a few inches of the table's surface. Neither of them is going to back down, not here, not now. Valentine again fights back, his meaty arm bulging and slick with sweat. It's really hot in here now and I down the dregs of a can of beer that sits on the shelf behind me, a few drips of the cool liquid spilling down my chin and onto my t shirt. Rod now has his arm pushed down at a really uncomfortable looking angle, his bicep straining.

The whole room is whooping and calling out, it's a primal sound, a battle cry ripped from the depths of our past, the simian hoots of our ancestors. People have

267

started to lay down money. A couple of quid on Rod, a fiver on Valentine. There's is punching and wrestling, as a playful aggression overtakes us, the beginnings of manhood coaxed out by the spectacle. Rod and Valentine both have sweat running down their faces and chests now, Max pouring cold water over Rod's head from a plastic bottle to cool him down.

For a minute or so neither holds sway, neither will yield, they are locked like that, eyes set on their own meaty fists, gripping one another, straining with all the strength their youth can muster. Valentine screams out, giving one final push and slams his younger opponent's hand down onto the table. The room erupts in cheers as Valentine leaps up, thrusting his fist into the air. There are arms around necks and slaps on backs, Max pushes through the crowd collecting pound coins and crumpled notes, mates shouting in his ear. Someone opens a fresh beer and hands it to Rod where he sits on the thick carpet, arms splayed out behind him. He downs the contents in one and crushes the can in his fist. A couple of girls from the year below me push their way tentatively into the packed, sweaty room and stand by the doorway drinking alcopops, amused grins on their over-made faces.

The victor gets lifted off the floor and paraded around the tiny room, his hands up on the ceiling, head inches from the light fitting, while arms of commiseration wrap around Rod's neck and shoulders. Valentine gets lowered down and the two opponents shake hands and exchange a few words before Valentine pulls his younger friend in for a crushing hug. Everyone loves this and we all start to cheer again with renewed vigour.

Rod grips Valentine's hand in his, You can be my wing man anytime, he says, feigning a stupid American accent.

Bullshit, you can be mine, replies Valentine.

We all laugh and Ethan breaks open a bottle of vodka, screwing off the cap and pouring a few shots for the two.

We all feel invincible, buoyed up by this spectacle, by the masculinity on display. We are unstoppable. Rod is right. Sometimes it is much better just the lads. We have begun the unstoppable march towards adulthood, towards manhood. For a few minutes those two young men encapsulate everything the rest of us want to be. Fuck my thin white body and long mousy hair, fuck my hairless chest and skinny wrists. I want to be like them. We all want to be like them. Those two young men from a small provincial city in the South East are fucking gladiators, they are Gods tonight.

THE SEED

Mate grab it, encourages Nails.

I'm trying mate but my arm doesn't fit, replies Tom, who has got his arm shoved into the machine up to the elbow, his grasping fingers just a couple of centimetres from the chocolate bar.

Let me have a go, I suggest, my arm's thinner than yours mate.

Alright go on then, offers Tom, pulling his arm out of the gap in the front of the machine, rubbing his elbow a bit as he frees it.

I reach in, my cheek pressed up against the glass and my fingers close awkwardly around the prize. I pull it out slowly and am greeted with a pat on the back as I drop it into Nails' waiting hands.

Nice one mate, he congratulates, who wants a bit?

The vending machine we are stealing from is old and sparsely filled. It consists of a couple of carousels that spin once money has been inserted into the slot, allowing the item closest the glass to be taken out through a flap like door at the front. The thing is that there is a space between the sides of the machine and the carousel part. This means that anyone with a skinny enough arm can reach in and take anything to either side of what is closest to the little door at the front. So far we have two packets of crisps, a chocolate bar, a bag of roasted peanuts and a piece of squashed chocolate cake.

The machine is on the third floor of the district hospital, the building in which all three of us were birthed mewling and puking into this world. We are standing next to the entrance to the paternoster, an old, clanky continuous lift system. It's made of a series of doorless boxes, all one on top of another, that move around in a huge loop from the basement to the top of the building. Once they reach the top, they travel over and continue back down. Getting on and off the thing can be a bit intimidating at first, but after a few goes it starts to get really fun. We like to fuck around in the wheelchairs on the first floor, racing each other down the narrow corridors, or balancing on the back wheels, our legs in the air. When we get seen by the security guards or one of the doctors, we leg it through the building and onto the paternoster to escape, standing up against the back wall as our adversary approaches, willing the small car to sink faster into the floor, hearts pounding in our skinny chests.

Nails breaks the chocolate up into several chunks and dishes it out. We all munch hungrily on it.

Doctor said we could go in at 2:30, what time is it Tom? I ask.

2:36 mate, he replies, glancing at the big watch around his thin wrist, let's go.

I don't like hospitals. I don't like the smell. I don't like the stark white walls or the grim faces.

When I was about seven or eight I woke to a terrible pain in my abdomen. It was like I was on fire, as though

272

someone had reached into my guts and was squeezing the life out of me. I screamed for my mum, and she and my dad came rushing through into my room, flicking on the light and wiping sleep from their eyes as they yanked the covers off me. I couldn't walk so my dad picked me up like a new born infant and bore me down the stairs and into the living room. I heard my mum calling an ambulance from the hallway before coming back into the living room and wrapping me in a blanket, prying open my eyes and peering into my mouth. My parents spoke quickly and sharply to each other, voicing their various concerns and I foetal and mewling clutched at my mum's arm as she stroked my face.

It's alright my dear, the ambulance will be here soon. It's alright, she whispered to me, tears in her eyes.

The ambulance arrived and my dad carried me out of the front door, into the misty blue chill of an English morning, and into the back of the awaiting ambulance, its lights flashing, the stink of exhaust fumes hanging in the still dawn air. He gave me a kiss on the forehead then rushed back down the pathway to the front door.

I'll come down later with the children love, he called back as I was laid on a stretcher, take care of our boy Veronica.

My mum said nothing as the ambulance doors slammed shut and we raced off up the road towards the district hospital, sirens blaring, the noise vibrating through the stuffy interior. The ambulance came to a halt and the doors swung open and I was taken out of the ambulance on the stretcher, banging through the heavy doors and into the sterile fluorescent interior of the emergency room, the sharp stink of disinfectant filling my nostrils. We were met by doctors, one of whom tied something to my wrist while the other talked to my mother as I was pushed along the corridor, my hands clutching my belly, knees brought up to my chest. I was taken to a room through another pair of double doors, the stretcher pushed up against the wall of the bright little room while the doctor pushed his fingers firmly into my stomach, all the time asking me where it hurt. A young nurse with the previous night's mascara still smudged beneath her eyes coaxed me off the bed and led me hobbling into the X-ray room. The door slammed shut and I stood alone, t-shirt pulled up over my skinny chest, ribs clearly visible beneath the skin, pressed up against the cold machine. There were three loud thuds as the x-rays were taken, then the door opened again and the nurse took me back to my stretcher. They performed another series of tests and took some of my blood, a sharp bite followed by a dull ache as the needle pierced my arm, my dark liquid flowing into a little glass tube. I was at last wheeled into a half empty ward, the doctors and nurses leaving through the swing doors at the far end, my mother sitting anxiously by my bed, warm hand upon my stomach.

We talked in hushed tones, the softness of my mother's reassuring voice washing over me, filling my heart and dampening the pain which was at last beginning to lose its edge, the initial sharp burning sensation slowly abating, becoming more of a deep indistinct ache. She tried to get me to sleep, but I was still in too much discomfort and felt uneasy in that bright clean ward with its harsh electric lighting, echoing coughs and machines.

The doctors came back and they called my mum away. I could hear the low drone of their voices from the hallway outside as I lay staring up at the ceiling lined with humming fluorescent tubes.

My mother came back in and sat by my bed, her hand on mine, and explained to me what was happening. They had first thought it was appendicitis and were all set to take me to the operating room, but as the pain was slowly dissipating they had reassessed their original diagnosis and now believed that the pain I was experiencing was caused by swollen glands in my stomach and that thankfully an operation would no longer be necessary. My mother left at about lunch time but told me she would be back soon and I sat upright in bed, eating ice cream and watching cartoons on a little black and white telly that was wheeled in on a small trolley.

My mum came back an hour or so later with a few of my favourite Action Force figures and some fruit and chocolate wrapped in a paper bag. She sat by my bed and I slept fitfully, dreaming of gigantic, brightly coloured plants that tasted like battery acid, awakening to an intense thirst, my bed soaked with sweat. My mum helped me out of bed and onto my feet, holding me steady as I took off my wet clothes and stood in that cold ward, half naked and shivering as she dressed me in my Star Trek pyjamas, still a little warm from the airing cupboard. The nurse came in and changed the sheets as my mother held me, rubbing my torso to keep me warm. I climbed back into bed and pulled the stiff covers up to my chin.

275

The evening crept on, the windows by my bed darkening, the yellow lights of the city coming to life. My mum told me that I would have to stay in the hospital over night, just so the doctors could keep an eye on me. I said I didn't want to stay but she assured me that I would be ok and that she would be back in the morning. She kissed me on the forehead and talked to the nurse briefly before plucking her handbag from the bedside table and walking out.

A young nurse brought a plate of tepid food which I poked and prodded at as Blake's 7 played on the black and white telly. The nurse came in and ordered me to drink some medicine from a little plastic cup, which tasted both sweet and bitter at the same time, and a few minutes later the lights turned off with a thud and I was left alone in the dark.

The initial silence was soon replaced by a plethora of alien sounds as my ears got used to the quiet. There was the constant beep of a heart monitor and the hum of some machine deep within the bowels of the old hospital, rumbling quietly as it kept the building alive. There was the occasional cough and the mumble of softly spoken voices somewhere at the other end of the room. A nurse would occasionally come in, leaving the double doors swinging as she clattered across the hard pristine floor on stiff shoes, hair pulled back tight against her skull. I tried to sleep but I couldn't relax, couldn't let go and so lay in that iron framed bed with its starched itchy sheets staring up at the ceiling, counting the tiles.

There was a short chord with an orange button on the tip by the side of my bed, and the nurse had told me to press if it I needed anything. I wanted to go home, my stomach was starting to feel much better and I longed for the comfort of my own bed, for the warmth of the open fire in the living room and the weight of my lazy cat on my knee. I wondered if the nurses might get cross with me if I pressed it, but I really wanted to go, to leave this place. I missed my mum and dad, my brothers and my toys.

I pressed the button and within a minute a nurse came trotting purposefully into the ward. She came over to my bed and asked me in a soft whisper what was wrong. She smelt of perfume and cigarette smoke and her lips were red with lipstick. I told her that I was feeling better and that I wanted to go home. She asked me if I could wait until morning, but I quietly insisted and she told me she would phone my mum. She took a look at my chart hanging at the bottom of the bed then walked off out of the double doors and I was left in relative peace and quiet once more.

Less than an hour later, the double doors swung open and my mum walked in, dressed in a long wool coat, her handbag hanging from her inner elbow, accompanied by the nurse. She came over to my bed and gave me a long hug, the cold air still clinging to her.

Let's go home love, she said to me, tears in her eyes. I'm sorry for leaving you here.

I swung my legs out of bed and slipped my feet into the trainers my mum had brought with her. They were blue with white stripes. My mum asked me if I could stand and I carefully put all my weight onto my feet and stood up unsteadily. She asked if I was alright and I told her I was fine. She packed my few things into a shopping bag and we walked across the ward, past those other poor souls in strange beds and out through the double doors, out into the bright lights of the corridor beyond.

We tentatively push the door open and one by one file into the small room. Debbie is sitting upright, her back propped up with pillows. There are various tubes in her arms and a monitoring machine next to the bed. It beeps steadily. My mouth still tastes of chocolate.

She smiles as we enter and gives a feeble wave. Her eyes look sunken with dark rings around them. The vitality and shine that she usually exudes has been sucked from her. She looks grey and weak.

How are you doing mate? I ask, my hands hanging awkwardly by my sides. I wish I could smoke in here.

Alright yeah, she replies weakly. There is a hoarseness to her voice and she coughs a bit.

Tom has pulled the curtains aside and is peering out of the window.

Mate, I can see Nugget's house from here, he informs us.

Nails sits down on the edge of the bed.

Kael been to see you yet? He asks, said he would come today or tomorrow. He lies.

Nah not yet, she replies. I don't reckon I really want to see him at the moment. My mum is here a lot, and the nurses have been really kind.

There is a moment of silence and we look about the room, Tom is tying his hair and Nails picking something off his trouser leg.

Don't suppose one of you has got a fag? Asks Debbie.

Don't reckon you'll get away with smoking in here, Tom tells her. They've probably got smoke detectors anyway.

It's fine, replies Debbie, I've already had a couple anyway. The nurses either don't realise or they don't give a shit.

Her curly, reddish hair is down, falling in waves about her pale neck. She is wearing a little bit of makeup and the top few buttons of her pyjama top are undone, exposing the upper half of one of her round breasts, nearly down to the nipple.

I reach into my pocket and bring out a packet of silk cut, offering her one.

Fucking silk cut, complains Nails, at least give her a proper fag.

Mate she's in the fucking hospital, I say, I don't want to kill her.

Nails just shrugs and grins.

His real name is Harvey, but he got the nickname Nails when he was in primary school for taking on a much bigger kid from a couple of years older and kicking the shit out of him. He's short, stocky and handsome, short brown hair, high cheek bones and a sort of rugged look to him. He's one of those lucky bastards who tans easily and looks like he was built for the outdoors. He joined the army on leaving school and is stationed up in Chatteris or somewhere. He says he really likes it. They teach him how to drive and shoot and also pay him a decent wage. He gets quite a lot of leave and always comes back down to The Borough to see us, and I give him a haircut before he goes back, always making sure it's short enough to be hidden under his beret. Him and Kael go way back and have always been really close. They are more like brothers than friends and Kael's dad loves the cheeky bastard.

Thanks Kei, says Debbie, pulling one from the packet.

Nails leans over the bed and lights the cigarette from a box of Swan Vesta matches, striking a couple of times before the match ignites.

Tom mate, have a butchers down the corridor and make sure no one is coming, suggests Nails.

Tom nods his head several times, pushing open the door and wandering out into the corridor.

Debbie takes a drag on her cigarette and rests back against the stack of pillows. I open the window as wide as it will go and waft my hand to get rid of some of the smoke.

I reckon I'll have one too says Nails.

I throw him the pack and the two of them sit on the bed smoking and chatting. I look on from the open window. The sky is overcast and there is a bit of rain in the air. Tom was right, you can see Nugget's house from here.

About a week ago Kael told Debbie that he wanted to break up. They argued and they fought, punches were thrown and hurtful things were said. At one point Debbie told Kael that she was going to kill herself. He told her to go ahead and that is exactly what she did. She downed a whole bottle of paracetamol and Kael sat and watched as she washed it all down with a few swigs of her mum's vodka. At some point she passed out and Kael called an ambulance. They took her to the district hospital and pumped her stomach. Luckily they got to her early enough and were able to save her life. The doctors said that she was less than an hour away from liver failure and that once that starts then there is no going back. Apparently it's a very long slow and painful way to die. One nurse explained that they get a lot of similar suicide attempts, teenagers with broken hearts, divorced mums with too many responsibilities and not enough money, middle aged men who have been laid off, unable to go home and face their families. They awaken from their slumbers to the concerned faces of friends and family, they feel good, rehydrated and rested, seemingly normal and often in high spirits, the attempt on their own life having failed, a renewed hunger for life ignited deep within. They wonder why everyone looks so distraught, why their faces hang like onlookers to a funeral procession. They want to get out of bed, to leave this place, to go home and hug their parents, their wives, their children. The doctor explains that there is nothing that can be done, that over the next three or for days liver failure will set in, that as the poisons in the body build they will become progressively worse, headaches, abdominal pain and intense nausea as they slip ever closer to the end.

Debbie skirted on the edge for a few days, dipping in and out of that black void, the doctors keeping a constant watch on her organs, on her liver function. After a couple of days she awoke to a new morning, the doctors announcing with relief that her liver and kidney functions were gradually returning to normal, that she would survive.

After a few hours they transferred her to a private room. She was on suicide watch for a couple of days and at that time no one was allowed to come and see her. Once her mum, sister and the doctors were convinced that she was no longer a danger to herself, they moved her into this more comfortable private room and started to allow visitors. No one has asked Kael yet if he wants to come. Me and Nails went over to his house a couple of days ago but he wasn't in. His brother said that he's just been sitting in his room smoking weed and listening to Bob Marley.

Tom pushes open the door and in a half shout, half whisper tells us that someone's coming. Debbie and Nails put out their fags in a half empty coke can and I chuck it out of the window into the bushes below. Nails finds Debbie's deodorant and starts spraying it around the room, while the rest of us wave our arms and hands about in a futile attempt to get rid of the smell of smoke. I fan the curtains next to the window and Debbie washes out her mouth with orange squash, spitting it out into the small sink next to her bed. We pull up some chairs and sit down just as the door opens and in walks a stout, rather serious and solid looking nurse. She must be in her late thirties or early forties. Her hair is in a long brown pony tail pulled tightly back from her face, and a pair of fat rimmed spectacles magnify her already large round eyes. She walks up to the end of the bed and takes the chart, eyeing it and occasionally flipping from one page to the next. She scribbles something on it and then returns it to its rightful place.

So how are we feeling today? She asks her patient, peering down her nose at Debbie and giving the rest of us a tertiary disapproving glance.

Feeling much better today actually thank you, says Debbie in her best innocent little girl voice.

Well you shouldn't spend too much time talking to your...she looks us over again...friends, you need to get some rest.

Nails looks over at me and grins and I grin back.

The nurse wrinkles her brow and lifts her nose as if smelling something and her eyes move about in their sockets. she is about to speak when Debbie pipes up.

Um, would it be possible to get something to eat, I'm feeling a bit hungry actually.

The nurse turns her attention back to her patient, a smile spreading across her face.

Why of course dear, she answers, I'll fetch you some fruit and yoghurt, it's a very good sign that your appetite is returning.

Thank you, says Debbie smiling broadly at the nurse.

But after you finish eating, you have to promise me that you'll get some sleep, directs the nurse as she leaves the room, closing the door behind her.

We all look at each other and Debbie starts to laugh, a proper hearty laugh that comes from her belly and the rest of us join in. She wipes a few tears from below her dark brown eyes and pushes her curly hair back away from her face.

Lads, I'm pregnant, she says, almost in a whisper.

I look out of the window to where a row of birch trees used to stand, their organic silvery trunks stark and solid against the dirty white angles of the hospital. In the winter their leaves would drop gently to the pavement and we would crunch through them on the way home from school, their huge branches swaying and bending in the wind above our heads.

MY HANDS

The bell rings for the end of art and we all push our stools under the table and make our way down the corridor, through the history block and down towards science. I'm chatting to Simon Mason. He's a mate from a couple of years back. Back in the forth year we would meet up every lunch time, sit on a bench, eat our sandwiches and take the piss out of people who walked by. Neither of us is very big, so it's a surprise we never got our heads kicked in to be honest. Looking back on it we were a couple of twats, but it was a long time ago, things change and people change.

He's got long hair in a ponytail like most of the boys in my year, Doctor Martens and a pair of black army trousers on his skinny legs. His face is a bit spotty and he's got this one big eyebrow that goes right across his face. We are walking and chatting and talking bollocks. The group of girls from our class pass us in the narrow corridor, chatting noisily about Twin Peaks and the gorgeous 'Agent Cooper'. I nod to 'Her' as she passes and give her a smile.

I'll talk to you later Kei, yeah, she calls out laughing as they all push by.

Mate you shagged her yet, enquires Simon, nudging me with his elbow, eyes still on the group of girls, a hint of their perfume still in the air.

It's not like that mate, we're friends, I tell him looking down at my shoes as we walk, my hands thrust into my trouser pockets, but he doesn't want to let it go.

She must have given you a BJ though mate, he teases, you're over there enough.

I ignore his comment, trying to change the subject.

You done your environmental science homework? I ask him.

Yeah did it ages ago he replies,... she's got nice legs though mate, I wouldn't mind giving her one myself, he goads.

Let it go mate, I tell him, you're starting to get on my tits.

Thought you said you were just friends, so let someone else have a go mate, he continues, knocking into me playfully with his shoulder.

Really mate, let it go, you're starting to piss me off now. I warn him again.

What's up mate can't take the competition? He teases grinning.

I ignore him and stare down at the floor feeling the anger like a heat building in me, I bite down and try to ignore it, clenching my fists and breathing slowly in and out.

He doesn't stop, have you fingered her though? Bet you have you dirty bastard, he grins that stupid grin again and I snap.

I grab his head by his long pony tail and slam it into the wall with as much force as I can muster. He looks at me, a surprised look on his face and stumbles, dragging his legs as he fights for consciousness.

I told you to shut the fuck up, I tell him as a group of third year girls pass by us whispering and gossiping. I can see tears in his eyes.

I fucking told you, I say, tears welling up in my eyes too, and I stalk off towards the science block, punching the wall as I go.

I turn into the boys toilets at the end of the history block, go into one of the stalls and close the door behind me. I take my bag off my shoulder, put the lid of the toilet down and sit there waiting for the anger to subside. My heart is beating and I can feel my face is hot and flushed. I hold my hands out in front of me and study the lines and creases that run across them. One day these hands will nurse and care for my boy, washing and bathing him in warm water. One day these hands will open a diary and my life will change forever.

HAPPY HOUR

We are in Joe's Garage. It's a pretty rough place really, a tiny little bar on West Gate tucked in between a few shops and done out in faux 50s American diner decor, with neon lights and chrome bar taps, the full nine yards. It has one saving grace however, Saturday evening happy hour. Beers are fifty p a pint and so it's always packed to the rafters with Trevs and Tracies, done up to the nines and stinking of cheap perfume.

We turn up early, at about six or half past, grab a table towards the back and Finn goes up to the bar to get the beers in. It's me, Tom, Nugget, Nails, Kael, Hardy, and Finn and his mate Lenny. I'm in baggy jeans and a tie dyed t shirt, my long hair down and a bit of fluff on my chin, while the rest of them are all done up in coloured shirts, dark jeans and leather jackets. Except for Tom and Finn, their hair is cropped short and shaved at the sides and they are all wearing too much fucking aftershave. I look well out of place.

Finn is the boyfriend of Tom's dad's bird's daughter if that makes any sense. Tom's dad got divorced years ago. He's a really nice bloke and being a doctor, he's pretty popular with the ladies. His new girlfriend is called Silvia and she must be a good ten years younger than him.

288

Everyone gets on with Silvia. She is easy going and fun, treats us a bit more like adults than some of the other parents. She's got a daughter called Mel. Mel's got long curly brown hair, a wicked smile and a really nice set of tits. She comes over to Tom's a couple of nights a week to babysit the kids. I say babysit but Tom is sixteen and his brother is thirteen so it's hardly necessary. She is in her early twenties and often brings booze and her really fit friend Andrea with her, so as you can guess we are always pretty keen to hang about at Tom's house on these occasions.

Now Finn is a fucking nutter. He's about four or five years older than us. He's got long blonde hair that he usually wears up in a pony tail, a nose that looks like it's been broken several times and shitty tattoos all over his forearms. He loves a good ruck, and it's almost guaranteed that a night out with him will have a violent bloody conclusion. Some of my mates are pretty hard but Finn is on another level, being out with him and his mate Lenny is like a license to fuck around and be a twat. It's protection. Lenny is a meaty, rough looking geezer with cropped short hair and tattoos on his hands. Finn is a beast and likes a good fight, but Lenny is pure aggression. A machine built to fight, fuck and smash shit up.

Finn comes back with eight beers on a shitty little tray and plonks them down on the round chrome table. Beer is sloshing about everywhere, but at fifty p a pop it doesn't really fucking matter. His hand is bandaged and he's got a massive welt on his head and a black eye. It's a familiar look for Finn. Nugget asks him what happened as he takes a seat, downing half of his pint in one go.

Fucking tell him, encourages Lenny doing the same. The pint looks like a kid's cup in his meaty fist.

It's all this cunt's fault, begins Finn, pointing an accusatory finger at his mate.

Lenny laughs, I was just backing the twat up, he retorts.

Fucking showed those cunts though eh, adds Finn winking.

A young couple push past us, squeezing into the next table. The bloke looks about fucking fifteen, a leather jacket a good few sizes too big for him, a bum fluff moustache and a massive fucking gold hoop through his right ear. His bird is all perm and cleavage, her fat arse squeezed into some cheap as shit dress from Next or Top Shop, eyes glued together with too much mascara, mouth shiny with lip gloss. Finn gives them a tertiary glance, before hunkering forward conspiratorially over his half finished pint.

So we were at that new Pizza Hut just round the corner, he continues.

The one near the arcade? Asks Nugget.

Yeah that one, nice fucking pizza, Finn goes on. He's got a massive grin on his face.

Let's just say we had a bit of trouble, interjects Lenny. He's already downed his beer, peering at his empty glass then up at me. He points a meaty tattooed finger in my direction.

You, what's your name?

Kei, I reply as coolly as possible.

Bit of a fucking pussy name in' it? He laughs, but any mate of Finn is a mate of mine, go and get some more fucking lagers in would you mate, he orders.

No problem I reply, getting up and walking the short distance to the bar. I get the barman's eye with a half raised arm and order eight pints. He looks me over once and I think he is going to ask for ID. Thankfully he doesn't and starts to pull the beers. I hear a burst of laughter from our table and I see Lenny standing up.

So I bit his fucking ear off and spat it in the cunts face... is all I catch.

I get four beers on the tray and carry them back to the table.

Fucking nice one says Lenny, slapping me across the back and slipping a fiver into my hand, and lose the fucking dreads mate, you aren't a fuckin Rasta.

Yeah I say, self consciously pulling at my hair, and cheers for the fiver.

I go back to the bar to get the other four pints. I get back, distribute the pints and sit down.

Finn is talking, his hands open, palms facing each other as if reaching for something, a lit ciggie between his middle and index fingers.

So anyway this cunt decides to do a runner, he smirks, and I'm left there looking like a right fuckin plum with the bill and about two quid in my pocket.

Lenny starts to laugh at this point, taking a big drag on his fag, his lip curling.

Finn goes on, So I decide to politely explain to the cunt behind the counter that I'm only paying for my food. I tell the twat that I don't know the other bloke, but the skinny wanker doesn't believe me and starts to try and call me out. Now I'm not having some little bender giving me shit, so I tell im to shut his fuckin mouf or I'll shut it for im. Now, he doesn't take too kindly to this and starts calling for his manager. There's about three of the cunts there now and they're all goin off on me, so I grab one of the mouthy twats and fuckin pop him in the mouth, and as we're struggling one of the other sneaky fuckers whacks me over the head with a fucking metal bar.

Bollocks, interrupts Kael, no way some bloke in Pizza Hut is gonna smash someone with a metal bar.

It's fucking true, cuts in Lenny, backing up his mate, when I got back his fuckin head was streaming with blood and his hair was all fuckin stuck together, looked a right fucking mess.

He laughs and reaches over the table to pull Finn's pony tail.

Cunt needs a fuckin hair cut, he adds.

Finn gives him two fingers and continues with his story.

So yeah, I'm fuckin bleeding from my head and fighting these three twats behind the counter, when Lenny ere fucking strolls back in like nuffing's happened. He quickly clocks whats goin on in the place and marches in through the door like fucking Rambo, and aren't I glad to see the cunt.

Lenny grins and downs his pint, wiping his mouth with the back of his hand.

yeah mate, you would have been fucked if I hadn't come back, he says, chuckling.

I was doin alright by myself mate, Finn reassures.

So anyway the staff are shitting it now cause there's two of us and they're backing off into the kitchen, but I've got a right fucking monk on so I say to Lenny 'lets fuck this place up', and we fuckin go at it.

Yeah, says Lenny, we start pulling up the stools and kicking in the walls. At one point this fuckin nutter lobs a chair through the shop window and the whole thing fucking smashes, they've still got police tape over it now if you wanna look. Then we yell a few more fuckin insults at the cunts hiding in the kitchen and Finn sticks his hand in the till and taxes a few twenties and we fucking scarper.

We saw a fucking shed load of rozzers on the walk back to your flat didn't we Finn mate, he says chuckling.

Fucking right we did mate, hid out at mine and smoked some weed and listened to the pig cars goin past outside we did.

Lenny reaches over and shakes Finn by the hand and Finn slaps his mate playfully around his meaty, shaved head.

Lenny laughs and puts up his fists, want a fuckin go do you mate?

You wouldn't stand a chance mate, replies Finn.

Joe's garage is starting to fill up now. Everyone is half cut and in the mood for a club and a dance, but it's still only seven thirty and we've got a lot more booze to drink. There are a few tarts in short skirts and too much make up at the bar and Lenny, Finn and Kael are giving them the eye. The crowd is mostly short hair and button down shirts, a few tattoos poking out here and there and the smell of cheap aftershave most likely half inched from John Lewis' that very morning. Everyone gives our table a

293

wide birth and Lenny and Finn lean back in their seats like fucking kings, still high on the destruction of the previous day.

Kael sparks up a crafty joint and Finn gives him a wink.

Someone get some more fucking beers in, orders Lenny, downing the last dregs of his lager. It's time to get fucking pissed lads.

L'APPEL DU VIDE

We are over at one of Kael's mates houses in Westwood, a bit of a dodgy bastard, a couple of years older than us. I reckon he once half inched one of my guitars. We are all drinking and smoking in the conservatory. We sometimes come to his house at lunch time because it's close to school, and play pool or just smoke and chat.

This fit bird Julie, a couple of years below me at school used to hang out here too. She's got long curly hair, big blue eyes and a really fit body, wide hips and a skinny waste, nothing to complain about up top either. So we were all mucking about and a couple of the lads tied her to a chair with those elastic straps with hooks on the end, you know the ones that people use to secure things to the rack on the back of a bicycle or the top of a car. So they had her tied up and one of them pulled her top up and undid her bra. She was struggling and telling them to stop and they were laughing and pointing. This big bloke then grabbed her tits from behind and started groping her. The other lads were watching with mouths hanging open. I didn't know what to do at this point, so I just grabbed my coat, made an excuse and walked out.

Where the fuck are you going you puff? came a voice as I left, but I had already stepped out into the rain.

It's not much of a party and there's a funny vibe. It's a mix of a bunch of people and most of them don't really get along. There's our lot from Thorpe Lea Road, Jimmy Doyle and his mates from Bretton and a bunch of lads from Westwood. Andy is there along with some others that I only really know through reputation.

Andy is a good bloke, a big lad and he fucks around a lot at school, but I reckon he's got a good heart in him. We used to fight a bit at school, he was big and strong and I was fast and wiry, neither of us ever really got the upper hand and so we fell into this kind of truce that eventually turned into a sort of friendship. He comes over to us and passes me the joint he's been smoking.

Good shit that mate, have a pull, he offers.

I do and he's right, I get the head rush from the tobacco first and then the warm touch of the weed starts to take hold. My eyes thin and a smile spreads across my face.

Debbie and Kael are here. She's been out of the hospital for a month or so and those two got back together shortly after she got out. Their relationship is as turbulent as ever though, very binary. Fucking or fighting. They are doing the latter at the moment and Kael is standing up yelling some shit while Debbie sits quietly in a low arm chair, in tears, cradling a glass of something strong. Fucking or fighting.

Kael's mum found out about the baby last week and fucking lost it. He locked himself in his room and when he refused to open it, she threatened to kick in his door and smash up his room with a golf club. They might be fighting about that, or something else. No one really knows or cares. Everyone is so used to it now that we hardly even register it anymore. It's like familiar background noise. No one tries to intervene, someone even walking over to the stereo and turning up the volume. At one point Kael flips a small table over and storms out. An ashtray and a few glasses smash on the tiled floor and everyone steps back as he stalks through the conservatory punching walls as he goes. Andy tries to talk to him as he passes, but I grab his hand and tell him not to bother. There's no getting through to him when he's like this. We all go back to our drinks and smokes and Debbie storms upstairs in tears.

Like I said there's a horrible tension in the air and the argument has just added to that sense of unease. I'm about to call it quits and commit to the hour long walk back to mine when one of the Westwood lads comes running into the conservatory. He's waving his arms about and talking in a loud animated fashion. I grab his shoulder as he passes and he turns to face me.

It's Kael, he says.

I run out onto the common. There's a big patch of land behind the back gardens of the terraced houses. It's all grass, still damp with dew, a few trees dotted about. I see Kael and his brother Tony a few metres away, hear a few angry shouts on the air and start to run over to them. Tony is at the base of a large tree, its branches nearly bare, a few stubborn leaves still clinging to it, and I notice Kael half way up, standing on a thick low hanging branch, shouting down at his brother. I jog over, calling out to them but neither turns. As I get closer I notice that Kael has got a leather belt tied around one of the tree branches and the other end looped around his neck. His twin brother Tony is trying to grabs his legs, yelling at him to get down.

Leave me the fuck alone, yells Kael, a wild look in his grey eyes, his blonde hair greasy and plastered to his forehead.

Kael, what the fuck are you doing mate? I call out as I approach the tree. He's about a metre up, his feet jammed into the space where two huge branches conjoin, his right arm around a thick branch, his other on the belt looped about his neck.

Who fucking told you to get involved? He yells, pointing an accusatory finger in my direction. Tony turns to face me slowly shaking his head from side to side, a look of defeat on his face. I give him a nod.

Come on mate, I plead, why don't you get out of the tree?

Who are you to tell me what the fuck I can do? Just fuck off and leave me alone, he retorts.

Tony gets a hold of one of his legs and Kael starts thrashing about violently, kicking and cursing. Tony gets a boot to the face and head a few times, but he doesn't let go.

It was the middle of another long summer holiday. Everyone's parents were at work and we were in Tom's kitchen smoking cigarettes and talking about girls, the back door wide open, a warm breeze blowing through the house. Tom had set up a dart board in the kitchen, but we had long since given up on the game and were now just fucking about with the darts, tossing them into cereal packets and letting them drop into the rubbery linoleum floor. Kael and Debbie had broken up again and we were happy to be able to hang out with our friend again.

Mate remember when you threw that dart into Gabriel's ankle, I said to my brother laughing.

Yes mate, he chuckled, the look on his face, standing there with that fucking thing sticking out of him.

I know mate, I replied giggling, bet it really fuckin killed.

Yeah mate, can't believe he didn't cry... screamed like a baby though, he added.

Fuckin pussy, grinned Kael.

I dunno mate, I said, looked really nasty.

It's just a dart, continued Kael, turning one over in his left hand, flicking a finger tip over the sharp point.

I can chuck one into *your* ankle too mate if you want, teased Hardy.

Alright mate, do it, challenged Kael.

Hardy faked throwing the dart, a big grin on his chops, but Kael didn't flinch. We all laughed.

Kei mate, bet you can't stick that dart in my hand, he continued.

Come on mate, I implored, let's fucking stop with the dart shit alright.

What's wrong mate, you too pussy to? I smiled at that, shaking my head, shrugging it off.

Come on mate, bet you can't, Kael continued to goad.

I picked up one of the darts and Kael splayed out his left hand on the kitchen table.

Fuckin go on then mate, he urged me.

I walked over and placed the dart on his hand between his thumb and index finger, in that soft fleshy area of skin and muscle. I looked him in the eye and he stared back.

What are you waiting for mate, fucking do it, he commanded.

I applied a small amount of pressure, the point of the dart pushing into his flesh.

Come on mate, he continued, don't be a fucking pussy.

I pushed harder, the sharp end of the dart now digging into his skin, a small bead of blood appearing near the tip.

Fucking stab it in, he spoke between gritted teeth, his right hand clenched, nostrils flaring.

I leant forward, placing my weight on the dart and I felt a pop as the dart punctured his hand, the point slipping through his flesh and into the kitchen table.

He looked at me, a half smile on his face, a tear working its way down his left cheek.

Get out of the fucking tree Kael, his brother is yelling.

I can see tears welling up in his eyes, a hint of desperation creeping into his voice. Kael kicks at him a few more times then jumps. The belt goes tight around his neck and for a few seconds he is hanging and choking, the full weight of his body on that old leather belt. Tony heaves him up, gripping one of his lower legs and releases some of the tension around his neck. Kael is kicking and yelling, but also gripping at the belt and his neck, now trying to release the buckle. I help Tony by grabbing Kael's other leg and we both lift him up, taking all of his weight on our shoulders. I get kicked in the chest and a knee smashes into my nose and it starts to bleed.

A knife? I shout to Tony.

What? he replies.

Have you got a fucking knife? I repeat.

Jacket pocket, he yells, trying to hold his brother still.

This teenage boy he shared his mother's womb with for nine months. This boy that crept into his room one early morning and shaved off his eyebrows before his first year school photograph. This brother that jumped in and got his face smashed in by some older kids down at the grange so that he himself could escape a beating. This man that hugged him when their dad was admitted to hospital for heart surgery. This bloke who is now hanging by his neck from a tree on a disused plot of land below a low autumn sky.

I let go of Kael with my right hand and search Tony's pockets for the knife. I find it and pull it free. It's a large flick knife with a wooden handle, inlaid with gold. It's the knife I used to carry, the one I pulled on Liam outside the community centre on that cold night. It's heavy and cold in my palm. I signal to Tony that I'm going to let go of Kael's other leg. He gives me a nod and I let go. Tony gets another boot to the head, Kael screaming now.

I'm going to fucking kill both of you cunts, I'll kick your fucking heads in.

I slide the knife into my jeans pocket and start climbing the tree from the other side. Kael tries to turn his head to see what going on but doesn't have any room to move. His arms are free but he can't reach behind his head. I reach the belt, push the knife into the loop wrapped around the tree and start to saw. The knife is sharp and I quickly cut through the soft leather. There is a snap and Kael slips

301

from the tree, his head striking the trunk on the way down, landing on his back in the muddy patch of grass in front of his brother. He immediately springs up and starts swinging punches at Tony. Tony doesn't fight back. He puts his hands up in front of his face, dodging the punches that he can, while all the time trying to talk his brother down. I approach them with my arms out, pleading with Kael to stop.

Kael, he was helping you mate, he's your fucking brother, I call out, what the fuck are you doing? My shouts echoing around the rows of red brick houses lining the wide empty patch of wasteland.

Kael, go home, you've fucking lost it, sniffs Tony through the tears and blood.

His face is scratched and bruised, his eyes watery, arms held up limply in front of him, still defending himself from his brother's onslaught. Kael is yelling and crying. Tears are streaming down his freckled cheeks, blood and sweat matting his hair, a wide purple contusion around his neck, just below his unshaven chin.

I'm going to fucking kill you both, kill you both, he mutters

He can hardly speak and with each word, he breathes in sharply. He tears at his hair and walks in circles. At one point he turns towards me and I back off slowly with my hands out in front of me. The knife is still in my left hand and I back away slowly.

You gonna fucking stab me mate, fucking go on then, he screams at me thumping his chest and spitting.

Mate, it's alright, nothing is going to happen, you are alright mate. I drop the knife behind me and put my hand into my pocket, pulling out a crumpled packet of cigarettes.

Have a fag mate and calm down, I say offering him the packet. He sniffs and wipes his eyes, his gaze flicking briefly down to the cigarettes, turning between me and Tony.

Your brother loves you mate, I try in vain to reassure him, he's on your side.

He pulls at his hair and lets out a cry. It's a desperate sound that reaches into me and pulls at something deep within. It's a cry of exorcism and of penitence, the last gasp of a man struggling with something that burns from within. I see the struggle in his grey eyes, the hopelessness of his condition. I desperately want to reach out and hold him, to tell my friend that I understand, that I can help, that whatever it is that is gorging on his soul can be excised.

I realise at that moment that this isn't some childish call for help, or a desperate act by an angst ridden teenager, no this is self destruction. This is the end game. This is real and it terrifies me. It terrifies his brother too. I can see it in his eyes. He looks worn out, defeated. His long hair hangs about his face in thick curls and his eyes are set in a hard stare. He is bloodied and broken. None of us speak, a cold wind sweeping across the common, flattening the grass, whipping my long greasy hair across my face. A couple of other people have ventured out of the house and onto that wide patch of land to get a glimpse of what's going on, beers in hand, jackets pulled around them. They stand motionless on the fringes, their presence amplifying the heavy silence. Tony turns and motions them away with a wave of his hand, but they stay, transfixed as we all are by this moment. I can feel the moisture from the grass beginning to seep into my trainers, the cold touch of yesterday's rain somehow now even finding me.

Kael raises his head to look at his brother and slowly shakes his head. Tony stares back at him, still and stoic. Kael turns to me, his grey eyes unfocused, his gaze fixed on something that lurks on the periphery, cheeks still wet with tears, then he turns and walks away.

Tony desperately calls after his brother, come back inside mate, have a joint and chill out.

Kael stops briefly and barely turning his head replies.

I'm sorry, he says, before walking off towards the main road where I eventually lose sight of him behind a row of trees. I decide to start walking after him, but Tony holds me back.

No, he tells me.

We both flop down exhausted on the grass and I lean back and stare up into the sky. It's wide and grey and dark, typical fucking English weather. As a young child I used to think the movement of the clouds was caused by the rotation of the earth. I had in my head an image that the sky was static, somehow held in place and that we were spinning below it. One day my father explained to me that it was the clouds that were moving and not us.

I'm sitting in my parent's dining room. It's 1983 and I'm sitting at my parents dining table. It's a big round polished wooden table with four ornate, yet sturdy legs. It can be lengthened with a crank and an extension slotted into the middle so that more people can be accommodated (something that only usually happens at Christmas when we have a lot of friends and family over). I rub my hand over the table's surface. I remember all of the knots and imperfections in the wood. I have sat at this table a thousand times. There is a large iron crank that runs through its centre and when I was smaller I would often disappear under the table and hang from this solid metal rod. It always smelled of oil and had the bitter tang of iron to it. I would hang upside down and do backwards somersaults from it as the adults drank wine and discussed grown up things. I loved being under there, under the table cloth, hanging from that bar watching the adult's legs cross and uncross, ladies shoes flicked off and put back on. Nothing could touch me under there. Nothing could get me.

My dad is sitting opposite me and my mum is hovering about in the kitchen, doing a bit of tidying up. My dad is looking over my ID again and trying to figure out what to do. He is smoking a cigar and he glances over at me and shakes his head.

I feel like I've met you before, young man he starts... perhaps, his brow crinkles and he takes another drag...did you used to work at The Development Corporation a few years ago? Is that how you got all this information about my family, about my son. His voice raises slightly as he says those last few words, and my mum comes into the doorway and looks on anxiously.

I glance up at my mum's concerned face and then back at my dad.

305

Look, I say, I didn't really want to show either of you this because I was worried that it might scare you, but I don't think I have any choice.

My dad sits upright in his chair and takes the cigar slowly from his mouth as I reach into my pocket.

My mum looks a little concerned, so I hold my hands out flat for a moment, palms down to reassure her.

It's alright m... Veronica, I say, trying to speak as softly and reassuringly as possible, It's just a phone.

A what? questions my dad.

Don't worry you'll see, I say.

I reach back down into my pocket and take my phone out, laying it face up on the table. Immediately as I place it down the lock screen comes up displaying the time and the wallpaper I have set. It's a picture of my son on his first day of middle school. He is smiling and his light brown hair is chin length, hanging about his smiling, tanned face.

My mother looks shocked and my dad just stares in wonder. He looks up at me and his lips part briefly, before shutting again, he looks over his shoulder at my mum who has moved closer and is now standing, mouth open behind my dad, one hand absent mindedly massaging his left shoulder.

What...what is that? enquires my dad, placing the half smoked cigar in the big glass ashtray in front of him.

Some sort of portable telly? You said you were from Japan, so I imagine it's..it's just..i've never seen anything like it.

I slide it the short distance across the table to him and he picks it up, turning it over slowly in his hands.

It's heavy, he says although not really to anyone.

306

He looks up at me, what do I do? he asks.

Touch the screen, I answer, gesturing with my right finger.

He hesitates for a moment, turning again to my mum, then places his hand on the screen.

The display comes to life and he starts a little.

He looks over at me.

Who is this boy? he asks peering closely at the screen, he looks...

That's your grandson dad, I reply.

DAD

Me and Hardy get home from school at about four and I realise I don't have a key. It's autumn and there are big piles of crunchy leaves on all the pavements, that familiar smell of winter on the air. Christmas is just round the corner and everyone has got that end of term feeling. It's cold and I don't really fancy the thought of waiting outside till mum gets back so that we can get in the house. Dad should be in, and the car is in the drive, but when we ring the bell there is no answer. Dad is off work again for a couple of weeks.

We head up to the garage for a smoke and talk about the day at school. Hardy is seeing this new bird in his year. Her name is Tracy and she's really nice. Hardy seems to be really into her. She's petite and pretty and her family just moved down to The Borough from Scotland. Her dad works for the unions so my old man is pretty happy about it all.

My Dad works of course, but he also puts a lot of time into his role as a local labour councillor. At election time he used to drag us out and make us deliver leaflets door to door in the local area, while he went canvassing for the party. He is very politically active. Years ago he went on a three day fast at the town hall in the city centre to raise awareness and money for the people starving in the

Ethiopian famine. We went down after school to see him every day with mum. He looked tired pale and emaciated but full of drive and enthusiasm. He has always been incredibly strong minded and selfless. I have never really known him and mum to fight, but recently something has been going on. He drinks a lot, and when he's pissed does a lot of stupid shit. He runs out into the street in front of the house, shouting at cars that drive too fast, or gets into awkward conversations with our friends. I love the old bugger, but I wish he would stop with the booze, not that I'm really one to preach.

A few weeks ago when he was supposed to have knocked it on the head, Hardy found a bottle of gin hidden in the toilet cistern and stormed out into the back garden to confront him, hurling the bottle against the fence and smashing it. I watched Hardy shout and cry through the kitchen window while my dad sat in a deck chair, his long beard and grey hair in an unkempt mess, stub of a cigar between those thin lips, trying to placate his youngest son.

We finish smoking and head back towards the house, hands shoved into our pockets. The house is dark and quiet. I see the cat rubbing his body up against the double doors at the back but other than that it seems empty. We try a few of the windows, including the one at the end of the kitchen, but none of them are open. It's really cold, the wind biting at my ears, my nose running a little and I need a piss. I look around and see a big garden shovel leaning up against the kitchen wall, my mum is putting in a new flower bed at the bottom of the garden near the garage. I pick it up.

What do you reckon mate? I ask Hardy.

I reckon we should do it mate, he replies smiling, mum might not be back for two hours and I'm getting hungry, there's some sausages in the freezer.

The kitchen window opens out on hinges, unlike the rest of the windows in the house that slide upwards on sashes. There is a gap between the window and the frame with just enough space to get the shovel tip into. I push the shovel into the gap and try to lever it open. It bends in its frame slightly but doesn't budge.

Let me have a go mate, insists Hardy, taking the shovel from me.

He forces it back into the gap, and with all his strength levers the window away from its frame. There is a crunch, as the latch inside is ripped from its housing and the window pops open and hangs limply on its hinges, swinging slowly back and forth.

Fuck me, I exclaim, mum is going to kill us.

Hardy holds the window open with his hand and I climb through the small gap and into the kitchen. It's dark and smells vaguely of cigar smoke and fried food. Hardy climbs through after me giggling.

Think the window's fucked mate, he says, dropping down onto the hard tiled kitchen floor.

I pull the window closed after him and look at the damage. The latch has been ripped out of the frame, splitting the wood across the bottom and one of hinges pulled nearly from its housing, the thread on the silver screws clearly visible.

Reckon we'll have to replace the whole fucking window mate, I say.

Shit, he answers, still at least we are inside. You hungry?

I go into the freezer and get out the bag of Waitrose frozen sausages.

We all used to go shopping together in Waitrose on a Thursday evening. Dad would drive us all into the orange lit multi storey car park in the big beige Volvo estate, always parking on the second level so that we could walk straight through to the shops. One of us would get to push the trolley and mum and dad would guide us around the aisles picking products from the shelves and putting them in, occasionally chastising us for riding the trolley like a scooter. We were allowed to get a packet of boiled sweets each and we would usually go for either Foxes Glacier Fruits or Glacier Mints. They were hard oval sweets individually wrapped in clear plastic. Hardy would scoff most of his in a couple of days, but I was always much more frugal and would still have a few red or black ones left in the top drawer of the dresser in my bedroom the following week.

Dad would pay for the week's shopping, usually about thirty quid, and we would pack it into a big cardboard box to be taken down to the pick up area so that we could load it all into the car and go home. Dad would always cook something really nice for us on a Thursdays like fish fingers and chips or masses of sausages and fried potato, once we had helped him unpack the food, and we would all sit in the living room and watch Star Trek on telly while we ate our dinners and talked. We would tease dad for asking obvious questions about that week's episode, and he would pretend to get cross and everyone would laugh.

311

We would go up one by one for a bath, Luka going last as he's the oldest, before getting into clean pyjamas, under fresh sheets and reading our books in the dim light of our bedside lamps. Dad or mum would come in later, give us a kiss and turn off the lights, dad's breath always smelling of cigar smoke and coffee. I would fall asleep to the soft low melody of my parents voices in the room below me and dream of spaceships and girls.

There are about ten sausages in the bag, but they are meaty bastards so we decide to cook six. There are some beans in the cupboard and Hardy turns on two of the electric hobs and gets a couple of pans off the shelf. There is a knack to cooking sausages from frozen. If you whack them in a pan that's too hot then they burn on the outside while still being cold on the inside and that is fucking horrible. You have to cook them for five or so minutes first in a relatively cool pan, and once they are fully defrosted then you can bang up the heat to get that nice crispy brown outside.

The beans are bubbling away (we both like them a bit over cooked) and the smell of frying sausages is making my stomach rumble. It's cold in the kitchen so I sit down at the far end next to the window that looks out onto the frosty garden, the trees bare of their leaves, a few birds pecking at the hard earth, my back pressed up against the radiator waiting for Hardy to finish cooking the sausages. He's prodding at them with a fork and they sizzle as the oil leaks out of them and into the hot pan.

Our current oven is quite new, my parents had to buy it after Hardy left a pizza in the old one for about an hour and the whole thing set alight. We ripped its burnt carcass out of the wall once it was cool enough to touch, and threw it out into the snow.

The beans and sausages are done. The sausages have turned a beautiful golden brown and the beans congealed into a sloppy orange mass, just the way I like them. I grab a couple of plates and Hardy dishes up. Three sausages and a big blob of beans each.

We grab some cutlery from the drawer and are about to tuck in, standing up against the work surface when dad walks in.

His long grey hair is a mess, tied behind his head in a short pony tail. His eyes are glassy and half closed and I can smell the booze on his breath. He's wearing a grey jumper with a Lowry scene on it, it's the only thing I ever see him wearing anymore.

Back from school boys? He slurs slightly.

Yeah we tried to knock but no one answered.

Yes sorry I was in the lav, he replies smacking his lips and looking at the food on out plates.

Have you made any for me? He asks.

No, says Hardy rather bluntly, thought you were out.

It's alright I'll just have a bit of your sausage, he says reaching for my plate. Hardy pushes it away.

Make your own, he spits.

Dad looks at him briefly as though he's going to say something but doesn't.

Make sure you put the plates in the dishwasher after you finish, he finally says in a somewhat accusatory tone, I'm not cleaning up after you.

You never do anyway, I accuse, and as soon as the words leave my mouth I regret it. I grimace a bit and Hardy gives me a look. It's the kind of look that only people who live daily with a certain situation can give or understand.

Dad looks weak and defeated, but I've had enough of his shit recently. I feel a twinge of pity.

It's late summer, the sun sinking below the trees that line the far side of the river, the smell of cut grass and the salty tang of sweat on my top lip. We are kicking a ball about in front of the old wooden goal posts, the white paint peeling from the wood. He runs about energetically trying to tackle us, the last half of a lit cigar hanging from his lips, sleeves rolled up over skinny wrists and long black hair slick against his high forehead. We clamber over the small broken wire fence as the sun sets and a cool breeze blows the dust into our eyes. We wander home, hair wet with sweat and knees stained with grass. He lifts me onto his shoulders and we all stroll back up the hill in the twilight, talking and laughing, muscles aching and stomachs rumbling.

His mouth is set in a thin line and his eyes look vacant and dart about as if trying to find a focus.

Like I said, I'm not bloody cleaning up all your mess, he grumbles.

We will eat in the fucking garage then, Hardy bites back, picking up his plate.

You do that then, announces dad.

Yeah mate, I agree, let's fucking go, I say.

It's freezing cold up there, says dad.

Don't care, replies Hardy, and we both pick up our plates, open the back door and walk back out into the winter evening.

Do what you bloody w... he starts to shout but Hardy kicks the door shut and we don't hear him finish.

We walk up to the garage, both with a tepid plate of sausages and beans, and sit up in that cool dark brick room eating in silence as the sun finally dips below the horizon and the darkness creeps slowly in.

WE THE ETERNAL

Christmas Eve in the Fox and Hounds and everyone is a good five pints in. They are playing the usual shitty Christmas music, Slade, Cliff Richard and such like, John Lennon being the only saving grace. There's a juke box up against a wall and we keep pumping twenty pence coins into it so we can hear something a bit less shit.

The place is rammed, lots of blokes from my year, Eli, Marko, Ethan, both of the Marks, James, Blake and most of the girls from my year. 'Her', Becky, Kyra, and Millie and Christine. Everyone fancies Christine and Millie. Back in the third year we all used to hang around the tennis courts at school to watch them play in the evening. Christine would always wear a short skirt over blue tennis shorts. She would keep tennis balls tucked into those tight shorts and we would look on in awe every time she pulled one out to serve, exposing a bit of thigh. Millie is cool, a bit of an indie girl and likes the same music as me. She's got beautiful dark features and long black hair that always hangs over half of her pale face. I have completely failed to get off with her at least twice.

I'm talking to Kyra and 'Her' and smoking one of the fags from a pack Tom brought back from Greece. These fuckers are strong and don't have any filters. Even the smokers in the pub complain about the smell of the things. I like them. 'She' looks amazing, rosy cheeked and a bit tipsy, blonde hair tied up behind her head in a loose bun. She has on a baggy wool sweater and jeans. She glances over from where she stands leaning up against the bar and smiles. I grin back.

My older brother Luka and lots of blokes from his year are also here. I love Luka. He is rapidly becoming an extremely accomplished guitarist and is probably the cleverest bloke in the pub. He's in his first year at Leeds University, doing astro physics. It's the same University and department that Brian May from Queen attended. I'm planning to go up and see him next year when I've finished school, chat up some college birds and get pissed in the student union.

His band played their first ever gig down at the embankment in the summer and it was fucking wicked, really loud punk and hardcore. The lead singer John wore the t-shirt I painted and we moshed in the open air and drank vodka from the bottle, then sat around on the grass in front of the stage and got stoned, pulling on sweaters as the sun set. My grandma went to see the gig too. It was really odd seeing a seventy year old working class woman with a blue rinse sitting in a field, watching a hardcore band while masses of unwashed teenagers danced and headbanged around her. Still she said she had a good time.

Luka is at the bar, so I signal to him to get me a pint and he mouths 'ok'. His hair is long, blonde and curly, tied behind his head in a pony tail and he has a pair of round framed gold spectacles perched on his nose.

When we were much younger he and I used to fight a lot. He would always win, being much bigger than me and two years my senior. We would punch and wrestle until he got me in a headlock or found some other way to restrain me and tell me that if I stopped struggling then he would let me go. I would never give up. I would keep struggling until my arm or leg was screaming out in pain, and still I wouldn't back down. Even when the pain forced me to tears, I would keep up and eventually he would take pity on me and let me go.

We once had a massive fight in the living room over something or other and I got so angry that I threw a heavy metal toy tank at his head. Luckily the thing missed him and instead went through the living room window, smashing through it and leaving a jagged foot wide hole in the centre. Let's just say that my mum was not at all pleased. Not only because I had tried to kill my older brother, but also because most of the windows in the house were still of the original handmade glass, uneven and filled with imperfections. I don't remember what punishment I received, but I hope it was harsh.

The older we get, the closer we become and I imagine that in the future Luka will be the one of us with three kids, a wife, a mortgage and a steady job.

I'm standing at the end of the bar, chatting away to Kyra and 'Her'. There are so many people here that it's going to be impossible to talk to everyone. It's a wonderful feeling to be half drunk and surrounded by all of your friends, all the people you love.

Can't believe you two the other night, I remark to Kyra, nudging her playfully with my elbow.

Me neither, she answers, picking at her short fringe, I never do stuff like that, a huge smile spreading across her face.

I thought you were going to chicken out, I grin, sorry I didn't come along with you, I tell her, taking a few swigs of my beer. Another horrible Christmas song comes on and a group of kids from the year below me push past us to get to the bar.

It's fine she replies, moving aside to let them in, it was really good fun actually, a bit of an adventure to be honest.

Best night I've had for a long time, 'She' agrees, grinning.

Me and Kyra were both at 'Her's' a couple of nights ago, just hanging out and chatting. We were bored and I suggested we all get stoned. The problem was we didn't have anything to smoke and it was getting late. I jokingly proposed that we go to Kael's old dealer on Gladstone street and try and get hold of something.

Now Gladstone street is a bit of a dodgy area on the other side of town, and we tend to stay away unless we want to score, or buy fireworks from one of the corner shops over there. Kael's old dealer is a bloke called Stony. He's a big Rasta dude with lots of dreadlocks and a nose ring. He's pretty chilled, but Kael says he's a scary cunt, up to all sorts of shady shit apparently. He lives in a house with a few other dodgy looking fuckers, and Kael reckons the house is being watched by the pigs.

319

To my surprise the girls were up for going, even seemed excited at the prospect. I half heartedly tried to talk them out of it, but they were restless and up for doing something stupid. I gave 'Her' a tenner and asked if they wanted me to go. They gave me some bollocks about it being a girls only night, and said they would be fine. I phoned Kael's house and got the address from his brother, Kael was out, then the girls threw on their coats, bundled out of the door, full of excitement and giggling nervously, and off into the cold night they went.

Be careful, I called after them and they shouted back.

We'll be fine, don't worry.

I waited in the house for a good hour and a half. 'Her' mum was out, so I was the only one there. I pottered about for a bit and made myself some toast, turned on the telly and flicked through the channels. There was nothing on so I turned it off and went out into the back garden for a smoke.

I love being in 'Her' house. It always feels so full of life and moments of being. Some houses are sterile and cold, but this one has a soul and a texture to it, some essence imbued in it from the lives lived within, the smell of home cooked food, the clutter in the living room, the half empty bottles of French booze up on the shelf. I love sitting upstairs on 'Her' bed, shoulder to shoulder, talking aimlessly into the evening in that way best friends do, in a bubble of shared understanding and intimacy. I am always so close to kissing her, but never have the nerve.

I have kissed a lot of girls in my time and done a lot more, but this is different. It is different because I actually like her. It scares me. The potential of something happening is enough for me. The idea that I am on the cusp of happiness gives me a feeling of control, but it's a fragile control and a single misstep could send the whole thing plummeting to the depths, and so this has become my routine. We talk and get close, I put my arm round her and we hold each other, but we've never kissed. Once we were on the sofa in her living room, my body pressed against hers, our lips just centimetres apart. I could feel her breath on my face and smell the earthy scent of her blonde hair. I was looking into her blue eyes and we were whispering to each other. I was about to lean in and kiss her when the front door opened and in came her mum. We immediately sat up straight on the sofa, 'Her' rearranging her hair quickly with her fingers and me trying to hide the bulge in my trousers.

That was the closest we ever came, and on those nights when sleep doesn't find me I often close my eyes, and in the dark repository of my own imagination I transport myself back there, our lips touch and we kiss as the trees outside the open window rustle and sway in the wind.

So I was sitting on the sofa reading an old copy of cosmopolitan when I heard keys in the front door and laughing and excited chatter outside. The door swung open and in fell 'Her' and Kyra, cold air still clinging to them, rosy cheeked and giggling excitedly.

Welcome back ladies, I said as 'She' reached into her jeans pocket and produced a small bag of weed.

Ta da, she called out theatrically as I took it off her hands and examined it closely. It looked good. Nice and green with full buds.

They were both chatting away, happily recounting their adventure to each other. I tried to listen, to understand what went on, but they were speaking too fast and interrupting each other as one anecdote quickly led into another. In the end I only caught glimpses of the full picture.

Kyra was too scared to knock, giggled 'Her'.

I wasn't, I just didn't know if it was the right house, and your voice ...excuse me but we are friends of Kael.

Kyra burst out laughing at her impression and both girls span around clutching each other by the wrists and collapsed in a heap on the sofa, sighing and wiping long hair away from their faces. I was feeling a bit left out, like someone turning up to a party when everyone else was already drunk.

Let's get stoned, said 'Her' in her best impersonation of me and we all sat down and talked about the night, while I skinned up a massive joint on the cover of the magazine I had been reading, Cindy Crawford eyeing me longingly through the mess of rolling papers and discarded tobacco.

Becky and Kirsten come over to join us too, drinks in hand.

What the fuck is that? I ask, pointing at Kirsten's drink as she wobbles over.

I don't know actually, she answers drunkenly, swaying a bit from side to side, Mark bought it for me, it's awfully strong.

She gives Kyra a kiss on the cheek.

322

Scored any more drugs recently dear? She asks giggling and we all laugh. Dancing Queen by ABBA comes on the juke box and Becky squeals excitedly.

Ohh I love this song, she shouts grabbing me by the arm and pretending to dance.

The pub is getting really full now and the bar is packed. All around me I can hear familiar voices and as people I know walk by I give them a nod, a shake of the hand or a hug. The windows are steamed up and the air is thick with cigarette smoke. A couple of blokes from the year above me push past, raising their chins in greeting as they do.

Gabriel here? I ask.

Yeah, he's over by the bar mate, with Sally, replies one of them, both hands raised above the crowd carefully carrying two very full pints of lager.

Cheers, I reply as they disappear into the crowd.

Want a proper fag? I ask Becky holding out the packet.

No thanks, those things smell horrible, she replies and takes her own packet of silk cut out of her pocket. I offer her a light and she grins at me.

I catch Eli's eye from the other side of the room and he and Marko start moving over, slowly weaving their way through the drunken crowd. Eli has on a Santa hat and the white wool cardigan he always wears.

Kirsten taps Becky on the shoulder and gives her a wink.

Eli's coming over, she teases.

Yeah, I would definitely shag him, says Becky putting on a bloke's voice and grinding her hips.

323

Lovely, laughs Kirsten steadying herself on her friend's shoulder.

The two lads reach our little group and tap their glasses to ours in turn.

Cheers we all say in unison before taking large gulps of our drinks, Kirsten downing hers in one go to a round of applause.

You are going to be well pissed Kirsten, remarks Kyra.

I think I already am dear, replies Kirsten laughing.

Luka and a couple of blokes from his year manage to make their way over and we all get together for a group hug.

Merry fucking Christmas, wishes Eli patting my back with his hand, and we all reply 'Yeah Merry Christmas'.

My head is buried in my brother's shoulder as we hold onto each other tightly. I am drunk and ecstatically happy. It's still barely nine and the long winter holiday has just begun. The future and the sirens that lie sleeping in its fold remains shrouded and far off. My mind is on other things. I think of music and getting my eyebrow pierced, of a new guitar and my cat. I hold my friends close to me and we promise each other that we will remain like this forever. I tell each of them that I love them and they do the same. It is said with sincerity and heart, with a knowledge that this moment is fleeting and yet eternal. We cling to each other in the hope that this bond will never break, that this moment, this beautiful pure moment will never wither and fade to be lost in the dust of the years, and as we spill out of that pub and onto the frosty quiet streets, embracing one another and calling out to the night, we know that we will live on forever, never succumbing to the years or the bleak winters they hold.

THE BOROUGH

T he Crown to town is a pub crawl well known to anyone who has ever lived here in The Borough for a significant length of time. The Crown is the first pub on the crawl, hence the name and it's situated on a long road that winds its way into the city centre, past corner shops and markets owned by various immigrant families. There are about ten pubs situated along the route, and like I said the first is The Crown, a cozy little place with an open fire and leather sofas. It's pretty far from the city centre so we all get a taxi out there and meet in the pub at about six thirty; have to start early or we won't make it into town. We all clamber out of the taxi and into the warm embrace of the old boozer. It's not very busy and I see that Blake, Ethan and Valentine have already commandeered a few tables in the corner and a couple of sofas. I wander over to the bar and order three pints. Me, Eli and Marko have decided to do rounds and I've volunteered to go first. The bar man pours three pints of Fosters and puts them on a tray for me. Fosters might be as week as piss but we've still got another good nine pints to get through before we make it into town, so I don't want to go mental. A lot of the others are just doing half's, but we are going to be here for a while waiting for everyone to arrive. I put the tray down on the table and distribute the drinks, everyone giving me a 'cheers mate' as I do. It's Svensson's birthday and he is sitting back on one of the sofas with about six or seven drinks on the table in front of him, mostly shots of something or other.

I wish him a happy birthday.

Cheers lads, he says lifting one of his drinks and giving me a nod.

Let me know when you run out of booze mate and I'll get you a bevvy, I tell him.

Get in line mate, he chuckles, get in line.

I laugh and pull up a chair next to Blake and Ethan.

Should be a good one mate, states Blake pushing his glasses up his nose.

Yeah I reckon so old boy, I reply.

I take a big gulp of my beer, it's room temperature and a bit flat but then again Fosters always is.

Mate The Hardons are playing a gig in Leicester next month, we should go, remarks Blake.

The Hardons are an Australian hardcore band with loads of really catchy songs. I can't remember who introduced me to them, but I really like them. Their songs are really simple to play, usually only two or three chords, but they've got some great melodies.

Yeah mate, I reply, I'm in, just have to ask my mum and dad if it's alright.

I'm sure they'll say yes, he assures me, your parents are pretty sound.

I reckon he's going to be well pissed tonight mate, I tell him looking over as Svensson knocks back another Southern Comfort and lemonade to a round of applause and pats on the back.

Yeah I reckon we all are mate, replies Blake.

Half way through my first pint and Rachel, 'Her', Kirsten, Becky and Kyra walk in. I catch 'Her' eye as she comes through the heavy wooden door and she gives me a smile. They head over to the bar to order drinks and I spark up a cigarette and try to act nonchalant. James and the two Marks are the next to arrive. They've all got the red eyes and slight grins of blokes who have had a few joints before coming to the pub. I like to smoke as much as the next bloke, but I always save it till after a night out. I like to be sharp chatty and on the ball when I hit the beers, but nothing beats a nice joint at the end of the night after a skin full.

Our drinks are soon finished and someone announces it's time to head to the next pub, The Locomotive. Just as we are leaving, Millie and Christine wander in wanting a drink. Svensson tells them to wait till we get to the next boozer and so the whole lot of us pile out onto the street, birthday boy leading the way to the next pub. Everyone is chatting and laughing as we walk down Lincoln Road and I hang back for a moment to wait for 'Her'. We make small talk and I ask about her dad and brother. Kirsten comes over and joins us as we walk, and we chat about school and exams and stuff like that.

We enter the next pub and order more drinks, downing them quickly, keen to move on to the next boozer. The Locomotive is a bit too local for our tastes. Lots of old boys who live nearby enjoying a few pints. They all look a bit pissed off at the sight of a bunch of noisy teenagers coming into their boozer but their tired

328

eyes light up when they see the girls. There are a few comments muttered under breaths but we couldn't give less of a fuck. Who are these old cunts anyway?

Onto the next pub.

The thing with pub crawls is, keeping everyone together as a group gets gradually more and more difficult as people get more and more inebriated. Everyone drinks at different speeds and pretty soon half of us have finished our pints and want to move on, while the other half are still only half way through. This poses a problem. We either order another drink and hammer it down as fast as possible, or wait it out for ten minutes while everyone finishes. Of course we order another one.

Just a vodka and coke or something I can down fast mate, comes the order from Eli as Marko goes up to the bar to get the drinks in.

By now everyone else has finished their drinks, so we down the vodkas in one and again we are all back out onto the street. Everyone is three or four drinks in at this point, everyone except Svensson who must have already had about seven. Seems to be handling it pretty well though.

Svensson is a bloke from my year at school. He's big and tall and has a mess of long blonde hair. I think his mum is Swedish hence the name, which everyone manages to mispronounce. He's really into esoteric funk music and 70s soul. He was the first of us to learn to drive so everyone sponges off him for lifts everywhere. He doesn't seem to mind though. He's not much of a driver, but a great bloke.

Off to The Triangle now. It's a weird little pub smack bang in the middle of a busy triangular junction half way down Lincoln Road. We are all half lit and wander in laughing and joking. The pub is full of locals and there must be a hen night going on, lots of middle aged tarts in short skirts and too much make up, off their tits on white wine and sangria. As we walk in a few of them whistle and Eli gets his arse pinched. He turns and gives them a nod.

Alright ladies, he greets, and they all burst into laughter.

We sit down at one of the free tables next to a window and I go up to the bar to buy some drinks. We are done with beers now and it's time to move on to something stronger. Double vodkas and cokes all round I think.

Me and Eli are sitting opposite each other, an ashtray, a couple of lighters, and a couple of packs of cigarettes between us. He places his pack of cigarettes on one side of his table and mine on the other.

No no you don't understand mate, he slurs, my house is my house and my home is my home.

I nod grinning in understanding, my fag hanging loosely from my lip, right eye closed against the smoke.

He puts his left hand on one of the packs of smokes.

Now this is my house, he says then places his other hand on the other pack, and this... this is my home.

I nod again and start to chuckle.

I think I understand mate, but just explain the whole thing again, I say laughing.

Eli leans back in his chair, taking a drag from his cigarette, nearly tipping all the way back. Marko puts his left hand out and rights the chair.

Listen lads I've got a joke for you, I tell them.

Alright, tell us mate, they say dragging their chairs in.

So there's this elephant standing around in the jungle, I begin, and it's really fit, beautiful legs and trunk and shit.

Eli and Marko lean in already giggling in anticipation.

Now this mouse comes along, takes a look at the elephant and thinks I wouldn't mind shagging that.

Fucking mice, always well horny, chuckles Eli, and we all laugh.

So anyway the mouse walks up to the elephant and starts to crawl up its back leg, I continue, It gets closer to the elephant's fanny and this monkey up in the tree realises what's going on and starts to get a bit you know... excited.

Marko mimics a monkey having a wank and nearly knocks his vodka and coke over in the process.

Woah mate calm down, calm down, chides Eli standing up, drink in hand to avoid any spillage.

A bit goes on the table, but Marko manages to save most of it. Eli sits down and scoops the liquid off the table and onto the floor with the edge of a beer mat, then sits down again.

Soz mate, he grins, carry on.

So the mouse gets up there and he starts shagging this massive elephant with his tiny mouse cock. He's really fuckin going at it and the monkey up on the branch is getting really into it and he's shaking the tree as he...

Auditions the finger puppets, interrupts Marko and we all start laughing again.

Fuck, so the mouse is going at it, I go on, and the monkey is shaking this branch as he wanks furiously and

331

suddenly, bosh, a coconut falls off the tree and lands square on the fucking elephant's head. The elephant goes 'oooh ahhhh' and the mouse says… the mouse says, I'm already laughing at the punchline before I've said it and can't get it out.

Says fucking what? Implores Eli, what the fuck does the mouse say?

So the mouse says… yeah that's it bitch take it all in, I finally spit out.

We all start to laugh, deep belly laughs that you can't stop, that take away your ability to speak, those laughs that only come at a time in your life when you are young, naive and completely without inhibition.

After a minute or so the laughing dies down, and we take a few exploratory sips of our drinks, giggling and wiping our eyes. Eli grabs his vodka and coke and shouts out, down in one. We all grab our drinks and hammer them back.

Whose fucking round is it? I ask.

Fucked if I know mate, replies Marko but I'll get em in.

Me and Eli cheer and the tarts from the hen night look over. Funny, they look much better than they did when we first came in. Eli gives them a wink and one of them waves back.

After The Triangle there is a long walk to the next pub. It's a bit chilly so I grab my Benny hat out of my pocket and pull it over my head, tucking my long greasy hair behind my ears. There is still a lot of traffic on Lincoln Road, people finishing late on a Friday night and heading back home to their lazy wives, husbands and ungrateful children, or just keen to get to the local and start hammering back those beers with the lads.

We waltz into The Six Bells, arms around shoulders and singing, the cold air and the exercise making us twice as drunk as we were. There is a shitty disco going on in the pub, lights, DJ, the full fucking monty, and we are all in a party mood. We crowd around the bar and everyone orders drinks. I'm properly pissed now and so is everyone else. 'She' is at the end of the bar talking to Blake, her hand on his arm. She looks beautiful and I want nothing more than to go over and kiss her. Svensson is dancing away on the tiny dance floor to staying alive by the BeeGees and Millie quickly joins him, drink in hand.

I turn to talk to Eli but he is no longer there, so I take a big swig of my drink, (how did that get there?) and head over to the table where Mayhew and James are sitting, looking out over the chaos.

Not pissed yet lads? I ask as I approach.

Nah, replies Mayhew, had a few too many joints before we left the house so not really up for too many beers.

It's all good mate, I reply swaying slightly.

Mayhew has on a black leather biker jacket and James is wearing his blue Dinosaur Jr t shirt over a white long sleeve t-shirt. I look at them both sitting there, eyes red and half closed. The dance floor is full and they are playing 'All That She Wants' by 'Ace of Bass'. Eli loves this tune but I fucking hate it. Pop music, man, I can't be dealing with it.

Mayhew gets my attention with a nod of the head and mimics rolling a spliff with his right hand, head tilted towards the door of the pub, one eyebrow raised expectantly.

Nah mate cheers, I reply, half shouting over the noise and placing my pint down on the sticky table, feeling a bit pissed actually...

That last syllable reverberates in the space around me, deep and echoey like a shout into an empty room and for an instant I am aware of another layer to things, a vast hollow space just beyond the misty pub windows, a dark vista lying waiting at the fringes of my numbed senses, subduing everything under a blurry thickness.

This is a dream, I whisper quietly to myself.

What's that mate? Quizzes James leaning in.

Um... just once I uh... I remember when we were in France, I answer, focusing my eyes.

When you were little yeah, nods Mayhew, joining in.

Yeah mate, I continue, shaking my head to clear it, well once we were in this tiny village down south called Bize or something, and we had this really long dinner, it was like ten courses or something, you know what the french are like?

Yeah man yeah, comes the reply from Mayhew.

So we finish dinner and we are walking back to the car park, fuck I must have been seven or eight or something and I suddenly had this feeling that I was in a dream.

What do you mean? Enquires James, wrinkling his brow.

Dunno mate, I reply, just like I wasn't really there, it's um hard to explain, but it felt really weird. I told my mum and she told me to sit down for a bit and the feeling soon passed...

The music has stopped briefly and there is a moment of almost complete silence. My voice suddenly sounds loud and intrusive and people seem frozen in time. I look at Svensson and Millie on the dance floor, hands raised high in the air, Svensson's blonde hair aflame from the lights of the disco. Eli, Marko and Jacobs are at the bar in conversation, Marko's mouth is wide open, his big white teeth exposed in a huge grin. 'Her' and Blake are deep in conversation, her keen eyes glued to his, her shapely legs tucked neatly below the bar stool. Becky, Kirsten, and Kyra are on the edge of the dance floor. Becky has her arm around Kirsten's neck and Kirsten's mouth is wide open in a laugh, Kyra smiling broadly, fag in one hand and gin and tonic in the other. Christine and Stuee and a few other people are waiting to get served at the bar, Stuee has his arm raised, but the barman is at the till, placing a handful of fivers into the tray. The place has a dream like quality to it, the air feels soupy and thick.

Time will take all of this and chip away at it until there is barely anything left. The words spoken, the things felt and learnt will mostly be lost, and those that remain will be twisted and unrecognisable or simply so decayed, that like ancient texts scratched into clay they will no longer be of any use. The dull seemingly meaningless aspects of the world I now inhabit will one day be shaped into things of beauty by the deft fingers of time. The ghosts of our past and the melodies of things once so prosaic will burst into symphonies once they are lost. If only I knew this, if only I could see the import of it all, then I could perhaps capture it, hold onto it a little longer, scribble the words spoken, sketch the faces of the beautiful people that surround me onto a scrap of paper that will reside yellow and fading in that shoe box along with all the other relics of this moment. Age transforms us into archaeologists of our own lives, desperately digging into memories to uncover those treasures lost beneath the dust of the years, things once beautiful and pristine but now damaged and worn away to almost nothing.

I push my hand through my hair in a desperate attempt to cling on to something real, something tangible and take a big drag on my fag to clear my head. It sharpens me up a bit but I need some fresh air. I apologise to James and Mayhew and push through the crowd, through the pub door and out into the cold crisp night.

The heavy pub door swings shut behind me, muting the loud pop music to an indistinct thump thump thump. I pull my coat around my skinny frame. The fag in my mouth has been smoked almost down to the filter, so I flick it into the drain and dig through my pockets for another. I pull out the box of Embassy number ones, but it's empty. There is a Shell garage just down the road, a stark, bright, beacon of light amongst the orange street lights, so I decide to have a wander down and let my head clear.

It's horrible and bright in the garage as I enter, classical muzak playing over the speakers set in the ceiling, and I realise how drunk I really am. I wander up to the counter and ask for a packet of Embassy, swaying a bit on unsteady legs, my tongue feeling swollen and unwieldly as I speak. The bloke tells me they don't have any so I settle for twenty B and H. I pay the bloke and get out of there as quickly as possible. I walk back down Lincoln Road, coat pulled tight around me and stumble into the warm yellow heart of The Wheatsheef pub, the last stop before we enter town. There's a local rock band playing on the small stage. They are doing covers of popular seventies rock tunes and they don't seem half bad. Eli spots me entering the boozer and waves me over. I waltz over to the bar and he hands me a Southern Comfort and lemonade. We clink glasses. Cheers mate, I say.

Yeah cheers old boy, he replies.

Eli is just as hammered as me and his speech has started to slur. Everything has become indistinct and amorphous, my warm heart solid and obvious in my chest, the passage of time skipping and stunted.

I fucking love you mate, I say to him.

He smiles, yeah me too old boy, he tells me, giving me a brief hug.

I think our band are going to be famous mate, he grins, we are going to be on The Word and play the Reading festival and shag loads of birds.

You reckon so? I ask.

Of course mate, you're a wicked song writer an we fuckin rock mate. He mimes playing his bass and I copy him.

Fuck mate we've got to do more gigs, I tell him, The Luckyleaf is good n' all but we've got to get more exposure if you know what I mean.

Yeah mate, he replies, I reckon we could do with a female back up singer too.

Yeah I reckon that would be wicked, but has to be someone fit, I add, and we both laugh

Of course mate, he replies, gesturing for a fag.

I pull the new packet from the left leg of my trousers, tear off the cellophane and tease two pristine ciggies out of the packet, handing one to him.

How about Millie, he suggests as he lights it, pointing over to her and Christine standing at the bar drinking shots of what looks like tequila.

Reckon she can sing? I ask.

Dunno mate, he answers, but we can ask her, she's cool too and would probably fit right in.

Let's ask her then mate. I reply as we touch glasses.

Cheers mate, we say in unison, before downing our drinks and yelling out into the crowded pub.

Eli nudges my shoulder and points up to the stage.

Look at these old fuckers, he says, we are much better than them.

Fucking right we are mate, we should be up there playing, I reply, tucking my long hair behind my ears.

The band finish their set and it's getting towards closing time. The bell for last orders just rang and there is a last minute rush to the bar for more drinks. Svensson is well wasted and stands unsteadily, one elbow on the bar, a line of shots in front of him. Ethan and Valentine are beside him, egging him on. He's going to feel rough tomorrow I reckon.

The band are unplugging amps and putting away equipment when Eli approaches the stage and gets the singer's attention.

Oy mate, he calls and the bloke turns to him.

Yeah good gig mate, Eli tells him.

Cheers mate, replies the singer.

He must be in his forties, long blonde hair ringing a balding scalp.

Actually we are in a band too, Eli continues, and I was wondering if we could get up there and play a few tunes.

The bloke looks a bit surprised.

No sorry mate the gigs over and we are off home, he says, shaking his head.

Go on mate, implores Eli, just one song.

Sorry mate, not possible replies the bloke. Gig's over.

Go on mate, don't be a cunt, let us do one song. Eli continues. His drunken mind is set on something and logic and pragmatism are no longer present.

Look I said no mate, insists the bloke, starting to get a bit irritated, now leave us alone, we've got a lot to pack up.

You lot are fucking shit anyway, derides Eli.

The bloke just shrugs and turns away.

Fucking twat, comments Eli under his breath as he turns away and comes back over.

Eli is more of a lover than a fighter, but he can handle himself if needs be.

One time we were outside Ronaldo's and Eli was talking to some bird. This bloke she was with got a bit uppity about it all, climbed up onto a low wall and kicked Eli in the face. Now Eli was on his own and this bloke was with a lot of mates, so twatting the bloke back would have been a bad idea. So Eli, calm as can be, pretended he wanted to make amends with the bloke. He put his arm round the lad's shoulder and led him across the busy road, telling him he wanted to go somewhere for a quiet chat. He talked to the bloke for a bit, seemingly apologising, even shaking hands. Eli waited for the lights to change at the junction and once the road was busy with traffic again he started laying into him with everything he had. The bloke's mates could see what was going on but couldn't get across the street because of all the cars, taxis and buses. Eli gave the bloke another couple of kicks then wandered off as his mates frantically tried to get across the road shouting threats and insults, but Eli had already gone leaving that twat bloody and bruised on the pavement.

But tonight isn't for fighting and as we leave the pub me and Eli approach the bloke, shake his hand and apologise.

It's alright, no harm done lads, he replies.

We push open the pub doors and we all spill out onto the street.

We congregate outside and everyone is talking about what to do next. Svensson and Ethan want to head into town and find a club. Christine, Kirsten and Becky seem up for it, but I'm not too sure. Not really a big fan of the club scene on a Saturday night, too many drunken loonies wanting to kick someone's head in. Most of us decide to call it a night and we say goodbye. We all give Svensson a hug and wish him happy birthday, then the group slowly starts to break apart, people peeling off and going their separate ways. Blake and Marko get in a taxi to Longthorpe and 'Her', Rachel and Kirsten get in another. I give 'Her' a hug and tell her I will phone her some time during the week. She smiles and tells me to take care. Millie and Mark and a few others are still chatting away on the street. I say goodbye to each of them in turn. They try to convince me to hang around, but I'm done with this night. It's time to head home.

Eli and I wander off chatting towards the bus stop and down into the underpass. As we get further from the city centre and descend below the street we are met with an unfamiliar silence. My ears still ring from the loud music and the noise of a good night out, and impressions, like images burnt onto a film pass through my mind. Our voices sound loud and echo down here in the underpass, and we unconsciously lower our speech to accommodate. We climb up the stairs at the other end and out onto the pavement leading up to Crescent Bridge. We talk about our band and the new songs we've written. It's late and the roads are virtually empty as we cross the bridge, walking slowly, hands shoved in our pockets and shoulders hunched against the cold.

As we reach the other side of the bridge that slopes down towards Thorpe Lea Road, I look back briefly and notice someone behind us. It's Millie. She is walking slowly, her coat pulled up over her shoulders, a thick black scarf wrapped around her neck. I don't mention it to Eli and as we get to the top of my street I say goodbye to him and give him a hug. He says, see you on Monday mate, then wanders off down the street. A few meters away he reaches into his jacket pocket and lights a fag. The fire illuminates his face for a second and then he continues walking. He doesn't look back.

I hang about at the top of my street and light up a cigarette and wait for Millie. As she gets close I call out to her and she smiles at me as she approaches. She looks beautiful, dark eyes with thick lashes, a bit of smudged lipstick, the scarf covering her chin and her dark curly hair hiding half her face.

You walking home? I ask.

That was the plan, she replies.

It's sort of a way to Bretton, I tell her, taking another drag and breathing the smoke out into the cool still air. She looks up at me with those dark eyes and blinks a few times.

Yeah I know, she answers, but I'm a bit drunk, wanted to walk it off before I got home.

I invited Millie to my fourteenth birthday party. I really liked her. We were in the same class and I thought she was the coolest girl at school by miles. We chatted sometimes and smiled at each other across the classroom, but I was always too shy to get to know her, trapped in that awkward skinny teenage body, still unsure of how to tackle the world or deal with the people within it. I didn't know how to stand or what to do with my hands.

My mum made me some invitations for my birthday party and I wrote in each one of them, putting them in envelopes and writing my friend's names on the fronts before licking them shut. I paid special attention to Millie's, writing her name in my best cursive hand and decorating it with a couple of flowers. I handed out the invitations the next day after our teacher had taken the register, Millie thanked me and told me she would definitely come.

The afternoon of my party, my mum helped me get everything ready. It was going to be held upstairs in the garage. We set up a stereo and my mum made sandwiches

342

and opened some packets of crisps, pouring them into a large orange bowl. She went back into the house and I sat alone up there listening to Cure tapes, my stomach tight with anticipation, nervous and excited.

My mates turned up first, everyone in jeans and sweaters, stinking of older sibling's aftershave. A couple of them had smuggled in a few bottles of wine and someone else had a half bottle of whiskey hidden below their denim jacket. I opened the windows and we drank the alcohol from paper cups. The girls turned up about an hour later. It was Christine, her friend Kerry Hadfield and Millie. They all looked amazing in jeans and tight t shirts, perms with far too much hairspray, cheap lipstick and thick mascara. I put on my favourite Cure tape and I awkwardly offered them some sandwiches and a drink. James handed them each a paper cup of whiskey and we were soon tipsy and rosy cheeked, laughing and chatting about first kisses and who liked who and all the other secretive, exciting preludes to adulthood. I sat next to Millie, her warm leg up against mine as we talked and gossiped, the night pushing quietly on, a cool breeze blowing in from the half open window.

I needed the toilet so I got up, pushing myself out of the sofa, excused myself, walked down the stairs to the lower floor and out into the garden. It was late spring and there was still a slight chill, the misty remnants of a rain shower hanging in the air. I went for a piss up against the back fence, the large silver birch tree rustling above my head. I could hear James and Mayhew chatting around the side of the greenhouse so I pulled up my flies and wandered around to see them. We talked for a bit about

343

girls and who we wanted to snog, passing a half empty bottle of sweet white wine between us. I told them that I thought I liked Millie. James teased me and Mayhew gave me a few words of encouragement. We finished off the bottle and went back up to the party. The music was on loud, some slow songs. A few couples were slow dancing and the lights had been switched off, only the glow from the street lights that lined Kirkwood Close offering any illumination. I looked around the garage for the girls. Christine and Sally were still sitting on the sofa, deep in discussion and Millie was in the corner, leaning back against the wall, her tongue in Martin Rutherford's mouth.

You can stay at mine if you want, I suggest to her.

She looks up at me from below her fringe, dark eyes glassy in the cold.

Ok, she replies, and I flick my half smoked fag into the bushes. I take her hand and we walk down the street towards my house. A gust of wind blows my hair into my face and my ears sting a little with the cold.

Hey you want to be in my band? I ask her.

Alright, but I can't sing, she replies.

Doesn't matter, I tell her, I can't either.

She smiles.

I unlock the front door quietly as my parents sleep above and we both slip inside, taking off our coats and hanging them in the cloak room. We join hands again and walk up the creaky stairs to my bedroom.

Something stirs out there in the darkness, something lithe and blessed, an angel or ghost of things that will one day be said, that will perhaps enable the birth of voices soft and perpetual. A middle aged woman sits alone at her dining table watching the tiny rivulets of the dying rain snake across the glazed roof of her conservatory, her iPhone face up on the table. She has an old shoe box of photographs in front of her and she takes out a handful from the top, splaying them out across the table cloth. She fingers through them, occasionally lifting one to her face and peering at it over the top of her reading glasses. Images of her and her friends at school, hair in plaits and bags on shoulders, a few pints in the local on a Thursday night, faces white with camera flash, messing about down at Ferry Meadows, dressed in bathing suits, messy perms and too much eye makeup. She picks one from the top of the pile, a photo from her hen night. She rubs her thumb unconsciously over the tan line where her ring use to be and looks over the faces in the picture. She smiles as she remembers those friends, those people that were once so much a part of her life, a life that now seems so long ago. Her eyes go to a group of boys in the background. They are all laughing, fags in their mouths, the table in front of them littered with empty pints. The boy in the middle is quite handsome she thinks, dark eyes and a few freckles around his nose, a white cardigan over his shoulders. There is a knock at the front door and she stands up, pushing her chair back and dropping the old photos back onto the pile.

LIZARDS

I t's my eighteenth, and rather than go out we decided to make a punch. We got the idea from one of Luka's mates at University. I went up to visit the old boy about a month ago and we got a big plastic bucket, dragged it down to the park near his house and filled it up with booze and fruit juice. We got some plastic cups and sat around on the grass playing old rock songs on a shitty guitar and smoking some rather potent hash under a vast grey Yorkshire sky.

We didn't have a clean bucket in my house so we grabbed the old cool box that we used to take to France on holiday, gave it a good clean and took it down to the garage. It's big, must hold at least a few gallons. We bought some cheap orange juice and white wine and told everyone who was going to turn up to bring a bottle of something. The thing is everyone decided to bring spirits, so now there are about ten bottles of vodka and gin, eight beers, some red wine and a tiny bit of fruit juice in there.

We mix it all up with a wooden spoon until it starts to froth like a witch's brew and we lean in to take a tentative sniff. It smells fucking potent. Luka grins and breaks out the paper cups. He's back from University for the spring holiday and it's great to see him. The garage is rammed full of people. There's Rod, both Mark's and James, Max,

Nugget, both my brothers, Eli, Marko, Blake and a few other people are popping round later. Not many birds, but that's probably for the best, cause I imagine things are going to get a bit messy.

We all dip our cups into the booze and fill them to the brim. Everyone says cheers, wishes me happy birthday and we gingerly take a few sips.

Fuck me, exclaims Rod, that's a bit sad rough isn't it Kei mate?

It is indeed old boy, I reply, it is indeed.

We all down our first cups and after a couple, the punch (if you can call it that) starts to taste much better. Luka puts our favourite tape in the player. It's a mix of stuff, from Thin Lizzy to Rod Stewart and Lynyrd Skynyrd. Freebird starts up and I lean back against the cold brick wall and take it all in. Nugget and Rod are chatting away about something or other, Rod leaning forward, his legs apart, one hand on his knee, a bent fag in his gob, eyes half closed and a massive grin on his chops. Nugget is explaining something, his hands moving in big obvious gestures in front of him, occasionally running a palm over his short cropped hair. My brothers and Max are all standing in the centre of the large room, arms around each other's shoulders, deep into the mood and music, Max moving his head to the tunes. Mark, James and Eli are all enjoying a massive joint in the far corner next to the stairs that lead up to the second floor, big plumes of smoke emanating from their mouths as they pass it around the group. It eventually gets to me and I take a big drag, sucking the hot smoke into my chest, that sickly sweet rush cutting through the warm comfort of the booze in my head.

We had a bit of a jam earlier before everyone turned up. Rod played the drums, I played the bass and Luka amazed us all as usual with his guitar playing. We did the usual stuff, some Chili Peppers, Pearl Jam and a reggae version of Stairway to Heaven. Rod sang on that one and Hardy took over the drums. Dan turned up half way through and played the bass for a bit, freeing me up to do a bit of singing. It was a great jam, we all really got into it and Luka hung a mic from the ceiling with some Gaffer Tape and recorded the whole thing on the four track. Can't wait to give that a hungover listen tomorrow.

My parents have renovated the garage, put a proper front door downstairs, redone the floors and put in some storage heaters. It resembles a proper house now. The bottom floor is still a bit rustic, the original stone floor and brick walls, but the upstairs looks really nice, plasterboard over the original brick and a large window in the wall at one end overlooking the garden.

Tom and Nails show up at about eight. Everyone is already well on the way to being wankered and we all cheer and give them hugs as they stroll in. Tom's tall and skinny with masses of beautiful, long, wavy, black hair. He's gregarious, funny and cheerful almost to a fault, and I've known him nearly my whole life. Our families used to go on holidays to France together, and while the parents sat around on rustic old chairs drinking wine in the shade of an ancient tree, we would swim in the river or explore overgrown gardens as the sun bronzed our skin. He's got a bottle of some sort of Chinese alcohol with him. His family spends a lot of time abroad and he's always bringing back weird bottles of booze. This one he got in Spain and it's got a fucking curled up lizard in the bottom of it. Actually make that two curled up lizards. As soon as I see them I know one of us is going to end up eating those bastards, and that it's probably going to be Nugget.

Tom's still got a bit of a black eye, the dark purple of a week ago now faded and yellow. He's been messing around with Finn's bird Mel and Finn found out. He went round to Tom's house, rang the door bell and as soon as Tom opened the door, bam, he smacked him one in the face. Didn't say a fucking word then turned and left. Tom's dad was well pissed off and tried to have words with Finn but you can't reason with a bloke like that. Tom was pragmatic about it.

I was asking for it really, he admitted.

Another few cups of punch in and everyone is well on the way. Eli and Nails are up for going to a club and meeting some birds, but I'm well happy here, surrounded by my mates and good music on the stereo.

A moth has flown in and taken up residence on Nails' black bomber jacket. It doesn't look like it wants to move and Nails keeps stroking its head with a delicate finger.

Steady on mate, teases Eli, reckon you might have pulled.

Don't talk about my bird like that, replies Nails grinning, his cool grey eyes on his tiny pet.

He's back on leave for a bit and well up for getting wasted. He says the army is fun but strict as fuck. He had

349

to clean the bogs with a toothbrush a while back for not making his bed properly. I don't reckon I could handle it.

Someone has got the playing cards out and a small circle of us are sitting in the middle of the garage playing Black Jack on a wooden stool pockmarked with cigarette burns and stained with rings from the bottoms of beer cans and wine bottles.

We used to have a sofa up here. It was a big old ugly brown thing with a faux felt finish, don't know who donated it, but we were grateful to have something to sit on. We spent most of our evenings, squeezed onto that sofa smoking and talking, hot cups of tea gripped between our knees. We came down one morning, opened the door and the whole thing had burnt down to its metal skeleton, the room full of the pungent smell of melted plastic, and there was a massive black patch of smouldering ceiling above the aftermath like a hole into the heavens. Suffice to say we have only been allowed wooden furniture since then.

Dan slaps down a winning hand and we all have to drink. Rod downs a massive cup of the death punch and screams

"Woooooo, this is great stuff".

I agree. Tastes like shit but gets the job done.

So what did you get for your birthday mate? Tom asks me. He's skinning up a massive joint with a big old cone at the end.

Got a Fender Jazz Master, I tell him, it's fucking wicked mate, white with a red tortoise shell scratch plate. I'll run in and get it in a bit mate, show you.

Wicked man, he replies, doing this thing with his fingers where he flicks his hand quickly back and forth, making the middle and index fingers slap together to produce a snapping sound.

He doesn't look up, still focused on the task at hand, tongue protruding slightly from the edge of his mouth, that shiny black hair obscuring half of his face.

You gonna have a swig of that mate? I ask him, pointing to the bottle of Chinese liquor.

Nah mate, not me, he replies, looks well nasty, reckon Nugget will be up for it though.

I reckon so too. He once downed a two day old glass of beer filled to the brim with fag ends for a fiver so a couple of lizards are going to pose little problem.

Tom twists off the top and takes a sniff.

Fuck me, he exclaims snapping his fingers again, that shit is well rank.

Give it here, I say, holding out my hand as he passes me the bottle. I eye it doubtfully, trying to decipher the foreign characters on the label, but my eyes won't focus. I'm pretty pissed now.

Having difficulty there mate? Enquires Tom laughing as I peer perplexed at the big green bottle.

Take a swig mate, I dare ya, he encourages.

I sniff at the liquid in the bottle and it doesn't seem too bad, the aroma strong but not unpleasant. I put my lips to the bottle rim and tip it back taking a small exploratory sip. Tom looks on grinning in anticipation. I bring the bottle back down and nod.

Not too bad actually mate, I tell him.

Oy Nugget, come ere mate, Tom shouts out across the room, I've got sumfing for you.

Kyra, Kirsten and Becky turn up at about nine and everyone cheers. We must be really drunk and they are going to have to play catch up. Becky is looking amazing tonight, jet black hair cut into a medium bob, smooth pale skin and a smudge of oily red lipstick. They all take a sniff of the liquid in the cool box and politely decline a cup, so Tom Hands them each a beer. The Chinese booze is half done and Nugget actually seems to have taken a liking to it, the big green bottle hanging limply from one hand, a lit cigarette in the yellow, nicotine stained fingers of the other, smoke curling up his arm. His light grey eyes stare intently at the mural on the opposite wall, as if searching for something, trying to find purchase on this chaotic existence. I wave my hand in front of his face and he snaps out of his trance, smiling.

Mate you alright? I ask.

Yeah bruvver, sound, he answers in a slur, just thinking about...

Hey Rod, he calls out to his friend, remember the sociology squidgy lemon days?

Rod just looks at him, confused for a short moment before bursting into his familiar raucous laughter and slapping his thigh.

The conversation is getting less and less intelligible, talk of old drunken exploits and conquests, half remembered jokes and piss taking. Mark Mayhew is sitting against the wall on the old guinea pig hutch, chatting away to James and smoking the biggest joint I've ever seen.

As the night progresses so does the level of intoxication. Everyone is in that loving mood, hugs all round and 'I love you mate' repeated over and over. Those of us from my year are at the point where school will soon be over. The University application process has begun and we are approaching the final exam period. There is a sense among us that things are at a zenith, a feeling of time moving on, an indefinable shift occurring. This small town is our world, a self contained microcosm, a safe bubble of existence, our home, but as we grow we start to see beyond its confines, our young minds beginning to define dreams that lie beyond its safe boundaries.

There is an exciting world out there, full of hope and opportunity, new people to meet and places to explore, we are hungry for change, for new paths and fresh starts. We yearn to move forward, and yet at the same time the prospect of cutting these ties of familiarity and friendship is a scary proposition. We are adults now, but we don't feel like it. We are still driven by childish instinct and the naive idea that we can become something more, that we can perhaps shape this world into something better, that we might perhaps even make a difference.

We are yet to find ourselves. Our hearts are still unmarked by tragedy, our minds still preoccupied with the trivial and the blasé. Like young animals birthed in a field, we totter and ruminate, doing our best to understand and to comprehend what it all means. We stumble and struggle, suffer and fall, but one day we will rise on strong legs and push onwards, at last becoming what we were meant to be.

Now I've never been one for planning for the future. My real skill is not giving a fuck. The rough friction of this short existence will slowly erode me, cut and damage me, but my core burns with an intensity that will never be extinguished. All the beauty and love that now surrounds me will one day whither away and be lost. These people that my heart now so aches for will forget me, and this beautiful moment will fade like the yellow bruise on my friend's face. I am completely oblivious to this truth and yet somehow painfully aware of it. It prods at me through the thin fabric of whatever it is that surrounds and engulfs me. I am afraid of everything and yet somehow know that nothing can ever really harm me. I have already given myself up to the monsters within.

I look about the room at the faces that I have known most of my life. I wonder if any of us will live to see thirty or forty, I wonder what the future holds for each of us, I wonder if we will have children of our own and settle down. I wonder if we will be rich and make our mark on the world or if the world will make its mark on us, use us up and leave us adrift, bruised and battered and begging for the end.

Someone out there knows, the being that has danced with this skinny drunk teenager, the harlequin that hides behind his grin and pulls and pokes at the future which lies hibernating somewhere in a forgotten realm. He knows that none of us will make it out of here, that one by one we will either fall or soar. One of us will lose a

354

brother, another will lose a twin. One will wander the streets lost and alone, a vagrant who sleeps under bridges and washes in hotel bathrooms, and another will dance in the fire light at the other end of the world. One will sail across the cold depths to discover the light that for so long has enticed him, and another will slowly change and blacken, falling to vice and temptation. We will all bleed and falter, struggle to possess the essence of what once seemed so clear and pregnant with purpose. A few will skirt on the edge, too afraid to look into the depths, too hollow to commit, unsure, like oil on a moist surface.

Most of us will fall in love and marry and a few will be happy. We will be changed, the world slowly eating away the things that could have made us great, locking away our passions and shuttering the windows that once so deeply betrayed our souls. We will face our demons with the same indifference the English have to the rain.

Tonight is about the end, but also the beginning. We have so much time and yet have none. The boat edges closer to the plunge and the abyss calls. The question is do we embrace it now, or keep paddling until our strength gives out and the current takes us.

Jacobs is hunched over on the hutch now, head in hands. He is pale and sweaty, his hair hanging in greasy curls about his face. He mumbles something then pukes up a huge amount of liquid onto the garage floor.

Whoa, we all call out lifting our feet into the air to avoid the splash of vomit.

He heaves again and more comes flying out of his gob. Eli moves over, avoiding the puddle on the floor and holds

Jacobs' hair back away from his face. It's a simple gesture but one of affection.

It's alright mate, he whispers, patting his friend on the back. Get it all out mate.

Perhaps outside might be a better place for that old boy, I say, not trying to be a cunt but that shit's gonna be a nightmare to clean up.

Jacobs gets slowly to his feet with some help from Eli and they move slowly to the door. Mark looks a bit better after a good puke and he turns to me as they walk out into the cool night.

Sorry about that old boy, I'll clean it up, he slurs.

Fuck it mate, I say, don't worry about it, get some air and you'll feel better.

Just having a whitey, he replies, too much fucking gange mate.

Go and have a sleep inside if you want, I tell him.

Nah mate, I'll just have a kip in my car, he replies.

Alright mate, I say giving him a pat on the back as he passes.

James is next to go. He stands up and says he needs some fresh air and just makes it to the door before throwing his guts up, mushrooms and orange juice by the looks of it.

Fuck me, exclaims Rod, sad bunch of lightweights, he laughs, downing another paper cup full of the shit that has already defeated two of us.

Reckon you're next mate, I tell him with a grin.

It's me, Tom, Luka, Hardy, Max, Nugget and Rod left. Everyone else has either called it a night or gone to puke somewhere in the garden. Eli and Nails ditched the party to head into town, the moth still happily clinging to Nails' top. They were itching to meet some birds and said they'd be back once the clubs closed. Good luck lads I told them as they left and they both wished me happy birthday and gave me a hug.

We are drunk, really drunk. The conversation has devolved into something almost unintelligible, slurred jokes and angst ridden emotional diatribes. Max is in a bad way and sits tilted to one side on the only chair with a back, his beautiful long hair matted together, the ends singed and split.

I was wrong about Rod. He's usually one of the first to go, but tonight he is holding his own like a trooper. He has one hand on his knee and is leaning forward, peering through eyes that are almost slits as a fag, smoked almost to the filter hangs loosely from his lips. It must be five or six in the morning and the birds are out. We have been playing cards, or at least trying to, but no one has any fucking idea who is winning. Rod dips his cup into the punch for another go. The fucking cool box is still three quarters full.

Everyone is nearly out of fags and the weed disappeared hours ago. I look down to my left and see the bottle of Chinese booze has been drunk down nearly to the bottom, the two lizards clearly visible, tails curled up and sleeping peacefully. I tip the remnants of the liquid into one of the paper cups lying about on the stool we are using as a table and tap the rim of the bottle into my hand until I can reach in and pull out one of the lizards. Luka and Hardy watch me, swaying slightly as though rocked

357

by some invisible wind. Once I've extricated both of the small reptiles from the bottle I examine them, then pass them round for the others to have a look.

Have a butchers at these, I remark.

Mate, someone's got to eat one of those fuckers, comments Rod, reckon you'll be tripping balls if you do, read that they are hallucijenik.

He stumbles over his words and we all laugh. Not a hearty laugh like before, a lazy drunken laugh that soon fades.

Gimme one, demands Nugget grabbing the one Rod has dangling from between his fingers by its tail.

Fuckin do it Nugget, we all cry.

He wraps it up into a ball, pops it into his mouth and washes it down with another cup of punch, spilling half of it down the front of his shirt. He hardly notices. He slams the cup down onto the stool then jumps up to his feet grimacing and slapping his thigh.

Fuck, that shit is well rough he spurts out, Tom mate you've got to do the other one.

Yes mate, we all join in, you fuckin brought the shit in the first place, eat the fuckin lizard.

Yeah eat the fuckin lizard, we all shout and start to chant

Li-zard li-zard li-zard...

Tom puts up his hands in a gesture of surrender. He has resigned himself to his fate, but the chant continues. Li-zard li-zard

Like Nugget, he wraps the thing up into a little ball, pops it into his mouth and swallows it. Rod passes him a cup of punch and he downs it, grimacing. Nugget throws his arms around his friend and they dance about like fucking loonies for five minutes while we laugh and cry out and clap our hands together.

Suddenly there is a thud and we all look round to see Max passed out and looking really pale on the cold stone floor.

We lift him back into the chair and try to talk to him. He isn't responding. His eyes are half closed and he's mumbling something incoherently. Nugget leans in closer to try and listen, quieting us down with a wave of his hand.

What's he saying Nugget? Enquires Tom.

Dunno mate, he replies, sounds like he's saying li-zard li-zard li-zard.

I'm in the garden. Astonishment quickly turned to fear and doubt as my parents looked at the photographs on my phone. I flicked through them, showing them images of me in my house in Tokyo, of Luka and the children in the botanical gardens in Cambridge. My mum saw pictures of her brother and sister as old people and she could no longer control her emotions. She burst into tears, trying her best to dampen her sobs, hand lifted to her mouth. My dad seized my arm and told me,

Stop

It was a simple command, but one that carried a great deal of weight and feeling. It was a voice fueled by a depth of

359

emotion I had never heard issue from this man, this father. I leave the phone on the table where it rests, humming with implication and secret, like a Pandora's box or The Ark of the Covenant at the end of Raiders of the Lost Ark. The power it holds is too much for my parents and we all in that instant realise the truth of what is happening. Something in the world has unravelled. The threads of this carefully woven existence have become tangled and knotted. My parents gaze into a future that they do not know and I peer into a past that had become muddy, faded and granular, a past that now sits across from me, surrounds me and consumes me, as clear and crisp as the daylight on the morning my father died. I start to feel dizzy and things slip in and out of focus. I struggle to my feet and pass through into the kitchen, past my parents who look on in silence, open the back door, my hand twisting the familiar knob and out into the back garden. I sit down at the old wooden table that sits in the centre of the lawn.

My dad bought the thing for fifty pence at a jumble sale many years ago and it sits slowly decomposing in the garden, occasionally covered with a table cloth on sunny days so we can eat outside. I can see my parents through the window of the kitchen, a window that Hardy and I will one day break through with a spade we find leaning up against the wall. My dad looks stern faced and stoic, his mouth in a thin line, brows low and creased. My mum is still in tears and dabs at her eyes with a small handkerchief.

I see movement in the windows set into the double doors of the back room to the left of the kitchen and notice two faces peering out at me. I smile and wave to them and the bigger of the two waves back. The back doors open out onto the garden and my parents would often open them in the summer to let a cool breeze circulate through the house. My dad would sit in his armchair, smoking and reading the newspaper while mum listened to classical music, spinning thread on an old wooden spinning wheel, her left foot pumping the pedal, hands delicately feeding the yarn onto the large rotating wheel.

I stand up and walk slowly towards the two faces pressed up against the window. One of them turns, grabbing the other by the shoulder, but the other doesn't move. He looks me in the eye and smiles. I smile back.

I approach them slowly, feet in the soft grass, waving as I do so. Once I reach the window I crouch down and place my fingers on the window pane.

Let him in, urges the bigger one.

Mum said not to talk to him, whispers the other trying not to be heard.

The double doors are already ajar and the larger of the two pushes them open. He must be about seven or eight and has a mess of uncontrollable hair. He has in his hand a stormtrooper figure. The other is smaller and thinner, hair cut into a short bob, and dressed in a brown track suit.

Hello, I say to them both and our gazes meet. Tears well in my eyes as I am suddenly caught by a deep yearning for this once forgotten place, for the the paint peeling from the edges of the double doors, the scent of freshly washed clothes and cut grass on the air, and the familiar calls of birds whose songs once coaxed me awake from beyond my open window. I catch a glimpse of my reflection in the imperfect glass of the doors and run a hand through my thinning hair.

Are you my mum's friend? Asks the bigger one.

361

Something like that, I reply, looking into the eyes of my younger brother.

Are you Australian? He asks, your voice sounds weird.

I laugh a little bit at this.

Actually I was born here in The Borough, but I live very far away in another country.

Japan? Ask the smaller of the two and suddenly I'm looking into the eyes of my childhood self and he looks back.

There is a weird buzz in my ears, like the feedback loop you get when you point a video camera at the tv it's plugged into, the universe trying desperately to reassert itself and correct this anomaly. I can feel my lips moving and the speech coming out of his mouth, or is it my mouth. I get the sensation of looking out through two pairs of eyes, each pair meeting the other, as though I'm looking down an endless tunnel, into the inner workings of something deeper and much more profound than I could ever comprehend. The feeling knocks me off balance for a bit and I have a moment of dizziness. I wonder if the boy feels it too, but he doesn't seem too bothered if he does.

Yes that's right, I reply a little surprised, how did you know?

He blushes, and lowers his face.

I listened to you talking to my mum, he mumbles.

I wonder for a moment if I should tell him, tell him not to marry that beautiful young Japanese girl that he will one day fall deeply in love with, tell him to run away from that poisonous bitch as quickly as possible. Tell him that he will meet another beautiful girl called Aya one drunken night, and that when they kiss for the first time beneath that railway bridge, he should hold her tight and never let go, tell him that he will one day have to make a choice between two women he loves, and that that one simple choice will alter his life forever.

But what about my boy, my beautiful boy? For the road to ruin and heartache is the path I must take. The boy is the only thing that matters. His existence rests on her. He was grown in her. My love for that cruel woman will bring that perfect boy mewling and puking into this world and without him life will have no meaning whatsoever. His light will carry me through all of the shit and hate and grime that my future holds and one day this child before me will emerge from the ashes of it all, a man with a boy in his arms and a new life ahead of him.

Choose Yuri, I whisper to him.

He lifts his head and looks at me with those soft brown eyes.

It's a girls name, I say, reassuringly.

Who is she? Asks my brother? Looking confused.

Someone your brother will know one day, far far in the future.

They both look at me quizzically and I see confusion but also intrigue in those young eyes.

One day your brother will have to choose, I continue talking to my brother as the other boy's eyes have become too hard to look into, like gazing into an endless abyss.

Choose Yuri I say again, and this time he slowly mouths the words, and my heart breaks a little knowing that he will have to live through all of that pain, but it will be worth it.

It's warm and the garden is green and lush. There is the smell of lavender and mint on the air, and I can hear children playing in gardens up and down the street. All

363

friends from years ago. One of those voices will be Tom and another one Kael. I long to go and find them, to look into their eyes, to see them as they once were, to gaze upon their faces once more before I have to go, but I know i never will.

Children, my mum's voice calls out from the kitchen, and the two of them go scampering off.

I stand up again, my left knee giving in slightly as I put my weight on it and I take in a deep breath of the warm summer air. It's a beautiful sunny day and the huge oak next door rustles and sways in the breeze. I stroll up towards the garage, my dad eying me suspiciously through the kitchen window as I go. It still has the old roll down garage door on it and there are three bikes leaning up against a pile of wood near the right hand wall. I step slowly into its cool, dark interior and breathe in deeply, eyes closed.

Do it for the boy, I whisper to myself.

My eyes slowly open and I glance gingerly at the digital clock next to my bed. It's two in the afternoon. I move my head slightly and the pain hits, a tight unpleasant stabbing sensation behind my eyes. My body feels heavy and my skin hurts in that way that signals the beginning of a fever. This is no fever though, this is the sweaty familiar embrace of a hangover and it's a fucking horrible one. I lie in bed for a few minutes and reach clumsily over for the pint glass by my bed. I grab it and down the dregs of the water that remain in the bottom. The water tastes stale and dusty. I kick my legs out of bed and put my feet down onto the cool floor. It feels good. I can hear voices from downstairs, sounds like Hardy and Tom. I push open the bedroom door and waddle down the landing towards the bathroom at the end. I've walked this landing so many times. I know all of its bumps and creaky floorboards.

I go into the bathroom, lock the door and sit down on the toilet. I pick up a shampoo bottle to read and just sit there. The window is open and a cold breeze blows about my naked legs. I feel really nauseous and wretch a little every time I cough. I fight the feeling for a few minutes, breathing in and out deeply, but finally I give in. I stand up, lift the toilet seat, kneel down in the soft carpet and throw up violently into the bowl. The first wretch is so strong that I pull a muscle in my stomach and have to lie on my back on the bathroom floor until the muscle loosens and I have to throw up again. After a few dry heaves I flop back onto the floor and let the cool sweat run over my skin. I shiver in the cold air, but it feels good. My mind flashes back to the booze and the lizards and I get up and heave a few more times.

I wipe my face with some toilet paper, then flush away the whole disgusting mess, remnants of another night, and walk back to my bed. I fall back into the warmth of my duvet shivering, head throbbing, imagining lying in a meadow on a spring day looking up at a blue sky, and sleep soon takes me once more.

Fuckin hell are you still sleeping you lazy bugger?

I peer out through half closed lids, the ghost of a dream slowly fading behind my eyes, and see Tom standing above me grinning.

Morning mate, I croak.

365

Morning? It's nearly fuckin four o clock mate.

Really? fuck me, I say, how are you feeling old boy?

Pretty good actually, comes the reply, reckon that lizard sorted me out.

Yeah I grunt, sitting up and wiping my eyes.

Max isn't doing too well though, Tom continues, his mum phoned Nugget this morning, apparently he was in a right old state when he got home this morning, puking his guts up, half unconscious. His old girl got a bit worried and called an ambulance, took Max to hospital to get his stomach pumped.

Fucking hell, I exclaim, I know he was wasted, but he didn't look that bad.

Yeah mate, I've seen im worse, agrees Tom.

Oh yeah and did you hear about Mark?

Jacobs? I ask.

Yeah man, says Tom excitedly, snapping his fingers, got fuckin pigged.

What the fuck do you mean? I enquire, where did he get to actually?

That's it mate, continues Tom, He only went and drove home.

What? he could hardly fucking stand up, I say.

I know, he said he thought he was giving Kyra a lift back to hers.

Fuck me, I reply, shaking my head.

Yeah, so he's driving home in that horrible blue vauxhall Chevelle of his when he runs out of petrol right outside the Westwood police station, so this WPC sees him with the bonnet up, fiddling with the engine and comes to help the old boy out. Thing is Jacobs is fucking

366

well pissed and as soon as the pig talks to him she goes and arrests him for drunk driving and takes him into the station.

Fucking hell that's well rough, I comment shaking my head, how did you find out?

Talked to James this afternoon on the blower, says Jacobs is well in the shit, could do time.

He won't do fucking time mate, I assure him. First offence and he's only eighteen, might lose his license though.

Yeah mate, he's really fucked up anyway, grins Tom shaking his head, poor bloke. I love Jacobs man, but he's fucked when it comes to the booze.

I lie back in bed and look up at the ceiling. There is a paper lamp shade hanging above my bed and it casts a familiar shadow on the walls.

HER

We are in Bogarts. Everyone is here. It's ten o clock, and everyone is four or five beers in, we are in the sweet spot, the point in the night at which everyone is full of love and hope and optimism. There are so many of us that we spill out into the beer garden. Bogarts is a small bar on a back street in the centre of town. I don't remember why we started coming here, I think it was to meet one of Luka's mates and since then you can't keep us away. It has just the right mix of clientele. You have the goths and indie folk in their donkey jackets and dread locks, a few townies out on the piss, making a quick stop before heading to a club, some locals sat in their usual corner nursing their pints and chatting and us, a weird eclectic mix of hippies, townie types and trendies. We don't really fall into any category.

I have always been friends with everyone. I have no prejudice. I love people from all walks of life, from bikers, and stoners to tarts and nerds and everyone in between. Our house is a hub for my large group of friends, a stop off point on the way to town. It's a place where everyone congregates and chats over cigarettes and tea in the evenings. The garage is the centre of our social lives. Everything starts and ends there, so many interactions and conversations, parties, fights, and encounters.

I look around the pub and realise I know ninety percent of these people. I can see Eli, Marko and Butcher over by the toilets talking and laughing. Luka and his mate Kizzie are standing, elbows resting on the bar, and knowing my brother, discussing physics or religion or some other esoteric subject. Kizzie nods thoughtfully as my brother talks. Hardy, Rod, Tom, Nugget, and Max are out in the beer garden smoking and talking bollocks, I can hear Rod's booming laughter from time to time, even through the noise of the bar. Ethan, Blake, Valentine, Svensson and a few others are all looking dapper, sitting around a small table near the door. Valentine is waving his arms around and everyone is laughing. Becky, Kirsten, Kyra, 'Her', Rachel and the rest of the girls from my year are at the bar. Kirsten is laughing so hard that she is nearly in tears and 'She' looks amazing, simple jeans and sweater, long blonde hair spilling over her shoulders. Becky is smoking a fag and wearing a bit too much make up, her arm around Kyra's shoulder. Kyra short and dark in complexion is relating some funny story to her friends. Millie is with Chris, the Marks and James. Jacobs managed to stay out of prison but lost his license for four years and has to do some community service, but all things considered it's not too bad.

Millie and I have been on and off since that time after the pub crawl. She joined the band and we've played a few gigs. I really like her. She is cool and fun and sexy as anything, but I am a narcissistic idiot who doesn't know a good thing when he sees it. I chase and chase and once I get what I want I lose interest. Fuck me sometimes, fuck me and my selfish stupid attitude. The world doesn't

369

revolve around me, and my solipsism will bring me to ruin. She's too good for me.

I am standing at the entrance to the toilet talking to some bloke I vaguely know from Luka's year. There is a bit of a queue to get in so there are a few of us out here. The toilet empties out and I go in for a piss. There are ashtrays next to the urinals and I stub out my fag in one before getting down to business. I rock back and forth slightly on drunken legs and grin to myself. I am happy.

I am going to Sheffield University in September and so are Kirsten and Stuee. Becky and Kyra are off to Leeds, the same University as Luka. It's only twenty minutes by train so we are planning to meet up at the weekends. I am surrounded by all the people in my life that I love. I have the attention of an amazing, beautiful girl and I'm in my favourite pub, drunk and a little bit stoned.

I finish up and walk back out into the throng. There is a good vibe in here tonight. No aggression, no twats starting shit, just happy people drinking and talking, enjoying the company of friends. I get another pint from the bar. It's pretty busy but I don't have much trouble getting served. We are in here a lot and the bar staff know me. I grab my pint and I walk out into the beer garden to see Rod and Hardy and the lads. Rod sees me coming and throws out his arms.

Kei old boy, come here you cunt, he shouts.

Rod must be pretty flush at the moment cause he's wearing his ring. He's got this big gold sovereign ring that he wears on his middle finger. It's an ugly fucking thing but it was a present from his uncle, and besides it's pretty good for inflicting damage on people. I'm sure that there are a good few wankers wandering around The Borough with an impression of that thing in their foreheads. Any time Rod is a bit skint on a Friday night he heads down to the pawn shop in town and sells the ring for twenty quid so he can go out on the piss. He's a resourceful bastard and always manages to scrape together enough money over the following week to go and buy it back, usually for twice what he sold it. The bloke who runs the pawn shop is getting a bit fucking fed up with the constant cycle and so every time the amount he can get for it goes down by a few quid. Still Rod doesn't seem to complain when he's six beers in.

I join the group and we talk and laugh.

Did you hear what this twat did? Asks Nugget, gesturing to Rod who is grinning, a half smoked roll up between his teeth.

Nah mate, I admit, but I can probably fucking guess.

We were in the Wortley, he begins, having a couple of swift jars before coming here and the doorman was on the fruity, you know the one next to the door?

I nod, taking a swig of my beer.

So the big bastard has racked up some reasonable corn on the machine, but he finds he's out of change, so he goes to the bar to get some more. So Rod, the cheeky bastard just wanders up and presses the collect button. Kaching kaching. Fucking half inches all the cash, then strolls up to the bar, stands right next to the bloke and orders two beers with a big fucking handful of quid coins. Even asks the bloke if he wants a pint.

What? Grins Rod, he looked thirsty.

What did the bloke do? I ask.

What could he do? He didn't see anything. Looked surprised as fuck though when he got back to the machine, Nugget laughs, and there's us two cunts with our fresh pints. I thought we were going to get decked, but Rod just gave him a nod.

Rod smiles and takes a big gulp of his pint.

So anyone seen Kael recently? I enquire.

Yeah, replies my brother, seen him just yesterday, went down to the field and had a few joints and rode about on our bikes.

By bikes he means motorbikes. Kael's mum bought a little scooter a while back, meaning to use it to get around town on while her car was in the garage. It wasn't long before Tony and Kael got hold of it and we were soon down at the field every weekend riding it about down there, doing jumps and doughnuts and generally fucking the thing up. After this Hardy bought an old Honda Cub from a family up the street. Kael, not wanting to be outdone got his hands on a 70cc Honda and after that it was all we did for weeks during the holidays, take the bikes down to the field and mess around. We've been chased by the pigs a few times but we know the area too well. We've been playing down there since we were tiny. They have no chance of catching us.

Is he coming down tonight? I ask.

Dunno mate, replies Hardy, the smile fading from his face, he said he would be in town tonight, but he's out with Clive and that lot, so they are probably dropping a couple of Es and going to a club, might see him after in the garage.

372

Kyra and the girls come out into the beer garden and Rod gives them all his usual greeting. They are all drinking double vodkas and coke and Rod stands up on the metal table and sings a song to each of them in turn. Everyone laughs and cheers at the end and the girls give him a kiss on the cheek. He does a stupid dance and downs his drink, howling into the night and we do the same.

Fuckin chuck it old boy, commands Rod, but I'm laughing so hard I can't summon up any strength.

It's a big fucking sign and made of solid wood, not one of those cheap chip board things. We are on Kirkwood Close, the secluded street that runs down behind the back gardens of all the houses on Thorpe Lea Road and we are trying to throw this huge sign, must be a metre and a half across, into my back garden over the high fence at the back. We get the top over the fence and we both push as hard as we can. The sign flips up and over the fence, landing on the other side with a really loud bang.

Fucking hell mate, I say, we are going to wake up the whole fucking street.

Don't reckon that's our biggest problem mate, replies Rod

What do you mean? I ask

Wrong fucking garden old boy.

We all walked back to mine over crescent bridge after last orders had gone at Bogarts. Everyone was in high spirits and we had some booze back in the garage, so as usual the whole crowd decided to come back to ours. Me and Rod got somewhat waylaid on the way back looking

373

for somewhere to buy some fags and it was then that we found the sign. The old solicitors office on Thorpe Road was up for sale, and a huge sign had been erected on the front lawn just in front of the large bay windows, facing the main road. It was about a meter and a half high and about the same across, the whole thing secured to two huge stakes hammered into the grass.

It was my idea to nick it and Rod was well up for it. We must have looked like a right couple of idiots, standing on the main road trying to pull this massive piece of wood from the earth. Anyway we finally got it out and it fell to the ground with a heavy thud. It was massive and far too heavy for even two people to carry. Luckily it had been constructed in two sections so we kicked off the bottom third and tested the weight again.

Reckon we can carry this, remarked Rod and I agreed.

But let's go around the back down Kirkwood Close, I suggested, can't fucking drag this thing all the way down our street.

We crossed Thorpe Road, which at midnight wasn't really busy at all, and down the thin path that led to Kirkwood Close.

I jump over the fence and into our back garden landing just outside the garage. The lights are on and I can hear music, a cloud of smoke emanating from a half open window. I can see the sign in next door's garden, crushing what looks to have been a well tended flower bed. I look down towards the house to make sure none of the lights are on and clamber over the fence into the garden of number 14. I whisper shout for Rod to come over, and a

374

second later his grinning face appears over the top of the fence and he drops down into the garden. We grab the massive sign and heave the thing over the bushes that separate the two gardens and into my driveway where it lands heavily in front of the garage door. Me and Rod follow, panting from exhaustion and laughing at the sheer fucking size of our prize.

I push open the garage door and we walk into the smoky interior.

What the fuck happened to you two? Asks Nugget, bottle of red wine swinging from one hand.

Got a bit distracted mate, I answer.

Nugget looks past me and sees the massive white slab of wood lying on the ground.

You fucking twats, he grins.

The garage is chock full of people and the stereo is on loud, Stevie Wonder's 'Superstition' blaring out of the speakers. Tom, Max and my younger brother are standing in the centre passing around one of Max's massive spliffs. Kyra, Kirsten and Becky are sitting in the comfy chairs, Kyra perched on the edge of Becky's knee. They are laughing, Kirsten talking loudly in her high pitched voice. 'She' is here too, sitting on the hutch against the wall nursing a bottle of something and chatting away to Luka. I plonk myself down next to them and ask Tom to hand me a beer. He rips one out of the plastic six pack and hands it to me.

Cheers, I say, and crack it open.

Luka has been rather busy himself and has nicked one of those road cones with a light on top. The light is activated by movement. Turning off all the lights and shaking the thing turns the garage into a fucking disco. Luka never does stuff like this. He is as straight as they come, but he seems really pleased with himself for the minor indiscretion. He's got that permanent, contented half smile across his face that always appears after one too many.

He gets up to go for a piss in the garden and I slide over to talk to 'Her'. She is wearing a tiny bit of lipstick and her hair is tied up behind her head, little strands have broken away and hang loosely about her face. Her eyes are blue and bright and I catch the familiar whiff of her usual perfume above the smoke.

Having fun tonight then Kei? She asks.

Yeah it was wicked, I reply, taking a swig of my beer and sweeping my hair back away from my face.

I'm quite pissed actually, she informs me giggling, and my dad's car is parked just outside your house, I hope it's alright.

Reckon it will be fine mate, I tell her.

Luka comes back in and changes the tape in the player. 'Maggie May' comes on and everyone cheers and starts to sing along. I give him the thumbs up and he smiles at me.

Hey remember that Viz comic with the colourblind kids? 'She' asks.

I start laughing at this, yeah and they are both in wheelchairs, I giggle.

Yeah, she continues, and there's a special school for them.

She starts laughing harder and so do I.

I'm colourblind. When I was in primary school I drew a picture of myself and coloured the face in green thinking it was skin tone. On one of those precious evenings, sitting shoulder to shoulder on her bed, talking into the night, I told 'Her' about this and she thought it was hilarious, and so the whole colourblind thing has sort of become a running joke with us.

Our laughing subsides and I lean back heavily against the wall.

I'm going to miss you mate, I say softly, without turning to her.

What's that? She asks, not really hearing me.

The music is loud and everyone is talking and shouting, it's a real party atmosphere. That's the great thing about having the garage. It's all the way down at the bottom of the garden so we can be as loud as we want.

I'm going to miss you when we go away to university, I repeat, turning to face her.

Luka hears me say this and gives me a knowing smile.

'She' brushes a few strands of hair away from her face and uncrosses her legs. She looks me in the eyes.

I'm going to miss you too, she tells me.

I close my eyes and nod, my long greasy hair falling down over my face, a big grin on my chops. I already know how this will play out, I have a sense of what will become. There is something about this night, something huddled beneath the darkness, as though each moment gives birth to an infinite number of narratives, a forever branching reality, each delicate step of mine disturbing the limpid waters of my fate, setting me along another path. Tonight feels too real, too vivid, the blue smoke hanging in front of my face, the touch of my greasy hair upon my warm cheeks, the cold air blowing in from the gap beneath the door and the smooth bumps of paint on the wall behind me. Could we really have carried that heavy sign, tossed it so easily over the fence? Like the remnants of lucid dreams, images flash through my consciousness, the crunch of fresh snow and the sting of the biting cold on my damp fingers as we run, the soft words of the mourning and the salty taste of tears, a tattooed girl with Egyptian eyes and the iron tang of her blood. One day we will awaken perhaps, pull back the heavy curtains that shroud that dark mechanism and finally be able to divine what lurks at its core.

'Fallin', by De La Soul comes on the stereo and I see Nugget's face light up.

I fuckin love this tune, he shouts, as he starts to dance, eyes half closed, lit fag hanging from his bottom lip and a can of Carling clasped loosely in his left hand.

I stand up and join him in the middle of the garage and we sing along together.

'Hey yo kid what's up remember when I used to be dope...'

We jump up and down, arms around each other's shoulders. I look over at 'Her' and she grins back at me.

My heart breaks a tiny bit, knowing that we will never be together, but this is enough I tell myself.

As a child I would fall often, scraping my knees on the concrete playground at school or coming off my bike in the patch of gravel surrounding the garages at the bottom of our road. My legs would be a patch work of scabs and purple bruises, souvenirs of those moments, reminders of long summer days, of games of hide and seek, the school nurse and the stink of Germolene ointment. My wounds would sting as I got into the bath and the sharp pain I felt would remind me of what I was, a being of meat and flesh, imperfect, flimsy and mortal.

The song ends and Nugget slaps me on the back as I sit back down next to 'Her' and she hands me my drink. Someone has opened the door to let some of the smoke out and a cold breeze blows in. The scent of autumn is on the air.

Can I go in and use the phone Kei? 'She' asks, lightly touching my arm. I've got to ring my dad and tell him I can't bring the car back tonight... it's getting really late, she adds, looking at her wrist watch.

Of course mate, I reply, actually I'll go in with you.

We both stand up and push our way through everyone. Nugget gives me a wink as we pass and I blush and give him a punch on the shoulder. He feigns injury and laughs.

Where are you staying tonight? I ask her as we walk out of the garage.

The night air is fresh and cool after the smoky humidity of the garage. The trees rustle above us in the breeze, the music and voices of the party in the garage softened and muted.

Actually Kirsten said I can crash at hers, she tells me, so I reckon we'll get a taxi together.

Alright, I say, nodding.

We reach the back door, crunching over the gravel and I push it open as quietly as possible. The kitchen light is on and as we enter we are met with a wonderful silence. The kind of comfortable silence that can only be experienced in a house you have spent your whole life in. It isn't just the absence of noise but something else, a

379

softening blanket of something that crowds out the sounds and intrusions of the outside world.

I have lived in this house for eighteen years and know every inch of it. I can close my eyes and walk about it in my dreams, feel the different textures of the carpets below my feet and the cool touch of the wooden door handles. I know its walls and ceilings like I know my own palms, each intricate line and imperfection. I know its heart and its breath, the low hums of its inner workings and the throbbing pulse of its arteries. This house has raised and mothered me, it has sheltered and protected me. It is a place of absolute love and security, a sanctum, a womb, my home.

The dining room with its big round table in the centre is still and peaceful. There is a hint of cigar smoke and roast dinner on the air, a bowl of fruit sitting stoically in the centre of the table, a couple of the apples starting to look a little over ripe.

I remember being so small that I had to stand on tiptoe to look over that table, I whisper to 'Her'.

She runs her hand over its surface, her fingers tipped with painted nails, gliding delicately over the polished surface as we pass by.

You want an apple? I ask.

I'm alright thank you, she whispers back, giggling.

She goes out into the hallway, picks up the phone and dials. I hang back in the dining room, door closed and wait for her to finish.

I pull out one of the heavy antique chairs from under the table and sit down, resting my elbows on the smooth surface, years of careful polishing exposing some of the wood grain next to where my hand rests, fingers splayed across its surface.

She finishes her phone call and comes back into the dining room, closing the door carefully behind her and taking a chair next to me.

Your dad ok? I ask.

He's fine, yeah, a bit drunk though.

Yeah tell me about it, I say.

There is a brief pause and she puts her hand in mine, squeezing gently as she does so. The clock above the dining room ticks loudly in the silence and I can hear the buzz of the fridge from the end of the kitchen.

Is it ok if I stay here tonight? She asks.

We walk up the stairs hand in hand and into my room. I push the door closed behind me with my foot, turn off the light, and we sit on the edge of the bed in the blue half light. We stay like that for a moment or two, hands resting awkwardly by our sides, a few words passing between us, then she moves over, places her hand gently on the side of my face and pulls me towards her. I take her in my arms and kiss her, gently at first but my tongue soon finds its way into her mouth and she reciprocates. She smells of cigarettes and floral shampoo, her body warm and solid as she presses up against me. This person who inhabits my daydreams and lurks on the periphery of my consciousness, suddenly rendered real and tangible. I touch and smell her, hold her to me, peer at her through the darkness, trying desperately to bring her into reality. We fall back onto the bed and I pull off her jeans and top. She straddles me and we kiss some more. I think I'm laughing as I kiss her and tug her knickers off around her ankles as she undoes my flies and pushes me inside her. She is wet and hot and grinds up and down on top of me. I kiss her stomach and neck and grab her head in both hands.

I love you, I say as we move together, her hands gripping mine, her long hair tickling my face, the rest of the world invisible, pushed to the periphery, all the nagging itches and mundane pains of being, forgotten and diluted.

Somewhere in the distance I hear the sound of music and people laughing.

I swing my legs out from under the covers and get out of bed. I pull the duvet back around 'Her' and give her a kiss on the forehead, she moans lightly and exhales slowly and deeply. I brush a few strands of hair away from her face, then cross the room to the large window that looks out onto the back garden and open it fully. It swings open horizontally in the middle so I am able to sit with my legs dangling out over the low kitchen roof and use the glass as a kind of table to skin up or put an ashtray on.

It's cold and I'm just in my boxer shorts, but the air feels fresh and cool. The lights in the garage are still on but the noise has died down. I imagine them all slumped back in their seats talking into the early morning, cigarettes smoked down to the filters, empty beer cans, their tops covered with ash. Part of me longs to join them, to share this exquisite night with them, but there is nothing in the world that would pull me away from that warm body wrapped up in my bed. I wonder what time it is. I find a half cigarette on the desk behind me and light it, coughing a bit as I take a drag. I turn back to make sure that she is really here, that this isn't just a hallucination, a dream conjured from the sweetest depths of all I am.

We all have our fantasies, building perfect worlds within us, sculpting the prosaic into something more, hoping that we will one day eschew the humdrum, that we will find that one golden thread that pulls us from the depths and sets us aflame, that one perfect virtue that allows us to finally take flight. We believe that meaning and purpose exist extant from ourselves, that these fragile moments will somehow illuminate or beguile us, protect and instil in us that delicate complexity that happens just beyond our reach. Is this it? The end? The only thing that could possibly bring me to bear?

I look over and see the duvet moving slowly up and down with her breaths. No life can sustain this, I think to myself, no one can go on getting exactly what they want. It has to end at some point. It has to balance out. People always say that we should never meet our heroes because what if they disappoint you, but what happens if you meet your hero and they are exactly as you imagined.

I finish my cigarette and climb slowly back into bed, next to her bed warm body. I prop myself up onto one elbow, and trace the contours of her face with the back of my finger. I gaze down at this beautiful woman asleep in my bed, in my home, and I cry.

GOOD WEATHER FOR ONCE

Everyone sees the world differently and so when someone dies it is, in a sense the death of an entire world.

My mother rocks me awake. I was dreaming of running across the rooftops in a slum in a far off city, jumping lightly from building to building as dark clouds gathered in the distance. The curtains are open and sunlight streams through the window. My cat sleeps peacefully at the foot of my bed. I look up at my mother's face and I know before she even speaks. Her eyes are puffy from tears and lack of sleep. She stares absently towards the small window set into the wall at the end of my room.

Such a beautiful day, she half whispers, as though talking to an unseen presence.

I got back from Sheffield late last night, taking the train immediately after lectures finished, and went straight to the district hospital. The nurse led me upstairs to the second floor and into a quiet ward. It was dark and peaceful, the quiet broken occasionally by the odd cough or clearing of the throat. My dad lay unconscious in an iron framed hospital bed. His gown was open at the front

385

and a series of machines pulsed and breathed next to him. His eyelids quivered as I spoke a few words, none of them carrying any real meaning or depth. My mother sat by his bed, her hand resting on his slowly beating heart, but there was no hope in that gesture. It was one of comfort and of a lifetime shared. It was an act of forgiveness and of letting go. We sat like that for an hour or so, speaking few words, the machines slowly ticking away the last moments of my father's life. The doctor came in and looked at his chart, marking a few things down and tapping the back of his finger on the heart monitor, before leaving us once again in silence. I went home, climbed into bed and fell into a fitful sleep while my mother and father shared their last ever night together.

The next few days seem slow and surreal. We all go about our usual routines but everything is covered in a blanket of something thick and opaque as though the lights have been dimmed. My mum calls my University to let them know I won't be back for a few weeks. Friends come over and we sit in the garage and drink and talk. The conversation inevitably turning to my father at some point. Distant relatives appear and offer condolences and the phone rings often, concerned people with the usual platitudes. I cry briefly on that first morning but sadness soon turns to numbness and then nothingness. Grief is a funny fucking thing. It's as though someone has moved to another country, a place far away with no phones or ability to communicate. Our minds are unable to truly grasp the concept of non existence and so the idea of death in itself has little meaning.

We don't mourn death, we mourn loss, and the true loss resides not in the metaphysical idea of death itself but in the gradual awareness that the individual is no longer a part of our existence and never will be again. It's an amalgam of tiny realisations that stack up over a long period of time, of moments that could have been shared, subjects that you could have talked about, events that will never affect them. My father never cared about his body, perhaps one of the reasons why his life ended as it did. His body was just a vessel for his mind and that that part of him has gone is the true loss here.

The funeral is quite a grand affair. If the measure of a man is indeed in how many lives he touches then my father was truly a titan. My dad was well known and loved in the community and I am delighted and amazed by the number of people that turn up to pay their respects. There are people from all walks of life and every race and religion, teachers, politicians, community leaders and friends. I briefly bump into the headmaster from our school and my old English teacher Mr Pateman.

I am wearing an ill fitting black suit, borrowed from a friend and I wander around in a daze greeting, shaking hands and accepting condolences. The service is held in the local crematorium. My father was a staunch atheist and so the service is secular and simple. So many people speak that I start to feel myself drifting away, stress, lack of sleep and too much alcohol taking their toll. After the service, the coffin travels along a conveyer into the back wall and a curtain lowers. 'Brothers in Arms' by 'Dire

Straits' starts to play and the body that once contained my father, a lifetime of knowledge, hopes and fears is burnt to dust, the last remnants of him spat out into a bright march sky in a thick grey smoke which is soon lost amongst the clouds.

We all spill out onto the grassy area outside, scowling slightly in the bright morning, and talk of him and his life. There are tears and handkerchiefs, arms around shoulders and weak knees. My mother stands stoically accepting hand shakes and hugs, wiping the occasional tear from her impeccably made up face. We drink as we always do and soon the loss and grief are lost behind a veil of inebriation. All my friends are here. 'She' accompanied me and for that I am supremely thankful. I cling on to her as we move about the crowd greeting and talking. I have never met anyone in my life who is as good with people as she is. She has this innate ability to bring out the best in everyone. She says everything with such sincerity and honesty that it is disarming. People just want to talk to her, tell her their intimate thoughts and feelings. She is a force of nature and I love her, I always will. I'm a skinny broken puppet of a human; paranoid, narcissistic, anxious and completely unable to grasp this fleeting existence of mine. She puts me on track, fixes my clipped wings.

After the funeral we all head back to mine of course. The house is packed full of mourners. It's only about two in the afternoon but everyone is already drunk. There are half finished bottles of wine everywhere and we wander about helping ourselves. Rod is here and is the centre of attention as usual. He tells jokes, and cheers people up.

He makes tea for the old ladies and charms them to smiles with his witty banter. I give him a hug and tell him I love him. He returns the gesture.

Love you too old boy, he says, grinning like a fucking idiot.

The house gradually gets less crowded as people make their excuses and begin to leave. 'She' says goodbye and I hold her, my nose pressed into her neck. She wipes a tear from her cheek and squeezes my hand as she leaves. I stand at the door, watching her walk down the garden path and cross the road to her car. I watch her pull away as I stand in the empty hallway gazing out onto the street before returning to the dining room.

My mum has already started to clear away the plates and glasses, Rod and Nugget stepping in to lend a hand.

Let us do that Veronica, offers Rod, you go and put your feet up.

Thank you Rod, smiles my mum.

She looks exhausted and emotionally drained. It's been a long and very trying couple of weeks for her. Luka gives her a hug, holding her skinny frame to him and I go into the kitchen to turn the kettle on. There is still lots of booze about and the few of us that are left continue knocking back the wine and talking. We are all sitting around the big round dining table, my mum still dressed in black, a cup of tea cradled in her hands. She looks so tired. I tell her she should go to bed.

Yes Veronica, agrees Tom, we will clear up in here.

We all nod in agreement and she stands up.

Thank you boys, she says, a little teary eyed.

She reaches beneath the right lens of her glasses and wipes her eye with her forefinger. She gives each of us a big hug.

I love my boys, she tells us before going out of the dining room and up the stairs to bed.

We hear her sobbing quietly as she ascends, and we sit in silence for a moment, reverent and drunk. My dad's favourite grey jumper, the one with the Lowry scene on it is draped over the chair in the corner.

At some point we wander down to the garage, bringing a few bottles of wine with us and sit about listening to music and talking. Luka bursts into tears at one point and I uncomfortably console him. I'm not used to seeing my big brother cry. Nugget puts some music on.

Let's get fucking pissed old boy, I say

We are all drinking out of bottles and we each raise one to our lips.

To Nigel, toasts Tom and we all follow suit.

Yeah, to dad.

Mate you've got no fucking idea, growing up here in fucking middle class Borough.

What the fuck do you mean? Nugget retorts, raising his voice slightly, my family is proper fucking working class mate, we've been through some shit.

Rod and Nugget are arguing about something or other but everyone is too drunk to intervene or even care. It's getting late and we've all had far too much fucking wine. The atmosphere has gone from sentimental to morose.

You're full of fucking shit mate, accuses Rod, standing up and pointing. I seen a bloke get fucking stabbed, saw the fucking knife go in mate.

Rod, sit the fuck down old boy, and stop talking shit, I mutter.

It's not fucking shit Kei, he retorts, turning on me, saw the fucking blade go in.

You're talking bollocks mate, Hardy tells him.

What the fuck is everyone ganging up on me for? He bites at us, could smash the fuck out of you fick idiots anyway.

Yeah you probably could mate, I tell him, but why don't you sit the fuck down and stop acting like a cunt.

I realise I'm probably pushing this a bit far, but I don't give a fuck. I'm drunk and feeling self destructive.

Luka tries to calm everyone down.

Let's all have another beer lads, he suggests.

We don't listen.

Kei mate, I know you just lost your dad n'all, but if you keep being a cunt I'll have to smack you old boy.

I just stare at him

Fuckin do it then mate, I challenge, standing up. He's a good half foot taller than me and built like a brick shit house but like I said, I really don't give a fuck.

Rod mate, intervenes Nugget coming between us and pushing Rod away with his left hand, you are the one being a cunt, we just put his old man in the fucking ground.

Why are you fucking pushing me Nugget? Accuses Rod.

Nugget pushes him again, cause fuck you, he answers.

Fuck you Nugget, grunts Rod, pushing back.

Nugget stumbles backwards over a stool and nearly falls. He immediately rights himself and charges forward chest pushed out.

Yeah what the fuck are you going to do Nugget? goads Rod.

They are face to face now and neither one is going to back down.

I don't see who throws the first punch, but pretty soon things get out of hand and we descend into a drunken brawl. It's me Hardy and Nugget against Rod. Everyone is fucking throwing punches and Rod is holding his own. It's a confined space so it's difficult to fight properly and we end up grabbing each other and wrestling clumsily, trying to get the upper hand. I get a fist to the side of the head and nearly go down. Hardy has got the garage door open and we all grab Rod and wrestle him, kicking and fucking screaming like a loon out into the night air. We slam the door shut and Rod hammers on it, cursing and threatening for a few seconds before giving it one last kick and leaving. I slump down in my chair and rub my head with my hand. Nugget rights a few of the stools and Hardy collapses on the floor with his back against the wall. I pull a box of fags from my trousers and share them round. We all spark up and take a few drags.

Fuck, apologizes Nugget, sorry old boy. He looks at me shaking his head. Sorry for fucking up.

Nah mate, I tell him, you were sticking up for me old boy.

Hardy's got a big welt on the side of his face and bloody knuckles.

Do you reckon I ought to go after him? He asks.

Nah fuck im, replies Nugget, he'll sober up soon enough and we'll have a good giggle about it tomorrow.

Everyone sits in silence, the light pitter patter of rain on the windows, a barely audible hiss from the stereo speakers.

I'm going after him, I announce, getting to my feet.

Don't bother mate, calls Nugget after me, but I'm already out of the garage door and onto the driveway.

The rain is coming down harder now and there is the distant rumble of thunder on the wind. I jog down the driveway, crunching over the gravel and out onto the street. My t-shirt is already wet through as I cross the road and I'm fucking freezing, but I don't care. Something deep inside me is telling me that I have to make this right. I see Rod's solid silhouette at the top of the road. He's walking quickly, head bent forward, hands shoved into his pockets, his drenched t shirt clinging to his muscular frame. He doesn't hear me through the rain as I catch up with him and grab him by the shoulder. He spins round and for a moment I think he's going to punch me and I raise my hands to my face.

He looks at me and I notice the tears in his eyes.

Mate I'm sorry, he sobs.

I grab him by both shoulders and tell him it's ok.

Don't worry about it mate, I urge, it's just a stupid fucking fight.

Nah mate, he replies, I really fucked up this time.

He is soaked to the skin, the rain running down his face, dripping from the end of his nose.

We all fucked up mate, I tell him, we're wasted, come back and have a fucking smoke, it's alright mate.

He looks down at the ground avoiding my gaze.

You have to let go old boy, he mumbles into the rain, you have to let us go, he tells me, looking up at my face, easily unclasping my hands from his shoulders.

Mate... I, I manage to gasp but he has already stalked off into the rain.

Just before he rounds the corner he turns round and looks at me. He looks right into me and I start to tear up. The stress and the grief of the last week have taken their toll. I haven't eaten properly for days, surviving on booze and fags and I'm freezing cold and falling apart. My long hair clings to my pale skin in tattered greasy ribbons and I can hear my heavy heart beating quickly in my skinny chest.

Rod raises his hands into the rain. It's a gesture of rage and repentance. I realise that there is something much heavier resting within him, something none of us has seen, something he has kept hidden away. Like all of us, he has that thing that lurks below the surface.

He bellows into the cold night.

I'm sorry!

THE LESBIAN BRANCH OF THE CIA

'm sure they're watching me, it sounds fucking stupid, but I just have that feeling. There's a couple of lesbian birds shacked up in the flat across the road and I swear they are watching me. We were in Bogarts last weekend and we got hassled by some undercover pigs. Me, my brother, and the rest of the lads were having a quiet pint on a Sunday afternoon and this bloke wandered up and sat with us. Nugget gave him a look like he was going to smash the twat. He was mid thirties, dirty blonde hair and the stink of shitty aftershave, the kind you might nick from Asda on a boring Saturday afternoon. He apologised for sitting at our table, making up some bullshit about there being nowhere to sit and started talking to us. Normal stuff at first. Where do you boys live? How long have you been coming here? You know that kind of thing. But then it started to get a bit weird. He called some of us by name and seemed to know specific details about each of us. He knew Max's name, at one point remarking,

'You're the funny one aren't you?' In a dry tone that none of us liked.

Nugget told him to fuck off and the bloke got defensive, putting his hands out and saying, I'm just in the pub having a chat lads, not after any trouble.

Anyway the bloke was starting to freak us out so we downed our beers, told him goodbye and left. I looked back as we were leaving and he seemed to be watching us intently. And now there's this.

I've got the telly on and I've moved the chair back into the alcove in the living room wall so they can't see me. The girls across the road have got a dog. It's big and black and whenever they duck out of view the ugly thing pokes its head through the lace curtains. Is it possible that they and the dog..? No mate it isn't. Stop fucking thinking about it and concentrate on the telly. Crappy daytime telly as usual. Some bloke jabbering on about something or other. I can feel their eyes on me. I peak out from around the arm of the big armchair and see the lace curtains across the road twitch.

Stop it mate. You are just being paranoid. Too much fucking coke that's what it is. It's true, we have been doing an awful lot recently.

It started like every other drug. We had a bit of extra cash and wanted to try something new. Kael got a small wrap and we snorted a bit one Saturday night. The problem with cocaine is that it makes you feel invincible and once you start then it's really difficult to go back to life without it. It's so much better than speed.

Amphetamines give you that horrible chemically rush, like drinking far too much coffee, you get shaky and twitchy. You feel things writhing under your skin and you sniff and scratch at itches that don't exist. Coke is a whole different fucking game.

It's turned into a regular Saturday night thing now. Everyone chips in twenty quid and we get as much as we

396

can. Max knows a bloke who lives up in Bretton who always has a bit extra to sell. We usually do a few lines then head into town to get wasted then back here to polish up the rest, usually popping in to rob the bakery on the way back.

It all started out innocently enough, a few loaves of bread and a tray of doughnuts. One time Mayhew tried his bike keys in the forklift and the fucking thing started up so we drove it around for a bit. Then it started to get a bit more serious, breaking into the office and stealing the petty cash and then the computer. We took the thing up to the garage to try and figure out what to do with it. The problem was we were all so coked up that none of us could engage in anything approaching civil conversation. We were all just jabbering away or waiting for our turn to talk. We were interrupting and arguing and shouting. In the end Max had had enough. He picked the computer up and threw the whole fucking thing out of the second floor garage window then stormed out. No one tried to go after him or apologise, no we just started arguing about how we were going to share out Max's coke now that he had gone.

Another time I went up to Leeds with Becky in her blue Metro. Me and Kyra bought a few grams of Charlie and went clubbing. I had a sudden bout of paranoia before we left for the club, visions of getting searched by the bouncers and thrown in a cell somewhere, and so I left my share under Kyra's bed. We got into the club no problem and Kyra was happy to give me a few lines, which we snorted through a fiver in the bird's toilet. When we got home everyone went to bed. There were about ten of us in Kyra's living room. It was winter and I was the last in and so got jammed into one of the corners. The radiators were all on full blast and I was having to sleep with my knees up in the air to keep my feet from touching the scolding pipes. The problem was that every time I was on the edge of sleep, my muscles would relax and my legs would stretch out involuntarily. My bare feet would connect with the hot pipes under the radiator and the pain would jolt me back awake. After a while I got fucking sick of it and got up. I remembered the spare coke I had under Kyra's bed and sneaked upstairs to retrieve it. Kyra was in bed with her bloke, but they were both well asleep and I easily found the small package of cling film where I had safely tucked it behind some old shoe boxes. I tiptoed out of the room and back down the stairs and into the dining room. I pulled up a chair, grabbed a copy of Cosmopolitan and started snorting coke and reading a rather informative article entitled 'ten ways to please your man'.

I must have been pretty engrossed in it because I didn't even see Becky wander in.

You are up early Kei, she said, opening the curtains onto a rainy Yorkshire morning. I hadn't expected daylight and it made me squint.

What fucking time is it Becks? I asked, a little annoyed and confused.

It's 10:00 in the morning mate, she replied, peering at me.

Have you been awake all night?

Fucking looks like it, I answered, I must have read this fucking magazine cover to cover.

Cosmopolitan, nice, commented Becky, we have to get going soon mate, have to get the car back by this afternoon.

Alright mate, I told her, keep your fuckin hair on.

We got packed up, said goodbye to everyone, then walked out into the cold rainy morning. In front of us where Becky's car had been parked the night before was a large, square, dry patch of road in the shape of a Mini Metro.

Your car's been nicked, I commented.

No it hasn't, it can't have, her voice came out all high pitched and panicky.

Then where the fuck is it? It was there last night and now it's gone, what the fuck else do you think might have happened? I had been really looking forward to getting in the car and falling asleep, listening to the slow rhythm of the windscreen wipers and the patter of the rain.

But who would steal my car? Becky was in disbelief, still staring at the large dry patch in the road.

I dunno mate, I replied, fucking car thieves perhaps?

The police found the car in a ditch three days later. It was smashed to bits and burnt out. Some little cunt had stuffed a rag in the petrol tank and set it on fire. Becky was quite upset. She had loved that little blue car, even gave it a name.

We ended up getting the train back to The Borough that day. Becky slept the whole way back while I drank three cans of Stella and stared out of the window as the grey English countryside swept by. I tried to get some sleep, but every time I closed my eyes all I could see was my father's face.

GLASS HOUSES II

You phone it mate, I say.

Kael nods and goes into his jeans pocket, pulling out the small crumpled piece of paper. He unfolds it and hands it to me and I read out the number written on it in blue biro, while he dials the number.

He holds the receiver gripped between his jaw and shoulder, using his right hand to fiddle with the curled up phone chord.

Is it ringing? I ask.

He holds up his hand, gesturing me to be quiet.

I hear a click at the other end and a voice.

Put it on speaker, I urge him pressing the large grey button before he can protest.

Yes I'd like to speak to private Makepeace if that's possible, he asks in his most polite voice. I nearly start laughing, but Kael gives me a look and the smile fades from my face.

We hear a voice in the background shouting out into an echoey room.

Private Makepeace, get your useless arse over here, phone!

There is a rustle and click and then Nails' voice comes on the line.

Hello?

It's Kael and Kei mate, wanted to phone and see how you are.

Alright lads, comes the reply, cheers for giving me a bell, but I don't have long to talk.

His voice has lost some of its usual strength and confidence and me and Kael immediately recognise the seriousness of the situation and give each other a look.

Um... Nails are you alright? Asks Kael.

These two have been best friends for years, forever getting into scrapes, and watching over each other. They are basically brothers, and I reckon Kael's dad would adopt Nails in an instant given the chance.

We can hear noise and shouting in the background and Nails' breath in the receiver.

No, he replies before hanging up.

Private Makepeace was a great soldier. He was built for the armed forces. He was strong, fit, tough, brave and had the ability to get along with anyone. Everyone loved Nails. He was what we all aspired to be. He was good looking and could handle himself. Me and him were about the same height, but while I was skinny and pale, he was stocky, solid and always had a suntan, even in the winter.

He had had a bit of a rough upbringing, his parents divorced when he and his brother were young and the family didn't really have much money. He often got into trouble at school for fighting or messing about, but he was always polite to the teachers and treated everyone with respect, he just wasn't built for an academic career and he realised this from an early age. He was a very physical being and needed a job that would take advantage of his

401

particular skill set. For this reason a career in the army was a great fit, and so he left school and enrolled as soon as he was sixteen. Whenever he had leave he would come back and we would hang about at mine or get pissed at the pub. He seemed to be getting along really well. He had taken up boxing in the army and was winning a lot of fights. Got a couple of medals in his weight class. He got in even better shape and was learning to drive and shoot and all sorts of other useful skills. There was a part of me that envied his determination and single mindedness, I knew that there was no fucking way I could ever do what he was doing.

So things were going really well for him until he got called up to do a tour in Northern Ireland. Once he was over there we didn't hear from him very often anymore. There would be the occasional phone call, and the times when he did come back on leave he seemed different, reticent and cynical. He told us stories about soldiers torturing prisoners, of kangaroo courts and interrogations. They would have to stand guard in the street and little kids would come up and spit at them and throw stones, yelling insults. They would have to stand stoically, rifles in hand and take it. He was drinking more and smoking more, his hair had grown longer and he wasn't shaving as regularly.

One day we were all sitting in the garage smoking and he told us that he wanted to get out.

He had a few options. He could wait it out, do another couple of years and then apply for a formal discharge. Another option was to buy his way out. It would be expensive but Kael's dad said he would put up the money.

402

The final option was to do a runner, to go AWOL and hope not to get caught. In the end he chose the latter.

On his next leave he just didn't return. He knew it was dangerous to hang about in The Borough so I told him he could stay at mine. I was in Sheffield at University and was living in a big shared eight bedroom house. He agreed and his mate Donnie drove him up one day. He slept on my floor, and in the evenings we would go out, get pissed and try to chat up girls. We would wake up early in the morning, me going to lectures and him heading into town to look for work. He couldn't get anything legit because of his situation so he was looking for cash in hand stuff. I knew he was struggling for money so I looked after him financially. It was fun for a while. The two of us living in that small room together, getting wasted and fucking about. At some point he developed a really bad cough. Neither of us was eating properly and we were smoking and drinking far too much. I went to the chemist and bought a massive bottle of black current flavour cough syrup and put it on the shelf. He would wake up every morning, cough his guts up then take a massive swig of it before heading out to look for jobs. It was gone in under a week.

We both started to get paranoid, maybe it was all the booze, or the lack of sleep, but we would duck or run when we saw a police car and started to stay in much more, playing Mario on my mate Tim's SNES and drinking cheap booze. One day Nails decided he had had enough. He woke up at five in the morning, packed all of his shit into a huge bag and left the house. He hitchhiked back to The Borough, getting lifts from truckers on their way down to London. I threw away the big empty cough syrup bottle and went back to my normal life.

When he got back to The Borough, Finn told him he could stay at his place and so he moved in. The problem was Finn and the people he lived with were dodgy bastards and so it was inevitable that the police would go poking around at some point. One day they did. Nails grabbed his bag and passport and Finn told him to hide in the closet in his room. The police were there looking for drugs, but they didn't find any. What they did find was a young man hiding in a cupboard clinging to his passport and with a bag full of belongings. The police questioned him and soon discovered the truth. They arrested him and turned him over to the appropriate authorities. He was taken to military court where he stood trial, and now he has to spend a year in Colchester military prison, a place nicknamed The Glasshouse.

CONTINENTAL DRIFT

We are driving through London in Tony's jeep, actually it's his dad's jeep, actually, technically it's someone else's jeep but for now that doesn't matter. It's me, Tony and Hardy. It's late summer and we've got the top down. We've got food and beer and a giant three litre bottle of lemonade with about half an ounce of speed dissolved in it. There is weed in the glove box and we are all in high spirits. We are driving down to Spain to stay in Tony and Kael's dad's villa. Apparently it's a really nice place in a rather exclusive resort. I heard Terry Wogan has got a place nearby. First things first though. Tony doesn't have any money so we have to pop in to see his mum so he can scrounge a few hundred quid. His mum and dad are now divorced and while his dad kept the house in The Borough his mum moved into Kensington with her new bloke Jake McQuillan, a famous Irish musician.

He had an accident, banged his head a couple of months ago and is confined to a wheelchair and has lost the ability to speak. He is going to a physical therapist though and the doctors are hopeful that he will make somewhat of a recovery. We park the jeep outside a row of exclusive flats opposite a small canal and Tony grabs his cap from the back seat, pulling his hair back into a ponytail. We enter the building and Tony presses the buzzer for his mum's flat. Her voice comes over the intercom and she buzzes us in. We go through the glass doors and into the lift to the second floor. His mum and sister meet us at the door, his little sister, a head of fuzzy red hair and a massive grin across her chubby cheeks throwing her little arms around Tony's waist and giving him a crushing hug. Tony ruffles her hair as we walk into entrance hall.

Hi Lyra, he grins.

The place is small but beautifully furnished and impeccably decorated. Tony's mum leads us through into the living room where we meet Jake. He can't really speak but has no problem communicating. We shake hands and he gives Tony a pat on the shoulder. Tony's mum prints off a route from the AA website while we all sit around chatting and drinking tea, then she takes Tony aside and gives him a wad of cash. We down our teas, make our excuses then decide to head out. His mum asks us to stay a bit longer but we politely decline. We've got a long drive ahead of us.

I like the short hair by the way Kei, she remarks as we leave.

He looks like a fucking skin head mum, says Tony laughing.

We head back to the car, Tony cramming the route printout in the glove box, it's a good hundred pages thick, all printed on that thin paper with perforations between each sheet and little holes running down both sides. We all climb into the car, Tony in the drivers seat, Hardy next to him, and me in the cramped back seat with all the luggage and booze. It's a beautiful sunny day, a blue sky above our heads and a light breeze blowing through the busy streets. Lots of people are out and about, lounging around in outdoor seating areas, drinking expensive sparkling wine from thin flutes.

Tony turns on the ignition and then immediately switches it off again.

What is it mate? Enquires Hardy.

Hold on a second lads, says Tony pointing across the road, I'm just going to nip over to the bookies, got a really good tip on a horse from my mate.

We protest a bit, eager to get going, but what can we do. It's Tony's car.

Me and Hardy wait in the car watching the posh twats walking up and down the street, sunglasses perched on foreheads, the rich birds tottering along in heels, clinging to the sleeves of their bloke's blazers, and the old, finely coiffured women with tiny little dogs on leads. I open a can of Stella and me and Hardy pass it back and forth taking swigs and talking shit, watching the world pass by.

After about thirty minutes Tony gets back, and he looks pissed off.

Sorry lads but the trips off, he announces.

What the fuck? We both exclaim in unison as he throws his wallet into the back and climbs into the drivers seat.

You fucking blew all your cash didn't you, accuses Hardy.

It was a good fucking horse mate, replies Tony, fucking cunt fucked me.

That was three hundred quit mate, I say, you put all of it on the horse?

Yep, to win. Lost the fucking lot, he replies.

We are going mate, protests Hardy.

Then what the fuck am I going to do about money? Questions Tony, turning in the drivers seat to face us, pulling his long hair out of its pony tail and retying it.

Dunno mate, figure it out, Hardy tells him.

Fuck, exclaims Tony banging the steering wheel.

Go and ask your old girl for more, I suggest.

No fucking way, replies Tony shaking his head, she told me straight up not to gamble it all away when she gave it to me.

Fucking guessed right didn't she, comments Hardy.

Tony sits at the wheel for a moment, turning the car keys over in his hand and staring out of the side window at the canal that runs by the road.

Actually lads I've got an idea, he says, hold on.

And with that, Tony gets out of the car, slamming the door behind him and jogs across the road through the slow moving traffic and back into his mum's building. I climb out of my seat and perch myself on the edge of the black jeep, my feet on the back seat. We spark up a couple of cigarettes and wait for Tony to return.

After about twenty minutes we see him emerge from his mum's building. He jogs across the road and gets back into the car, a big fucking smile across his unshaven face.

We are back in business boys, he tells us, fucking borrowed two hundred quid off my little sister. She's been saving it for a year, but I told her I would pay her back.

Well fuck me let's go then, urges Hardy.

Yeah what the fuck are we waiting for? I add.

Tony starts the car, puts it in gear and off we go.

A bloke in a high visibility jacket knocks on the driver's window and motions Tony to wind it down. He's a skinny chap, thinning blond hair and pock marks on his cheeks. Tony rolls down the window and the bloke leans in, giving the interior of the jeep a quick once over. He tells us to leave the queue and bring the car over to a small parking area next to the customs booth.

We are in the line to get on the ferry from Dover to Calais and this is the last shit we need. Tony pulls out of line, driving the jeep the short distance over to where the bloke is pointing and turns off the ignition. The bloke pokes his head in through the drivers side again and asks us all for our passports. I've got them all together in my bag so I fish them out, being careful to keep the big bag of weed hidden, and hand them to him.

There a problem? Enquires Tony nonchalantly.

No mate, just a random check, won't be long, comes the reply.

The bloke walks back to his booth and sits down. It's quiet in the car with the engine off and we watch the slow procession of cars driving up into the bowels of the huge red ferry ahead of us. One of these things capsized a few years ago. Some fucking idiot didn't secure the back doors and water started to leak in. The whole fucking thing flipped onto its side and a lot of people drowned. I hate big ships on open water, the gaps between their hulls and the dock, and the thin sliver of black water between.

We can see the bloke in the rear view mirror. He is on the phone, the receiver held between his chin and shoulder. He occasionally glances over at the car.

Tony looks nervous and keeps looking back over his shoulder, his hand fiddling with the gear stick.

What's up mate? I ask, he won't find the weed and all the speed is in the lemonade, I'm pretty sure he isn't going to ask for a swig, I add.

Nah mate it's not that, he tells me.

What then? Asks Hardy, starting to look nervous himself.

I'm pretty sure this car is stolen, replies Tony.

So it turns out Tony's dad won the car in a poker game from this bloke who runs these dodgy car auctions. He gets his hands on a lot of shady motors, repaints them, files off the serial numbers on the chassis then sells them on. There is a slim possibility that he acquired the car legitimately but let's just say it's unlikely.

Let's just hope he doesn't run the registration plate, says Hardy.

Of course he's going to check it, replies Tony.

I hear the rumble of the ferry's huge engines coming to life. There is the stink of petrol on the sea air.

After about five minutes the bloke in the booth puts down the phone and steps out onto the concrete. He has another last scan at the passports in his hand and walks back over to the car. We are all shitting it as he peers at the rear registration plate and approaches the car, signalling Tony to wind down his window again with a circular motion of his hand.

He gets to the window and pokes his head back in, briefly scanning the front seats and dashboard.

So where are you boys headed? He asks.

Hardy pokes his head forward from the back seat to talk to him.

My dad just passed away, he begins, and so we are off to Spain to spread his ashes on his favourite beach.

I nod in agreement and hang my head, trying to look as despondent as possible.

The bloke gives the interior of the car one last cursory glance then hands the passports back to Tony. We all thank him, and Tony turns the key and starts the ignition. As we pull away the bloke tells us to drive carefully and we once again join the long line of holiday makers hoping to leave their troubles behind, drink far too fucking much sangria and get horrible sunburn somewhere on an overcrowded beach with a bunch of other pasty white racists. Fucking hell I love the English abroad.

The ferry trip is reasonably uneventful. We have a few beers and stand up on deck watching the white cliffs disappear into the haze, before retreating back below deck to have a smoke and watch Tony blow a lot of cash on the fruities. The Channel is pretty rough and the ship yaws from side to side, the view through the windows cycling between blue sky and grey sea, people stumble along below deck with trays full of pints, swaying dangerously from wall to wall, the metallic groan of massive structures under immense pressure beneath our feet.

An announcement comes over the tannoy telling us we will shortly be docking, so we down our beers, stub out our cigarettes in plastic ashtrays decorated with various beer logos and head down below deck. None of us can remember where we parked the car and so we wander around in the bowels of that massive ship for a fucking age before finally clapping eyes on it.

We all clamber in as the ship pulls into port, the clang of heavy equipment ringing around the cavernous interior of the ship. The massive doors in front of us open with a slow groan, the bright sunlight from the opening creeping across the cars and trucks in front of us. Tony starts the engine as the chains are released from the wheels and we drive off the ferry, down the ramp and onto the European continent. We stop briefly to take the roof down and have a quick gander at the route printout, then Tony floors the jeep and off we go.

Hardy is sitting in the passenger seat navigating and I'm in the back with the beers and the speed lemonade. The roof is down and we are making good time, cruising along a motorway that will carry us most of the way down through France. We are all well pleased with ourselves and the conversation is flowing, fuelled at least on my end by beer and the occasional swig from the big bottle of cheap fizzy drink laced with methamphetamines. There are a shit tonne of toll booths along the road and the cost is starting to mount up.

You see, I told you we should have just taken the fucking plane, moans Tony as we stop at one more and chuck a few francs into the little tray.

I know mate, but where is the fuckin fun in that? I reply, I love this fucking car man, we are free to go wherever we want mate, we are on a fuckin road trip old boy, just the lads, no fuckin worries.

I take another swig from the lemonade.

Tony put some fucking tunes on old boy, I suggest, and none of that fucking drum and bass bullshit, I add, I wanna hear some real fucking music.

Tony puts a cassette in the tape player and Bob Marley comes on.

Nice one man, I tell him.

I crack open another beer and take a big swig.

I feel fucking good lads, I tell them. This is going to be a wicked holiday.

Tony just sighs and keeps his foot on the pedal, powering that little black jeep onwards. I've got a lovely buzz going on and I grin to myself as I stare out of the window and watch the scenery flash by, small farms and freshly harvested fields, little villages full of stone houses and brand new multiplex cinemas, stark white monoliths of glass and neon. I lie back in my seat and stare upwards.

The sky looks just like it does in England, I say.

It's nighttime and the roof is up, we are speeding through tiny villages on country roads as I desperately try to follow the route. It's printed on a massive long roll of paper perforated between sheets so that it folds up. Hardy is sleeping in the passenger seat and I'm in the back trying to follow the fucking thing using only the small light set in the car's ceiling for illumination. It's pretty dark and although there are a few orange street lights on in the larger villages, it's pitch black once we head out onto the small winding roads that cut through the French countryside.

Turn left and you should see a sign for a village called Picquigny, then from there we should follow signs to Amiens, then straight through to fucking Paris, I call out, the crumpled route in my hands.

Pig.. fuckin what? says Tony, mate you've got to slow down, you are doing my head in.

I know mate, I've just had too much fuckin speed old boy and I can't fuckin stop talking, I reply.

Mate you better soon, or I'm going to come back there and smack you.

I laugh and go back to shouting out french village names and drinking from the lemonade bottle. I reckon I'm pretty fucking good at this navigation shit. I'll get us there, don't you worry about that. Just follow the instruction, its like anything in life, follow the instructions and you'll be fine. Shit I ripped it a bit, no problem, I know this fucking country like the back of my fucking hand.

Tony mate, why don't you let me drive, I call out from the back seat.

You've never driven a car in your fuckin life mate, comes the reply, and I nod in agreement.

Tony is doing a fantastic job of piloting this vehicle but I reckon I could do better, given the chance.

True enough, I reply, but there's a first time for everything.

Fucking Paris at rush hour, what are the chances? The sun's out and my eyes hurt. The light and the noise, everyone fucking honking their horns and the stink of exhaust fumes fills the car. Hardy is driving and Tony is trying to sleep in the passenger seat. Good fucking luck I think. It's alright though. Fucking Paris, the yellow brick art nouveau buildings cut into the blue sky and the haze of the city softens the tall buildings in the distance into indecipherable shapes. The lemonade bottle is half empty already, *or is it half full?* I laugh to myself and look down at the route. Fucking thing has become impossible to read, don't know why they would use such an indecipherable font. Is it even in English? Fuck me, I'm thirsty.

Anyone got any...It's cool, Ive got some lemonade here. French drivers are fucking crazy. I heard somewhere that in England traffic lights are compulsory, in France they are optional and in Spain purely decorative. I'm starting to think it's true. Hardy navigates around the Champs-Élysées. Horns are beeping and Tony is shouting and giving two fingers to every cunt who cuts in front of us. There are cars coming from every angle and Hardy is in an unfamiliar car and none of us has slept for twenty six fucking hours.

We finally find our way onto the expressway that dips below the streets of Paris and the traffic starts to ease off. Hardy puts the little jeep into low gear and fucking steps on it. The tunnel is concrete and the growl of engines echoes around the yellow lit interior as we join the mass of traffic. There are trucks traveling across Europe, holiday makers with cars stuffed full of unnecessary shit and people on their way to work, the radio on, eyes gluey from another shitty night's sleep. We've got the top down again and I'm looking out of the back of the jeep towards the entrance to the tunnel. I notice a long dark line on the road behind us.

Think the car is leaking oil lads, I call out, my voice lost amongst the clamour.

The rest of the drive is like a bad dream. Moments of clarity punctuating one long vivid hallucination. None of us has slept for two days now and the beer and speed is all gone. More village roads and motorways, and faceless people in deserted midnight petrol stations, little oases of light in the darkness. We pass into Spain at about two in the morning, the skinny old man in an ill fitting uniform sitting in his little booth, not even bothering to check our passports. As we drive past he leans out of his booth and yells.

Eengliiish!

Tony slams on the breaks and the car skids to a halt. He goes to put the car in reverse but Hardy stops him with a hand on his shoulder.

Leave it mate, he says.

We drive through endless nameless towns, white concrete blocks of flats and kids on mopeds, dusty roads and slick beautiful people lined up outside a nightclub, stray dogs sniffing at their feet, faceless shadows hidden from the lights of the city, huddled in alleyways, ghosts that will vanish with the first touch of the sun. The night seems to go on for an eternity and I slip in and out of consciousness, never truly awake but never fully asleep. The sun touches my face and wakes me. I put my legs up on the edge on the jeep and fall back into a fitful sleep, the rumble and vibration of the road below me, dreaming of big ships and stardust.

At some point the jeep dies, spluttering and coughing as Tony steers it into a petrol station. I awake to harsh sunlight, below a cloudless sky. I wipe my eyes and climb out of the back of the jeep. My clothes are cold with my sweat and stink of cigarette smoke and car upholstery. We congregate around the front of the car and Tony opens the bonnet, pokes around a bit in the engine, then starts to unscrew the radiator cap. I begin to shout out for him to stop, but it's too late. A jet of boiling hot steam and water bubbles into the air and over the hot engine, as the pressure is released. We all jump back and Tony curses, his hand scolded by the boiling water. He goes into the petrol station office and tries to talk to the bloke behind the counter, me and Hardy watching him from the jeep. In the end he gives up and leaves, shaking his head as he wanders back across the dusty forecourt. The man behind the counter wipes his eyes and goes back to watching his tiny colour telly.

We fiddle around with the engine for a bit, but none of us has any fucking idea what we are doing. We leave the thing to cool down and Hardy fills up the radiator reservoir with a bottle of mineral water. I wander off to some bushes for a piss. I get back and Tony climbs back into the jeep and tries the ignition. The fucking thing starts up, the stereo coming back on full blast and we all give a half hearted cheer. We clamber back in and Tony

417

pulls out of the petrol station and onto a deserted road, gunning the engine as we drive away.

I am just starting to doze off again, my head heavy with sleep, the edges of dreams creeping into my perception, when the car suddenly skids to a halt, pulling me back to consciousness.

What the fuck, I yell out, angrily jerked from my sleep.

Tony doesn't answer just spins the car round and starts driving back the way we've come. The mad bastard is going the wrong way down a motorway and Hardy is yelling at him to stop.

Tony you fucking twat you're going the wrong way, he's shouting.

He doesn't stop

What the fuck is it? We are both yelling at him, Tony mate, for fucks sake..!

We reach a toll booth and the official comes running out as he sees us, shouting and waving at us to stop. Tony skids to a halt and starts reversing. He spins the car round and pulls into a lay-by, engine still running.

Fucking hell mate, what the fuck are you doing? Hardy's voice is edged with anger, his hands still gripping the dashboard.

Tony turns to us, his grey eyes darting about and unfocused.

When we stopped at that petrol station, I left my fucking wallet on the roof, he says.

Yet again Tony is left with no money.

We drove back along the route we came and eventually found the petrol station. We looked around for his old brown wallet, which contained about three hundred quid and all of his cards, but we didn't find it. I tried to talk to the bloke in the office in broken shitty Spanish, but it was no good. The thing was gone.

So here we are in some shitty hotel in southern Spain eating cheap bread and trying to get some sleep. Tony is still raging about his wallet and that thieving fucking bastard in the petrol station. We tell him to give up. He's never going to find it. What we need is sleep and some time to think about what to do.

We wake up with the sun from a fitful sleep and after a quick breakfast of stale bread and bottled water head out into the already hot morning, clambering back into that sun baked car. We are all starting to hate the confines of this fucking thing. I think we all had this idea in our heads of this romantic drive along the roads of Europe, stopping off at little villages, eating fresh oysters by the sea and fucking the local girls under the rafters of old rustic barns as the sun dipped below the horizon. In actuality the whole thing is a nightmare of Kafkaesque proportions. Hours cramped up in this sweaty little jeep with only each other for company, surviving on snacks and stale water, strung out and sleep deprived. All of us now share the same desire. Our only goal is to arrive at that fucking villa without getting arrested or dying on a deserted road in this god forsaken jeep, surrounded by empty crisp packets and cigarette ends.

After about another six or seven hours of driving we finally reach the dusty outskirts of the villa complex. My brother is driving and I am in the passenger seat. I'm trying my best to stay awake but it's been three days and none of us has had any real sleep. Hardy is nodding in and out of consciousness too. I can see his eyes focused on the road ahead, desperately trying to stay awake. He sees something in the road ahead of him but is too tired to avoid it. Luckily it's only a plastic bag.

We pass a sign that says 'beware of bandits' and we keep going, too tired to really register anything anymore. Tony doesn't really remember the way so it's just a question of driving up and down the same roads until we find the entrance. As long as we can get in the complex then we will be ok. We drive down deserted roads and along dirt tracks with broken wire fences on either side, through ghost towns with boarded up petrol stations, stray dogs scavenging in the dry scrub. They bark and scurry away as we pass, these three lost souls in their dusty black carriage.

We cross a small bridge that runs across an empty dike and turn a corner and there in front of us are the entrance gates. Tony fishes around in the glove box for the villa keys and we pull up to the complex. Tony gets out, holding the key ring to a panel set in the gate post. There is a loud clank and the large iron gates swing slowly open. Tony climbs back in the car and we drive slowly into the villa complex as the gates swing shut behind us. Everyone breathes a sigh of relief and the mood in the car suddenly lightens. The sun is just peaking up over the horizon, beyond the pristine white villas, and in the distance, through the haze I can see the sea sparkling blue and green under a clear morning sky.

I kick the covers off me and reach for a bottle of water. It's fucking boiling in here and the air has a strong chemical smell to it which sticks in my throat. The window is open and someone must have been spraying the plants outside with pesticide. I roll out of bed and wander through to the kitchen in just my T-shirt and pants. There are two bedrooms in the villa. A smaller one with two single beds and a master bedroom with a big double bed in the centre and an en suite bathroom. Tony is in the main bedroom, it's his dad's place after all, while me and Hardy are stuck together in the singles. We've got an agreement that whoever pulls gets the double for the night, which seems fair.

Tony is in a pair of blue shorts, top off, belly hanging out, a half finished fag hanging loosely from his lips. His long dark hair is down and he's got an open can of beer on the work top. He is leaning over the electric cooker, a wooden spoon in his hand, peering into a big saucepan filled with some sort of pasty looking gruel.

What the fuck is that? I ask, as I walk over.

Hummus mate, comes the reply through a cloud of smoke.

I wrinkle my nose and take a swig of his beer.

What? It's fucking Greek mate, he tells me.

Looks it, I reply.

And get your own fucking beer, he scolds, grabbing the can back from my hand.

Tony needs a lime for the hummus so we go out of the front door leaving it open behind us. There are a few shops down in the centre of the complex, but Tony doesn't feel like taking the long walk. We spot what appears to be a citrus tree in the garden across the street from us so we trot over, have a quick look around to make sure no one is watching, then Tony vaults over the wall, grabs one of the fruits from the small tree and returns triumphantly clutching his prize.

We are walking back when an old lady comes out of the villa next to ours. She's got greying blonde hair, still damp and pinned up behind her head. She's in a dressing gown and slippers and she's clutching a copy of The Sun newspaper in one hand. The old girl seems to be crying as she approaches us and Tony asks her if she's alright.

Haven't you heard? she asks us, rubbing the corner of her eyes with a small white hanky.

Heard what? We both ask.

It's Princess Diana, she's dead.

Four double vodkas in and things are getting pretty lively. The food and booze on the complex are cheap as fuck and at last it's starting to feel like a proper holiday. Me and Tony are in a small karaoke bar in the main entertainment area of the complex. It's a small town square done out to look like a quaint Spanish town with seating in the middle and a host of bars and restaurants surrounding it, catering to every taste. There's a chippy, a Chinese place and a curry house. It's pretty fucking mad really. Here we are on the beautiful coast of southern Spain and we just had a curry and are sitting with a bunch of other pasty English bastards, getting drunk and listening to some old fella do a rather convincing impersonation of Frank Sinatra. The bloke can certainly sing.

After the curry Hardy had a bit of a funny turn, went white as a sheet and looked like he was going to puke, so he wandered off back to the villa for a kip, taking a short cut across the golf course. Tony and me watched him disappear into the night. Hope it isn't food poisoning. I don't fancy the idea of the three of us all puking and shitting ourselves to death in this beautiful place.

Can't believe she's dead mate, says Tony
Fuckin hell yeah, I reply.
It's all over the news in all the bars and restaurants. Massive piles of flowers outside Buckingham palace, shaven headed English blokes with neck tattoos crying like little fucking babies. I couldn't really give less of a fuck to be honest. She was a nice lady, don't get me wrong, but this public outpouring of grief on such a massive scale is just a bit embarrassing. Some of these blokes on the telly wouldn't bat an eyelid if some poor bastard got beaten half to death in a gritty boozer somewhere in Peckham, and here they are bawling their eyes out for some posh tart they've never even met.

It's all a load of bollocks if you ask me. Still by the looks of the crowd in here I should probably keep my opinions to myself. Especially considering we were driving down the exact same road where she died, just twenty four hours earlier in a fucked up jeep that was leaking oil.

That fucking photographer should get the fucking death penalty, I hear a voice from another table announce, followed by mumbles of agreement from the rest of the bar.

I down the rest of my vodka and get up to go for a piss. The telly is showing images of Diana and her bloke as they leave a hotel. They are grainy and look as though they've come from a security camera.

There are a couple of girls hanging around, but the whole place is actually quite quiet. Tony says we are a bit late. Apparently mid July is very different, hundred of young people out to get wasted and shag the night away.

Last year Kael pulled some bird and shagged her in one of the sand traps on the golf course. Tony said that when he turned up Kael had a massive grin on his face and there was a deep imprint of his arse in the sand behind him.

We head back at about two in the morning, wandering slowly past darkened villas and still, pellucid swimming pools, the cool moon in their waters. Hardy is fast asleep when we get back and I flop down on the bed next to him, my head spinning. I reach one leg out from under the covers and place it on the cool tiles, letting the warm depths of my dreams overcome me.

We wake up the following afternoon to another hot day beneath the scorching sun and drive down to the beach. We buy loads of cheap beer and some bread and ham from a small supermarket on the way. We park the car under the shade of the tree and eat and smoke, looking out over the clear blue ocean.

We rent a jet ski and mess about on the water for a couple of hours. Tony drives the thing in the same way he drives the car, with reckless abandon, jumping off waves and speeding through the wakes of large boats, narrowly missing the heads of unaware swimmers, bobbing up and down in the warm ocean. We come off a couple of times, thrown into the blue waters, swallowed for a second by the smothering silence, the noises of the busy beach muted for a moment before we push back up into the bright noisy world above. We swim back and clamber back onto the jet ski laughing and choking on salty sea water.

When we are a good distance from the shore, Tony cuts the engine and we drop into the deep dark water. The jet ski bobs and floats next to us, our legs dangling down below us into the tenebrosity. The water is warm, almost body temperature and small waves lap up against the jet ski with their little white fingers. We bob up and down, lost in that huge ocean, the bright strip of white beach on the horizon. It is silent save for the sound of the moving water and as I peer down below me into the plunging depths I imagine sinking into that inky dark abyss until it swallows me whole and I am never seen again. I get a sudden feeling of vertigo at the idea of what lies below me, images of lost souls and dark shadowy things with rows of sharp teeth and I swim quickly back to the jet ski, keen to get my body out of the water and safely back on the shore.

Tony, I say, I think our time is running out mate.

Nah man, he replies, we've got ages

He floats on his back in the calm waters, looking up at the sky.

We are in a club. It's not a very nice club and it's not very busy either. The music is shit but the booze is cheap as fuck, so here we are. We are sitting at a small table covered with an array of alcoholic drinks. There are a couple of girls dancing next to us. We ran into them at the beach after jet skiing and they just started hanging around. One of them, the better looking of the two has definitely got a thing for Tony. The other one is alright, nice face but she's a bit on the big side for my liking. Still it's pretty slim pickings around here so we will see what happens. We are all thoroughly drunk again. Hardy is downing double vodkas like no one's business and I'm on my fifth or sixth double vodka and coke. Like I said the booze is horrifically cheap here and the shots are more than generous.

The British aren't built for clubbing on the continent. We are used to pubs closing at eleven and the clubs kicking out at two in the morning. Over here things work very differently. People don't go out until after midnight at least, and the clubs don't really get going until about two in the morning. Suffice to say we have peaked far too early. The Spanish people don't get pissed like the English. We drink to forget, to escape the cold. We drink for confidence. We use it as a crutch. It breaks down the the years of conditioning telling us to push our feelings deep down inside, to repress our self expression and to continue on regardless of what shit life throws at us. We drink too much and too quickly. It's a lubricant, helping us to slip through life with as little resistance as possible. We drink to fight. We drink to live.

Spanish people are different. They turn up to the club at three in the morning, lively and beautiful, tanned and full of energy. Life for them isn't just about surviving, it's about experiencing and getting what you can from this short existence. It's about letting go and allowing life to carry you where it will. While we fight against it, trying to batter it into submission, they let it take them. They dance and talk and move with fluidity and a smoothness that is alien to us. We are pasty, white, drunk and full of hate and cynicism, our movements blunt and violent, lacking in any subtlety and our language sounds harsh and guttural. Hoses are brought out and the dance floor is filled with white foam. The bodies writhe and move within it as we sit morose and lacking, self destructive, full of the dreams that only the young can ever possess.

I don't know what time it is. All I know is that it's late and I'm so drunk I can hardly think. We were in the car, then on a beach somewhere, I took off my shoes and paddled in the surf. I talked to the girls about something or other, but my tongue felt like it belonged to someone else and words came out twisted and meaningless. I smoked and sang and jumped in the pool outside our villa. The water was cold and I couldn't feel my body. Tony told me to be quiet and I yelled something. I stumbled into the house with Hardy and Tony and slumped down in the living room awakening to darkness and silence and a feeling of unease.

I remember Tony going into his bedroom with that girl and Hardy smoking outside, watching the clouds slowly traverse the star filled sky, stars which spun in circles and danced about my head.

I lie there for a few moments trying to get my bearings.
I wonder what 'She' is doing. Wonder if she will ever
forgive me, if she will ever see my true purpose. I love her
I think, or perhaps I just love the way she defines me,
makes my grip on this slippery reality a tiny bit stronger.
I'm a sickly little deity that relies on the belief of others
for his own selfish existence, their delicate fingers shaping
me into this being, my plight, my purpose just a reflection
of what others actually desire. I always get the sense that
no one truly likes me, that I am just another minor
character in their stories.

Are we all but ghosts, ephemeral shadows, soon to be
lost and forgotten, buried beneath the unfathomable
weight of the centuries to come? I just can't get a grip on
things. Perhaps I really am a narcissist. I wish I could talk
to 'Her'. She would know what to say, she always does,
but I know that I'll never ask. For now I have to live like
this, absent and alone. One day this will all come crashing
down. These friends that I hold so dear and this now, this
present that is so real, so tangible and solid will be gone,
withered away by the years and I will stand alone on a
precipice, unwilling to jump but too afraid to hold on.

Our actions, and the events that shape us into who we
are are purely and absolutely out of our control. It's only
with hindsight that we are able to put them together and
structure them into some sort of narrative. Time
continues unimpeded by the wishes and hopes of us mere
mortals and long before the sun swells and swallows our
planet, we will be lost in time. Some of us will continue,
stumbling along until they at least find some semblance of
happiness, able to close their eyes and shutter their ears

to the call of autumn. Others will become lost, wading out too deeply to thrash about in the surf trying to find purchase, to find a foothold. Perhaps one day someone will once again hold them to their breast, absolve them of their struggle, set them free and pull them from the hungry maw of fate. In the end we will all return to the earth amongst the tears and flowers, our lives reduced to words, our existences only finding form in the melancholic utterances of those lucky few that remain. We will persist for a time, but one day someone will speak our names for the last time.

I stand, pushing my legs out and placing my feet on the cool slick tiles. I shuffle towards the square of pallid blue light from the window quivering to the edge of my vision. I kick off my shoes as I approach the large wooden door, my now naked feet sticking slightly to the floor with each shuffling step. I reach forward and twist the door handle, pushing the door open with my shoulder and half stumbling out onto the terra-cotta porch. The moon gazes down upon me, her subtle visage shimmering beyond the leaves of the lofty palm tree at the centre of the court yard. A slow, gentle breeze envelopes everything, imbuing the night with a slow subtle movement, a low trembling breath, a soft ushering whisper, an epiphany spoken to the slumbering unconscious. I push on.

I reach the pool's edge and I wait, letting the stillness overtake me. I imagine lying half asleep in the back seat of that jeep as we climb into the Pyrenees, the sun sparkling off the Mediterranean as I slip once again into the numb solitude of sleep. I imagine the hot sun as I awaken to another day, another quiet cacophony, and a half remembered dream, the world once more thrust into my view, the still, persistent yearning of my being once more conjured into form. I think of the warm embrace of home, of the cracked paint on the front door and the stiff sash windows, of the creak of the stairs as I ascend in the pale fold of night and of the low rumbling murmur of voices from beyond its red brick walls.

I gaze down into the dark, still water, a vague shadow of me reflected on the glassy surface, an outline of another being, a figure from another time and place, another losing battle against the unyielding entropy that will one day lay all of this to dust and cast us all into the deep. I step into the darkness, one foot sinking into the water. Why do I hold on so tight? Why do I persist? I move forward, down the steps, wading into the cool water. It soaks my jeans, seeping up into my crotch, stealing my breath for a second, pulling me closer as I push on. I hear laughter and the excited chatter of happy voices carried on the breeze from beyond the golf course, remnants of another soon to be forgotten night, the last words of those mortal few that remain. I shiver as I let the water engulf me, sinking down up to my neck as it laps at my ears, the clean chemical stink of chlorine filling my nostrils, the deep hum of the pools filtration machinery barely audible above my long slow breaths. I stand on tiptoes now, my head back, face to the stars. I breathe in and out through my upturned nose. My hands float loosely by my sides, my body weightless, shapeless, reduced almost to nothing, hanging motionless below that enraptured moon as I let myself sink below the surface.

After my father's funeral I found the pile of books that he was planning to post me to help with my philosophy degree. I opened one of them, it was 'The Theory of Beauty' by Edgar Frederick Carritt and as I flicked through the pages a small piece of paper fell out onto the table. It was yellow with age, the edges crumpled. On it was my dad's familiar scrawl, words he must have written when he was still at university, as he stood at a juncture, as he was passing into adulthood, yet still weighed down with all the childish baggage of youth. On it was written the following:

'What more ghastly image can be called up than that of a man betrayed by his body who, simply because he did not die in time, lives out the comedy while awaiting the end, face to face with that God he does not adore, serving him as he served life, kneeling before a void and arms outstretched toward a heaven without eloquence that he knows to be also without depth?'
Oh to lie asleep in the soft brown earth, with the long green grass waving gently above your head, with no yesterday, with no tomorrow, able to forget love, able to forgive life.
Underneath it he had written in slightly larger script,

P.S don't drink.

EPILOGUE

After my father passed away my mother, never one to lie down and let life walk over her was soon back on her feet and living life the way it was supposed to be lived. She had spent too much time bowing to the wishes of others, her energies always focused upon the selfless and it was finally time for her to shine. She started to paint again and got in touch with old friends she hadn't seen in ages. She travelled Europe and redecorated the house. Her eye for interior design was always flawless and with the children out of the way she could finally have the house she had always dreamed of. She commissioned a beautiful rustic wooden bench for the garden where she would often sit and drink tea, below the old apple tree. She found love again with a wonderfully kind RAF man from Nottingham called Harry. Whenever I was back from Japan over the Christmas holidays I would stay with her, and when my jet lag woke me early in the morning I would head down to the kitchen, knowing she would be up, and sit by the window at the end of the kitchen (the one Hardy and I had wrenched open all those years earlier) gazing out into the garden, watching the birds eat bread from the frosty ground.

She was diagnosed with breast cancer in 2002 and had a mastectomy, followed by chemo therapy. She seemed to make a full recovery and for a time things were good again. The cancer returned like it always does, but she was strong and fought it until the bitter end. She died on a frosty morning in 2005.

She had been moved from the district hospital into palliative care at Thorpe Hall, a grand stately home on the edge of The Borough that had been turned into a Sue Rider hospice. It was a cold spring morning and my wife and I walked though the grounds of the hall, a wide open expanse of grassy uneven land, dotted with cows, a low mist hanging over everything. We were led up to her room and I stroked her hair and talked to her about the beautiful morning outside and my recent new life in Japan. I held her swollen hand and she told me she was sad that her wedding ring no longer fitted her finger. She urged me to stay as she dipped in and out of consciousness, and I told her I would come back and see her the following day, that she should get some rest. I had no idea how close she was to the end.

The last words she ever spoke to me were

Kei, what are you doing with your life?

She passed away early the next morning. I saw her stiff emaciated body, skin pulled tight over her face like the mummies in the British museum and I wept like a child. She was interred in a huge room with wooden beams that swept up to the ceiling above her. She was alone in the centre surrounded by church pews, small windows high in the ceiling letting a little yellow light spill through and illuminate her pale skin. Her left hand hung stiffly next to her face, red curls around a pale mask. I was thrown by the beauty of it all and my breath caught in my chest.

After we left Thorpe Hall, I went down to the registry office with Harry to register her death, then spent most of the day talking to relatives, brewing endless cups of tea and making funeral arrangements. At some point in the afternoon I apologised to everyone, I was exhausted and couldn't go on. I climbed the stairs, collapsed onto my bed and fell into a deep sleep.

The funeral like my father's before was full of well wishers and friends. Our house was once again crowded with people, alive with conversation and activity. My mother had always been a great entertainer and would have loved the idea of so many of us being in her house, in her beautiful home, remembering the woman who had raised me and nurtured me, who had sat at my bedside tending my fever, who had scolded me for staying out all night and worrying her half to death.

My friends were all there and we shared hugs and a few tears before once again retiring to the garage to drink and listen to music on that old cassette player, to forget.

The house was sold a year or so later and my older brother took a few last photographs of it before it was gone from our lives forever.

Another family live there now forging new memories and lives within its walls.

A few months later we scattered my mother's ashes into a swollen stream near her brother's cottage in the lake district. My wife was angry with me for some reason that morning, unconcerned as usual with the feelings of others, and so I stood alone on the pebbled bank as the last remnants of my past life were swept away in the churning waters of the stream that had watched us grow year by year into the men we now were. My uncle placed a gentle hand on my shoulder. I shrugged it off and stared into the clear waters, wishing that they would also carry me away.

Luka went to work on a cruise ship, playing the guitar in a band and traveling the world. He met a wonderful girl, got married and bought a house in a quiet village outside Cambridge. She got pregnant but lost the baby a few days before she was due to give birth. She had to go through the pain of giving birth to a child that she would never raise, that neither of them would ever know. The experience nearly broke them, but like my mother they bounced back with renewed strength and vigour. They had two more children and they live happy, simple lives surrounded by good friends and loving family. Luka makes a living playing the guitar and bass and is still an amazing musician and the cleverest person I know. I go back to see them once a year with my son and every time I do, I feel as if I want to stay there forever. Perhaps someday I will.

Hardy didn't turn out so well. He was the strongest of all of us, but somewhere along the line something broke in him, but that's a long story, one for another time...

od eventually became the lead singer of a rock band called Huge Baby. They became somewhat famous, touring as the support act with AC DC and Napalm Death. They released an album to moderate critical acclaim and I read about my old friend in the pages of Kerrang magazine one hungover morning in my small room in Tokyo. Rod returned to The Borough, the conquering hero, playing a gig in a local club. We all went along and moshed in front of the stage. We got drunk together in my garage afterwards just like old times.

His id soon got the better of him however, and at a drunken recording session one day he got into a heated argument with the producer and threw a chair through the glass partition, nearly maiming the sound engineer. The rest of the band had been struggling with coke and heroin addiction and they were soon dropped from their label.

Rod became an alcoholic, my brother occasionally seeing him on the streets of The Borough wandering aimlessly around town or slouched against a wall in the Asda car park, his hair long and unkempt, a bottle in hand. He moved down to London and continued to spiral into addiction, sleeping rough and washing in local hotel bathrooms. He eventually got arrested for something or other and did some time in prison. He got off the booze and went back out into the world a new man. He soon reverted to his old ways however, of drugs and alcohol.

I Skyped him during the riots in London when he was staying in a bed sit on housing benefits, behind him were boxes and boxes of iphones and other apple products. He was trying to get back into music and so I bought him a cheap electric guitar and amp to help him along. Don't know if he still has them or if he sold them for booze and I don't care. I love the man and it was a gesture that didn't require any reciprocation.

A couple of years later his older brother John died. He had been feeling ill for a week or so and went to the doctor for a check up. They did some tests and he was diagnosed with a rare form or highly aggressive cancer called double punch lymphoma. That February he had been a healthy active young man and by the end of March the same year they were lowering his body into the ground. Hardy went to the funeral. Rod's family were all Jehovah's witnesses and so it was a strange affair. Almost a celebration, his family certain that they would once again meet in the afterlife. Last thing I heard of my old friend was that he had given up the booze and the drugs and become a born again Christian.

Nugget still lives in The Borough and has a large family. He travels the world and is often in Asia and the Middle East. I've seen him a few times, and although he has mellowed a great deal since his teenage years, he is still the same as ever. No one calls him Nugget anymore

Marko runs a very successful classic car business, buying and selling old motors, which came as no surprise to anyone. Eli was my best friend all through the last years of school but once we went to University we soon lost touch. I know he was working for a clothing company and living in Leicester but apart from that I have no idea. I hope he is happy.

Kael drifted around for a while, never really finding himself, moving from one thing to another. Debbie had a baby when she was fifteen. They named him Silas. The two of them continued their turbulent relationship. They broke up eventually and Kael moved in with his dad. They sold the house on Thorpe Lea Road and got a place in a village somewhere.

One day Kael woke up, had breakfast, told his dad he was going to go and buy some credits for his mobile phone then hanged himself in the garage.

He was more a brother than a friend, fearless, erratic and full of love. He had always seemed so strong and unafraid and it pains me to imagine the hollow that must have existed within him, a hollow that we either didn't see or perhaps mistook for something else.

I think some of us are simply born with that brutal seed already within us, the enticing call of the void and the warm embrace of its promise as apparent and inexorable as our shadows. It is simultaneously a comfort and a curse, a cold aching pain, a dark mystery and a chance for infinite redemption.

After the funeral there was a lot of talk about him and his previous suicide attempts, at one point I turned to my brother and asked him what he thought. He began to cry and in a weak voice replied simply

He was my friend.

Debbie soldiered on, raising their son Silas by herself, whilst at the same time getting an education and working hard to bring in enough money for both of them. Silas went to University, got into programming and has recently released his own game. He is twenty nine years old, older than his father will ever be.

Tony, Kael's brother I think was deeply affected by his twin brother's death. They always fought and bickered, but deep down there was a lot of love between the two. He is also still in The Borough. I sometimes talk to him on Facebook. I love the bloke like a brother, but we don't really have much in common anymore.

The last time I saw him was shortly after we returned from Spain. He was renting a small house near the fish and chip shop in West Town. He had moved in with the girl he met in Spain and her five year old son. Me and Hardy went round his for a barbecue one day. Tony was outside in the concrete back yard, top off, fag in his mouth, prodding at a half cooked sausage on the grill, while the kid ran around like a maniac.

We stayed for a beer but made our excuses and left shortly after.

Tom got into the pharmaceuticals industry and married his long time girlfriend. They have a couple of beautiful children and again I sometimes see him whenever I'm back in England.

Nails worked for the postal service for a while after getting out of prison and perhaps he still does. I haven't seen the old boy in years but I follow his life on Facebook and he seems to be really happy. He's also married with children.

The two Marks and James are still about. I talk to Mark Mayhew a lot and he has even bought a couple of my paintings. He is the same as ever, a good friend with a kind heart. James has a partner and a few kids. He lives a very private life, avoiding social media. He apparently also has one of the largest Lego collections in the Uk.

Finn got into an argument one day with a girl in a rough old pub in Bretton. He lost his rag and broke a bar stool over her head. A couple of days later he was in the bath with his bird when he heard the doorbell ring. He got out, dried himself off, threw on some trousers and answered the door. At first he couldn't see anyone there, so he leaned out further placing his hand on the door frame. Someone hacked off his thumb with a meat cleaver and a group of blokes pushed him back into the small flat stabbing and slashing at him with knives and machetes, leaving him bloody and half dead on the old cigarette burned rug. His girlfriend who had been cowering in the bath, trying not to scream came out to find him in a bloody mess, yelling for an ambulance. Apparently the girl Finn had smashed was the sister of some Irish travelers and you don't fuck with a pikie's family.

He was whisked away to hospital, crashing twice on the way and lost about four pints of blood. They had half severed his thumb, nearly cut off his right knee cap and stabbed him some forty times. It took him a long time to recover but he eventually pulled through.

He popped up on Facebook a good few years later covered in tattoos and looking as dodgy as ever. I have no idea what he's doing now.

Max got into journalism after a number of career changes and now lives in Nottingham with his adopted son, wife and the children from her former marriage. I'm happy to say that he hasn't changed in the least.

Millie got really into outdoor sports, climbing and canoeing and the like and lives with her husband up in the Lake District, close to where we spread my mum's ashes. Luka passed her in the car recently when he was up there on holiday. I'm not sure if they talked. She seems happy.

The girls: Becky, Kirsten, Kyra and Jacqui all still stay in touch. Jacqui works for the local government, locating and prosecuting individuals and companies that damage the environment. She always had a big heart.

After University Becky got into a relationship with someone we knew from school. Things were good and she seemed happy. He went to sleep one night and never woke up, carbon dioxide poisoning from a faulty heater.

Becky bounced back like she always does and a few years later found love again, got married and recently gave birth to a beautiful little girl.

Kirsten got married when she was still in her twenties to a big friendly policeman. They bought a house and a dog and had a couple of children. These things rarely last however and they ended up getting divorced but remain friends, sharing custody of the kids. Kirsten found someone else and settled down and her eldest recently got accepted to University. Kirsten and I used to sit together all the time in Mr Pateman's English class, attentively listening to him explain the subtleties of 30's poetry or the imagery and themes of King Lear. She helped me edit this book.

Kyra is happy and full of life. She doesn't seem to have aged one bit. She was always focused and strong, completely unafraid of life and willing to accept its vicissitudes. She found a good man and has two beautiful children. I am pleased to say that my old friends are all healthy and happy, but I miss them.

As for 'Her'. She spent some time in France before returning to England where she met a gentle honest man, fell in love and got married. I bumped into them both in Bogarts shortly before moving to Japan. I asked her what she loved about him, and she whispered the answer into my ear, smiling.

They have three beautiful girls and live in a small village not so far from my brother. The house is open and warm just like my old friend, and her husband is just the kind of person I would expect her to be with. She is a teacher at a rather prestigious school and I am certain that she is popular with her students. She is still gregarious and funny, intelligent and optimistic. We have stayed in touch and I realise deep down that I will always know her.

What about Lucy? That beautiful barmaid from Bogarts, who stole my heart. Well to be honest, most of that was a lie. It's so easy to deify those people that we no longer have any interaction with. She was the most beautiful person I have ever seen in my life. I don't believe in love at first sight, but even twenty years later, I still think about her almost everyday, and I still have that small yellow post it note with her number on, safely tucked away in a drawer in my small flat in Tokyo. My feelings for her were real enough, but all the rest was just a product of my narcissism. In a sense she was never a real person to me and perhaps that's why I idolised her so completely. It's very easy to idealise people when they exist on the periphery. It's simple to take your idea of what someone should be, and shape that into something that fits your narrative or caresses the secret hopes and desires that you keep locked up safely within.

The truth is that apart from a few small interactions and the occasional conversation, we barely even knew each other. I did see her outside Charters as we left that night and I did speak to her briefly, but everything after that I'm afraid was a fabrication, a fantasy I sometimes fall asleep to. We didn't go for a walk by the river, we didn't hold hands and we certainly never kissed. I don't remember what I said to her on that spring evening by the river, but it was probably something prosaic and uninteresting. After we spoke, I turned my back and walked away. I looked back once, but she had already gone.

To be honest I don't really remember any of the details of that last time we met in April of 1999. I might have been on my way into the pub and met her while she was coming out. Maybe it was the other way round. It's possible that it wasn't April and that I wasn't with my brother, Hardy. It's possible that her clothes and hair were completely different to how I described them, and it's impossible to say for sure how our conversation went. The only thing I can be truly sure of is that that was the last time I ever saw her and how I regret not saying the things that come so easily to me now.

Lucy Mary _____er died in 2009 of a brain tumour. Doctors noticed something was wrong when she had a seizure during child birth. The tumour must have been aggressive, because by the end of the year she had already succumbed to her illness. She had a small funeral and there was a short obituary in one of the local papers. I would have had no idea that she had died were it not for a drunken fit of self agrandisement one night. I decided one day to try and get in touch with her. I scoured Facebook and finally contacted Millie's younger sister, who I knew used to be friends with Lucy and she replied to me a few days later with the news. It affected me a great deal more deeply than I thought it would. I am reasonably certain that if Lucy were still alive that she wouldn't even remember me. I would be barely a footnote in the story of her life. Memory is fallible and the past hungry for compliments and so many of the details concerning her and indeed other people and events contained within this book are also probably far from accurate.

The shades of feeling however, at least from my side are real. Our lives and the experiences that shape them are a product of the people that touch us no matter how briefly, and those that have become ghosts are often the ones that linger the longest. I felt I needed to tell someone about her, as in some small way if someone else is made to remember her, then perhaps she will exist a little longer and the world needs as much beauty as it can get.

I also feel a twinge of guilt. I was never a big part of Lucy's life, and there were people who loved her a great deal more than I ever did or could. I sometimes feel like I have hijacked her memory, that I have no right to remember her the way I do, that I'm a tourist.

In retrospect I don't wish that we had fallen in love or even had a relationship. I simply wish that she, like so many others in this story, were still a part of this world.

So what about me?

Well I'm still alive, if not a little damaged.

My son moves a bit under his covers, one small hand reaching up to wipe his eye. I tuck him back into his blanket and take another drink of my beer, that familiar buzz starting to come over me. The sun is setting and the clouds hang, kissed with golden filigree in a sky the colour of the sea that hot summer in Spain. I had a plan, a plan to bring this all to an end, but I found love in the most unexpected place. I found happiness.

445

There are many different shades of happiness. There is the happiness that comes from creating or achieving something, the happiness that you feel drinking with good friends or family, the happiness you get when you fall in love and realise the other person feels the same way. There is happiness that springs from comfort, from that feeling of warmth and security when your loved ones sleep safely and silently as stormy winds shudder the windows in their frames. There is the happiness that stems from a kind gesture or the generosity of strangers or seeing a bond between a parent and child. However, nothing can compare to the deep all encompassing happiness that comes when I am alone with my boy, when we are together in our own world and everything outside seems muffled and softened to melody, when we share an experience or joke or a moment that defines that instant in time, a moment in which I realise that I am truly content with what I have and that no outside force however strong can break that, a moment in which I discover the true meaning of what it is to be happy. For happiness has nothing to do with having what we want, but in wanting what we have.

If not for him my story would have been much shorter. I now realise that this life is no longer mine to command. The precipice moves further and further away with each centimetre of his height, scribbled onto the wall in biro, with each new word spoken or Saturday morning shared. I now very rarely hear the call of the void. The voices of those I have lost have stilled, and the rush and roar of those plunging falls, although never absent now seem very far off. One day this bizarre yet beautiful ride will end, but it will not be by my hand, for I have a future now, and when at last the darkness consumes me and I lie asleep in that soft brown earth, the green grass swaying above my head it will be with the God I love and not with the woman I do not.

I know it's you.

The garage is cool and smells of old wood and oily bike chains. The warm summer sun doesn't penetrate in here and there is a cool dampness on the air.

Your father is having a difficult time believing it, but I would know my boy anywhere.

I turn and look into my mother's eyes, blue grey, soft and a little wet with recent tears, they speak the words that she cannot voice. She has a pair of large round brown sunglasses pushed up onto her forehead, sweeping the curly red hair back from her face. Her pale skin is mottled with rusty freckles, teased out by the long summer days and she stands in the wide doorway, a cup of tea cradled in her bony hands.

I don't know why you are here, she continues, but I know that it's you my love.

I can feel a lump building in my throat and tears beginning to well up in my eyes. I sniff and close them tight in an attempt to stem the emotion.

Little bright specks and shapes dance and swim across my vision and the world starts to unravel. The solid brick walls of this old building hum and vibrate and I can hear the roar

447

of the sea like that trapped within the heart of a slick sea shell. I remember falling or jumping and the calls of a thousand birds, white birds with plump bodies and pinions of alabaster, held aloft and flung about by the wind in a sky the colour of bronze.

She speaks again but her words are becoming more difficult to discern, distorted by static and stretched into something with a further depth of meaning and purpose.

In that place you come from..?

Yes, I reply, eyes still closed against the halo of sun surrounding her.

Are we still..?, you know..?

I know, I reply nodding and slowly open my eyes.

I gaze into her grey eyes and smile, and she smiles back. She moves towards me and pulls me to her. I bend my head forward and press my face into her shoulder, her hand tightly gripping the back of my head. I see her body laid out in a dark room full of church pews, one hand stiff and swollen and held above her face, beckoning towards the void that has claimed her. I see the smoke from the crematorium as it curls up into a clear sky that consumes the last remnants of my father, and the empty house, stripped of its furniture and carpets, the halls echoey and unfamiliar.

I want to tell her about her grandchildren and my brother's house in the Cambridgeshire countryside, nestled among undulating hills and fields of golden corn. I want to voice all the beauty and delights of a future which to her is as of yet unwritten. I want to speak of thunderclouds over Tokyo and the charcoal ink in my skin, of cherry blossoms; orange in the firelight, and drinking wine in the grounds of that French chateaux under a full moon. I want to tell her to

448

keep an eye on dad's drinking and to get regular breast exams. I want to tell her to stop spoiling her youngest son and to drive carefully, to avoid that big black dog in the south of France and that when I wake up screaming, a fire burning in my belly, not to worry. I want her to hold my beautiful boy to her chest and whisper into the night, to bear the only beauty I could ever conjure and see me as I truly am. I want to say all of this and more, but I know that my time is up. I can feel the fingers of the things that dwell in those dark places and the whispered promises of a thousand voices urging me onwards, the future and the past mixing and merging into one.

You and dad live long and happy lives, I whisper, before closing my eyes one last time.

LUCY
202229

1